C000175256

Separation

for

Beginners

Joe Portman

Separation
for
Beginners

Joe Portman

WELBECK

Published in 2022 by Welbeck Fiction Limited, an imprint of Welbeck
Publishing Group Based in London and Sydney.
www.welbeckpublishing.com

Copyright © Joe Portman, 2022

The moral right of the author has been asserted.

All rights reserved. No part of this publication may be reproduced,
stored in a retrieval system, or transmitted in any form or by any means,
electronically, mechanical, photocopying, recording or otherwise, without
the prior permission of the copyright owners and the publishers.

Separation for Beginners is a work of fiction. Names, characters, lyrics, business,
events and incidents are the products of the author's imagination.
Any resemblance and inclusion to actual persons or entities, living or
dead, or actual events is purely and entirely incidental and coincidental.

A CIP catalogue record for this book is available from the British Library

Hardback ISBN: 978-1-80279-174-7
Ebook ISBN: 978-1-80279-177-8
Trade Paperback ISBN: 978-1-80279-176-1

Printed and bound by CPI Group (UK) Ltd, Croydon, CR0 4YY

10 9 8 7 6 5 4 3 2 1

For Vicky

Chapter 1

I want to say two things. The first is about love. Even if it descends into a hell, causes pain and loss and a broken heart, if you have loved the way I loved my wife then you know what it feels like to be truly alive. I loved every second of it, right up until Claire divorced me a year ago, which felt like pure pain.

Pain for me, not for her. She's having the time of her life.

Which is great.

The second thing is more of a practicality. When your kids reach adulthood it's important, as a parent, to have your own interests and passions. Your children need to believe you're going to be fine after they move on. They want to know that you don't live for them, through them, because of them, that they aren't the project for which you abandoned all other projects.

And that's why I regret that when my twenty-three-year-old daughter told me she wanted to move back home to live with me for a while, I fell to my knees, burst into tears and pulled at her coat as I thanked her.

It's Monday morning. The kettle boils as I stand in a winter suntrap in the corner of my kitchen, and, for a moment, I am back in my happy marriage; a solvent, content father of two little kids in my thirties, a man loving the battleground of raising teenage children in my forties, still speechlessly in love with his wife after all these years. I am everywhere and anywhere except where I really am, until the kettle clicks and I open my eyes and see two mugs on the worktop. This mistake I have made many times in the past year. I return one mug to the cupboard and make myself, and myself alone, some tea. I no longer take it back to bed. Nowadays I stand at the bi-fold doors that separate my kitchen from the back garden and drink my tea there.

My forehead rests against the glass as the sunlight tries to bully its way into my face. I hear laughter from Susie's room. I hold my breath and listen, hoping that my daughter is alone in there, on the phone. Then I hear the low rumble of a man's voice and know that the boyfriend has stayed over, and I will not have the pleasure of breakfast alone with my girl.

I take a shower and I shave. There are two sinks in the bathroom I had fitted after my divorce last year. Ever the optimist, I often picture my ex-wife shoulder to shoulder with me in there as we get ready for bed. The lock on the bathroom door has been broken for nine months and, now that Susie is living back home with me, we have a protocol of singing or humming loudly when we're in there. The alternative is me getting my act together to fix the lock and that is out of the question.

When I return to the kitchen from my bedroom, in the time it has taken me to dress, the bathroom has become a pigsty. I stop in the hallway to take in the view, impressed by the speed at which it is regularly reduced to a dripping, steamy, towel-strewn warzone with, this morning, the bonus of the toilet roll unfurled down to the puddles on the tiled floor, so that the damp is slowly ascending the paper.

In the kitchen I find Susie shovelling cereal into her mouth while watching something on her tablet. The radio is on too. The kitchen table is littered with the contents of her bag. She

2

is wearing a work skirt – there's a name for the shape of these skirts, long but tight around the legs, straight out of *Mad Men*, but I don't know it – and a collared shirt. Her jacket is on the chair back. It's interview day. Again.

I slice a bagel, put it in the toaster and kiss the top of my daughter's head.

'Bathroom looks like a bomb hit it.'

Susie nods and, with a mouth full of food, says, 'I know, he's a pig.'

She and I both know that she, not her boyfriend Niall, is the cause of the mess but I enjoy slagging him off and she enjoys going along with it, as a gift to me and to deflect from her own student-esque domestic standards. Impeccably turned out and as effortlessly stylish as her mum, Susie leaves a trail of destruction behind her. Niall, meanwhile, is fastidiously neat despite looking like the missing link.

'Why is Niall staying here so much?' I ask.

'Because he's my boyfriend and I live here. You remember how it works?'

'I mean, you always used to stay at his place on the nights you were together.'

'Until his landlady turned into a psychotic cow.'

'You considered upgrading, or going back to one of your exes? Mark, the good-looking one, or that guy from The Isle of Sheppey . . . No offence.'

'He was from The Isles of Scilly.'

'Same difference.'

'Yup, that's what you said to him.'

I nod at the memory. 'He was a bit touchy.'

'So were you when he said, "I get why you're not the most successful travel agent."'

I scowl at the memory.

'Yeah, not him then,' I say.

'Not anyone, because I'm going out with Niall.'

Then she hands me a typed sheet of paper and a wad of cash. I stare at it blankly.

'What's this?'

'A tenancy agreement, Dad, and five hundred quid.'

She cocks her head to one side to observe my reaction. She can seem so deceptively confident and confrontational in the moment.

I hand it all back to her. 'You're my daughter.'

She puts the cash in a jar on the shelf. 'I'm also twenty-three and living rent free in your house.'

Niall's voice comes from the other side of the kitchen island. 'It's a flat, not a house. Used to be a house.'

I didn't know he was in the room. I rise to the bait. 'Where the ballsack are you?'

Susie sticks her tongue out, the way she did when she was three to let food she didn't like fall out of her mouth. 'Ugh, do I have to hear you say things like *ballsack*?'

'Sorry, love.'

'Doing my Shavasana,' Niall says. 'None taken, by the way.' He gets up from the floor. 'Encourage your daughter to dump me, take away the first person who has ever made me feel good about myself, say what you like about me.'

'Cheers,' I say, 'I will.' I stare at him. Specifically, I stare at his trousers. 'What are you wearing?'

'Harem pants.'

'Doing panto this year? *Aladdin*?'

Niall's trousers are like a tracksuit but with a low, saggy bottom that hangs way beneath his arse. I've seen them worn, but not in this hemisphere.

'Don't you like them?' Susie asks.

'They're hideous. Why? Did you buy them for him?'

'I made them for him.'

'They're brilliant. You're very talented.'

I flash my daughter a toothy smile. She scowls at me.

It's kind of Niall to remind me that this flat I live in was once a house, but I couldn't be more aware on a daily, hourly basis that the house it once was is where Claire and I raised Susie and her brother. It's the house I put my adult life into and loved. It's the house I presumed Claire and I would grow old in together.

To be fair, the harem pants suit Niall. He is dark-haired, and he is handsome beneath the chubbiness and facial hair and languid approach to oh but everything, that makes him seem like a man constantly in the process of waking up. He rarely wears shoes and this morning he is, as so often, topless despite having a less than cast iron physique. And yet despite it all, miraculously, unfairly, he possesses what my daughter describes as charisma. He throws his semi-clad self onto the kitchen sofa. My sofa. My baggy old favourite place to sit. He digs between the cushions and finds his tablet there. He wipes the crumbs from it and gets down to what he will describe as work.

Susie hands me the tenancy agreement again. 'A contract can say what I should pay you back . . . one day . . . when I have a job . . . if it's well paid, after my student loan.'

'I don't want your money,' I say. 'And I'll never kick you out.'

'Excellent news,' says Niall.

'Which doesn't apply to you,' I say.

Susie coughs meaningfully at Niall and he obediently puts down his tablet and offers to make tea. Money from my daughter. Tea from the tosser. I sense some kind of pincer movement here. They want something.

'I'm going to work,' I say, even though I'm not. 'And Susie's got an interview, so everyone has somewhere to be.'

I stuff the contract into my back pocket and leave. Susie follows me into my bedroom.

'Dad,' she says. Or to be more accurate, '*Daaaad*.'

'*Yeahhhhhhss*.'

She hesitates.

'Daddy.'

Daddy. Shit. Emotional blackmail alert.

'Niall's landlady is being very difficult indeed and I wondered if he could move in.'

I don't conceal my horror. 'Oh, Christ. Please, no!' I say paternally.

'Thought so.'

'I just so want to be on my own, with you.'

Yup, that sounded pathetic enough. Not that I was acting, I may be hopelessly out of touch with what to do with my life, but I know that I don't want anyone other than my family in this house right now.

Niall appears in the doorway and tries to appear cute, holding on to the top of the door with one hand and looking bashful. I think he even tries to wink at me and I feel a tiny bit sick in my mouth.

'It'd mean I'm here more . . .' Susie says. Little vixen. 'Not at Niall's half the week. You and I will spend more time together.'

'But so will me and Niall.'

I take a set of keys from my bedside table and go outside. Susie follows as I head down the side of the house where what used to be the window of our dining room is now the door to the upstairs flat. Opposite the door, I notice a beast of a bramble sticking out of a flower bed. This thing is huge – it has a trunk, not a stem. I tut at it but that doesn't make it go away. Niall appears and puts his arm around my daughter, and they watch as I attempt to pin the bramble back in amongst the shrubs, because getting the secateurs and dealing with it properly is as likely as me fixing the lock on the bathroom door.

'*Rubus fruticosus*,' Niall informs me. 'Tricky bastards.'

Susie digs her elbow into Niall. 'Play Dad your landlady's message.'

Niall takes his phone out of his pocket and does so.

'*Niall, you fucking tit . . .*'

I'm with the landlady so far.

'*. . . if you think you're staying another night under this roof you are deluded, and the same goes for your little tart.*'

Susie points to herself and nods with theatrical disgust. Niall pauses the message and tries to look grave.

'That's not nice,' I admit.

'That's what we're dealing with,' my daughter says, as the bramble springs back out on to the path.

'Bollocks,' I say, to the bramble.

'Niall has to smuggle me in and out of the place, Dad. And FYI, the five hundred quid in the jar is from him cause unlike me he's got a job.'

I laugh under my breath. 'Right.'

'What?' Niall says. 'I work. Just because I don't make a song and dance about it.'

I'm aware that Susie is looking at me lovingly (it's not a huge stretch for her, she does like me) but with that slightly censorious thing she does with her left eyebrow. So, I don't look back at her. Instead, using my fingertips to avoid the thorns, I wrap the bramble behind a large thingy plant. I'm not totally sure what it is – only lived here twenty-three years – but it's got green leaves.

'I'm not having a contract with my own daughter.'

'Then you have my word, I'm going to pay you back and not stay here for ever.'

'A verbal contract,' Niall says. 'A non-parol agreement. Just as good.'

'Whatever,' I say.

The bramble leaps back out at me and catches my cardigan, the cashmere one Claire gave me on my first birthday as a divorcee. This weed is alive and taking the piss out of me. It's more alive than I am.

'So, Niall can stay?' Susie says.

'Possibly.'

She leaps up and claps her hands together, then comes over and kisses me on the cheek. I can't acknowledge or enjoy the kiss because the bramble is sticking into me.

'You have a different definition of the word "possibly" to mine,' I say.

Claire said to me when the children were becoming young adults that we should always let them make their mistakes under our roof, where they were safe and loved. This one's for you, darling.

I take the contract out of my pocket and rip it up and toss it in the bin because I am the master of this house and I am in control. The bramble comes with me, clinging to my elbow. 'Fucking thing!'

'Dad!'

'You swear constantly!'

'I'm young. You're eight hundred years old, for fuck's sake. Please don't swear.'

'And how about relocating that torn-up paper to the recycling bin?' Niall says.

I shoot him a withering look (intention). I stare at him and appear to have something in my eye (reality).

Susie backs him up, nodding. 'Come on, Dad.'

For the record, I do recycle. But the dramatic effect of ripping up my daughter's contract was better served by throwing it into the nearest bin. Still, I do what I'm told, taking the torn-up contract out of the bin and putting it in the recycling box, with a bramble clinging to me, because I am

8

in control here. Susie and Niall embrace, the sight of which inspires me to yank angrily on the bramble and get swamped by a whole mob of the thorny bastards unfurling from the shadows.

'Brilliant, Pete,' I mutter. Calmed by self-loathing, I manoeuvre my arms out of the cardigan and leave it hanging on the thorns, ignoring my daughter and her mistake in human form. I let myself in the side door and head up the newly built stairs to the other flat, which is a blank and blinding vista of fresh white paint. It's hard to see where the walls stop and the ceilings begin. Dennis is finishing off the snagging. Dennis has done a great job. Dennis has let me down. The flat is ready to be flogged and I'm not ready to let go.

'Bang on schedule, Dennis.'

'Yup.'

'Useless bastard.'

Where I'm standing was our bedroom. This is where Claire and I listened to Susie tell us that she and her boyfriend Abe wanted to sleep with each other. She was fifteen, he was sixteen. They had been going out for two years. Where Dennis's dust sheets lie folded on the floor is where the three of us sat on our bed, holding hands whilst Susie talked. After she left, Claire said she wanted her daughter to be safe, not losing her virginity somewhere that didn't feel nice. She wanted her to continue talking to us both, not having secrets.

We spoke to Susie and Abe the next day when Erland (our son, conceived in Sweden hence the name) was out. I told Abe that if he slept with a fifteen-year-old he would be at risk of getting into trouble. I told them exactly what Claire and I had agreed, using all the words that my wife had handed me as a gift. If, when Susie was sixteen, they still felt they were ready to sleep together they could do it here. Claire said that it didn't mean they could take the mickey, and Susie's room was not the honeymoon suite. And when Susie and Abe split up three weeks after they had slept together, Susie came straight to us with her bemused, broken heart. She came to us because Claire had guided me through the right way to be a dad to a teenage girl. Our daughter never stopped talking to us because we never alienated her. We were so good at this, Claire and me. I wanted nothing to change and, foolishly, I didn't see why anything ever needed to.

I call the shop before anyone will be in and leave a message to say I'm working from home today. I do this three or four times a week, but I stopped doing the working-at-home bit a long time ago. I tell them to call if there are any problems, but you need customers to create problems so I don't expect any – unless you call the plummeting income from my dying travel business, using up all my savings to avoid making three good people redundant, and sliding into thirty thousand pounds of debt 'problems'.

Being the wise old owl that I am, I choose to ignore all that for another day, and take my book to the kitchen to kill time until Susie is back from her job interview for the role of Assistant Trend Analyst for another fashion brand I've never heard of. This is a big one; they all are. She really wants this one; she really wants them all. She needs this; she truly does.

I lie on the sofa, open my book – Robert Harris, *An Officer and a Spy*, if you're asking – and am on the brink of enjoying it when Niall saunters in, kneels down and writes something on my TO DO list on the fridge door.

'What are you doing?' I ask him.

'Writing stuff down.'

'I can see that.'

'Then I don't understand the question.'

'I'm aware that you're adding something to my DIY to-do list. I'd like to know what.'

'More to-do's.'

'What to-do's?'

'DIY to-do's.'

I bite my lip. 'It's *my* list, not a communal one.'

'It's not really a list, is it? "Fix bathroom door lock" and "Buy super glue" doesn't really amount to a list.'

'What are you adding to it?'

'And please tell me the super glue is not for fixing the bathroom lock.'

'What are you writing on my list, Niall?'

'"Put a lock on Susie's bedroom door."' He smiles innocently at me. 'Be nice to have some privacy.'

I look at the floor and take a deep breath. 'If you feel strongly about it, maybe you should just do that yourself.'

'I don't want to take liberties,' he says, and ambles out of the room.

I look out at the garden rather than throw a heavy object at the back of his head. Claire would not be pleased at how I've let the garden go. Me, I like the Miss Havisham's garden look. Niall has offered to tidy it up but I took offence. It's not that I'm a snob, but what with him not being good enough for my daughter, I don't want to have to thank him for anything.

Niall returns, urgently, muttering, 'Ooh, ooh, ooh,' and adds another thing to my list, saying out loud as he writes, '"Cut – free – cardigan – from – brambles".'

Our garden wraps round three sides of the house. We're at the top end of a long, steep terrace of three-bedroom houses built between the wars. From the front and back garden, you can see across town to the Surrey hills. Claire loved the garden and we both spent very happy times out here. I would do the grunt work and she would plant and prune and have a picture of it all in her head. Basically, she'd tell me what to do.

There are three spots where we laid slabs for a garden bench to catch the sun at different times of the day, and we would take one end each of the bench and move it to where the sun was shining. It never occurred to us to buy more than one bench. For both of us, coming from working-class stock, we instinctively lived within our means. It should be the stuff of legend how much time I have spent in this garden and how little knowledge I have accrued about what any of these plants or bushes are called.

I am standing near to some coppery-coloured things, cutting the cardigan away from the brambles, when Susie arrives home.

'How was the interview, love?'

She marches past me to the front door. From the hallway I hear her scream, 'SHITTING SHITEY SHITWANK!'

I find my sobbing, disillusioned daughter in the kitchen, hugging Niall. He holds her in one arm and stirs soup on the hob with the other hand. He sees me and whispers solemnly, 'Susie did not, repeat did NOT, get the job.'

'You don't say.'

She throws herself into my arms. I would do anything to take this away from her, this bewilderment that a 2:1 in Fashion Design and Commerce has led to three years of unpaid internships, poorly paid bar work and job rejection after job rejection. And a debt similar in stature to my own. I don't know what to say to her.

Niall puts a bowl of soup and a plate of buttered soldiers on the table.

'Parsnip and nutmeg . . .' he whispers.

She smiles and snivels. 'My favourite cheer-me-up soup.' She gives Niall a kiss and sits down next to him. 'He always makes me lovely soup when it's my period or I'm pissed off.'

I'm fine with chit-chat about periods because I'm fifty-three not ninety-three. Don't know why I'm even mentioning it.

12

I look at Niall sitting next to Susie, where I ought to be, and something brilliant occurs to me.

'So . . .' I say.

But I stop and tell myself to be more mature and to rise above my own childish idea.

Nah.

'So . . . Niall, you made that soup two hours ago, when Sooz was in her interview. Does that mean you presumed she wouldn't get the job?'

Niall shoots me a WTF expression.

'You just went straight ahead with the cheer-me-up soup because you didn't think she'd be good enough?'

My daughter pulls fractionally away from Niall as she thinks about this.

'Unless that's celebration soup as well as cheer-me-up soup?' I add. 'But soup's not really a celebration liquid, is it? You didn't believe in my daughter.'

I take from the fridge a bottle of Prosecco given to me four or five months ago.

'I had a bit more faith,' I say, holding up the bottle.

Susie weighs this up, looks at me, looks at Niall, then at me again. 'That bottle's been there for months, Dad.' She kisses Niall. 'Thanks for the soup, gorgeous man.'

Niall kisses her and, behind her back, gives me the middle finger.

Chapter 2

The sun rises on the back of the house, finally, in response to my unspoken requests for it to do so since I woke at four o'clock. Most mornings I wait here for the day to begin, tired from the outset, in a darkness that feels overwhelming. I hold on until the daylight brings its vague, undefined offer of hope that today something will change. Life is a useful distraction from the problems it is responsible for in the first place.

It's a mystery to me that I don't have more friends.

Once upon a time, I would open my front door and collect the milk from the step with the sound of two boisterous children filling the place as they descended from the bedrooms upstairs. I don't think a day passed back then without me thanking Claire for our son and daughter and acknowledging the shitstorm she went through to grow two human beings inside her and deliver them in the most painful, unfit-for-purpose way that a bunch of blazer-wearing men in a wood-panelled boardroom could have devised, had they been charged with the task.

This morning, my view of the street is tainted by the sight of a brashly liveried estate agent's car pulling up outside. Martin, who is handling the sale of the upstairs flat for Claire, gets a *For Sale* board from the boot of the car. I step outside in my M&S dressing gown and Matalan slippers, looking like Jason Bourne.

'Morning.'

Martin is wary of me, which is good.

'Morning,' he says. 'Sorry it's early, my day is rammed. How's it looking upstairs?'

'All right, I suppose. Not finished, though.'

I inspect the *For Sale* board as it goes up. Martin nails a smaller sign beneath it which reads, *1st floor flat, newly converted, 2 bedrooms, balcony.* I ask him if there's any need for all that detail and he chooses to ignore me. He's learning fast.

'Now, Martin, to reiterate,' I say. 'No viewings without me there. I've got a questionnaire to be filled out by anyone who wants to view.'

He doesn't ignore this. 'Really? Maybe we should leave that for when someone's made an offer.'

'No point getting people in who I am not going to agree to live underneath.'

'Right . . .' says Martin. 'It's not a great idea, to be honest. And it's Matthew, not Martin.'

'Really?' I say doubtfully, as if he might want to check his birth certificate.

Niall wanders out, wearing Susie's bathrobe open over his PJs and looking windswept. 'Morning, all,' he says, and smiles at me as he lifts his top and rubs his belly (he does this) and sighs happily at the blue sky.

'I love Saturdays,' the belly-rubber says.

'How profound,' I say. 'How do you distinguish them from weekdays?'

'You know, the traditional way – working and not working.'

'Right.'

Matthew makes his exit. 'We'll speak soon,' I tell him.

Niall inspects the *For Sale* sign. 'This must be hard for you.'

'Not at all. This way, I get to stay in my own home.'

Niall shakes his head in the manner described on page 72 of the *101 Ways to Patronise Your Elders* manual.

'No, no,' he says, 'I'm not having that. It must feel awful. That flat up there is like a monument to lost happiness, a mausoleum of broken dreams right on top of your head, every day of your life.'

'I'm perfectly happy, thank you.'

'How can you be, right? The family seat, sliced in half, and the heart of it – the yolk of the egg, if you will – the wife and mother, scooped out – to continue the egg metaphor – as she pursues a more interesting existence as a lone goddess on the highway of life.'

'You should write,' I tell him.

'I have thought about it. It's 2019, Pete. The world's changed and you've yet to find your place in it.'

'I'm impressed you know what century it is.' I march to the front gate. Niall calls after me. 'Thank God we're here for you, is all I'll say.'

I turn. 'Yeah, I've noticed you're a man of few words.' I remove the smaller sign, the one with all the detail. 'Well, I'll tell you something, I'm not selling that flat to just anybody. I'm going to do some serious vetting up there first.'

'That's a helluva departure from the travel business.'

I stare at him, incredulous. 'Not vetting, you tool!'

He stares back. 'I know!'

But I'm not entirely convinced he does.

'Anyhoo,' he says, 'do you want to hang out? Your daughter's . . . resting.'

The sight of him repulses me so much, I resort to going into work.

Saturday is the busiest day of the week for a high-street travel agent. When I arrive, this fact is backed up by the presence of not one but two whole people on the pavement looking at our bountiful window display. There are no customers inside the place – that would be crazy – just my staff of three, who disguise with varying degrees of success their surprise at seeing me.

Josie greets me brightly. She is nineteen and shy but has a certain spark about her. 'Morning! Can't wait to show you what I've done.'

'That sounds like your social-media tone of voice,' I say, beelining to my hiding place in the kitchenette at the back of the shop.

'Right,' Josie says. 'Instagram. It looks amazing.'

'Tea, anyone?' I call out.

'No, thank you.' Josie.

'No, thank you.' Mrs H.

'Strong with one.' Simon.

I would rather push a fifty-foot-high dung ball up a hill than try one more time to explain to Simon that, after twelve years, I know how he has his tea. And given that 'Strong with one' are just about the only words he ever says, it'd be a shame to cut them off.

Josie appears beside me. 'I'll show you on the iPad.'

'We've got an iPad?'

'No, Grant my boyfriend has got an iPad. Look, this is our Instagram account.'

'We've got an Instagram account?'

She hands me Grant's iPad and takes over the tea-making whilst I look at an array of mouthwatering photos of a hundred or so of the most stunning destinations on Earth. smithsholidayworld is our Instagram name, I learn, and we seem to have put up one hundred and twelve posts from all over the planet, with information about each place and the claim that we are the best people to send you there and meet your every need.

'We have forty-eight followers,' I say.

'Twenty-eight related by blood or friendship to me,' Josie says, 'and twenty people who have followed us from hashtags because they travel or they are in the industry. We'll grow that. I want two thousand.'

'Where are the photos from?'

'Libraries, Unsplash. It's fine, we're allowed.'

I pay Josie sixteen thousand pounds a year plus commission and every time she sees me (which isn't as often as it should be) she seems grateful. She walks to work every day from her mum and dad's home in Merriment, possibly the most inappropriately named housing estate in the UK. Though I can't say that for sure because my former love of travel hasn't taken me to many of them, despite both my parents being born on large, sprawling estates in South London.

I loved my parents and never fell out with them – I still miss them – but I couldn't wait to leave home and never had to worry that I wouldn't be able to afford a room somewhere as soon as I got a job. Sure enough, I was gone at the age of eighteen, working and living in cheap digs; I never went to college, and by my late twenties, with only a tiny deposit, Claire and I were able to buy a three-bedroom house, the one we've recently cut in two. No such effortless entry to property ownership and home-making awaits the Josies and Susies of this world.

Mrs Harrington slides her reading glasses off her nose and lets them hang on their chain as she swings her seat to face us in the kitchenette. 'I have to say, it does look good, the Instagram thing.' She is in her seventies, wears tweed skirts and has a bow-legged invincibility to her that is not uncommon in the Surrey suburbs. Part woman, part Winston Churchill.

She's my bookkeeper, accountant, business manager and fellow travel agent, and she was my parents' first employee fifty years ago. Mrs H likes Josie. I think she admires her energy and the way Josie seems to believe she is lucky to be where she is, even though I see her as working five and a half days a week for a salary that gives her few options at a company that has no future.

When Josie isn't busy, she writes in the Moleskine notebook I gave her, a notebook given to me at some event years ago, which then sat in my drawer. Ideas about travel? A diary? A very long suicide note focusing on the need to escape her job? I've no idea. It's not my business what she writes in there so furiously. I asked her once, six months ago, because I had called her in for a chat and to make her redundant. But I couldn't do the deed, even though I had promised my business banking manager at RBS that I would. I asked her if she was happy and she told me she loved it here. So, to pad out the meeting, I asked her what she wrote in her notebook. She blushed and stuttered, and I immediately regretted asking.

'You really don't have to answer,' I said. 'I don't know why I asked, I guess I just meant that I'm really pleased it's of use to you.'

'Oh, I love this notebook,' Josie said. 'Ideas, I just put down all my ideas.'

I gave her a raise.

Mrs H does have a first name – it's Mary – but when I took over the business and tried to use it, neither of us felt comfortable. She's always been Mrs H. That's what Josie calls her. Simon calls her 'Hello there, err . . .' As Claire once observed, 'Simon says . . . absolutely fuck all.'

That's the crew: Mrs H, silent Si and Josie. None of them earning much, yet together paid a combined total in excess of my profits.

There's a knock on the window. I look up and see Peggs, one of my three best friends (alongside Claire and my oldest friend, Ed). Peggs has his baby boy strapped to him. My face lights up. At least, I presume so, because my heart does. Josie goes, 'Awwwww,' at the window. Si glances up, shows no reaction and returns to his screen. Mrs H waves Peggs in.

'Here's my little lad!' I call out. I hurry over to them and start tickling and cooing at the baby. He laughs and giggles and kicks his legs, just missing Peggs's nuts. In a couple of months' time, Peggs will need to wear a box.

'Who's gorgeous? You're gorgeous!'

Si looks at me like I'm insane. I care not. This little lad, this late, unexpected gift from the gods, is one of the bright stars in my universe right now. I bury my head in his tummy and he squeals with laughter, or fear.

'I could kill a sugary coffee, Pete,' Peggs says.

He looks tired. Mrs H and Josie wave at the baby as Peggs follows me into the kitchenette. I put the kettle on, put a heap of instant coffee and sugar in a mug and when I look up, I see that Peggs is close to tears. I put a hand on his arm.

'Hey,' I say. 'You want to pop out for a nervous breakdown whilst I look after this little fella?'

Peggs nods. He breathes out heavily. 'If I could just have ten minutes in my own headspace. I've been up with him since five, but it's only eleven now and I just need to switch off for a moment – got the whole day ahead and I want it to be good for him.'

'Come on, hand him over. Course you need a break. Where's Summer?'

'I booked her into a day-spa thing with her sister. She's exhausted and hasn't had a treat for months, want her to totally chill out. The two of them never get to be alone.'

'Good for her,' I say.

'I don't even need to leave the shop. I just want to slob for ten minutes, look at some footballing bollocks on social media, you know, veg out.'

I hand him a mug of coffee in exchange for a ten-month-old human and point him to the sofa where our customers are cordially invited to sit back with a brew in one of our slightly stained-by-age mugs and peruse our very lovely, colourful holiday brochures. I think I see a small cloud of dust kick up when Peggs sits down.

I play with Mick. And I love doing it, but I'm going to call him 'the baby' or use a string of off-the-cuff nicknames because, to be honest, as a name 'Mick' isn't doing it for me. I'm hoping he'll grow into it, or that Peggs and Summer will change it.

Peggs sits upright on the sofa at first, drinking his coffee and enjoying whatever he's enjoying on his phone. He's my curator of social media, emailing me links to articles he's read or debates on Twitter. He keeps me less not-up-to-date than I would otherwise be. I follow a total of seven people on Twitter, check into it on a monthly basis and never contribute. Peggs follows a couple of thousand people, hungry in his reading of politicians, progressives, music journalists and anyone involved with Crystal Palace FC. He's been an active member of the Labour Party since he was twenty. Until he met the love of his life at the age of forty-nine and became a dad at fifty-two, he gave money and time to charities and local organisations and the political party to which he has a critical, not blind, devotion. He's everything I'm not, and I love him.

He is also, now, fast asleep in my shop. He remains that way for fifty minutes, in which time I play with the baby, change him, and feed him the bottle I find in Peggs's backpack, warming it in hot water first. I put on the baby carrier, strap mini-Peggs to my chest, check that his heels aren't lined up with my gonads for when I start tickling him, and take him for a walk.

By the river, I feel that wonderful shift in a baby's weight that tells you they have fallen asleep. I cradle his head until I find a bench by a tree to slouch on at an angle that allows my handsome little companion to lie across my chest. I am the happiest man in Old Woking and that is quite a claim given that Woking is the thirty-seventh-happiest town in the UK. This sort of thing, the baby stuff, I love it and I was always good at it. Apart from the time I dropped Erland on to a radiator and then pranged the car taking him to A&E. But my family hardly ever mention that.

The thirty-seventh-happiest-town thing, I made it up. But not the bit about how happy I am when I can hang out with Peggs's son; that's all true.

Peggs texts me:

Where are you?

By the river. Good sleep?

The best. On my way.

I wonder if I should diversify my business and charge people to pop in and take a nap on the sofa during the day. For insomniacs, I could offer a deluxe service in which I talk them through the demise of my business and send them into the deepest sleep of their lives. For depressives, a guided tour of my divorce from the woman I still love, to make them feel better about their own situation.

I'm sitting on a gold mine.

It feels like a magnificent triumph when a parent whose child you are looking after returns and you have their child fast asleep. Peggs sits down beside me with the lightness of a feather.

He whispers, 'You want to come to "Monkey Around" with us?'

'What's that?'

'New soft-play place. He'll sit in a pen full of colourful plastic balls, drooling on them and picking up another cold, whilst fit mums in their thirties feel comfortable chatting to us 'cause they think we're a couple who have adopted.'

Work or Monkey Around. There's no choice to make here.

Chapter 3

Aside from being left with a bone-aching sense of emptiness and yearning afterwards, I enjoy my FaceTimes with Erland in New Zealand.

In a precious moment when Niall is out of the flat, Susie and I call him. It is eight-thirty in the morning in Cable Bay. Erland is on the veranda of his mobile home on the vineyard he works on. As ever, he looks sunkissed and languid, with the glow that working outdoors bestows. The sun is low behind him. He has sent us many photos of this landscape in the last two years and every one of them makes me happy for him and reminds me of an old version of me I dare not dwell on.

Erland takes the mickey out of his sister for having a degree and no job. She calls him trailer trash and laughs at things he says which she'd find offensive from anyone else. Then they move on to me.

'Dad's started swearing a lot.' (My daughter.)

'He thinks we'll like him more – it's pathetic.' (Son.)

'Fuck off, both of you.'

After the call I suggest a movie and pizza to my daughter.

Watching *La La Land* is my idea of a slow death, but the fact that Susie wants to and Niall returns and says he dislikes the idea, means I feign enthusiasm. The film is what it is but my daughter cuddling up next to me on the sofa and Niall being relegated to the floor makes it all worthwhile. I don't reckon he'll go the distance and, sure enough, forty minutes in, he cracks.

He pauses the film and announces, 'A chronological history of psychological torture in western civilisation goes: first, the rack, then waterboarding, then musicals. I am fearful of what this movie might do to my mental well-being.'

'I think you'll find musicals have been around a tad longer than waterboarding,' I say.

'Water torture dates back to the fourteenth century,' he replies. 'It was documented as a practice in Pennsylvania in the 1300s.'

'Pennsylvania's in America, Dad,' Susie adds.

'You two deserve each other,' I mutter.

I'll miss this sort of nonsense if my daughter ever moves out. Which, of course, she will, and must. What sort of father wishes his daughter to remain unemployed so she doesn't leave home again?

'Would you guys mind if I bugger off to the pub?' the druid gardener asks.

'Not at all,' I say.

Niall is on his feet in a nanosecond. And, yes, you heard me right, Niall is a druid gardener. That's his job. It gets better; 'druid' is spelled wrong on his pick-up truck ('Drewid') and, controversially for a man in his profession, he seems to work from home. His career is what rolling one's eyes was designed for.

'Sooz, you mind?'

'Do as your conscience dictates,' Susie says.

This comment means he'll go but not be totally relaxed about going, and that is excellent work on my daughter's part. Niall hesitates before continuing out of the room. I turn up the volume one bar to cement the illusion of me

24

loving the film as much as my daughter but still we hear Niall call out.

'Guys, someone's stolen that five hundred quid.'

I call back, 'I paid the builder with it.'

'Why are you looking at Dad's rent money just before you go to the pub?' Susie shouts.

His face appears at the door. 'I was going to take twenty quid out of it 'cause I can't be arsed to look for my card.'

He has no filter. It's what makes him so annoying and so honest. We listen to the front door shut and I enjoy the prospect of a few hours in a Niall-free universe. Things then improve further when Susie pauses the film. 'It's shite, isn't it, this movie?'

'I believe so,' I say.

She switches it off. We remain slobbed out on the sofa eating Revels. We were always good at lazing around together as a family. I know it's not an Olympic sport, but we aced it.

I lob an unidentified chocolate at her. 'Any work leads, darling?'

'Fu—' She stops her potty mouth on this occasion, I don't know why. 'Nothing. And don't just send the orange ones my way.'

I stop myself saying that something will turn up. I'm unhappy but I don't want to die just yet.

'Nothing,' she says, 'except for another email from Mark in Stockholm talking about the job there.'

'Poor Mark. Doesn't give up, does he?'

'No . . . he doesn't. It's a good offer, a real career, makes you think—'

I lob another Revel at her, in the hope that she'll stop thinking. She catches it in one hand and eats it.

'Seriously, Dad, if I get another orange fondant from you, I'm gonna scream.'

'Like I know what's inside.'

'That must be your superpower.'

'That would be me all over. "Your superpower, Mr Smith?" "I can see inside a Revel."'

'As long as you use it for the forces of good, not evil.'

'Bloody cold in Stockholm.'

'Tropical here, of course.'

Always got a clever answer, my kids. I wish we hadn't sent them to such a good local comp – there were plenty of ropey ones to choose from.

Susie goes to say something but stops herself. We sit in silence. The right thing to do now is to tell my daughter to take the job in Stockholm if that's what she thinks she should do. That's what a good father does now.

'It's so brilliant having you back home,' I tell her.

She switches the TV on again. 'Watch a *Queer Eye*?' she says.

It's one of our treats. Soon, we are in Japan, with a woman called Yoko. She's my age and has turned her home into a hospice because she wants people to have a better death than her sister had. The Fab Five work on getting Yoko to take some time away from all the, you know, death and be good to herself. By the end, we are sobbing our eyes out, and go to our rooms emotionally drained. It's been a great evening.

I am woken at a quarter to midnight by a scraping sound. I go to the front door and through the window to the side of it, I watch the mottled shape of Niall bent over as he tries to get his key in the lock. A minute of this, whilst enjoyable in its own niche way, tells me it ain't ever gonna happen. I crouch down and lift the letter-box flap.

'How's that going, Niall?'

'Tricky little devil, this one.'

'Good night?'

26

'Epic. Can you stop the building moving about?'

I open the door. Niall tracks with it, stepping into the hallway, bent over, still trying to get the key into the keyhole as he shuffles in.

'Strictly speaking, now that you're in the hall, the need to get that key in the lock has passed.'

'Eh?'

'You're inside the house.'

Niall straightens up and looks around. 'It's a flat, not a house.'

I glare at his glazed eyes and return to bed. Feeling lonely, I break my no-phone-in-the-bedroom rule and get mine from the kitchen so that I can enjoy the company of the seven people I follow on Twitter: Ed, Peggs, Susie, Claire, David Baddiel, James Naughtie and Sir Ian Botham. There's a text from Claire, sent at ten o'clock this evening.

> If you're in the mood for some pillow talk, my solicitor says he's chasing you for a signature. There's no rush but every time he chases you, I pay for the privilege. Sorry x

We are doing it our way, and our way is that we agreed almost everything between ourselves, Claire taking the lead and me being monosyllabic and using all my strength not to derail the process or delay it; courtesy of which heroic effort, I still retain a portion of my dignity. Then, when it came to the detail of our home and provisions for the children, she hired a solicitor and we all sat down in a room together. We did this to limit the cost, and to make it clear we were not at war. It felt good being in that meeting room, Claire and I being reasonable and bright together. It was almost romantic. It reminded me of Sunday evenings when we'd have a drink and talk about the kids and what they needed, things they'd said to each of us, what to watch out for about them, funny moments from the week. And then we'd go early to bed.

I have hardly seen Claire since that meeting a year ago. Once the divorce was done, I steered clear of seeing her at first, not because I didn't want to but because I still wanted to so much. In time, she stopped suggesting we meet up, having been blanked for so long, and I took offence at that and refused (to an audience of me) to contact her, out of principle, as the one who had been dumped. And she went back to being busy whilst I waited for her to make the effort to get in contact again, because them's the rules and I'm an idiot.

I'm pretty sure that's how we came to not be seeing anything of each other. But we do text and we talk about our children, who are no longer children.

As I make a cup of tea, I hear my daughter laughing in her bedroom. Then, the low rumble of Niall's voice and Susie laughs again. I sit on the kitchen sofa in the dark and read Claire's message a few times and formulate an answer. I enjoy this version of being with her, which is why I prolong the moment and don't simply reply, *Will do x* and go back to bed.

Draft 1, just to get it out of the way:

Send more filthy lawyer talk, now x

Because we did send messages like that to each other once.

Draft 2, just in case she wants to abandon her 'more interesting life' project and come back to me:

Sorry, will sort first thing, been distracted, the business is going down and Susie really needs me around a lot and I'm thinking of a whole new life, somewhere, somehow, and am behind on my paperwork. Let me pay for the chasing bills, no reason why you should have to. Will sort first thing. Sleep deep xxx

That's a brilliant text. It's a cry for help and a broadcasting of my qualities and struggles, with a tantalising hint that I might move away thrown in (how she'd miss me then). I should send that. Except, it's mostly untrue (Susie doesn't need me, she needs a roof over her head until she gets a job), it's mainly pathetic and it's too long, and Claire will reply by being excited for me moving somewhere new.

Draft 3:

> Sorry, just so busy since Susie moved back in, what with her choosing to live with me and not you, will sort asap, just keep forgetting to during the catalogue of high-quality, cherishable, never to be forgotten father-daughter moments. X

The capital–X kiss is a good one because, on the one hand, it seems like a big kiss (and could be, if the receiver chooses) but on the other it's just the quickest way to text after a full stop, so can seem nonchalant on the sender's behalf. I'm not sure 'cherishable' is a word. 'Perishable' is, 'cherishable' I have doubts about. But that aside, it's a work of art as texts go. I send it, then another offering to pay for the lawyer's chasing letters. What a combo! Brilliant.

She replies immediately:

> Cheers xx

Wait.

What just happened?

My text was designed to open up a highly charged, flirtatious back-and-forth.

Cheers?

In bed I become paranoid that she is only awake at half-past midnight because she's with someone. It takes me a while to consider that, if that was the case, Claire probably wouldn't break off from the orgasmic (bound to be) pleasuring which her physically perfect (bound to be) partner is giving her, to text me about the solicitor.

So I turn to social media, and distract myself with Sir Ian Botham's excellent life.

Unless she's awake because she cannot sleep after so sensational (better than anything that went before) a sexual experience as the one she's just had, and her mind has turned naturally enough to the job of clearing me out of her life completely so that she can devote her time to more of the same.

This is why I have a rule about putting my phone in the kitchen at nine o'clock every evening. I'm wide awake now. It's my own fault, and a bit Claire's.

But I'll blame Niall.

The next morning, I forget to sing and Susie walks into the bathroom, shrieks and does an about-turn.

'Please fix that fucking lock, Dad!'

'Will do.'

I am in a rush because I want to get into the kitchen before what's in the kitchen moves. What's in the kitchen made me so happy when I first saw it five minutes ago that the desire to get back to it distracted me and made me forget to sing. I hurry back and, yes, joy of joys, it's still there. On the sofa. Barely moving. Making a faint groaning sound. A hungover Niall experiencing genuine suffering.

'Good morning!' I shout.

His body is limp. His eyes look like a koala's arsehole, almost cute but all wrong.

'How are we this morning?' I say, clapping my hands together. I hear Susie run a bath as I get eggs, mushrooms and bacon from the fridge. I slam the bread bin shut.

'I said, how are we this beautiful morning, Niall?'

Niall sees what's going on and sits up. 'Never better,' he says weakly.

'Sure?'

He nods.

'Fancy a fry-up?'

I notice a little gag in his throat.

'I'll pass.'

'But you're all right?'

He looks me defiantly in the eye. 'Me? Tip-top. Yourself?'

I nod and set about making breakfast. 'Let me know if you change your mind.'

Niall gets up and slides open the bi-fold doors. 'Bloody weeds . . .' he mutters.

'That's right, you get some air.'

Niall disappears out of sight. By the time he reappears I am sitting down to a feast and he is wiping his mouth and taking a few deep breaths. He looks a bit perkier.

'Nice and fresh out there,' he says and lifts a slice of toast off my plate on his way to the sofa. He throws himself down, takes a bite and talks at me with a mouthful. 'You going in today?'

'Yes, I'm going bloody in! We've not folded yet, you know!'

'Just asking.'

'Are *you* going to work today?'

He waves his tablet at me. 'Been at work since six, same as every day.'

I snort at this. Because I'm twelve. Truth is, I'm disappointed that he seems to have ended his suffering with what must have been a textbook tactical vomit on one of the flower beds. I'd hoped for a day of his head slung over the toilet, Pete Smith style.

31

'What you doing at work today then?' he asks me. He lifts his T-shirt and pats his belly as he talks. It is beyond me how anyone, other than a mafia hitman, can feel this at ease in someone else's home.

'I'd like to understand your work better,' Niall says. 'People can know each other for years and never really understand what they do at work.'

'We're not going to know each other for years, Niall.'

'Paint me a picture. A day in the life of a high-street travel agent.'

I sigh and regret how theatrical it sounds. 'I go to my shop. We sell flights and holidays to people. And I've got a trade fair coming up, actually, so am very busy.'

Niall weighs this up. 'And what do high-street travel agents do at trade fairs these days? Burn effigies of Tim Berners-Lee?'

'Who?'

'My point exactly. The man who invented the World Wide Web.'

Shit. I knew that.

'Oh. That bastard.'

'Where is it? Southend?'

'Er, no, Berlin, actually.'

'Cool. Very cool. I'm impressed. Want me to look up some cheap flights for you?' He waves his tablet at me again. 'Takes a second.'

There's a plethora of fine retorts to this and I would use one of them if I could, you know, think of one.

Chapter 4

I am in the bath listening to opera when Josie FaceTimes me. Josie thinks that FaceTime is a phone call. I decline the call, turn the music off and voice-call her back.

'Judy at Adriatica called, but only wanted to talk to you,' she says.

'That's fine, Josie, I'll call her.'

'She said you've got her number.'

'I have.'

'You sound echoey.'

'Must be the line. Thanks, Josie.'

'Okay, bye!'

Judy from Adriatica will be wanting to discuss our relationship, the one in which Smith's Holidays is named as one of her Italian travel company's lead agents and gets priority access and discounts in return for booking a lot of punters on to their holidays. Judy will be wanting to talk about the one-way-ness of the relationship. She'll be looking to end the relationship.

Rather than call her from the bath, I put my music back on but decide on a change of mood. Red Snapper. Great band. Perfect music for letting you all in on a shocking secret – this is not a fantastic time to be a high-street travel agent. None of Susie or Erland's friends have ever set foot inside a travel agency. As teens, I'd see their faces wrinkle with confusion at the concept of what I do. They'd want to be polite to you, because you're old and they're in your house and they like you on account of generally decent feedback on your parental performance from your child. But despite the good manners, I could almost hear them whimper, '*I don't understand,*' and see them tighten the grip on their phones as if to say, '*My travel arrangements are in my hand – what are you talking about?*'

At some point during my mum's funeral I should have noticed that half the people who had been at my dad's funeral five years earlier weren't there. I should have done the maths on the fact that my core customers were making the same one-way trip to the ultimate unknown destination, and that this was not good for business. But I was too busy cremating Mum and stuff. No, that's an excuse. I was averting my eyes from business reality long before my parents departed.

It started well enough. I learned the trade from them and found that much of it was already in my brain by a process of osmosis. They loved their work almost as much as they loved each other. (I'm not even going to start on my parents' marriage. They were dynamic, happy and very much in love. None of which helps.)

I added a new side to the business, scuba-diving holidays in Europe; I set up partnerships and got to dive Sharm, Gozo, Lofoten. I grew it and took in Bonaire and Cuba. My parents placed their faith in face-to-face contact remaining the heart of a successful travel business and I failed to modernise their thinking because we ticked along, and I only ever wanted to tick along so I could leave early enough to do the school run and be with Claire and the kids as much as possible. I have been to forty countries on this planet and, once I was married, nothing ever beat the feeling of walking through my own front door.

When you're a father of young children you get the chance to do the right thing every day of your life: protect them, feed them, make them feel safe and good, choose to laugh with them instead of getting annoyed. You have a partner who makes you feel stronger every day, helping you correct your mistakes, appreciating the things you get right. Every single facet of it is nurturing to one's soul and self-worth. Now, there's no one to get things right for. No one needs me. I am in an undiluted, non-stop partnership with myself, my fiercest critic.

There's a knock on the bathroom door. At least, I think there is, but the music is so loud I can't be sure. I ignore it anyway. Then there's a banging on the door. I ignore that too and Susie calls out, asking me if I've had a heart attack.

I reach for my phone to turn the music off.

'Er, no, don't think so. Not a big one.'

I switch back to some classical music. I installed a Sonos system when my flat was complete, spent a week transferring my CDs to it instead of going into work, and am already informed by Susie that it's out of date. 'The classic purchase by a man of a certain age,' Niall called it, shortly before I clubbed him to death in my dreams.

Susie marches in and stops dead when she sees me.

'Do you mind! I'm in the bath,' I say.

She tilts her head sympathetically, switches the music off and kneels down by the bath, the empty bath in which I sit fully clothed reading *The Romford Pelé* by Ray Parlour.

'Why are you reading in here?'

'It's nice. I like it.'

'What's wrong with your bedroom?'

'I don't like my bedroom.'

35

It's true. It was the playroom and then became a small snug where Claire and I used to sit and read. I don't like it being my bedroom.

'Living room?' Susie asks.

'Gandalf is in there.'

She sighs, like a mum with a teenage boy she doesn't know what to do with. 'Dad . . .'

'I'm reading.'

'It can wait. Did you put that potted tree in front of the *For Sale* sign?'

'Not exactly in front.'

'Totally obscuring it.'

'Yes.'

'Houses are sold online anyway, not from passing traffic.'

'Then it doesn't matter.'

'Dad . . . I need to talk to you.'

I return to my book, which is a ridiculous thing to do when someone is talking to you, but I don't realise this until I am holding the thing up to my face. When we played hide-and-seek, Erland would stand in the middle of the room covering his face and consider himself invisible. Erland was two. That's the level I'm at right now.

'Must be a great book,' Susie says.

'Yeah. I mean, it's not Joyce.'

'Dad . . .'

I put the book down and turn to her, to listen to what I don't want to hear.

'I'm taking the job in Stockholm. I can't keep working as an intern. I graduated nearly three years ago and it's getting me down. I have to take this job, Dad.'

My daughter wipes away the tear that has already escaped onto my cheek.

'I'm going to tell Niall now.'

36

'About moving to the tundra or the fact that your new boss is a handsome ex-lover who still has a thing for you?'

'We were nineteen, it lasted four months, we never . . . *did* anything.'

'Oh dear, unfinished business.'

'No.'

'That's how Niall will see it.'

'Which is why I'm not going to tell him about Mark, just about the job.'

'What if I tell him, for my own amusement?'

'What if I tell Mum you've taken to lying fully clothed in the bath listening to Mozart, for my own amusement?'

She has a point. This isn't my finest hour. 'It's Puccini,' I say.

Susie gets to her feet.

'Good luck, love.'

'Thanks, Dad.'

Left alone, not allowing myself to sob without a lock on the door, I see myself for what I am: an ageing man with his business and family disappearing in front of him, lying fully clothed in a bath, and I hate myself. I've even got my shoes on. My daughter heading to Sweden, my son on the other side of the world, Claire on a journey of her own. Well done, Pete. You're the man.

Claire and I were still together when Erland went to New Zealand but I think he knew that Claire would leave me before I did. I don't mean that she told him, but that he could see it coming and that he wanted to get as far away as possible. It can't be fun to watch your mum grow bored of your dad.

When Susie was born, I got Erland from nursery and brought him to meet his sister. For one brief moment, all four of us were sitting quietly on the hospital bed. Claire, exhausted, elated, looked at us and said, 'Two is perfect. Let's quit while we're ahead, let's not change a thing.' She was right, it was perfect. But when it came to not changing a thing, I took that a bit literally for the next twenty years. The trick would have been to – well, if I'd known what the trick was, things might be different.

For a change of scene, I get out of the bath and go and stand at the kitchen window, so as to look pathetic in a different part of the flat.

Niall comes in, looking off-the-scale distraught. 'She's going at the weekend!'

'I know.'

We immediately have a problem here in that I am so full of self-pity I'm all out of sympathy and in any way giving-a-shit about Niall. I try to break this to him gently by not looking at him. The garden has my full attention, along with the depressing prospect of being left alone in this flat. I had no idea she was going so quickly.

'Don't you think that's kinda short notice?' Niall says.

'She's got to work, Niall.'

Typical me, putting my daughter's needs first. But yes, I do think it's fast, until it strikes me that she probably made up her mind days ago, if not weeks, and what has taken longer is knowing how to tell the two of us. The one thing – and I insist the only thing – Niall and I have in common is that we spend our days looking forward to Susie coming home. This is both pathetic and back-to-front, given that we, allegedly, have jobs and she doesn't. Didn't.

I hear a weird sound from behind me and when I turn, I see that it is the onset of a wave of snotty, whelping sobs. Niall is inconsolable. Tears are streaming down his unshaven face. His shoulders are heaving. He looks like a toddler who has dropped his ice cream. I'm so shocked I approach him as if to offer comfort but find myself hovering uneasily just beyond reach, as if he smells of wee, until I am saved by the doorbell.

'I'd better get that.' I move fast.

Niall grabs my arm. 'I can sort accommodation with a friend, so you needn't worry about me.'

I look at him, incredulous. 'I don't.'

I open the door to Matthew and a couple in their thirties.

'Just doing a viewing, Peter.'

I step out and shake hands with the couple. 'Pete Smith. I own the flat.'

'I thought a Mrs Smith owned the flat?' the woman says.

I don't like her. I turn to Matthew and ask why he hasn't told me about the viewing, as agreed.

'I did text you,' Matthew says.

I reach for my phone but can't find it. I am still patting my pockets when Niall appears, snivelling, his purple face strewn with tears, and looking like he's just taken a beating. The couple are horrified by the sight of him.

'Must have put my phone down,' I say. 'Sorry. Fair enough, go ahead.'

Matthew rolls his eyes, which I think is unnecessary.

Niall takes my phone from his pocket. 'Here it is. Got you a present, was doing it just now when Susie broke the news. It's a thank-you for everything.' He hands it to me, wiping his tears and snot away with his sleeve.

'That's my phone. You got me my phone?'

'No, I signed you up on Tinder.'

I splutter in front of the couple.

'I've created you an account and everything,' Niall says proudly. 'As a thank-you.'

'*What!* How did you get into my phone?'

'Guessed your passcode. Susie's year of birth . . . original.'

'How dare you!'

39

Niall looks aghast at me. 'That's insanely ungrateful.' He is genuinely hurt.

'But I'm not gay!' I splutter. 'I love gay people and people of every possible description and, you know, absolutely everyone, but I'm not gay.'

'I don't think Tinder's the same-sex one,' the woman says.

'That's Grindr,' her husband says, too enthusiastically for his wife's liking.

'This is a gift from me to you,' Niall protests. 'I put a lot of thought into this. I thought and thought and thought about it, a lot.'

The couple are backing away from the door now and Matthew is trying to usher them round to the flat entrance.

Niall steps towards them but his bulk, and his grief at Susie's news, and his outrage at my ingratitude make it seem like the lunge of a desperate man. 'I could have just given him wine, but I really thought about it ever such a lot – what do you get for a man who needs to get back on the bike, you know?'

I blush at this description of me because, whilst I don't want this couple (or anyone) to buy the flat, I do want the general public to think I am rarely off the bike.

'Is this sex site on my phone now, for everyone to see?' I ask. 'People will think I'm a pervert.'

'No,' Niall says. 'People will think you're a perv if you don't have it . . . "Look at me, I'm sixty years old and perfectly happy to go without sex and love for the rest of my life . . ." equals sexual deviant.'

'I'm fifty-three, you horse's arse!'

Niall turns to Matthew and the couple again. 'Am I right?'

'I'd be on it if I wasn't fortunate enough to be married,' the man says.

His wife grits her teeth. I can't tell if they're a double act who will be laughing about this after the viewing and rushing home for a quickie before going back to work, or if they're on the edge of an abyss and each hoping the other one will step over first.

Matthew looks uneasily at the couple. 'We should get upstairs,' he says.

'Well!' Niall huffs. 'You're welcome. Bloody hell! You try to do something nice!' He marches back inside to the kitchen. The couple look dubious and I see an opportunity to kill off this viewing.

'That sweet grizzly bear of a man,' I say, raising a brave laugh. 'Or should I say, child in a man's body, because that's all he is. He just loves people and gets over-excited, but you'll get to know him properly and learn he's no real danger, despite what the authorities say.'

I bid them good day and listen to the footsteps above as they view the flat. They are gone in less than five minutes.

It is shortly after four in the morning. I can count on the fingers of one hand the number of times in the last year I have slept later than four o'clock. And I'm talking about a severed hand with two fingers left on it. My waking terrors are fed by the terrible twins of debt and divorce.

Rather exotic is the fact that I wake up the same way people wake from nightmares in movies: sitting bolt upright, gasping for breath. In my case, this four a.m. ritual comes not because of a bad dream or a dodgy screenplay but because I think I am having a heart attack. I know that I'm not, that my mouth is dry and I can't swallow and this seems, in half-sleep, like being unable to breathe. But the part of my brain that knows that one day, given the extreme nature of my financial plight and mental distress, I might have a heart attack always believes that today is the day.

That would be very me; dying of a heart attack, brought on by the stress of mistakenly thinking I was having a heart attack.

41

When I wake like this, it is always to a very definite thought or fact sitting at the front of my brain, and usually it is one of the following:

One – why the people I have known in the travel world for decades have totally ignored my emails to them about merging or buying me out.

Two – my belief that the stress I feel over my work means I'll die soon and become a distant memory to my son and daughter who, by middle age, will have lived as much of their life without me as with me.

Three – not dying but my children being ashamed of me and preferring to hang out at the lovely big house Claire buys with her next husband, who is nice, successful, good-looking, solvent and hung like a tapir.

Four – the fact that I feel unable to share my money problems, work worries and general self-loathing and feeling of failure with anyone, thus calling into question all my close friendships.

Despite all this, there is something about my kitchen at four-thirty in the morning that I enjoy. The silence. The growing light. Coffee. Telling myself today will be different. But enjoying that time is only a relative value, it feels good compared to what has preceded it: the fake coronary, staring at the ceiling scared, despairing and lonely, feeling unconnected to lifelong friends. Compared to my four-to-four-thirty-a.m. slot, coffee in the kitchen is the Maldives. Compared to being asleep in bed with my ex-wife, it's a damp day on the Isle of Sheppey.

I know that there are millions of people who would be thrilled if they had to start again from fresh with what I have. And they'd be a lot more grateful than I am feeling. But I'm not and I don't know what I'm supposed to do about that.

I switch my phone on and see a text Claire sent me last night.

Thinking of surprising Susie at the airport to see her off. You going? X

Can't go. She's all yours. Lovely surprise for her x

When morning comes, Susie packs for Stockholm while I pack for the trade fair in Berlin. We both leave tomorrow. I chivvy Niall to get his things packed up, but he reminds me that, given his approach to material possessions, leaving here will take him approximately three minutes. He is, anyway, too busy lying on Susie's bed taking items out of her suitcase and throwing them across the floor and begging her not to go. It's pathetic but I don't say anything as he's kind of doing my job for me.

Chapter 5

Niall is in the kitchen, making breakfast. His tablet is propped up against an industrial-sized tin of olive oil and on the screen is what looks, I have to concede, like a work-type thing. He has three hobs in use. The oven is on and the grill door open. Niall glances up at me and winks but says nothing. He takes the coffee pot and pours me a cup, stirs in a half-spoon of sugar just the way I like it, then takes a milk jug from the hob and plunges it until the milk is a creamy, frothy texture and pours that into my coffee. He stirs it and winks again as he hands it to me.

Why he doesn't look overwhelmed by cooking a breakfast with more than two constituent parts to it is beyond me.

'That's nice,' he says. His voice is a purr.

'What's nice?' I ask, but Niall doesn't seem to hear me. Which is fine.

I go to the sofa with my coffee. I hear the shower turn off and Susie singing. This is the last time I will hear that sound. The next time I have breakfast in here, I'll be alone. I had been living in the flat for two weeks before she asked to move in and for most of that time Dennis was still here finishing things off. I've not really been truly alone here, and I wish I didn't have to go to a trade fair but could close the door when Susie and Niall leave today and face up to the solitude. After Claire left, there was a period when I felt excited about the future, the openness of it, the limitless possibilities; it lasted for twenty minutes and then I wanted her and the children back and that's pretty well where I'll be again with Susie gone.

'Can you repeat that?' Niall says. 'I didn't get you.'

'I didn't say anything.' I say.

'No problem.' Niall says. He looks across at me and smiles. 'Hungry?'

'No,' I say.

He grinds pepper into a saucepan, confidently, the way TV chefs do.

'Why don't you put this down to experience and stop worrying?'

'What?' I ask.

He looks at me. Smiles vacantly. 'What?'

'What?'

'I'll talk to you later.'

'Eh?'

I cannot wait for this man to leave my home.

'It's Niall,' he says. 'Talk turf to me.'

'For fuck's sake, Niall, are you off your head?'

'One sec,' he says, to the scrambled eggs. He looks at me, pulls his hair back, and removes an earpiece. 'What?'

'Nothing, I thought . . . nothing, Niall, just . . . nothing.'

He is confused by this and returns to his call. I am a dinosaur. I still think that if I am in a room with one other person and they are talking, they are talking to me.

Susie enters looking stylish and pumped up. She leans over the pans on the hob and smells the food theatrically. By the time she's done this, Niall is, of course, handing her a cup of her favourite coffee, grown in an organic, off-grid, fair-trade, politically neutral corner of a former war-torn nation, ground by Buddhist monks, and walked here by druids who leave no carbon footprint, to be mainly drunk by speccy, T-shirt-wearing digital disruptors (I don't know what they are, but Josie talks about them being our problem at work) and by us three.

Susie sits down next to me and cuddles up. She sips her coffee and sighs with pleasure at the taste.

'All packed?' I ask her, with huge originality.

She nods.

'How are you feeling?'

'Really excited,' she beams.

What a bitch.

Niall is talking into his hair again. 'Okay, team, ladies and gentlemen, I'll be AWOL for the morning, trip to the airport, so you've got Sally to call if you need. Work hard, work happy.' He taps his tablet, moves it aside and starts serving up the food, which looks incredible.

I turn to my daughter. 'Really? You have "nervous", "unsure", "sad to be leaving me", all at your disposal, but you're going with "really excited"?'

'Yeah, sorry. I just need to get there before I think too much about it, and get started.'

I put my arm around her. 'Good for you,' I say, into her hair. 'It's going to be fantastic.'

Our itineraries see me leave first, heading out to my taxi in the hope that Susie and Susie alone follows. But never a great respecter of personal space, Niall is there too. He is fully clothed for a change but with bare feet, just in case I might momentarily forget that my university-educated daughter, the first person on my side of the family to get a degree, is in love with a man so lazy he has become the only gardener in the universe who works exclusively in a kitchen.

Susie and I hug, and I don't want to let go. For once, I grow up and do the right thing (I don't weep openly) and put a credible smile on my face.

'Good luck, darling, I'm so proud of you.'

'Thank you, Dad. Visit me soon.'

'How soon?'

'Give me a month to settle in.'

'Oh, okay. Knock 'em dead, darling. You're brilliant.'

'I love you, Dad. Enjoy Berlin.'

I had planned to be warm and kind to Niall at this moment, seeing as our cohabiting days are now over, but when it comes to it, I can't be arsed. I'm fucking miserable about Susie leaving (to be fair, Niall's not over the moon) and I'm weighed down by the stark reality of the truth about my trade fair in Berlin, so I don't even look at him as he makes to hug me. I head for the taxi and, without turning to him, say, 'Bye, Niall,' in a chirpy voice. It's immature but makes me happy.

As the taxi takes me away, I look back, like in the movies, in the expectation of seeing my daughter waving longingly at me, like in the movies. But she's already gone back inside, and I see, instead, Niall dragging my pot plant out of the way of the *For Sale* sign. The close-up of this moment, just like in the movies, is of his bum crack protruding from his jeans and that is exactly the image I deserve.

What I referred to as the stark reality of the truth about my trade fair in Berlin is that it's being held in Birmingham. The German capital was the first name that shot out of my mouth when trying to paint an interesting version of my life to Niall. Berlin sounded cooler than Birmingham at the time − and always will − but I have to ask myself, was it worth lying and having to pretend to my own daughter that I am now heading to the airport when I am going to the train station?

In Birmingham, I am surrounded by successful travel people with ideas and energy. I do not feel comfortable.

Now that I have all the time in the world to reinvent my company and myself, I cannot tell if I have no motivation to do it or no idea how. I enter one stand where, in a neon-lit cubicle, a questionnaire about my business concludes that we have a digital presence of 2, on a scale of 1 to 10. The three people on the stand are mute with embarrassment as I thank them and leave. One of them hands me a printed brochure, which seems ironic. I hide it in my bag, in case everyone else here was sent a link.

The evenings are sociable, as is a trade fair's wont. On the first I have a drink with a travel agent called Jack Kinney. He's a nice bloke, lives and works in Stroud but his first-ever job was for my late Uncle Ian in Cheltenham.

'How important is the digital side of things, Jack, d'you think?'

He looks at me curiously, like he's waiting for the punchline. When he realises it's a straight question, he says, 'You can no longer exist in business without a significant digital presence.'

I nod. And as I raise my drink to my lips, mutter, 'I'll get one tomorrow.'

He laughs affectionately. 'You crack me up,' he says.

I do not ask him why he never replied to the email I sent him eight months ago, suggesting he buy me out and have a presence in the south-east. Don't ask questions you don't want to hear the answer to. It's why I haven't asked Claire too much about her decision to leave. Which isn't to say I didn't ask her why she was leaving me; I just didn't let her answer. I would start those conversations, but I would scupper them too, or pull out, before they went anywhere. Instead of asking her why she didn't want to be with me any more, which I needed to know but didn't want to hear, I would ask her, 'Why don't you love me any more?' because I knew she would reply, 'I do love you.'

'Then don't leave! Why would you want to leave someone you love? That makes no sense, Claire. That's not logical, it's not wise. Love is everything.'

'I love my mum but I don't want to live with her.'

'I'm like your mum to you?'

'Wrong thing to say, not what I meant. I can try to explain why I want to leave.'

'No, thanks.'

'Then what is this conversation about, Pete?'

'Trying to make you feel as shit as I do, Claire. Derr!'

'I'm way ahead of you on that front.'

'I really, really do not believe that is the case, all due respect.'

And so it went on, shadow-boxing around the theoretical possibility of talking about 'us' without ever doing so because I didn't want to be formally notified of the fact that Claire was bored of our life together. I knew she was because I had watched her grow that way for two or three years, as Erland and Susie's departure left Claire exposed to undiluted marriage. I pretended it wasn't happening or hoped it would sort itself out and that, if I didn't bring it up, she would be too kind to mention it, let alone act upon it. And she didn't want the conversation either, because she knew it would lead, inevitably, to her hurting me by saying she loved me but didn't want to be with me, and she has never wanted to hurt me.

I would like those men whose wives or girlfriends turn toxic on them and treat them horribly to know how lucky they are to have something to hate, to have a separation they want and that will instantly improve the quality of their lives. I am jealous of them all. I would love to dislike my ex-wife. It would give me something to do and nothing to miss.

Day two of the trade fair is a blur. I listen to a couple of talks and it's all in a language I understand but can no longer speak.

I wander aimlessly and no one notices. Watching this industry of mine rattle and hum warns me that I am in serious trouble and that applying for jobs I am not qualified for at four-thirty in the morning is not a plan, not a fresh start, it's just serving up guaranteed rejection.

By the end of the second day (by which, FYI, I still do not have a digital presence) I can't hack the thought of a second evening. I go for a walk by the Grand Union Canal towards the centre of town. I could do with hearing a friendly voice and decide to call Ed or Peggs. My social life seems to have reduced down to these two and our monthly breakfasts, and there is a certain symmetry to that given that these two are where my social life started, years back. Or the symmetry would be pleasing if I was ninety years old. Fifty-three seems quite young to be down to two people.

Social anthropologists amongst you will be shocked to learn that Claire was the driving force behind our social life. It's not that anyone has turned against me, it's just that most of our friends were her friends and when a couple split into a self-depreciating, very-sad-at-his-divorce, directionless bloke and the inspired and inspirational bundle of understated but brilliant ideas that is Claire Smith (who wouldn't hang on to a surname like that?) and given that of the two of us Claire is better to listen to, better to be with, and better to look at, well, given that choice, who you gonna call?

Right now, Peggs will make me laugh and a call to him will guarantee that I either get to hear the baby gurgling and making noises that are getting ever closer to his first words, or I'll at least get to hear Peggs talk about the little fella. But, given that I want someone to wave a magic wand and find me a job and income and purpose, Ed's my man. Ed and I have known each other since we were four years old.

'Where are you?' I ask.

'In town, overnight. Had a lunch and staying up for a couple of days with Debs.'

He doesn't ask me where I am because I tend to be in the same place. Debs is Ed's wife of twenty-six years. She's a lawyer and works four days a week, staying in their London flat. Ed joins her up there and sees friends, goes to bookshops, nice restaurants and music gigs. This is his life nowadays. He is in the process of retiring and lives in Moreton-in-Marsh, where Debs joins him for their three-day weekends. All of us hate him on principle. All of us being Peggs and myself.

'I say "with" Debs but she's out at a sodding party I wasn't invited to.'

'Hosted by someone who has clearly met you, then.'

'Hop on a train to town and I'll buy you dinner,' Ed says. 'It's only forty minutes – come on, Smithy!'

I don't tell Ed I'm in Birmingham. I am in sight of New Street station. 'Yeah, why not,' I say, feeling a surge of hope at the prospect of seeing a friend.

'Excellent!' Ed says. 'Be good to see you without that wanker Peggson.'

I stride towards New Street, checking the train times as I go. The last one back to Birmingham is at half-eleven. It's an hour and a half to Euston now, so I'll be in London by seven-thirty. I'll spend three hours on a train tonight in order to spend three hours with a mate; the way I'm feeling, that's well worth it.

The brief period of my youth which I spent living in London was in a rented room in a flat-share on the Caledonian Road, above a pub which had become an Ethiopian restaurant. I was never that big on clubbing, always preferred a pub, but I did my share of nights out in the nearby warehouses of the then-abandoned industrial savannah of King's Cross and York Way.

To my untrained eye, the Euston Road doesn't seem to have changed in thirty years but crossing through St Pancras and into King's Cross, it is impossible to reconcile the place with what I knew then. The weight is oppressive, of feeling that I was somehow better off back then as a twenty-year-old than I am now, storming towards old age and unable to afford to step into any of these shops or restaurants and heading to meet the man I will have known for fifty years next year, on the basis that we both understand he will pick up the tab. I sometimes feel physically sick at where I've got myself to.

And I never thought I would have to take a deep breath and summon my strength before entering a restaurant to see my oldest friend. All my life, the whole point of my friendships has been how easy they were, the total absence of self-awareness. Now, that's all gone, and the deep breath is a preparation for the upcoming performance of my long-running one-man show, *Everything Is Fine*.

My work was never a talking point with my friends. I paid my bills and, naturally enough, went on really good holidays with my family. My wife and I jointly kept our children housed and fed and clothed, safe and happy. I was there for breakfast and, on the days when Claire did the school run, I was back for their bath and bedtime. I did all this without breaking a sweat, and I loved that effortless solidity was my identity, my thing. It's what earned me my place alongside a high-earning barnstorming friend in Ed and a brilliant mind and conscientious citizen in Peggs. I was the guy who was calm, tanned and always with my family. And I hate the thought of admitting that my career seems over and I'm at that unemployable age, and that I'll be returning to an empty home in a couple of days; but if I don't admit it very soon, I think my brain might explode, if my dorsal aorta doesn't get there first.

Ed and I embrace, as we always do, and it feels great. I hold a second longer, another one of the small cries for help I've been sending out for a year or so.

'Look at us,' Ed says, 'spontaneous bastards. You should come up more often.'

'Absolutely.'

He orders a beer and I order a Negroni. I'm not a big drinker but I like a Negroni. I got a taste for them on a work trip to Florence years ago. Then, when the kids were teenagers, we had four summers when we went back to the same villa in Italy because we loved it so much. It was remote and had a pool and there was one simple restaurant within walking distance on the hillside, and we'd go there most evenings, the four of us, surrounded by olive groves and the stupefied pleasure of having been in the sun all day, falling asleep whenever your body asked you to, moving from sun to shade and back again, eating fruit and bread and cheese and hanging out with your wife and children all day, saying yes to your teenage kids whenever they asked for your time or attention, listening to them turning into young adults, having hysterics over the stupid things you all say.

Fucking hell.

The restaurant we liked had views across the hills to Assisi. The terrace was covered in pine needles and the menus were handwritten and small. The air was warm but not stifling. Claire would wear her shorts and flip-flops and have a light shawl she'd hug around her. If we went later in August, she'd wear faded denim jeans in the cooler evenings. Her skin would be nut brown and her freckles out and I would start the evening with a Negroni and feel it slip down my spine and I would believe I could stop the clock and have this moment for ever.

Ed leans forward. He's a kind, impatient man. It has served him well in business. He likes getting to the point.

'How are you? How are you getting on?'

'Not too bad,' I say.

He makes eye contact. 'Yeah?'

'Work's not great.'

'You can't take that personally.'

'Absolutely. That's what divorce is for.'

When the drinks come, he chinks my glass and says, 'Good to see you.'

I'm not sure how Ed or anyone I know would react to me no longer doing the only job they have ever known me to do. But suddenly I am curious, and as Ed talks about a case Debs is working on and consumed by, both loving and worrying about it in equal measure, as she always does, my mind produces a beautiful short story of a fantasy of Ed finding me a job through a colleague or a mate – decently paid, nice people – which makes me feel good about myself and takes my worries away.

'I'd quite like to just work for someone else,' I say to him, when we fall into silence. 'Not have to worry or think about it, just turn up.'

'Just turning up no longer cuts it,' he says. 'You've got to want to do the job or be able to pretend. You losing the travel bug?'

I shrug and smile politely. I can't believe he thinks I've still got it.

'You look a bit tired,' Ed says. 'You seem a bit . . .'

'I'm fine.'

We look at our menus in silence. Soon, my focus goes, and I stare at the words and get lost in my own thoughts. For a moment, I think that if someone whispered in my ear to ask me where I was, I wouldn't know.

'Yum bloody yum,' Ed says.

I put the menu down and drain my drink. 'I keep waking up at four in the morning thinking I'm about to die and that by the time they're middle-aged Susie and Erland will have forgotten me.'

Ed looks over his menu as if someone's just told an offensive joke. 'Jesus, mate! That's not my idea of "fine". How often does this happen?'

'Just about every single night for the last eight months.'

'*What!*' Ed is horrified and that feels nice. 'Look, it's not going to happen – you're not going to, you know . . .' He stares at me with his mouth open.

I smile and nod. 'I know,' I say, even though I don't.

'Is this about Claire, or work being not so great – what?'

'It's difficult to separate them. Doesn't help that both Susie and Erland are now a long way away.'

'That's perfectly normal.'

'So is not being deliriously happy about it.'

'There's no point feeling like that. Our children are adults.'

'I guess the waking up early is quite a bit about the business.'

Ed leans closer. 'How long have you been stressing about work, Smithy?'

When you hit rock bottom, you presume the people closest to you have worked it out. It's a revelation to me, in this moment, how little Ed thinks about me and my situation in between our monthly breakfasts. When his son was expelled for taking cocaine at the age of fifteen and would disappear for days, I couldn't stop worrying about him. I was calling Ed three times a week.

'Two years,' I say.

Ed sits back, disgusted. 'Okay, well, that's a ridiculous length of time not to mention it. How much capital have you got left?'

I laugh to myself. 'None. Just debt.'

I see the barely disguised horror on Ed's face. 'You've run out of money?'

'A long time ago.'

He has so much to say about this that, fortunately, he doesn't know where to start. It's unfathomable for Ed that someone he knows and loves is in this situation. He's worked hard and always had his eye on the prize. His only regret is that Debs isn't retiring too. He wanted them to be together all the time and to travel, but she loves her work and believes a relationship is stronger for not doing everything together every day – by which reckoning, mine and Claire's should be impregnable by now.

'I'm going to say those three magic words to you,' Ed says. 'Steak and chips.'

I look away.

The last year we went to the villa in Umbria, the owners told us it was up for sale. We did think about it. Claire and I lay in bed discussing it, playing it through, a life lived there. With the children, we'd all joke about it. 'When we live here, we'll have this here, and that there.' And one evening, at dinner, as I sipped my Negroni, it was a sixteen-year-old Erland who said, 'You realise that if we moved here, the first time we strolled out for the evening and sat down right here at this table, it would all feel different. Not as good. It wouldn't be like this at all.' And he was right, of course.

'I could do with you checking in on me,' I say to Ed. 'I'm a tad alone with all this.'

'Mate, we'll talk every day from now on, and I'll come see you next week and we'll sit down and work on a game plan.'

I could weep with gratitude. 'That's exactly what I need. Thank you.'

The waiter comes across to us and Ed takes control. 'Steak and chips twice. Rare for me. Thank you.' Ed hands him the menu. The waiter looks at me. 'Medium rare, please.'

I smile my thanks at the waiter and then, as I let my eyes wander across the restaurant, I say to Ed, 'You been horse-riding recently, you pseudo upper-class twat?'

I sense Ed's relief at a change in the conversation. He settles back and his jaw relaxes and he tells me more about the riding stables he and Debs have put money into near Stow.

'I'd love to see you on a horse,' I say.

'I'm getting better,' he says. 'It's never too late to learn. But Debs is in a different league.'

'We've always known that.'

'No argument there. Talking about men who snagged women way better than them, do you see Claire? How is it?'

'It's fine. Really. She's good.'

We fall into silence, in which we drink and avoid eye contact.

'I mean,' I say, 'it will be fine. Eventually.'

'Smith,' Ed says gravely, 'it really will.'

I head back to Birmingham on a high. There's a warm, gooey feeling about being heard and cared about.

I miss train carriages being dark enough to see outside at night. I would like to watch the darkness over the south of England outside, but instead I can only look at the reflection of me and the dazzling strip lights and other late-night passengers.

I text my daughter and then my son.

I love you. Dad xx

I text Claire.

I'm really missing the children tonight. I just wanted to say that. No agenda. No reply needed x

But I get one.

If it helps, just remember that Susie screwed up your sleep patterns
for the first four years of her life and is currently unemployable in the
UK, so she can't be all that.

I watch the little pulsing spots on my screen as she types
another message.

But I know what you mean, I'll miss her too. Very much. I know you
weren't saying it, but I want to say, gently, that you and me being
together wouldn't change that, we'd still be missing the children, we
just wouldn't be alone feeling that way x

I reply thus:

I'm not alone. I'm taking a quick break from my Tuesday night orgy x

I hear that orgies are very good cardio x

Absolutely. I look radiant the following day, despite the clap x

Do you recommend them? X

In some cases, yes. But not for you. I think a book club, all female,
would do you the world of good x

You're always looking out for me x

You are welcome x

Always looking out for her. She has no idea how true this
is. Every time the doorbell rings.

Ed's words of support play musically in my head as I remove the nonsensically thin strip of purple blanket that adorns the foot of my Premier Inn bed. His promise to be in touch every day makes me feel less invisible and I sleep deeply and wake to what feels like a brave new morning and a future with potential. All this is lacking detail but replete with va-va-voom. I even consider a wank but instead I text the ex:

> Perestroika is the term used to describe the end of central planning in the Soviet Union and describes the period of warming relationships between Gorbachev's Russia and Reagan's US.

Oh, come on, what man hasn't sent that text to his current or ex-wife at some time or another?

Claire doesn't reply and that makes me feel stupid and very, very lonely. Then I feel useless. Then ugly. Finally, invisible again. And all this is before I even start on the possible scenarios preventing her from getting to her phone.

Four minutes after I send the Perestroika text, she responds at last and I'm Julie Andrews singing on a hilltop.

> Thank you for your interesting fact-filled missive. Duly noted. I'm guessing that you breathalysed at 6, 7 or 8 last night when you texted me from your orgy?

> I was one Negroni down so 6 is fair, I think. Hard to remember, I was so busy being not alone.

This is brilliant on my part. It's an admission of how lonely I am conveyed in humorous, non-tragic terms that suggest I am on the brink of great things whilst leaving the door wide open for her to return to the stimulating repartee-Vesuvius that is her ex-husband.

I possibly need to explain two things. Firstly, the breathalyser. It's not complicated: we have both sent each other messages since being divorced that betray a certain looseness of tongue or thought and usually these come later in the day. The first time I did it, she let me off the hook next day by guessing a mark out of ten for my alcohol levels the previous evening. This was generous of her and took what I had said off the table (and I was sober). Even kinder of her, she has made similar mistakes and given me the opportunity to be generous back.

Secondly, Perestroika. Some of you know that Russia's leaders weren't always the liberal, free-spirited, open-minded capitalists of today. It used to be a grey, oppressive place that took a dim view of same-sex relationships. Perestroika was the route from the latter to the former and Perestroika was, and remains to me, a monument to the uniqueness of the woman who gave me two children and thirty years of happiness. Claire had, and presumably still has, a habit (she did it four or five times a year, for many years) of sitting up in the middle of the night and saying things in her sleep which were both audible and incomprehensible, and bananas, and of which she would have no recollection the next morning. There were some real gems ('Peter, take the teddy bears out of the room and we'll never mention it') and some more run-of-the-mill mutterings, but one night four years ago, in midsummer, I was woken by her sitting up in bed and digging her finger into me, looking both perplexed as hell and utterly beautiful in the low light of a summer night an hour or two before dawn. With a searching voice, she said, 'So, what exactly is Perestroika?' Then she lay down on her side, with her beautiful, sleek back to me and the curve of her hips disappearing into the sheet, and slept soundly until her alarm. And it is without doubt one of the most consuming moments of love and adoration, among many, which I ever felt for her.

But, hey, I'm sure your partner has done the same thing.

Chapter 6

I surprise myself by staying in Birmingham for a further two days and nights and seeing the trade fair through to the bitter end. I've paid for the hotel, can flirt with the industry without embarrassing myself, and read in bed for two solid evenings whilst continually checking my phone – for what or who, I have no idea. In other words, I delay for a little longer the return to my empty flat.

Susie texts from Stockholm as my train approaches Woking. She has completed three days at work and it's going well. She's nervous but it feels great to be in a job. Mark is not too involved and is leaving her direct boss to look after her. Stockholm seems beautiful. She can't wait for me to see it. We'll take a ferry out to the islands.

I haven't heard from Ed since I saw him, but Susie's message puts me in a good mood and I have some purpose in that before Ed visits next week to help me sort out a plan, I must work out how much I need to earn, how long before I need to start earning it (two years ago) and which one of my overdrafts to raid for a visit-Stockholm fund, which Ed doesn't need to know about. I'll spring–clean the flat tomorrow (there, I've said it, flat not house) and enjoy the silence and get some thinking done.

It is early evening on Beaconsfield Road. I still love coming home to this street after so many years. The taxi drops me off and I drag the pot plant back in front of the *For Sale* board before I go in. (I've perked up, not grown up.) I step back onto the pavement and look down to the twinkling lights of town and up to the dark shape of the hills on the horizon.

Woking at its very best. In darkness.

I turn and face the front door, make my way tentatively up the path and let myself in. I stand for a moment in the hallway and acclimatise to the emptiness. Susie is well and truly gone and she has taken her background noise with her. The radio or a speaker on somewhere, the sound of her singing to herself or laughing on the phone. All those sounds have gone. The flat is silent. I won't have to sing any more when I'm in the bathroom.

I am still holding my bag. For a moment, I wonder if I will ever move from this spot. Yes, I feel happier now that I know Susie has safely started working life in a Stockholm that my imagination had turned into the favelas of São Paulo until I heard from her, and, yes, I feel more positive having blurted it all out to Ed and knowing that he is going to be there for me, but this will be a journey of highs and lows I realise as I stand here. This moment is a low. I'm lonely. I can't move for wanting my family.

I then find myself sitting on my bed, still wearing my coat. I don't know how long I've been there. I try to tap into what it is I am feeling. I'm not a man of huge self-analysis (you gasp with shock). If I feel pissed off or worried, I take that and live with it until the feeling goes away or, possibly, it strikes me now, I get used to living with it. I'm from Surrey, where we don't do introspection; we have commuting to do and squash to play and a new Waitrose opening somewhere soon.

I run a bath and finally remove my coat and then I keep going to the other extreme and strip off. Why not? This is my flat and I finally have the solitude that divorce offers. I want to learn to relax in my home again. As a family man, I was a very relaxed human being. Or, as Claire came to see it, monumentally dull. Fine lines.

I stroll naked but for my socks into the kitchen, take the bottle of Prosecco from the fridge, pour myself a glass and take the glass and bottle into the bathroom. I add some bath foam to the water and put on Beethoven's Seventh.

It's all absolutely tremendously fucking lovely.

The water is hot. I've overdone the bubbles. I don't go as far as lighting a few tea-lights, but I do consider it. I take a sip of my drink and sink down into the water. I duck my head in, listen to the sub-aqua rumbling of the taps filling the bath and the gravelly cellos and remind myself, much as Ed did three nights ago, that I have a lot to be thankful for. I come up for air, settle back, shut my eyes, listen and drink.

It's all going to be okay.

And then the door opens and Niall strolls in, pulls down his jeans and underpants so that his hairy bum cheeks are two feet from my face, and takes a noisy slash.

'Yo,' he says.

Because the column of wispy dark hair rising from Niall's arse crack is the last thing in the world I want to see, I can't take my eyes off it. I am enraged and close to tears.

'WHAT – THE – *FUCK* – ARE YOU DOING HERE?'

Niall looks at me like he doesn't understand the question. 'Having a wazz?'

I reach for my phone and turn down the music. He wiggles his bum as he shakes and zips up. He turns and smiles amiably, looking as he always, but always, does, as if he's just come out of hibernation.

'Through gritted teeth' is not just a phrase, it's scientifically accurate: I'm doing it right now. 'I mean, why are you in this flat when you moved out three days ago?'

'Ohhhh . . .' he says, forgiving me my stupidity. 'That. Didn't work out, wasn't nearly as nice as here. It wouldn't be fair on Susie coming home to that when she flies back to see me. And you don't want me living somewhere grotty.'

'I'm okay with it.'

'No, no, no. The worry would kill you. You're a worrier.'

'Where are you planning to live then? From today?'

Niall rests back against the sinks and sees the bottle.

'Oooh, bubbles, shall I get a glass?'

'No, you shall not get a bloody glass.'

'You're going to drink a bottle by yourself?'

'I am now.'

'What are you celebrating?'

I look at him, as murderously as one can when naked in a bubble bath.

'What?' he says.

I take a deep breath. 'Am I a naturist, Niall? No, I am not. Do you even live here any more? No, you do not. So, please leave me the fuck alone to have my bath.'

Niall looks hurt and heads to the door.

'Wash your hands!'

'Make up your mind.'

He walks back to the sink and washes his hands, as I bury my head in mine.

While I'm getting dressed in my bedroom – angrily, as if stamping my feet through the leg holes of my undies is going to teach somebody somewhere a lesson – the smell of Thai green curry reaches me. I take my glass and bottle and follow the aroma like a Bisto kid to the kitchen where I find Niall chopping up vegetables with his customary expert exuberance. There is an armful of fresh ingredients on the work surface, not all of which I could put a name to, steam rising from a pan on the hob, coconut milk and lemongrass in another. For five seconds it all looks like a high-end Lurpak ad until Niall pauses to pop one hand down his trousers and scratch his crotch. I start a text to Susie asking her to call him and tell him to get the hell out of my house but stop myself. She deserves to be left alone to get on with her new life.

I notice that the kitchen is impeccably clean. I inspect the rest of the flat. The whole place is spotless. Even the windows. It's like my fantasy of how I was going to have it by the time Ed comes to stay next week. I poke my head back round the kitchen door.

'Second time, yo!' Niall calls out when he sees me. 'You hungry?'

'Make yourself at bloody home.'

'You're a right sweary Mary today, aren't you?'

I tip a packet of chilli crackers into a bowl and settle down on the sofa with them and the bottle of Prosecco, which is making me feel ridiculous now that I am not alone.

'What about your last place? Go back there. Now.'

Niall laughs, but not at me – with me, as if I am joking.

'Right. Have you met my landlady? But seriously, this is way better than any other place on offer.'

'But this place isn't on offer.'

I really want to drink my bubbly but feel self-conscious about the flute in front of Niall. Oh, for a bottle of beer I could swig manfully then hurl at him.

'The property system in this country is legalised apartheid,' Niall says.

'Then go squat in Guy Ritchie's house.'

'Who he?'

You go out of your way to reference someone a younger person will know, and it falls flat on its face.

Niall takes a chilli cracker from my hand as I am putting it to my mouth, throws it back in the bowl and takes the bowl away.

'These ruin your taste buds. Wait for your dinner.'

I bow my head and count to ten; this prevents it from exploding. I get up and go across to the druid gardener, stand as close to him as I can, and stuff my mouth full of chilli crackers until my cheeks are bulging.

I'm fifty-three.

Niall doesn't blink at this. 'Squatting is a young person's game. Gets embarrassing at my age.'

'You're twenty-six!' Bits of cracker shoot out of my mouth. 'It's the perfect age for squatting!'

He looks at me disdainfully. 'I'm thirty-one.'

'Sooz told me you were twenty-six.'

'Did she? Oh, bollocks. We need to get our stories straight. To be fair to her, I did put twenty-six on my profile.'

'Your profile!'

He stops, busted. 'Look, sit down, stop stressing, have some proper food.'

He steers me back to the sofa. As I get comfy, my hand touches something cold and soft, like a slug, and I leap to my feet, repulsed. When I investigate, I find a slice of pizza down the side of the cushion. I hold it up to Niall and lose my rag completely.

'FOR FUCK'S SAKE, NIALL!!'

He freezes, like a toddler seeing something scary. I hold the slice of pizza right up to his face.

'COLD FUCKING PIZZA! DISGUSTING!'

He looks terrified, and I think I feel a bit terrified of myself and what I must look like, but I don't need this, I need to be alone. I'm sleep deprived and heartbroken, with chilli rice wedged so hard between my teeth that I don't know if it will ever come out. I want my privacy.

66

'Sorry,' Niall says, grabbing the pizza and wiping the sofa clean. 'Yeah, that must have been me, this lunchtime. Ironically, after I had done a clean of the whole place.'

'WHICH IS ALSO VERY PRESUMPTUOUS OF YOU!'

'Please stop shouting at me. Stop stressing and have something to eat.' He hands me a bowl of food. It looks and smells superb.

'I'm not stressing,' I say, calming down.

'Right, yeah, you seem relaxed.'

'But I will have some food.'

'You're the boss.'

I eat and the sort of subtle, fragrant, sweet curry flavour I love hits my taste buds and I can't stop myself groaning with pleasure.

'Oh, my God,' I say softly. 'Ohhh . . .'

'Now you're relaxed.'

'You can really cook.'

'You bet your granny's saggy bum cheeks I can cook.'

As Niall inserts that image into my head, I start making those cartoon eating sounds as I chew: 'Mmmm, mmmm, nom, nom, nom.' I don't mean to but I do. Then I notice Niall standing at the hob, studying me.

'You know,' he says, 'You make the same noises when you're eating that Sooz makes when she's, kind of getting turned on. Exactly the same. The family resemblance is very strong.'

I look out of the window. I clench my jaw muscles.

'What?' Niall says. 'There's an atmosphere.'

'You're not staying,' I mutter. I put my bowl down. 'I've got stuff to do in my shed.'

'But what's wrong? We were having a nice time.'

'I was having a nice time until you walked in on my bath.'

I stand up, as slumped and lifeless as I can, to convey to Niall that I want to be alone. I try to erase the memory of me losing my mind and shoving pizza in his face, and the image of Granny Lou's bottom.

'I'm sorry,' he says. 'But for the record, you weren't singing.'

'I was playing music at a very high volume,' I say.

'I was desperate, and you've only got one lav.'

'I'm sorry there aren't more lavs for you here, Niall.'

'I'll knock in future.'

'Niall, there is no future.'

I open the bi-fold doors and take one step towards the freedom of the shed.

'I've done something?' Niall says.

'You've said something, Niall. But that's not the point. I live here, you do not. I need some space in my life right now.'

'I think you need people. And what did I say? Please tell me, I hate getting things wrong.'

Little fucking sod, how did he get to be on the defensive?

'You do not make comments to a man about his daughter being turned on.'

He hangs his head. 'Sorry. You and I get on so well, I forget we're not mates. And it really was just an observation, not a laddy thing, I'm not like that. I just find things fascinating and want to talk about them.'

He is crestfallen.

'Look, do something for me. Don't find my daughter fascinating. She's not an interesting experience in your colourful life journey. Treat her as sacred, not fascinating.'

'Absolutely. I promise.'

'And at the age of thirty-one, you should be mature and experienced enough to understand what it's like for me as a dad, what I do and don't want to have to hear.'

'Honestly, Pete, I don't know,' he says, with that plaintive, slightly bemused honesty he seems to have. 'I have no experience of what it's like to be a dad or to have one.'

'Well . . .' That takes the wind out of my sails. Which is a shame, 'cause I really fancied tearing him to shreds for being so fucking inappropriate and for being in my fucking flat uninvited and for Ed not having fucking called and for Claire fucking off.

And, yes, I do think my swearing has got worse.

When I get to my shed, I do three things. Firstly, I wish I had brought my bowl of curry with me. Secondly, I regret not bringing the Prosecco. Thirdly, I realise that Niall has used my name for the first time and, crazy though this may sound, it felt strange to hear it.

Honestly, Pete.

Strange, in a nice way.

I occasionally hear my name, when I see a friend or my colleagues, but I used to hear it every day. *Pete. P. Peter.* Though mostly, of course, *darling*.

The shed is unique in being the one place that hasn't been altered by Claire going and dividing the house into two. Her bike is no longer here, but otherwise it is unchanged. I could come in here and pretend that I'm still married and she's popped out to the shops (on her bike, you see).

In the corner is a plastic box containing my old scuba equipment. If I am looking for a shed-based project to use to get away from Niall over the next day or so whilst he arranges alternative accommodation, then sorting this stuff out fits the brief.

The familiar objects inside remind me of a life once lived, both vivid and at the same time distant. My dive logs, goggles, some different mouthpieces and regulators, and a few knick-knacks from around the scuba-diving world. It all smells of salt and the musty insides of the catamarans and small boats that I would live on for a few nights when I was diving.

I lived in this town until I went travelling when I was twenty-one years old. Claire was raised in Boston, Lincolnshire, one of the few places in the UK with a weaker pulse than Woking. We bonded over the facelessness of our home towns. Like a fourteen-year-old pretending to enjoy the taste of cigarettes with his mates, I did not let on to her that I loved growing up where I did. We met in Grenada and had our first kiss eighteen metres below the surface of the Caribbean sea, at the *Bianca C* shipwreck. I wasn't always the person I am now.

I was twenty-two by the time I reached the Caribbean to do my Open Water Scuba course, eight months into my trip around the world. On day three, we left the open-air classroom and teaching pool and went beneath the waves, and I fell in love with being underwater. I had already fallen in lust with Claire English. She was willowy and confident and pale, having flown straight out from a Lincolnshire winter, and she was frighteningly comfortable in her own skin. She didn't talk unless she had something to say, she was funny but in a detached, cool way, she looked as if she liked everyone and would be equally happy if none of us were there.

After the second day of the course, we sat together in Esther's Bar in St George's amidst a dozen other scuba students and our instructors, and I don't care what you think of clichés or rose-tinted specs because I loved her from the very first time we got talking. I have always loved being with her — that has never faded. I desired her there and then, wanted her approval, and still do. It won't surprise you that I didn't have the guts to kiss her that evening but the next day, we paired up to dive. We didn't say anything about it, we just drifted towards each other as the pre-dive talk came to an end and the time to buddy up for our first day in the sea arrived.

When you train for your PADI licence, one of the skills you have to demonstrate is being able to 'buddy breathe'. If you run out of air for any reason, like a defective tank or being so horny for your buddy that you've been hyperventilating and consumed an hour's worth of air in half the time, you have to be able to share your buddy's mouthpiece and breathe their supply of air. Sitting cross-legged on the ocean floor, observed by one of the instructors in a test for our licence, I removed my regulator, taking the whole rig off my back and laying it on the sea bed, and as per what we had been taught, calmly held my breath until my buddy, Claire English of Boston, put her air supply to my mouth and shared it. Then we swapped and I shared my air with her, and then, when we were both done, our tanks back on our backs and our instructor moved on to the next pair, I removed my mouthpiece again and gently removed hers and kissed her under the ocean. It was unforgettable. It was romantic. It was fantastic. We both nearly drowned.

Three days later she was gone, her two-week holiday over, her accountancy exam results looming. I stayed on in Grenada for six months and trained as an advanced diver and then qualified as an instructor. I didn't look at another woman. I can be pretty certain that no other woman looked at me going by the law of averages in the years leading up to this time. This being the late 80s I was not emailing or texting Claire, and me being a young man obsessed with diving, I was not writing letters to her either. But I did know three things: her number, her address and that I was going to go and see her the moment I returned.

And to be fair, I did send her one postcard in those six months. It was a photo of the island's translucent green sea, on the back of which I wrote, *How's Lincolnshire? Pete.*

I returned to England in the autumn of 1989. I had been away for two years and spent the majority of that time working as a scuba instructor in the Caribbean and on the Great Barrier

Reef. I landed on 17 October and on the nineteenth I drove from Woking to Boston and knocked on the door of her parents' terraced two–up two–down.

'She's in London,' her mother told me. 'Who are you?'

'What's she doing there?'

'She lives there, in Dulwich. She's got a job with Touche Ross. Who are you?'

'We met abroad last year, in Grenada.'

'Oh, so you're him. I've seen worse. Why haven't you called?'

'I sent a postcard.'

'It had three words on it, you idiot.'

'I thought it was funny.'

She looked at me for quite some time, the way older people can pull off and I couldn't then and still can't now.

'It was funny,' she says. 'But not half as funny as you driving up here. Come in for a cup of tea and a wee and I'll give you her address.'

She made me sit down and have a cup of tea. She made me go for a wee. She gave me Claire's address and with a tinge of pride told me, 'She lives in *Dulwich Village*.'

When Claire opened the door of her flat on Langmead Street to me, I said to her, 'This flat is not and never has been in Dulwich Village. It's close enough to tell your mother you live in Dulwich, but this is West Norwood, officially and spiritually. There's nothing wrong with West Norwood, but Dulwich Village it is not.'

I figured this gave her time to decide what she felt about me appearing. And I figured I was being hilarious. The rest I will keep in my own sweet, soft, soppy head. I will simply say this: I often shut my eyes and re-live knocking on Claire's door in West Norwood that evening and the look on her face and the hours that followed. And to simply recall it all makes me happy in a way I do not expect to ever feel again, which is not to say I am not or will not be happy, but nothing will ever be quite like that day and the times it led to.

I look out from my garden shed towards the bi-fold doors. The light in Niall's bedroom is still on and so is the bathroom light. That is promising; it suggests he is heading to bed. Those bi-fold doors cost a lot of money, look fantastic, do indeed create a sense of 'throughness' between garden and kitchen as advertised but, more than all of that, they were one of the telltale signs that Claire was running out of things to do with me. Couples who are getting bored but don't know it yet often go for bi-fold doors. This applies when just one of the couple feels unhappy, I learned. It's a project that will give them something to talk about for a couple of months and will be something they can enjoy together for a couple of days on top of that. But it doesn't have to be bi-fold doors. Some couples who are utterly fucked but haven't fully faced up to it buy a second home or book an extreme sports holiday, have another baby, convert their loft or go to swing dance lessons. Others, with more of a predilection for lighting the touchpaper, sleep with other people.

Me? I had slim-profile bi-fold doors written all over me.

I open my dive log from Grenada for 7 March 1988. *Bianca C wreck dive, day two of Open Water PADI cert test. Eagle rays, reef sharks, nurse sharks, giant morays and barracuda.* At the end of the entry, I have drawn a small heart with a C in it. The date of our first kiss.

Since telling me she wanted a divorce a year and a half ago, Claire has behaved kindly and she's never had a dig at me, despite having the ammunition. She's been fair and she's been efficient. She blamed herself for becoming stagnant even though it's me she's bored of. She has wept over hurting me but been clear about not wanting to spend years feeling unfulfilled

73

when she is free to change her life and millions of people don't have the luxury of choice. She has always had a knack for implying that she would be letting down the oppressed everywhere if she didn't take the action she is taking. It's a gift and it's very hard to argue against when you're – well – me.

She is calm and steely and elegant and a beautiful kisser, tender even after years of kissing me. Her eyes are curious and full of openness, just like her mind. She snorts when she laughs. She can carry a room, but she'd prefer not to. She always made me feel like I was the exact person she wanted by her side. When we made love, which was often, she made me feel wanted and good. She appreciated the fact that I knew the difference between a vulva and a vagina, even though I did, secretly, look them both up in the encyclopaedia before we moved in together. In time, she earned twice as much as me and gave the impression that it was effortless and unimportant.

Obviously, I am super pleased with myself to have lost her.

Chapter 7

Something is different this morning. It takes me a while to work out what it is. Flower beds that are weedless, shrubs cut back perfectly, and trees pruned. The soil is dug over, everything has shape. I put a coat on over my dressing gown and go outside to take a closer look. The moss has been scraped off the bench and the wood re-oiled. Niall has done all this without me noticing. He has done it beautifully.

But he's not staying.

At nine o'clock, I am sitting on my refurbished garden bench, having a third coffee of the morning, asking my morale to allow caffeine to do the job of a year's good sleep, and watching Niall horizontal on the kitchen sofa where he's been on his tablet since six o'clock, same as every morning. I am still in my dressing gown and coat and slippers. Susie FaceTimes me.

'Eh, up, old man.'

'Hello, gorgeous!'

I mute the phone and shut the bi-folds.

'Why d'you mute me? Where are you?'

'In the garden,' I whisper, close up. 'I don't want Niall to know it's you and have to share you.'

She laughs this off. 'He wouldn't care. I speak to him every day.'

'Oh.'

I'll take offence at that later.

'Eh, up, old man . . .' is Susie's traditional way of starting a call with me. Either that or, 'Put me on speaker so you don't have to put a cold phone to your ear,' because once, just once, when I had put my phone in the fridge and a carton of milk on the kitchen table and couldn't find my phone for hours, I stupidly told my children about it.

Young adults are like hyenas with your mistakes. It's humiliating and, ultimately, good for the soul.

'How's Stockholm?'

'Oh, Dad, it is so good.'

'Where are you?'

'By the waterfront. Look . . .'

Susie flips the image and pans across central Stockholm and the river.

'How are you?' she says. 'How was Berlin?'

'Both good.'

Susie sits down on a bench and smiles at me. It's wonderful to see her.

'You exploring?' I say.

'Totally. Such a nice city to wander in. You taught me how to see a city – you've always been brilliant at that.'

That's nice.

'Dad, I really am telling Niall he's got to sort a place out. I'm so sorry.'

'Thanks, love, sooner the better. I want the place to myself.'

'Promise. I'm so sorry.'

I shake my head. 'Don't worry about it, just concentrate on enjoying Stockholm.'

We smile at each other and miss each other and don't need to say it.

'How's the job?'

'It's amazing, Dad.'

She pulls a face.

'What?'

'It's just a bit confusing how amazing it is.'

'Darling . . .'

'Yes?'

'Just go for it.'

She smiles and nods. 'I love it here.'

'I love that you love it there.'

I don't, by the way. I want her to like it there but prefer it here.

'Work's really good. I don't see much of Mark.'

She's possibly one of the worst liars in the world, and I'm very proud of her for that.

I think the on-trend word is 'decompress'. That's what I do, sitting on the end of my bed after saying goodbye to Susie. I picture her out there, putting her phone away and getting on with her day, exploring, wandering, seeing, thinking, growing. And, actually, I do feel happy for her. Really happy, as long as she stays safe.

Susie makes me laugh and I can laugh at myself with her. Why can't I do that with everything else? Instead of pretending everything is fine, why don't I go the other way and say, I'm a bit buggered and I'm stumped for ideas and you've got to laugh really. I'm the last guy left selling holidays from a shop, with an underpaid nineteen-year-old called Josie being the only thing which prevents my website from looking like a 1975 Little Chef menu. I'm the guy lucky enough to already own his own home and to have an ex-wife who has treated him well. I'm the guy who puts his phone in the fridge and the milk on to charge and has a hairy druid gardener living uninvited with him and really wants him gone but cannot bring himself to place his belongings outside and change the locks. All of this, I could laugh about.

Maybe I should talk like this, more openly. Or maybe I already did – to my oldest friend, who hasn't been in touch since.

I wonder what time it is in New Zealand and send a message to Erland asking if he wants to have a chat before he turns in for the night.

In the kitchen, I find Chewbacca on the sofa in front of a paused cartoon, talking to someone in a garden far, far away whilst he, without seeming to notice he's doing it, re-wires a food blender of ours that broke three years ago. He gives me a thumbs-up. I make myself a cup of tea and retreat to my bedroom.

Five minutes later, he walks in without knocking.

'Come and see this, it's incredible.'

'Can you knock first, please?'

'Oh, yeah, sorry.'

'You talk to Susie every day and don't let me know how she is?'

'You want me informing you how your own daughter is? Would that go down well?'

'No.'

'And you've got opposable thumbs, so texting or calling her is always an option.'

I look away breezily. 'Feel free to sod off.'

'Pete! I'm serious. Come and look – this will blow your mind. Come on!'

I follow him into the kitchen where he stands me in front of the TV to show me the thing that will blow my mind. What's it going to be? A breakthrough in a cure for cancer? Atlantis? A correct use of VAR? Alan Shearer shutting up? Mark Zuckerberg discovering on *Who Do You Think You Are?* that he is a direct descendant of Satan? He presses play to un-pause a cartoon and starts bobbing along as we watch a song which is like a sort of children's cartoon homage to the rave scene I so studiously avoided, out of fear, in the late eighties and early nineties.

'Stick, stick, stick, stick, sticky sticky stick stick!' the lyrics go and it's impossible not to move in time to it. Well, I say 'in time'; I'm male and fifty-three, but I am moving involuntarily. And I'm watching a large cartoon dog dressed as a lumberjack (he's got a tiny peaked cap on his enormous head) and some other little animals and a stick insect with eyes. I think the stick insect is the one singing the song, but I'm not sure of anything these days.

'Stick, stick, stick, stick, sticky sticky stick stick!'

It's contagious, it's ridiculous. It is not how I expected the morning to go. It's brilliant, but not as funny as watching Niall. He rubs his belly as he bobs around and when the stick insect starts appearing from all angles of the screen he bursts into uncontrolled laughter: eyes-screwed-shut, tears-streaming, purple-faced, bent-over-in-hysterics laughter.

I fight manfully not to laugh, and I don't know why.

'It's the best thing I've ever seen,' he says. 'It's genius. I could seriously die happy now.'

'Now you're talking,' I say.

The song ends and Niall sits down, breathless, and returns to reassembling the food processor, humming the tune to the stick song and bobbing up and down.

'Had to show you that,' he sighs.

'Why are you watching kids' TV?'

'A friend messaged me to watch it, said he'd wet himself.'

Niall switches the TV off.

'Your friends watch CBeebies. That figures.'

Niall looks confused. 'Er, my friend with a two-year-old boy, yes, she does. Why do you have to complicate everything?'

'I don't understand why you're showing me this.'

I didn't even want to say that! Watching Niall lose it to a dancing dog dressed as a lumberjack is one of the funniest things I've seen in a long time, but I cannot bring myself to enjoy any of it when I simply need to be alone and for my bank account and personal life to finally collapse on top of me until one of my friends finally notices and pulls me from the rubble.

'Because,' Niall says, 'it's *funny* and brilliantly clever and whoever made this knows their acid. Can I tell you your problem?'

'No, you can't.'

'Your problem is that you are incapable of thinking I have friends who have children and so it never occurred to you that is why I'd end up watching this.'

'Well, that's quite a niche problem to have, isn't it? Probably not going to hinder me too much in life.'

'Unless it's the tip of the iceberg.'

I don't like the direction this conversation is taking.

'Niall, I'm going to have another cup of tea, because I'm a crazy bastard. Can I make you one?'

'Yes, please. What's going on?'

'You like talking so I'm going to indulge you and have a chat. Unless you need to get on with your . . . er, work?'

'If a . . . er, work calls comes in, I can take it.'

Whilst I make a cup of tea for us both, he plugs in the blender and it fires up first time.

'There you go, good as new. I can make some organic pesto for us now.'

Au contraire, Niall. I can put the blender back in the cupboard and continue to buy Tesco's one-pound pesto now.

We sit on the sofa together. I turn to face him.

'Niall, listen to me.'

'Listening.'

'Somehow a week has passed and you're still here.'

'Six days, but do go on.'

'I'm a man needing to start anew, and I have to be left alone. What are your options?'

'Nothing great, to be honest. This is probably the best place for me.'

'Okay . . .' I take a deep breath. 'Go with me here. You need to make a slight adjustment in your thinking. You clearly have some options in terms of friends you can stay with until you've found a place to rent. The only mistake you are making is in thinking that here is one of your options.'

'With you in principle, but why wouldn't I just stay here, in practice?'

'Then you're not with me in . . . Look.' I pinch the bridge of my nose and it helps me stay calm and collected. 'You have to move out within forty-eight hours. I wish you well. And when Susie is visiting, if she's staying here and not at her mum's, you'll get a warm welcome from me, if I really muster all my strength.'

He is gazing at the floor.

'That was a joke,' I explain. 'You were meant to laugh, snap out of it, get up and tell me I'm a great bloke and you're going to leave now. Literally, just leave now.'

'I was just thinking there's a far better chance of Susie coming back, permanently I mean, if I'm here.'

'Nice try. I don't think she's leaving Stockholm any time soon.'

Niall shakes his head. 'I can't ask my friends, it's humiliating. It changes the dynamic. I don't like begging. And I've looked at hundreds of places to rent online, just rooms, but it's impossible with my take-home earnings and I love it here with you.'

'But I don't love living with you. I want to be alone.'

'That's so fucked up 'cause I genuinely worry about you being on your own.'

I laugh at this and check my phone. 'You don't need to worry about me.'

'Why do you keep checking your phone?'

'I don't.'

I do. I've been checking it constantly since I got back from Birmingham, I've even been walking around with it in my pocket, which I never usually do.

'I'm expecting a call,' I say.

'Who from?'

'This conversation is about you moving out – stick to it.'

'Stick, stick, stick, stick, sticky sticky stick stick. A call from the ex?'

'Don't call her that. I hate that word. And none of your business.'

I say this aggressively and it kills the atmosphere. Why am I like this with him? I wouldn't beat myself up for ripping into him for fun, but when it just makes me feel more miserable, I don't get why I'm doing it. I want to say something to override my hostility, but I can't think of anything. The words 'Can you please move out?' are so dominant that I can't find anything else.

So, I just say what's true. 'Fucking Ed. I'm expecting a call from Ed. Let's leave it there.'

And it does me good to realise that that is what is making me so ill-tempered.

'And I'm sorry I'm being short with you. Make a call to a best friend and aim to go tomorrow. Please.'

'Is Ed your best friend?'

'Yup. But you can't ring him, you have to call one of your best friends, not one of mine.'

He smiles politely at my attempt at levity.

'You sound mad at him,' Niall says, never one to take 'Let's leave it there' at face value.

I don't mean to respond but for some reason I do. 'He said he'd call.'

'Call him,' Niall says.

'I'm not doing that!' I yell, outraged. And I overreact by leaving the room.

Niall follows me into my bedroom and stands in the middle of the room. 'Knock, knock,' he says.

'No, Niall. Actually knock on the door on the other side and then wait for an invitation to come in.'

'I think you need to meditate. I'll show you.'

'For Chrissake. No!'

'Then go for a nice walk. You need to.'

Niall starts walking on the spot, and smiles encouragingly at me, nodding his head.

'Niall, I know what walking is without a demo.'

'Great, then go for a walk.'

'No! That's what I used to do with Claire.'

'Riiiight . . . you can't really stop doing everything you and your— the woman who was formerly your wife, used to do. All I'm saying is, don't mope.'

'Wait a minute! Why are we even . . . I want to mope! That's the point! This conversation is about you leaving so that I am free to mope full-time.'

'Yeah, that's a good idea.'

When I've got him out of my room it strikes me that what I need is peace, space to think, and that my shop is one of the quietest places in the developed world.

On my way in, I text Josie and ask for her, Mrs H and Silent Simon's coffee requests.

Boss of the year. We're going out of business, but he bought us a posh coffee once.

When I arrive, I ask Mrs H to print out the monthly bookkeeping top lines for the past two years. The way she nods and sets to it suggests she's been waiting for this day for

83

some time. She spreads out the paperwork in the privacy of the back office, on a table by the window on to the alley behind the shop. The alley is nothing much to look at (it's an alley) but the terrace of small houses that back on to it have tiered gardens with trees and, in summer, climby things. None of which I can see because of the state of the windows. I let the office cleaner go months ago and resolved to do a decent clean of the place myself once a week. Sit down, my child, you'll be staggered to learn that I have not kept to that resolution.

'Have your coffee, Mrs H. We'll start in ten minutes.'

I clean the windows, then open them. There is a fresh scent in the alley from the gardens. There can't be many alleys you can say that of. It's one of the perks of living in a town where taking a wee outside is punishable by hanging.

The office feels a degree or two brighter, even though there are streaks of dirty water on the glass. It's an improvement; I'll take dirty water over dirty dirt any day. Mrs H joins me. She is sprightly.

'Lovely coffee, Pete, thank you. Now, is it reality-check time?'

I nod and we spend an hour talking everything through. The poring-over-the-figures bit takes ten minutes of that time. It's not complicated. The business costs this amount, it earns that amount. The first amount is larger. We talk about shavings rather than big cuts, and we talk about what could be done and we, inevitably, talk about my parents, but I zone out to some extent because I realise that the conversation has to be about something else and with nobody but myself. Am I going to transform the way we operate to make us viable again? Would I know where to start or how to do it?

I have earned between thirty and forty thousand a year every year of my life since I came back from travelling and joined my parents' business. I'm from that lucky generation – I own my home in a quiet, lower–middle–class part of town. It's nice but not swanky, but it's mine. I have no cash and no pension or savings. For the last three years I have earned nothing at all, made no profit, and accrued some debt. In the first two of those years, Claire's income propped me up. When she left, I spent money converting our house into flats because I refused to move away, which would have been the sensible thing to do. But I'm the guy who went to his builder behind his ex-wife's back and asked him to come up with a conversion that was the easiest one to reconfigure into a house again. Optimistic; yes. Romantic; I think so. Stupid; undeniably. I even thought about putting the staircase into storage, but Dennis talked me out of that gem of an idea.

Then one day, a slip of the tongue on Dennis's part reveals to Claire that I wanted to keep the stairs. Her heart melts, she returns and we're on fire for the rest of our lives. That's how these things work, right?

I spend the afternoon looking at websites. I read articles documenting the terminal decline of the high-street travel agent and others that suggest these articles are wrong. I spend an hour or so looking at a company in Kent. We have one thing in common: we are a family business. That meaningless detail aside, they are everything I am not. Successful, growing, oozing a love of travel and expertise. I'd buy a holiday off them.

But it's what I'm thinking and feeling as I read their website that interests me. Or it's what I am not feeling.

Jealous.

I don't envy them. The couple who own it remind me of my parents, to look at their headshots. I'm happy for them. I'm impressed by them. I appreciate what a good job they and their sons are doing. I have no idea if the branches they have acquired in towns across Kent in the past decade have been saved and nurtured or if it's been the night of the long knives, but they are doing a brilliant job.

And I am not jealous.

Because it simply does not seem to pertain in any way to my life. Which makes me realise I have stopped being a travel agent but forgotten to shut down the travel agency I run. I do not have a single idea or impulse for transforming this company into something else. I just want it put out of its misery without having to make anybody redundant, because I want to be liked and I hate making people unhappy.

I go to the door of the office and look though at Mrs H, Josie and Simon. It's ten to five. Josie opens a drawer and takes out her Moleskine notebook. Mrs H puts highlighter on sections of the printouts we were looking at. These are for my benefit. It's my homework. Simon is bent low over his desk, peering at his computer screen. A client's booking? Poker? *Angling Today*? Could be anything. With him, it could be all three. He is the before of a before-and-after ad for posture problems.

Eight minutes to five. By five-thirty it could be over and done with. In ten minutes' time the conversation could be over. I'm shutting the business down and, with huge regret and a terrible sense of guilt, letting you all go. By this time tomorrow, I could be free of that burden and rid of the hairy biker back home. Faced with a void, things would have to change for the better. Surely.

Mum, Dad, I'm really sorry. There was a way to keep this business alive, but I just haven't the ability or desire – I'm not sure which – to do it.

I can smell freedom.

I return to my desk where I sit, head bowed. Inertia. The word enters my brain. It's a deadly disease. Do I have it? 'Inertia Creeps' starts playing in my head.

For fuck's sake, I used to listen to Massive Attack! Loud! I travelled. I lived beneath the sea. I bought a house with my wife. I took over a business. My family never wanted for anything. We laughed and played and took long flights to places. I've been to every continent apart from Antarctica, which doesn't count anyway. I sprayed my kids and their mother with the garden hose on the trampoline in the summer and dried them off and put them to bed and made love to my wife in the living room that night listening to Massive Attack.

What the hell has happened to me?

I'm sweating. I go to the door again and open it. Josie puts down her Moleskine notebook and looks at me. She is red-faced and exhales loudly.

'You okay?' I ask her.

She nods, hurriedly, but looks nervous. She is sweating too. 'Look . . .' I say.

Simon looks up. I have all three of them now. 'Look, please don't feel obliged, might be the last thing you want to do, but I fancy a pint and I've been a bit absent lately and it'd be nice to all have a drink so if any of you fancy coming to the Cricketers, I'd love to buy you a drink.'

Simon shrugs and nods. There is no sense that he might have any other plans or need to consult with another human being. Mrs H says, 'Lovely.' Josie checks her watch.

'Can we go to the Grasshopper?' she says, stuttering apologetically. 'It's just that, well, I've sort of planned to go there. Or . . .'

I step forward instinctively because it looks as if she's about to faint.

She says, 'No. You lot go to the Cricketers. I'll go to the Grasshopper. Or, come if you like. I don't mind.'

The rest of us look a bit confused.

'The Grasshopper is fine by me,' I say. 'But, Josie, if you've got plans already don't feel you have to, you know . . .'

She looks at the floor.

'Grasshopper is more on my way,' Mrs H says.

Simon puts on his jacket and stands by the door.

The pub is busy and a group of Josie's friends account for one corner of it. Her nerves seem to have gone and she even brings a girlfriend of hers up to the bar and introduces me.

'This is Mr Smith, my boss. This is Chrissie.'

Chrissie shakes my hand and beams a smile. 'So nice to meet you,' she says. 'You're a bit of a legend.'

She laughs, but it's kind and polite the way she talks to me and I suddenly realise that, despite my regular absences from work, Josie talks highly of me. It sparks a certain joy in me for approximately one billionth of a second until I realise that I would rather drive off a cliff than tell her she's out of a job. I buy a round, hand Josie and Chrissie their drinks, and take the others to our table gripped by an urgent resolve to use all and any contacts I have left to find this young woman a better job. The conversation between Mrs H, Simon and me is stunted but perfectly pleasant. I do feel a certain lightness at simply being out and at having spent some hours in the office. The fact that I have used those hours to confirm the oblivion of the business is a mere detail.

The landlord steps onto a raised stage the size of a table. He switches on a mic and we discover that there's a comedy night starting in fifteen minutes. A few whistles from Josie's mates tell us that's why they are here.

'We'd better cram in all our chit-chat before that starts, then,' Simon says.

Every small firm needs one chronically sardonic single male in the team, just so that no one else ever need fear being the biggest git in the company.

Mrs H, who seems to have morphed into the Queen Mother now that she's out in public, grips her handbag to her stomach and says that she won't stay for 'that sort of thing' but that 'it's nice to be out'.

We have nothing much to talk about, the three of us, and I turn to cast an eye out across the rest of the pub and nearly jump out of my skin when I find a young man standing over me, offering his hand. He is wearing cut-off tracksuit bottoms as shorts and a vest that reveals tanned and very muscular arms and shoulders, a couple of tattoos and a scar. He has cropped hair, a second scar above his lip, and possibly the most handsome smiling face I've ever seen. His eyes sparkle with warmth to the same degree that his voice is rough and ready.

'Mr Smith, I'm Grant, Josie's boyfriend.'

I know a little about Grant from Josie. That he's lovely and that he's a scaffolder.

I stand up. 'Hello, Grant, good to meet you.'

As we shake hands, he lays his left hand on top of my right. His smile is strangely disarming.

'It is such a pleasure to meet you,' he says. 'Josie thinks you're the business.'

I am speechless. Really? I want to say. I think I'm a useless, washed-up piece of crap.

Grant flashes his smile at Simon and at Mrs H, who looks like she wants to adopt him. Unless she wants to . . . No, gross.

'Nice to meet you all,' he says. 'Don't want to interrupt, just wanted to say hello.'

'Good to meet you, Grant,' I say.

He returns to Josie and their friends, and I see Josie glance across to us.

Mrs H offers the kiss of life to our conversation by making the ridiculous claim that when she first knew me, I looked like Grant, and describes my scuba-diving adventures back in the day as swashbuckling. I can sense Simon flinch to fill up his sarcasm water-gun, so I change the subject.

'I suppose,' I say, in a sweeping admission of defeat, 'that the bigger companies were always going to barge us off Bonaire and Sal and certainly obliterate us from the Red Sea but I wish I'd bought a property or two in one of those places back then.'

Regretting not buying property somewhere cheap that then became expensive: the conversational refuge of the living dead.

And Simon is happy to join this death march of a chat. Whitstable. Cape Verde. Harlem. Costa Rica. Ramsgate. That's his list of places he wished he'd seen coming.

Mrs H has her own list and doubles up on Whitstable. Without stopping for breath, she grabs the Kent link by the throat and tells us that her grandparents used to come out of London to work the hop fields and that was their summer holiday. All I can hear is Tim Brooke-Taylor doing the cardboard-box sketch. I almost miss Niall. He's annoying but at least his references are contemporary.

And then the worry about what to talk about, and the wretchedness of what we are talking about, and the perversion of thinking I could prefer Niall's company to someone else's – all these things go out the window and the evening turns on its head because I see something and then I hear something, and, for a moment, my head cannot compute what the two things mean.

What I see is Josie, standing at the far end of the bar clutching her notebook. She is looking at her feet and she is shaking. And her back is turned away from the bar. For a split second, there's no possible reason for her to be where she is.

But then the landlord's voice blares out of the speaker system. 'Ladies and gentlemen, as you know, from time to time, we have our open-mic night here at the Grasshopper, and tonight six people have five minutes each to show us what they can do. First up, we are very proud to welcome a local girl doing only her second-ever stand-up, so a warm welcome please to . . . MISS . . . JOSIE . . . CHAMBERS!'

My mouth drops open. I instinctively want to run and stop her, the slow-motion rugby tackle, but that tells you everything about me and nothing about brave Josie Chambers, who steps on stage to a riot of cheers from Grant and their friends.

When I say Josie is clutching her notebook, I mean gripping. With trembling hands. She looks terrified, but she barely hesitates before starting.

'Good evening, I'm Josie Chambers and I live in Merriment. You all know Merriment, you've all driven past it, the housing estate built in 1968 by DEFRA to house cattle and named by the famous London advertising agency Piss, Take and Fuckyou.'

The open mouths of Mrs H and Silent Simon are all I need to know that they, like me, were ignorant of what quiet, demure, shy Josie Chambers has been writing in her Moleskine notebook all this time.

'All my family live on the estate – me and my sisters, my mum and dad, my grandmum. There's one member of my family doesn't live on Merriment and that's Dodi. You know what's cool about Dodi?'

'No!' someone from her group calls out.

'What's cool about Dodi, Josie?' someone else shouts, on cue.

'I'll tell you. She's my great-grandmother. How cool is it to have a great-grandmother!'

There's a round of applause. Josie holds up an imaginary glass. 'Cheers, Dodi.'

She takes the mic off the stand. 'Dodi lives in Martyr's Green . . .'

There are a couple of stray shouts of support for the village, which is a few miles away.

'. . . and I would say I get a call from Dodi a couple of times every week, and I go over to see her every week too. She claims not to be a fan of the phone but she's rarely off the thing. And I have to tell you people, if my great-grandmother calls, she usually starts the call by saying the words, "Do you remember . . .?" and I have to warn you, if my great-grandmother calls and starts with the words, "Do you remember . . .?"'

She nods and waits.

'You do *not* want your name to be the next thing that comes out of that woman's mouth . . .'

There's sniggering from the audience.

'Because if it is . . .'

She looks out at us, narrows her eyes.

'. . . you're fucked. It means you've either got cancer or died. 'Cause those are the two things my great-grandmother likes to talk about.'

Josie holds her hand to her ear like a phone.

'"Josie, you remember old Mrs Coot?"

'"Hi, Dodi."

'"Remember the woman Coot?"

'"I think so."

'"You must do – she lived on Ripley Lane when I lived on Ripley Lane."

'"Thirty years before I was born."

'"You must know her, she used to come in with marrows from that wretched man's allotment."

'People, if Dodi has called to tell me Mrs Coot has cancer, Mrs Coot has probably died of it by the time I pretend to know who she is. Oh! And don't think it makes any difference coming out with an outright "no".

'"Darling, you remember Percy Bachelor from Windmill Lane?"

"'No, Dodi, I never knew him – I categorically don't know who that is at all."

"'Well, he just passed. Very rare form of leukaemia. Betty Wright called and told me."

Josie takes a deep breath and smiles at us. 'So, a man I don't know at all, who lives in a village I have never lived in, has died. What am I meant to say to her? "Does leukaemia count, Dodi? Not proper cancer, is it?" But I don't say that, I just respectfully mutter, "That's sad."

"'It is. I thought you'd want to know."

'WHAT?!! WHY, WOMAN?!! I was having a nice morning!

"'Anyway, how are you?" she'll then ask.

"'Okay, I guess," I'll say weakly, 'cause I'm distracted by the image of Percy Bachelor – who I have to make up from scratch in my head because I don't know him – lying dead in a bed, hooked up to some dreadful life-support machine that has just been switched off. And I wonder if Dodi and this Betty Wright character are competitive.'

Josie puts her hand back to her ear as a phone again.

"'Hello, Betty love, how are you?"

"'Hi, Dodi. Percy Bachelor has leukaemia."

"'I know, Betty, I've known that for some time."

Josie fist-pumps furiously.

'Take that, Betty, I already knew. Haha.

"'Well, he's dead, passed yesterday. Thought you'd want to know, Dodi."

Josie slumps and her face turns angry.

"'That fucking bitch! How the hell did she find that out before me? Fuck that!"

'Meanwhile, Betty Wright is dancing around her wardened accommodation. Do they have a scoring system, five points if you know someone's diagnosis before the other one does, ten points for a death? Bonus points if the terminally ill person has told you personally and you can prove it? You gotta be able to prove it.

'"Thanks so much for letting me know about your diagnosis, Percy. If there's anything at all I can do – and, um, look, I know time is of the essence – but could you possibly just put it in writing to me?"'

'Last Christmas, over a glass of stout, my great-grandmother actually said to me, "You know, I'm really hoping you have a nice year ahead, have some fun, be happy. I worry about you – sometimes you sound a bit down."'

Josie pauses, then yells, '"WELL, WHAT THE FUCK DO YOU EXPECT, WOMAN? WHENEVER WE SPEAK I'VE JUST BEEN TOLD SOMEONE IS DEAD OR DYING!! OF COURSE I DON'T SOUND HAPPY. MY OWN GREAT-GRANDMOTHER IS GOD'S OWN MESSENGER OF DOOM!!!"'

Mrs H is laughing but her lips are pursed together as if wanting to register her shock at the language. Si's pint glass is glued to his lower lip as he watches with a weird, snarling smile of disbelief lighting up his face. The pub is buzzing. I look over at Grant who is watching Josie adoringly, nervously, willing her on.

Josie takes a sip of water from a bottle. She wipes her brow. She moves loosely now and I suspect she knows she has the whole place behind her, and that pale voice and apologetic faltering start she returns to now, is deliberate.

'Now, this isn't really connected to anything but I only have a few minutes so I thought it might be a good use of our time to have a little chat about our arseholes.'

Mrs H spits her drink into her glass. Si, through some strange amphibious trick, smirks whilst downing his pint. The pub hushes. Josie allows her voice to grow stronger again, and make the whole thing seem accidental, off the cuff.

'And, specifically, about the fact that . . . Isn't it amazing that our arseholes don't wear out? I mean, what manufactured part, even titanium, lasts for that long with that sort of use?'

She does the maths for us, counting on her fingers. 'Two craps a day — yes, I'm just talking about women for the moment, that's six hun . . . seven hundred and thirty a year, live for seventy years, that's seven thousand three hundred times by . . . that's about fifty thousand usages . . . so between fifty and a hundred thousand usages depending on diet and gender. And it never wears out! No one dies of a worn-out arsehole, no one has an arsehole replacement at fifty. We should be building bridges out of this stuff. Let's amend the organ donor forms now and rebuild Britain with Percy Bachelor's arsehole! Let's take it to Parliament. No one, but no one, takes their arsehole with them to the grave!'

When her five minutes are up, the place erupts, the whole place this time, not just her corner, and she suddenly looks made of paper — as if the noise could crumple her. She makes it off the stage and collapses into Grant's ridiculously large arms. He engulfs her and kisses her, and she laughs and cries. She comes across to us, drenched in sweat, still shaking. Her cheeks are red and her eyes are searching for clues as to how she did as if her ears can't fathom the applause which the landlord is waiting to die down before he introduces the next act. All barriers are down now, cast aside by sheer joy, so I hug her and I can do nothing but stare at her, shaking my head, unable to put into words my admiration. Mrs H smiles bravely when Josie looks to her; she seems happy that Josie's act went down so well but bemused by the content.

Ironically, the only one of us who can find anything to say is silent Si, who does not do hugging, but raises his glass and mutters, 'That was funny, that. Really good.' Praise indeed. At one point it looks like he might even get out of his seat.

95

A work day that I had dedicated to hard-nosed cost-cutting decisions is rounded off by me using my least buggered credit card to buy a few rounds for the Josie Chambers fan club and my own staff. I resolve to keep them on the payroll for eternity. I walk home in a state of euphoria at Josie's talent and guts, bobbing my head around as I sing, 'Stick, stick, stick, stick, sticky sticky stick stick,' to myself. It's the best evening I've had in some time. It's the only evening I've had.

Chapter 8

I am sitting on the toilet reading more fabulous prose by the bard Ray Parlour and listening to Zoe Ball (massive crush 1990s to the present day, Claire fully aware and not entirely supportive) when Niall bursts in.

'I'm bloody in here, Niall! Radio's on!'

But Niall is excited. He seems to be panting like a dog. He's clutching his phone and holding it out towards me.

'Susie's coming back for the weekend! She's boarding any minute!'

I nearly leap off my seat, which would be bad. Instead, still somewhat forgetful of where I am, I call out, 'Hello.' Niall hands me his phone and it is then that I discover Susie is on FaceTime.

'Are you where I think you are, Dad?'

I look at Niall in disgust. 'Niall! Chrissake! Yes. Yes, I am. What's wrong with you, man?'

'Why are you both in the bathroom when Dad's . . .'

My daughter's voice recedes as Niall takes the phone back and heads for the kitchen.

'Well, I'm excited to see you even if old misery guts isn't,' I hear him say.

'SHUT THE BLOODY DOOR!'

I'm too happy about Susie's surprise visit to bother explaining to Niall how many all sorts of wrong it is to hand me my daughter on FaceTime when I'm seeing a man about a dog. What's the point? It's not my job to change him. It's my job to evict him.

I find him in the kitchen, on the sofa with a stack of recipe books. He's buzzing with excitement. 'She can't live without us, dude. She just can't live without us.'

I remind him that today is the day he moves out.

'Peter Smith!' he says, as if he's my mother, or Frankie Howerd. 'That would be crazy. Seriously. Massive mistake. Either Susie would come and spend the weekend with me at my mate's flat or she'd say, "No way am I kipping on the sofa-bed in a shithole," and we'd both end up here anyway.'

'Tell me more about your mate's flat. That is the only thing in what you just said that interested me.'

'Seriously, it's a non-starter. Awful option.'

'Again, all I'm hearing is the word "option".'

'Seriously, no way, she'd never forgive you for making me live there.'

'I get it – if you start a sentence with the word "seriously", it means you are about to talk bollocks.'

'I guess Sooz and me could stay at her mum's for the weekend.'

Bastard. That's below the belt. That's chemical warfare.

'You can stay the weekend, as our guest not lodger, and you're leaving Monday morning at the same time I go to work. And if you make any reference to being intimate with my daughter in front of me, I'll beat you to a pulp.'

Niall smiles patronisingly, the facial-expression equivalent of a pat on the head. 'There's no way you could, old chap, but point taken, I'll be really respectful about what I say. And it's good to know you're going to give work a try on Monday.'

I make a cup of tea. I don't make Niall one and when he gets up to make himself one, I spread out on the sofa. Not allowing him room on my kitchen sofa has become a ritual these past few days. Intellectually, I am regressing, and my starting point wasn't exactly Brian Cox.

'Did she say why she's coming back?' I say, switching on the evening news.

'No. Very tight-lipped, she was. She's seeing her friend Rebecca who lives near Heathrow tonight and coming to us super early tomorrow morning.'

Niall is stirring his tea when he suddenly lets out a loud, melodramatic 'OH!' that makes me spill mine.

'What the . . . ?' I gasp, jumping up into a power stance fashioned by the boiling fluid on my crotch.

He stares at me demonically. 'Oh, my God! Oh, my God!' he says.

'This'd better be good.'

'I just died!'

'That is good.'

'No, I mean, I just diiiiied. Oh, my God!'

He freezes and a beatific smile contorts his face. 'She's pregnant!' he whispers.

He starts fanning his own face, like he's auditioning to be the gardener on *Queer Eye*.

'I'm having a hot flush. I'm gonna be a dad! I'm so ready for this. No, I'm too young. No, I'm so ready for this!'

I take my phone off the counter and make an urgent call. 'Tell me one thing before you board, that you're not pregnant.' Now it's my turn to smile. 'That's wonderful news. See you in the morning, love.'

I hang up and ignore Niall. Sip my tea. Watch the news.

'Well?' he asks.

'You're not gonna be a dad.'

'Oh.'

'Which is good news for the universe.'

Niall slides down the kitchen units until his arse hits the floor. He puts his head in his hands. It's the Mickey Rourke 1980s school of acting, without the good looks or harsh lighting.

'To summarise, Niall. You can stay for the weekend but you're not hogging Susie, and you are moving out on Monday morning, and as soon as I have changed my jeans you are going to help me clean up this flat.'

'Great,' he says. 'I love a tidy-up!'

'So, you're over the not-being-a-dad thing?'

'The what? Oh, yeah. Anyway, it's an act of supreme selfishness to bring a child into this messed-up world.'

'That's the spirit.'

I leave and go to my room. I lie on the bed and decide that this is the right moment to be gracious towards Claire, with whom Susie has opted not to spend the weekend. Yes, folks, Claire's daughter has chosen to be with her dad – that's me, not her, me, her dad, not her mum, me-not-she, her dad, me – so I'll invite Claire round. I hate to think of her all alone whilst Susie and I are spending quality time together. I'll invite her round, the flat will look great, our daughter will be in it, with me, out of choice, and I'll be laid-back, in great form, cook something so good (Niall will, in fact, cook) that she'll want to know who else I've been cooking for. Yes, I'll do the mature thing and text Claire.

Hi. Susie here for the weekend. Last-minute thing. You'd be very welcome for dinner tomorrow evening, get a chance to see her. Px

Pitch-perfect.

There's a knock on the door, which rules out Niall.

'Who is it?'

'Eh? What do you mean, "Who is it?" Who do you think it is?'

100

'Do come in, Niall.'

The door opens a sliver and Niall peers around.

'Peter,' he says gravely.

'Niall . . .' I reply.

'Can I be candid and make a suggestion?'

'Do you think that's wise?'

'I do, yes. Look, it is my opinion that amongst your huge array of life skills, house cleaning is not included. I am good at it and I kind of enjoy it. The place is already a tip even though I cleaned when you were in Berlin, but I reckon that if you leave me alone for a few hours, I can have this place spotless. Go out for the evening, see friends, sit in the pub. Read. Let me do it all, as a thank-you for letting me stay the weekend and so that the flat actually looks better after cleaning it than it does now.'

He is so much more eloquent than me, despite looking like a used condom on a Spinal Tap tour. But he could be laying a trap, because he's also brighter than me. I'm unsure, but he's right to say I'm crap at cleaning the place and I do want Claire to see it clean and lovely.

'All right. Thanks,' I say.

My phone pings. I shoot Niall a you-can-go-now look and he does. I throw myself on the bed and gather my book and my phone to me to enjoy a little texting with the woman I love before getting stuck into the next gripping chapter of the greatest book about someone from Romford in more than two years.

Going to be in Stockholm all next week with our darling girl and I am tied up all weekend but thank you for the invite and have a gorgeous time with Sooz. X

What

A

Total

Fucking

Whore.

I hate losing at divorce-text. And why does she use the phrase 'tied up' instead of 'busy'? The hate you feel for the people you're in love with is a hate like no other.

Three hours later, I wake from the sort of long, deep nap normally reserved for the weakest residents of an old people's home and I find the flat spotless. There's a note from Niall saying he is doing a shop for the weekend. It seems a shame to mess up the flat so I take my book to the pub and have a beer and a bowl of chips there whilst I contemplate a weekend with my daughter and feel an unfamiliar sensation that might possibly be happiness.

The next morning further proof that there is no God comes in the form of hearing Susie's key in the front door whilst I am getting dressed, meaning Niall gets in ahead of me. He is hugging my daughter by the time I appear in the hallway.

'Let her breathe, Niall.'

Susie breaks from him and gives me a kiss and a hug.

'What a treat,' I whisper.

She smiles but seems distracted. Niall hugs her again. He is beaming. She rests her head against his chest. Niall takes a tenner out of his pocket and hands it to me.

'Make yourself scarce for a couple of hours – go to the flicks or something.'

They both laugh. I do not.

'Really though, Dad,' Susie says. 'Could you pop out for a bit?'

They both look at me expectantly.

For fuck's sake! If they're going to act like teenagers, they can go and make out in the park.

'Fine,' I say.

Niall reaches out to get his tenner back, but I pocket it. I get my coat and my book and leave them to it.

'The tenner was a gag,' he says.

'So is me spending it.'

I sit in my car outside the house, and read. When a neighbour – I don't know her name, you'd have to ask Claire – smiles at me as she passes, I decide that sitting outside one's own home isn't the best look so I drive off and do my own shop of the sort of premium junk food that Susie and I consider a treat and which Niall will hate.

When I get home, Susie is in the kitchen and Niall is nowhere to be seen. I kiss her forehead as I pass, and I unload the shopping.

'Thanks for giving us some space, Dad, I needed to—'

'Don't walk me through it.'

'I needed to talk to Niall as quickly as possible. To tell him I'm seeing Mark. I've slept with Mark.'

Only now do I see that she's been crying.

'How did he take it?'

'Oh, he's delighted, naturally. Really pleased for us.'

Hear that sarcasm? I taught her that. So proud.

'I'm confused, Dad. I do love Niall. It's just . . . I really don't know.'

'I know, darling.'

I give her a hug and it allows me the chance to smile over her shoulder, where I can't be caught. She starts crying and through her tears she says, 'I can't say for sure Niall and I won't end up together.'

Children. They give you hope and destroy it in the next breath.

We sit together in the kitchen and after a few minutes, when I feel she's had time to get over him, I ask her what she fancies doing.

'Dunno.' She blows her nose and smiles the brave smile. 'Am I horrible?'

Yes, darling, you are, but it's only Niall so don't worry about it.

I do not say this.

'No, you're not. If you didn't feel bad about it that'd be horrible.'

'Shall we stroll into town together?' she says. 'Just hang out? Nothing special.'

Nothing special? It sounds like paradise.

'And I'd like to pop in to the shop and say hello to Mrs H,' she says. 'I promised her I'd let her know how I was getting on.'

'She'll like that. You can tell her Stockholm is great and you've already shagged your boss.'

In the old days, we all worked on Saturdays, without fail. Busiest day of the week. Me, my parents, Mrs H, the full team. We'd each take another day off instead. Mrs H had Mondays off so she could have a delayed two-day weekend. Mum and Dad took the same day so they could do stuff together. When my parents retired, I brought in Si and the first thing I thought when he joined was that I could now take Saturdays off, not because this made any sort of business sense but because I wanted to have proper family weekends. And I recognise now that there's something I should have picked up on, that when the business became mine to run as I saw fit and breathe new life into, the very first thing I wanted was to do less.

It's late morning as Susie and I walk into town along the river. There are spits of rain but it's nice. When we get to the pub on the water's edge I ask Susie if she wants to have lunch there later. She does so I go in and book a table.

'Brilliant,' Susie says as I come out of the pub, and I wonder if she's being sarcastic, or forcing herself to say it, given her life in Stockholm which, I imagine, must be a sight more exciting than this. She and Erland have always seemed happy hanging out with us since they've become adults. Even as teenagers, save for the occasional meltdown over nothing much, they didn't want anything outrageous from us. They seem happy these days with small treats like a pub lunch and time at home together, but I wonder if Susie is patronising me today and desperate to be back in Sweden, and if she and her brother might have been bored shitless by me all this time but don't have their mother's option to divorce me. This self-loathing, it's cancerous. There's no part of you it cannot reach.

'You okay?' Susie is looking at me.

'Yeah,' I say.

Just now, when I walked into the pub, I had a shudder of fear that I would see Claire in there with a man. I still feel shaky now because I am imagining how I would handle it, going up to say hello or misting over and losing the ability to speak. And I wonder if I ought to move away, not far, but to a town or village where Claire does not live. If that would be nicer for everyone. But if someone asked me now, 'Where would you most like to go?' I wouldn't have a clue.

Susie threads her hand through my arm and squeezes it. We cut up away from the river towards the centre of Old Woking.

'What do you mean?' she asks.

'What?' I ask.

'What do you mean, "back in time"?'

'Did I say that?'

She laughs a little. 'Yes.'

I smile and shake my head. 'I've no idea. The pub. It's like going back in time, all the beams and stuff.'

'Right.' She looks at me curiously. 'And the waitresses with iPads, Sky Sports, espresso machines. Yeah, it's like old Mrs Miggins's ye olde ale house and brothel.'

'Depends how you look at it, I guess.'

She squeezes my arm again. 'I guess.'

'Tell me more about Stockholm.'

Predictably she starts by telling me it's in Sweden, but as she talks and we head up the high street it's good to hear the energy in her voice. She's like the old Susie, the Susie who went to university and played hard and worked hard, not the Susie who got despondent about finding a decent job. She just needed to be needed. Who doesn't?

As she talks, the worries seep back in. Our conversations consist of me drawing information out of her, talking about her news, her thoughts, and avoiding my own. Will she and Erland always be happy with this or will my self-deprecation grow wearisome and be exposed for what it is: a man with nothing to say? Maybe it already has been and they gear themselves up to talk with me, gird up their intellectual loins. I entertain all this paranoia whilst simultaneously enjoying a day out with my daughter. Who said men can't multitask?

I don't really *think* any of this is true. Neither of my children is impressed by people's status or money or achievements, unless those people are funny and genuine and kind. Susie's idea of a good time *is* watching *Groundhog Day* with me and the two of us muttering lines before they come out of the characters' mouths. For a decade we've been weaving these lines into everyday conversation, and it forms a bond, it really does. We like each other. We dig each other. I get her, she gets me.

'"This is a man we're talking about?"'

We roar. Every time. As long as the line is deployed skilfully.

But these things are the last stand of the Pete Smith family dynasty. When Susie and Erland get much further away from their childhoods, we won't be doing those things. So, I need to be able to do something with my weekends and go to a job that interests me, otherwise I am in big trouble.

For now, Mrs H's delight at seeing Susie and the two of them hugging is enough to put a big smile on my face. Susie and Josie, who don't know each other well, hug too in that way that young adult women can do so warmly and openly. They head to the kitchen to make tea for everyone.

I look out onto the high street and something is different. The view feels changed. I realise I can't see Superdrug. Come to think of it, I can't see Specsavers next to it or the boarded-up branch of RBS either. Why? Because there's a huge poster stuck to our window. I go outside to look at it. It's a poster advertising the NGA – National Governance Association. I read it. The NGA wants more school governors and have I ever thought of sharing my skills and time to help make our children's education better? Mrs H joins me, looking concerned.

'I hope you don't mind, Peter.'

'Of course not,' I say.

She's been a governor at a local primary school for – what is it now – two hundred and forty years. She tells me there's a nationwide recruitment drive for new governors. She says another three or four times that she hopes I don't mind the poster. I repeat that I don't, whilst wondering if she could have got a slightly bigger one to seal off the last vestiges of sunlight from the shop.

'You keep that poster up as long as it's needed – it's wonderful all the work you do for that school.'

We go back inside. I sit at my desk and watch a lovely scene unfold as Mrs H takes a call from a customer (yes, you heard me right, a customer) and my daughter and my youngest employee chat to each other excitedly. The shop door opens and in walks Silent Si, holding a Tesco sandwich and a bottle of Cherry Coke.

'Hi there, Si,' my daughter calls out.

As Si retreats to his desk he does a little wave to Susie that is a fulsome declaration of his inability to communicate with women and of the physical impossibility of him attempting to hug one without inadvertently headbutting her. And I feel a sting of affection for Si I had never thought possible.

Chapter 9

As we stroll back to the pub from the shop, I tell myself not to think about how quickly the weekend will go. Live in the moment, Pete. Live in the beer–battered–fish–and–chips moment with your daughter.

We have a table at the window and watch the light rain on the river on which Claire and I used to take the kids kayaking.

Susie presses her face up against the window. 'What are those things called?'

'Concentric circles,' I say. We watch hundreds of them, creating a repeating pattern across the river's surface, each one perfectly formed by a single drop of rain.

Neither of us has a drink. Susie hardly touches alcohol, and I don't want to get sleepy. The idea of a less energetic version of myself is terrifying.

She smiles at me. 'Love you, Dad,' she says.

'Love you, girl.'

'So nice to see everyone at the shop. Josie's amazing.'

'She told you about her stand-up?'

Susie looks blank.

'She's a stand-up comic,' I say.

She sits upright, as if disgusted. 'Shut – the – fuck – up! Really?'

I nod my head.

'Josie?'

I nod again.

'How do you know that?'

'Because we watched her do five minutes of potty-mouthed stand-up.'

'Oh, my God. I can't imagine her saying a rude word.'

'People are amazing.'

'Amazing people are amazing,' Susie corrects me. 'People are also arseholes.'

'According to Josie, arseholes are amazing.'

Talking of arseholes, my debit card gets rejected when I pay the bill and I get a hot, tingly feeling down my spine that I often feel these days when I pay for things. I glance back at our table from the bar. Susie is head down in her phone and I swap to a credit card without her noticing.

The rain has stopped, and Susie says she wants to buy me a coffee in the new place down by the river. It's an old boathouse, long and narrow, bare inside, containing many men with beards. No lack of dungarees either. The option to have a hemp latte should you have chosen to depart planet Earth completely.

We're sitting on a couple of beaten-up leather armchairs near to a woodburner when we hear someone behind us say, 'Oh, my God!'

Susie and I turn and, in unison, return the compliment. 'OH, MY GOD!'

Susie leaps up and throws herself into the arms of the woman standing over us. I move with less grace and speed, but equal enthusiasm, and I know there's a huge soppy smile on my face as I embrace Mary Blair, who was once upon a happy time Susie and Erland's babysitter. When the ooh-ing and aah-ing stops, Mary stands back and inspects Susie and tells her she's beautiful and grown up and when Susie informs her she lives in Sweden the "Oh, my God"s start again. I dislike the phrase, "I live in Sweden." I prefer, "I'm in Sweden for a bit." But what self-respecting twenty-three-year-old who has just landed a job in Stockholm wouldn't want to declare that as her home? Stockholm v. Woking. Not a fair fight.

Mary joins us. She must be in her early thirties now. I don't think Claire or I have ever bumped into her since she went off to college. She's a hypnotherapist and loves it, changed career from working for the council after she got divorced because she had a child in primary school and one in nursery and needed work to fit around the kids. I think that Susie and I both want to know what sort of a dickhead doesn't stay married to Mary, but we don't delve. She seems dynamic, smart, switched on. She helps people quit smoking, get over depression, recover from PTSD. She asks Susie more about her job, if she has a man, at which Susie glances at me and says, 'Not sure,' and I love that she is too considerate of Niall to talk about Mark.

Not that I give a shit about Niall, you understand.

And not that she was considerate enough of Niall to not sleep with Mark.

But anyway . . .

Mary is a human being who bears no resemblance to the girl we love the memory of. She has lived a lot since we knew her. She tells me she heard about me and Claire and that she's sorry and that she always 'thought the world of you as a family' and that it's been wonderful bumping into us. We all agree on that and then she has to go.

'I have to pick the kids up from the twat,' she says, laughingly, unapologetically.

If she is sad, or downtrodden, or lonely, she knows how to hide it.

'"Twat" is an interesting choice of word,' Susie says, after Mary has gone.

'It is?'

'I think it is. Twat to me says, "He left me, he landed me in it with two young kids, but he's an arsehole and I'm better off without him and he's the loser."'

'The man who leaves her is a loser.'

'Niall would never leave me,' Susie says.

'But you'd have left him eventually,' I reply. 'If you, you know, hadn't already.'

'Wise words, Dad.'

'Sod off.'

She smiles at me. I stick out my tongue.

'Let's watch *Queer Eye* all afternoon,' she says, 'then have a takeaway with a film.'

I put my coat on. 'Tremendous idea.' I'm a pig in shit.

We watch five *Queer Eyes* in all, or four and a half. We are midway through what we have promised each other has to be the last one when Susie gets a text.

'Niall's back. I told him he could sleep here. I didn't think he would, to be honest.'

She pulls an apologetic face. I wear one of utter dismay and whinge, 'Why would he want to? Why doesn't he go to a mate's?'

'He hasn't got many mates.'

'That's pathetic!'

She shrugs. 'He wants to talk it through, I guess. I owe it to him.'

'Not at all awkward.'

'I know and I'm really sorry, Dad. You want to go out for the evening, see a friend?'

'I haven't got any friends.'

They talk all night, in her room. At least, they are talking at eleven when I turn in and still talking at five when I wake with the terrors. Normally, when my day starts like this, I can scramble by my fingertips out of the wormhole to the relative safety of telling myself how fortunate I am: I have my children and a home and the worst case here is where I sell this flat and live somewhere small and cheap and get slowly back on my feet again. As shit-hitting-the-fan scenarios go, it's a decent one. But I am embarrassed by that scenario and I'm embarrassed that I'm embarrassed; that the thought of downsizing in front of my kids and merely surviving whilst their mum thrives . . . well, you can see just how badly I am doing with problems a big chunk of the world's population would volunteer to have.

I am lost and this is where I need to get a text from Ed: *I'm here for you, you need to talk? I've found a job for you, I know a guy who needs a guy* . . . or some buddy-movie crap like that. Isn't that what a friendship deserves after fifty years of getting it continually right? But I'm not going to text him at five in the morning and he's not going to respond. He is living his life. He signed up to be my mate, not my counsellor or personalised recruitment agent.

We are alone with this stuff if we're not in a relationship, and often even when we are. I was with Claire for more than a quarter of a century and never in that time did I tell Ed or anyone else a single deeply personal thing about myself – because I had Claire. Ed must have wondered what the hell was happening when I opened up to him. What was this weird stuff coming out of my mouth? Of course he said all the right things, he was just trying to get through the moment and order a steak.

At six o'clock I hear Niall go to the living room. I read until seven and then I get up. I find Niall asleep on the living-room sofa and a note pinned to Susie's door: *DO NOT DISTURB. NEED SLEEP.*

Thus, a precious Sunday with my daughter consists of me tiptoeing around my own house because her ex needed to talk for an entire night. If I didn't hate Niall before, I sodding well loathe him now as I watch the clock tick towards Susie's departure. When she does emerge, she staggers into the kitchen and hugs me.

'Poor you,' I say.

'Poor Niall.'

'Hungry?'

She nods. 'Very and I need a quick shower. Have you cooked?'

'I'm taking you for a pizza and then I'm driving you to the airport. I want all the time with you I can get.'

'I'm sorry today didn't happen.'

'Don't worry. You did a nice thing giving Niall time to talk.'

She smiles at me sleepily.

'Nicer than being unfaithful to him,' I add.

'Bugger off.'

I pray that Niall will sleep through Susie's departure, but I am not heard. He emerges, looking like he's been run over. He says nothing as he makes himself a cup of tea. I watch from the kitchen sofa. He sits at the table and gazes vaguely at the garden he has made look so good.

'Sorry,' he mutters.

'What for?'

'Ruining Sunday.'

I sit forward. 'Look . . .' I notice Susie reappear in the doorway but continue with what I was going to say. 'Look, Niall, I don't want to kick you when you're down, but I want some time with my daughter so I'm taking her out now and you're not coming. But you're welcome to stay here tonight, as planned.'

'Totally understand.'

Susie smiles at me.

114

I turn back to Niall. 'Before, you know, definitely moving out tomorrow.'

'See you,' Susie says. She doesn't know whether to hug him or leave him be.

'See you,' Niall says. He doesn't look at her.

Susie hesitates again and then leaves the room. Niall hears her open the front door and fixes his eyes on the garden as he starts to cry. I get up, rest a hand on his shoulder and then I leave too.

Over lunch we talk a bit about Stockholm, but Susie's heart is not in it. She feels guilty. Life's not fair. If this was happening to Erland, I'd wonder how his ex-girlfriend could be so cruel. But Susie can do little wrong in my eyes. I've always seen that as my job: to support her, make her feel safe, tell her she's wonderful and beautiful. And, yes, growing up we most certainly talked about values and treating people well, and she does not need me to tell her that being unfaithful wasn't great. And if I'm honest, she has not just capsized a relationship with someone I wanted to be my son-in-law and the father of my grandchildren.

The pizza is rushed and when Susie offers to pay I worry that she saw my card get rejected in the pub yesterday. I don't let her. She eats half her pizza in the car as we drive to Heathrow.

'Should be fun having your mum in Stockholm next week.'

'Yeah,' she says. She doesn't take the subject any further – and why should she when I have made conversation about Claire far from relaxing.

An airport in which you say goodbye to your child is a different place to an airport you fly from. The former is a place of muted, liquid sound that tries but ultimately fails to be a balm on the sadness of separation. When I watch Susie wave for the last time and disappear to the departure gates, I know that I am empty, and things have to change. I wonder if I will see this moment as the end of being a dad. My children will for ever be the most important thing to me, but this is the moment I can no longer claim that they are what I 'do'. Susie and Erland are no longer here, and I officially 'do' nothing. And I must change that.

As I head home there's a part of me that wants to stay out, but I don't have the personality to just keep driving and see where it takes me. I also know, being from Surrey, that to keep on driving means either going round the M25 in circles or reaching the coast within a couple of hours and having to turn back. I am not on a dead-straight open road in Arizona or Utah, the M3 is not Route 66 – I can't drive all night like Roy Orbison.

So I head home and, in true Jack Kerouac style, stop for a family-size bag of Revels in Sunbury which is so irritatingly dominated by peanut ones that I feel even less inclined than I might have done to accept Niall's thesis, delivered upon my return, that he and I are in the same boat.

'Given which,' he says, 'it makes zero sense for you to make me leave tomorrow. No one understands you more than me right now.'

Turns out, I should have kicked him when he was down, in the goolies, because he seems to have regained some of his sparkle.

'Remind me . . .' I reply. 'It's you who's been dumped by my daughter, not me. She's pretty happy with me as her dad. So we're in different boats. Mine's still afloat. And can you step away from the front door and let me come in.'

Yes, this conversation is taking place on the front doorstep, where Niall has scampered like a trusty hound to greet me upon hearing the key in the door.

He takes a few paces back into the hallway. I finish entering my own house and take off my coat.

'If you think she's happy with the job you're doing as her dad then I'm happy for you.'

'What's that meant to mean?'

'I belong here right now, by your side, that's the point. We're both heartbroken.'

'Susie dumping you is not what brings you and me together. On the contrary, it's the final nail in your coffin when it comes to living here. You are now my daughter's ex-boyfriend and I knew you five minutes.'

Niall's face crumples with incredulity. 'But I'll be homeless!' He saddens his eyes, like a Disney puppy.

'No, no, don't do that! You know full well that I'm exactly the sort of human being who would struggle to put you out on the street.'

'That's any normal human being! Everybody in the world should struggle with doing that!'

'I am going to my bedroom and you are not following me. You have your own journey to make, away from here, tomorrow morning.'

I am fully submerged in a piping-hot bath when, right on cue, Niall walks in and stands at the toilet.

'You might not make it to tomorrow morning, Niall. Get out.'

'I feel relaxed about the situation,' he says, unzipping.

'Oh, good, that's a weight off, I hate the thought of you not being relaxed.'

As he does his wee, he talks crap. 'Because of the non-parol agreement entered into by both parties, yourself on the one hand and myself and Susie, myself remaining entity to that party in spite of Susie's departure, on February the twenty-seventh of this year. Said verbal agreement evidenced by the acceptance of the sum of five hundred pounds by you, legally binding and to be upheld by a court if someone, in this case you, breaches the agreement, said agreement having reached completeness with all and any terms and conditions having been reached and agreed regarding terms, also on February the twenty-seventh of this year.'

Niall takes a breath.

'Now let us be clear, I am not saying any of this because I intend to remain here indefinitely. I don't. You want me to leave tomorrow and I intend to but it's important to be aware that my efforts to do so are *despite* the verbal agreement that would allow me to stay.'

I am momentarily stunned into silence by this barrage of legal jargon.

'I know you love chatting to me when I'm taking a bath, but I don't feel the same way so let's continue this fascinating-but-irrelevant-because-you're-moving-out-tomorrow debate some other time.'

Niall wiggles his arse and zips up. There's a commendable consistency to his weeing procedure.

'It's always some other time with you.'

'What?! No, forget I said "what" and just go away.'

'Telling Susie you don't want her to go abroad, telling your wife you love her, never doing any of your DIY list, giving up drinking midweek . . . some other time.'

I am livid at this, but it's hard to do my anger justice when naked.

'I do DIY.'

'Yeah, that's the thing to pick up on.'

Niall washes his hands.

'I don't want Susie to live abroad but I wouldn't say that!'

'Why not? You're usually quite selfish when it comes to wanting what's best for you not her.'

I get to my feet. The bathwater sloshes out and across the floor. 'GET OUT!'

He leaves. My bath is ruined. I dry myself and march to my room. While I'm dressing I hear a shuffling in the hallway and Niall starts talking to me through my bedroom door.

'It would have carried more weight coming from you. And now she's gone and met someone else, possibly more charismatic than me and definitely more wealthy.'

'Possibly more charismatic? Of course he's more charismatic!' I call back. 'And better-looking, athletic, with a log cabin in the woods, nice knitwear, likes a sauna.'

'There's no need for that,' Niall says.

I think there was a need for that, and I think that there's a need for more.

'If you had a proper job and were putting down a deposit on a place, then she might have stayed.'

'Because your daughter is that shallow or wants to be kept?'

Shit.

'Anyway,' he goes on, 'do you know what it's like trying to get a first-time mortgage these days, if you're not earning fifty grand a year and haven't been left a hundred grand by your Great-Aunt Jemima?'

'These are rhetorical questions, I take it.'

'No, they are not! Rhetorical means not answering them, right?'

'Look, Niall, I can't get dressed whilst arguing with a door.'

'AKA avoid the questions. Do you know what I earn?'

'Yes, I do. Twenty grand. You told me.'

'Twenty thousand pounds a year.'

'Yeah, I think I just told you that.'

I open the door. He is sitting cross-legged on the floor, so close that his nose must have been touching.

119

'I still mean the world to her!' he says. 'Her exact words! And you're going to risk incurring her wrath by casting me out.'

I look at Niall as if he's got me thinking, as if his line of argument might possibly work on me. I wait until I see a glimmer of hope in his eyes.

'It's great you understand that I'm casting you out. I thought I was going to have to explain it to you.'

'I bet he bloody well is gorgeous and Swedish and naked all the time!'

'He's not actually, he's English. I mean, yeah, he's good-looking from what I can remember but probably not as good-looking as you're imagining.'

Niall stares at me. I wonder why for a moment, then I hear what I've just said.

Again, shit.

Niall looks pale. 'You know him! She *already* knew him? Who is he?'

I shut the door again.

'Tell me he's not an ex-boyfriend,' he calls through.

'They never slept together.'

'*Unfinished business!*' he wails. 'How could you?'

'How could I what? I didn't do anything.'

'YES, AND ISN'T THAT JUST YOU ALL OVER!' he shouts, so melodramatically that I laugh.

That evening, as I wait for Susie's message to say she is safely back in Stockholm, and feeling drunk on the exhaustion of a year's bad sleep, I do two things that are out of character: I register my interest in becoming a school governor and I google 'Mary Blair hypnotherapy'. Her website congratulates me on *taking the first step towards a better life*. It offers to free me of anxiety and asks me to imagine a life in which I feel *calmer and clearer*. It invites me to rid my life of old habits and negative thinking. It suggests that perhaps I have been *thinking about making a change for a while but haven't quite got around to it*. And I wonder if she's written all this since bumping into me yesterday lunchtime.

The only thing more terrifying for me than going to see a therapist of any sort is going to see one who calls me Mr Smith and was our teenage babysitter, someone I should be flawless in front of.

But.

But.

Mary Blair knows who I am and, from the stuff on her website, knows everything about me. She's a lovely person and I trust her. And my hand is hovering over a keyboard just waiting for permission to ask for help. Mary Blair is an adult now, has been for some time; she's got two children, one husband, one divorce and is two careers into adulthood and aware that grown-ups like me do not have life sussed. She'd be out of work if we did.

I fill out the contact form on her website at nine o'clock and submit it. Ten minutes later, my daughter texts me from the most expensive train in the world to say she's on her way into Stockholm and that she loves me. At nine-thirty I get an email from Mary Blair saying it's 'brave and brilliant' of me to have reached out and when would be a good time to have a no-obligation telephone consultation? Would I like to seize the day and book in for a preliminary chat at eight-thirty tomorrow morning before her first appointment?

Brave and brilliant.

That's me all over.

Chapter 10

I am awake at five, which is usual, but fall back to sleep again, which is not. I get up at seven-thirty, feeling nervous and, I think, curious. I ignore Niall on the kitchen sofa as I make a cup of tea, because it's a game and in this house we've always enjoyed silly games, and because my call this morning has a clandestine feel to it. I shower and dress and eat breakfast and check my watch a lot.

Mary calls bang on time, with me holed up in my bedroom.

'Peter, it's Mary. Good morning.'

And that's my first question addressed: what will she call me? It was always Mr Smith. It is now, of course, Peter.

She tells me what hypnotherapy is and is not. She assures me about confidentiality.

'So, what has got you to this point, contacting me?'

'I think I need help seeing things differently and I've no idea about how to get help and then we bumped into you. It is no more thought out than that.'

'That's great.'

I need help. I've admitted it as a thought bubble above my head. But to say it out loud to someone I can burden with it, because I am paying them for their time, feels okay.

'You may not know yet, but what do you think you want help with?'

'Being happy,' I say.

I could talk about Claire, and work, and money and empty-nest syndrome (if Niall would sod off and allow me the luxury of a syndrome) but that feels like me offering the answers. If I strip it down, what do I want? To be happy. I don't want to break it down and go deep, I just want to be happy.

'Yes,' I say, 'I want help being happy.'

I bet I'm a breath of fresh air to her. Short, clear answers, not too much detail.

'That's a good thing to want, Peter.'

See?

'So try and break that down for me in detail. What's in the way of being happy?'

Bollocks.

Don't give answers, just problems, get your money's worth. The whole point of this is to get outside of my own head.

'I'm a bit lonely. Miss my wife. No self-belief. Financial problems. My business is buggered. Kids have left home. Can't sleep.'

'Okay.'

'I'm in a wormhole. Can't see solutions.'

'Brilliant,' she says.

And brave. That's me.

'What we could do in a first session is talk about loneliness, your friends, Claire, some of your success as a father and a professional, and we could do some visualisation that puts the good things and the bad in perspective.'

'Sounds good.'

It is not difficult to imagine being hypnotised by Mary Blair's voice.

'All I need you to do is turn up and be honest in a safe space.'

'I just want to mention,' I say, 'at this point – you know, from the start – that I'm not depressed. I don't suffer from that and I wouldn't want that in my files or anything. I want to be happier but I'm not, you know . . .'

'I hear you,' she says soothingly.

I picture her writing 'Depressed and delusional' into her notes.

Then she says, 'Let's leave it there,' which are the same words Claire used when yet another attempt by us to discuss her decision to leave me disintegrated into us not daring to say anything that mattered. And at the end of that discussion, I'm pretty sure I whined at her through my snot and tears, 'You can't leave me, you just can't, you don't do that to someone, that's not our story.'

And Claire slumped and said, 'Let's leave it there, darling man. Please.'

Why didn't we go to counselling? Two reasons. The first was my refusal to go to counselling. A significant factor, in hindsight. The second was that Claire gave up suggesting it, because of the first reason. And what with me not being averse to a spot of hypocrisy, when she finally agreed that there was no point in going, I suggested we go.

'Let's leave it there, darling man. Please. We're not suited to shouting or being unpleasant and I finally agree with you, there's no point in us talking to anyone.'

'Why would there be no point?'

'What? You suddenly want to' – here she used her fingers to denote speech marks and impersonated me – '"lay bare our relationship to a complete stranger and pay for the privilege"?'

'I'm simply saying I would like to know why there's no point.'

Rather than dignify this with an answer, which was not only beneath her but probably beyond her, she suggested we both write down what we'd like to discuss if we did go to counselling and make clear what our agenda was. I thought 'agenda' was a brutal, corporate term for trying to save our marriage until I saw Claire's list.

'This is an exit strategy, not a plan to rebuild our marriage,' I told her.

'It's a plan to keep our friendship after marriage.'

'But the point of relationship counselling is to save our marriage.'

'No, it would be to work on our friendship.'

And then I left the house and drove away, with the intention of booking into a hotel for three or four nights and switching off my phone, just to put the fear of God into her, make her worry herself sick about me (and confirm my adolescent levels of maturity − although that might be unfair on adolescents) until, an hour down the A3, I realised I didn't have any spare contact lenses and turned back.

'Think about it all and let me know if you'd like to book a session,' Mary says.

Her professional voice has a lilt to it that reminds me of East Coast academia, Harvard, Boston bookshops, podcasts by *New York Times* journalists who sound casual but are devoted to changing the world. Or my idea of them at least, given that I know no one from Harvard, have not been to Boston and am basing my entire knowledge of American podcasts on *The Dropout*, the only one I've listened to.

'I'll book now, Mary.'

'Great. What works best for you − daytime, early evening? I work some Saturdays.'

'Honestly, I can do any time, any day.' I laugh at the gaping chasm that is my diary.

'You want to get on with this, right?'

'I think so.'

125

'How about end of today then, six-thirty?'

Fuck! What, really? I'm doing this?

'Fine.'

'I'll send you a confirmation email. That has the practice address and there's a thing at the bottom about where to park, and also payment details.'

'Okay.'

'And Peter?'

'Yes.'

'Well done.'

I get an email from Mary before I leave the room. As well as all the details she promised, she has set me some homework. I must write a list of the things in my life I want to change; practical things or ways of thinking. Anything. Everything.

I decide to make myself a proper coffee to do this. And crazy though it might sound, I feel better already. A little bit more open. Less lonely. I feel the same way I felt after spilling my guts to Ed over dinner – but better, because this time I know there'll be some follow-up from the listener, because I'm buying the follow-up.

I go to the kitchen and put the coffee on and hardly notice myself tell Niall he can stay a couple more days whilst he sorts himself out.

'Really?' His face lights up, in a lovely childish way, like he's been offered an unexpected treat.

'Sure.'

Then his face sinks into confusion. 'What's going on?'

I shake my head. 'Nothing.' And as I watch the coffee simmer and steam, I feel nervous about my appointment in that exciting, risky, adrenaline-fuelled way I once knew.

I hand Niall his espresso, and he takes it tentatively. 'Is this a trick?'

'No. You've been dumped. That's a horrible feeling.'

'It is. It really is.'

'Listen,' I say. 'I have some homework to do and I want to do it in peace on that sofa, my favourite spot, so get out of my spot, leave me alone and don't disturb me until I tell you I'm done in here.'

'Okay.' He gets up. 'What sort of homework?'

'That's private but whilst I do my homework you have to do yours. Write down a list of all the places you could go live right now, pros and cons of each. Don't include this place. Then we'll look at the list and I'll help you make the right choice.'

'Blimey, you sound strangely engaged. What's happened to you?'

'Okay?'

'Okay. Fair enough. Thanks.'

He seems confused and tries to come at me with a hug, but I swallow-dive towards the fridge and look inside until I can be confident that he has aborted the manoeuvre.

In blissful solitude, I work on my list. I drink my coffee. I look at the garden. I get distracted by thinking about Claire's body. I return to my list. It's short (the list, not Claire's body):

Remove worry over money.
Get over Claire. (I do not want to be with someone else.)
Feel happy about my children and don't just miss them and worry about them.
Get my mojo back.
Get over feeling of abandonment by oldest friend.
Achieve the above and as a result become so irresistible, Claire returns.

Niall wanders in, holding a pencil and paper. I have finished my list and am browsing podcasts that might make me more interesting, or at least seem it.

'Done my list,' he says, chewing his pencil and checking his piece of paper.

'Me too.' I fold mine up and put it in my pocket. 'How many places on your list?'

'Six, but only four really. None of them great, to be honest.'

'One of them will work.'

'Coffee was awesome, thank you.'

'You're welcome. Write down another list. I'll dictate.'

'Okay.'

'House rules for the next few days.'

Niall rolls his eyes.

'Respect each other's personal space. Don't hog the kitchen sofa. Knock before entering my bedroom. Never enter the bathroom when I'm in it. Talk less. Cook more.'

Niall writes all this down then wanders across and hands me the pencil and paper.

'That was mostly rules for me, not you. And they – well, it's almost as if you don't want me here.'

'What an idea.'

'Right, now you write down my rules.'

He strides back and forth in a statesman like way, dictating, and I do an over-the-top mime of writing, waving the pencil like a conductor above the surface of the paper.

'Fix the bathroom door lock. No further lamenting the loss of Bowie in communal areas. Repeating the words, "Ugh, social media, why can't people just talk to each other?" to be punishable by adult circumcision. The phrase, "They used to make movies that meant something," to be phased out by Tuesday evening. Warn me before you commence a two-hour candlelit bath so I can take a leak first. No Radio Two. Go to work every day.'

'Done?' I ask.

'Done,' Niall says. 'Thwack it up on the fridge door.'

I stick my house rules on the fridge and make myself some toast.

'I'm not going to put this on the list,' Niall says, 'but I mention it as an advisory, that you consider phasing out incessantly calling Susie "my daughter" when you talk about her. It places an unhealthy emphasis on her as your possession. Technically, she is your daughter, but really she is Susie Smith, beautiful human being, university graduate, professional fashion buyer trend thingy, working in one of the most vibrant cities in the world, not just your daughter.'

'Did you say, "Technically, she is my daughter"?'

He nods. 'You use the term to express your superiority over me.'

'"Technically, she's my daughter." You sticking with that or you wanna withdraw it?'

He can't tell if I'm serious or not.

'You are her dad, granted . . .' He is less sure of himself now. 'She adores you. You do not need to constantly remind me she's your daughter, is all I'm saying.'

'Long speech, Niall.'

'Yeah, well . . .'

'Long enough for me to toast two pieces of bread.'

Which I now butter and marmalade. Yes, here, in my kitchen under my house rules, 'marmalade' is a verb.

'I think you're right, Niall. I'll do as you ask. I'll refer to my daughter as something other than my daughter.'

'Sweet.'

'Your ex-girlfriend, perhaps. Yeah, that works – your ex. Or if I'm feeling wordy like you, I'll call her the beautiful human being that decided to dump you. On days when I'm feeling less chatty, I'll just call her Mark's girlfriend. Better still, Mark's lover.'

'"My daughter" is fine.'

'I think so.'

'Like I said, it wasn't mandatory, it's not on the list, it was a word of advice coming from a good place – nothing for you to take offence at, just an advisory.'

'Like your legalese, don't you?'

'I slip back into it sometimes, yes. Can't help it when you've been trained like I was.'

'Like you were what? Trained as a what?'

'A lawyer.'

'In what way *trained*?' I snort as I say this and immediately sense that I'm going to regret it.

'First class hons in law from Gonville and Caius, Cambridge, then law school. In that way.'

'Oh.'

I did not know this.

'Why didn't you go into law?'

'I did.'

'Why didn't you stick at it?' I ask, because I am president of the Norman Tebbit society.

'Because it was full of cocks, it's a system that favours the wealthy and people work too hard.'

'So you chose to pack in the law and become a gardener?'

'Yup.'

'And don't tell me, you're discovering that, stone the crows, there's not a huge demand for druid gardeners here.'

'Not at all . . .'

'What a shock.'

'There's plenty of demand. Word of mouth and all that.'

'You'd possibly be busier if you left the house from time to time – it's a key part of the job of gardening.'

'It's a flat, not a house.'

'Yes, true, but that word "house" slips out. I can't help it after this being my house for a quarter of a century.'

130

'I feel your pain. As I've often said, I'm here for you and the anger you feel about that.'

'I'm not angry.' Jealousy and git-ness get the better of me and I let loose. 'You work from home, from my home, from my favourite sofa. What allows you to be the only gardener who works from home?'

He shakes his head dubiously. 'There's a lot going on there if we unpick your words and tone. But let's stick to your fundamental problem here.'

'Oh, yeah, and what's the fundamental problem, Niall?'

'Semantics. By which I mean, language.'

'I know what "semantics" means.'

'You keep employing the word "gardener" and it seems to be causing you a lot of confusion and stress.'

'I'm not stressed.'

'But if you get your language right and describe me and think of me as a CEO, you'll be less confused about my work–life balance.'

'I'm just pointing out that, flat or house, you and your tracksuit bottoms spend your time in it, merging with the sofa and dicking about on your tablet, not gardening.'

'No, Peter, I am on my tablet from six every morning, without fail, five days a week, coordinating eight gardeners and sometimes other teams who we bring in depending on the job. I run the company. You and I are both CEOs. I make sure, as we take on every job, small or large, that every year fifty per cent of our work is for charities and/or is means-tested work for people who are badly off or isolated. I pay my colleagues – and they are called colleagues, not staff, by the way – what my company, which is me, considers an amount that is morally acceptable, twice the minimum wage, and I never work them at weekends because time away from work with family or friends is a company ethos, and for all these reasons I make very little money for myself, twenty thousand or so. I am looking for investment so that I can spend more time out on site again, as I miss it, and grow the business so as to retain all the badly-off clients but have more high-paying ones too so that I earn more and can get my life sorted out. Tea?'

He goes to the kettle.

'If you're making,' I mumble, and pretend I've seen something interesting in the garden. He could have saved himself a long speech and just told me that he is everything I am not.

'And you're all druids?' I ask.

'Nope.'

'Well, that's misleading.'

'My name's Druid.'

'What?'

'My surname is Druid. D–r–e–w–i–d. I'm Drewid Gardening. It's a fairly standard thing to use your own name as the name of your business.'

'I didn't know that.'

'Because you never asked me anything about myself or my work until now.'

This stuns me into silence. It's true. I didn't even ask Susie about him. That is how far up my own self-pitying arse I have disappeared.

'So you're nothing to do with druids, even though you could pass as one?'

'There you go.'

'And all that stuff about paying proper wages and being morally sound?'

'It's how we roll.'

It's going to be tricky lifting that mug to my mouth when I feel about two inches tall. I avoid looking him in the eye

132

when he gives me my tea and I retreat to the shed, claiming to have something important to do there. Which is true, if you call polishing the brass bits of my old scuba equipment important.

The shed smells nice, as is the wont of sheds. I sit on my grandmother's old rattan chair, put my feet up, drink my tea and call Peggs.

'Hey, hey,' my old friend answers. I can tell he is either feeding the baby or changing his nappy. 'Can't chat right now, buddy,' he says. 'Trying to get a bottle down this one.'

'How is he?'

'All good, all good. One day he might even sleep.'

'He will. I'll leave you to it.'

'Thanks. Looking forward to breakfast next week, bud.'

'Bring that beautiful boy with you,' I tell him.

It goes so fast, Peggs. Enjoy every moment of this, even the difficult, sleep-deprived, middle-of-the-night ones. When you have a baby and a toddler, it never occurs to you that it is only for a very short period of your life that they cuddle up to you in that all-consuming way, their little hands clamping onto your neck or hair or ears. It often hurts like hell – one's back is never the same – but it's the best feeling in the world.

I shut my eyes and I am on Horsell Common on a Sunday afternoon in July. It is 2000. Claire and Erland are walking ahead of me beneath the yew trees. Erland is wearing a pirate's hat that my mum and dad gave him for his fifth birthday. Susie is in my arms, her head resting on my shoulder, her legs wrapped around my chest and her arms around my neck. She has been running after her brother most of the afternoon and now her three-year-old legs are tired. She is whispering to herself, making up some story with an amalgamation of characters from all her favourite stories and films, especially *The Aristocats* and *Lady and the Tramp*. I am trying to bottle the moment, the weight of her, her hair in my face, the grip of her tiny fingers on my skin, her breathing and whispering, my happiness. I have done a pretty good job of it, because it is still so vivid to me today.

I am returned to reality by Mr N. Drewid shouting out to me from the kitchen.

'Do you possess a barbeque?'

I consider it a step in the right direction that he hasn't worded this question, 'Do *we* possess a barbeque?'

I do possess one. My feet are resting on it right now. I bought it a year ago and it's still in its box.

'No,' I call back.

Why? Because I think it's funny? No, because I desperately want to be left alone.

'I'm going to go and buy one and do Thai. My thank-you for these extra few days.'

I can't muster a reply. But I do make a mental note of the fact that he is already calling the extra two days a few days, in return for which I'll let him go and buy a bar-b so I don't have to move my feet, then sell the one I have and make a little cash.

I can hear him singing. The only offence I would bring back the death penalty for is being chirpy. I haul myself out of the shed, look at the garden Niall has transformed into a perfectly proportioned universe, and call out, 'We do have a barbeque – I was lying. It's in the shed.'

'Aces! That's saved me a small fortune.'

He would have bought me one too, despite having so little money. He doesn't seem to dwell on the weirdness of a grown-up lying about owning a barbeque, he just gets excited about what he's going to cook on it. This is the last thing I need right now, to discover that even Niall is a better human being than me in every single way. I need to feel good, which

I now realise probably means not admitting to anyone, least of all the girl who used to babysit for us, how I really feel about myself. I'd actually rather hang out with Niall than look Mary Blair in the eye and talk about myself. So I send payment to her for this evening's appointment and I email her to cancel it, explaining that I have to work late.

I feel relieved. Therapy? What was I thinking?

Niall hands me a plate of food, not that the word 'food' does it justice.

'That's beef in oyster and coriander sauce,' he explains. 'They call it Tiger's Tears. That's tamarind sauce, grilled spring chicken, and that's green papaya salad.'

He hands me a sheet of paper. 'And that's my list of places I could live.'

I stop gawping at the food and look at the list. There are six names on it.

1. Mum and S/D
2. The X
3. Bodger and Psychic
4. PS
5. Aimz
6. Y

The first four have crosses next to them. The other two have question marks.

'Let's work through them in order,' I say.

'Oh, let's.'

'And remember, you are going to one of these, so there's no point being negative.'

Niall casts me a look, not one brimming with affection, and slumps back.

'Okay,' I say, 'number one, Mum and S/D. S/D?'

'Stepdad.'

'Where do they live?'

'Buckhurst Hill. It's in Essex, which is just above and to the right of London.'

'Hilarious. Great, your own mum, who probably misses you dearly. I'll drive you there.'

'You know I have wheels.'

'But this is funnier if I offer to take you, to underline how much I want you gone.'

'Funnier? You mean there's something less funny than that?'

'Yeah, you living here.'

'There's a good reason I put a cross next to my mum and stepdad.'

'What's the reason?'

'Suffice to say, I'd rather not. Family stuff.'

'Number two, the X. Ex-girlfriend, I take it.'

'Nope.'

'Then who?'

Niall looks at me neutrally. He keeps eye contact and mutters, 'Ex-wife.'

I stare back at him. 'Say what?'

Niall sits upright suddenly, slaps his thighs and runs his hands through his mane of hair. He smiles brightly. 'Ex-wife. Long story.'

I trip over a few barely formed words, which never fails to impress.

'Wh . . . eh . . . bu . . . why didn't I know? Who is she? Did Susie know?'

'Of course Susie knows!'

'Then why the hell didn't she tell me?'

'Oooh, I wonder why, looking at you now, purple-faced with fear.'

'It's not fear, it's outrage.'

'Same difference. I'm thirty-one and I've been married. If you think that's weird then you really need to open a fucking newspaper or step out of your house. You and your wife were very very, very lucky!'

This is the first time Niall has ever sworn at me. I think that's significant but don't know why. So I move on.

'Number three, Bodger and Psychic. And you're still claiming you're not a druid?'

'They would have me.'

'Great. Offer of a lift still stands.'

'To Harris. Ta, it's about a fifteen-hour drive, I think. I really would prefer to live somewhere that doesn't involve me abandoning my career.'

'There probably *is* a demand for druid gardeners on Harris.'

'You keep on trucking with the druid line of humour, even though it's based on nothing. Don't let me stop you, it never grows tired.'

'Bodger and Psychic are nice normal names, Niall.'

'Well, Bodger is a nickname, obviously.'

'Whereas Psychic . . .' I snort with laughter.

He looks at me curiously. 'That's her name. Her parents gave her that name.'

'That's her actual name? Psychic?'

'Yeah.'

'Why didn't she change it when she got to eighteen?'

'Why would she change her name?'

''Cause it's Psychic.'

'I'm not following.'

We are staring at each other now. Same room, different universe.

'Soooo, number four, who's PS?' Although as I say this, I realise I know the answer already.

'Peter Smith. Good friend.'

I strike through option four.

'I told you not to include this place on your list.'

'Put me in detention.'

'This is Susie's place. Why would you even want to be here, reminded of her every day?'

'Because I miss her.'

'But that's a good reason to leave, to add to all my reasons.'

'I don't think she was unfaithful. I think she's saying that to make it easier for me, the fact she wants to split up. She's trying to give me a reason to dislike her.'

'Er, interesting thought.'

'It makes more sense.'

'You're a bit all over the place, aren't you?'

'Yeah, I can only dream of having my shit together like you.'

I push the list of names closer to him. 'Keep going.' I load my fork with food. 'I see options five and six have question marks by them. Exciting potential. The question marks refer to the question, "Shall I move in there today or wait for tomorrow?"'

'More comic gold from PS.'

'Thank you.'

'The PS'ter. The PS-de-resistance.'

'Option five. Aimz. Spill,' I say.

'Aimee is an old school friend. It's always been platonic.'

'Colossal self-restraint on her part.'

'She's in a relationship with a nice guy and I texted her about my situation and she said it would be fine for a short while but I'm worried it will affect our friendship and I'm worried she's saying yes but her boyfriend might be less keen. I don't feel comfortable taking her up on it. I already regret asking.'

'Aimee sounds great and I think you should live with her immediately.'

'I can't, I shouldn't have asked her. So that leaves number six on the list, Y. The YMCA.'

'Oh, sod that, you're not going there. You put that on just to get my sympathy. What about your ex-landlady, who was rude about Sooz and you left to come here?'

'What about her?'

'Now that Susie's not involved, can't you rent that room again? It was fine apart from her disliking my daughter, wasn't it?'

'She's number two on the list, my ex-wife. It's not a healthy situation.'

I absorb this information.

'So . . . the woman who resented Susie being in her house was your ex-wife?'

He nods.

'Puts a slightly different perspective on her attitude, doesn't it?'

'Not really. Rude is rude.'

'You just float around, don't you, Niall, oblivious to people's own angle on things, unfiltered, asking for what you want, being gobsmacked when it isn't what other people want.'

'I'm not an unpleasant person, I think.'

'I agree. You're kind and decent, but you don't see things from other points of view. You don't have structure. If everyone behaved like that society would collapse.'

'What if only I behave like that?'

I look at his wide-eyed expression. He's serious. There is something so lovely about him, but I simply cannot take him being here.

'Move out,' I say, resting a hand on his shoulder. 'And thank you for the food.'

Chapter 11

It's Josie's day off today but she is sitting on the sofa in the window, the nice big sofa for the hordes of people who want to relax here whilst they browse our printed brochures arranged in pleasing fan patterns by Mrs H every morning for the past half a century. Josie is writing in her Moleskine notebook.

I don't ask her why she's in because it could make her self-conscious, and that is the last thing I want to do. But later, Mrs H tells me that Josie often comes in on her day off to write, as she finds the shop gives her lots of ideas. It makes sense that my business inspires comedy. Not that I'm personalising everything and feeding it into my own sense of self-worthlessness.

Josie leaves at lunchtime, having barely looked up from her notebook, and at three in the afternoon, silent Si breaks ranks with the universe and speaks.

'Look, we haven't had a single person in today, and the phone isn't ringing and I've updated every piece of content on the website. I've just changed the girth of the gridlines on the destinations pages. Would you mind if I go home? I've got some DIY to do.'

I don't mean to, but I stare at him, taken aback by the longest sentence he's ever produced. I look at Mrs H and she is waiting to take her cue from me.

'Sorry, I didn't mean to—'

'No,' I say. 'Of course you can, Si. Of course.'

'What's your DIY project?' Mrs H asks.

'Front door. I've already stripped it and put in a lot of wood filler. It's a rescue mission, but you wouldn't believe what a decent front door costs new.'

This is turning into a state of the union from him.

'Go for it,' I say.

'Cheers.'

Mrs H and I watch him go.

'Maybe he's going to a job interview,' I say.

'Couldn't blame him,' Mrs H says, then apologises.

We look at each other and I smile. She takes a seat opposite me and sighs, the way a consultant does before confirming test results you already know are shit because of the pain you're in.

'That chair you're sitting in,' I say. 'It's placed there so that people wanting to spend money in here can sit on it when I sell them the thing we do. They pay for the thing we do and that's the money we all live off.'

'That's the idea,' says Mrs H.

Mrs H is such an endearing name when your business is ticking along and everyone is enjoying what they do. But on a sinking ship, the fact that I have to remind myself what her name is — it's Mary Agnes Harrington — and that I know almost nothing about her, seems a little sad.

'Mary.'

'Yes, Peter.'

'What have we got left in the pot?'

'I'll email a summary to you now. I prepared it last week, so it's still accurate.'

'But in summary.'

'You owe a lot of money but, you know . . .'

141

I look at her with enough cluelessness to prompt her to finish that sentence.

'You own this place.'

'How would you be, if . . .?'

'I would be absolutely fine. I'm seventy-two and I've been in work since I was sixteen.'

'How old is Si?'

'He's forty-three.'

'Hmmm . . .' I mutter.

'Yes, not the ideal age.'

I picture this place as another boarded-up high-street shopfront and it makes me feel sick. After Mrs H leaves, I remain in my chair and think about the seven letters I sent out to larger travel companies raising the suggestion of merger. It's not that seven people have said 'No' or 'We'll be in touch' – there has not been a single reply or acknowledgement. I don't exist.

Seeing the *For Sale* sign outside my flat and the light inside, indicating Niall's presence, puts the finishing touches on my bad mood. I want to be left alone.

I take my shoes off at the front door and tiptoe past the light beneath Niall's door. I get myself a beer and a dangerously noisy party pack of crisps and creep into my bedroom where I remove my jacket in silent slow-motion and settle down on the bed with my book. I have done plenty of stupid things in my life thus far but trying to eat a crisp noiselessly in my own home is now right up there. I only get as far as opening the book when my phone goes.

'Yo, Pop!'

'What do you want, Niall?'

'Just to let you know, I'm heading to the kitchen to cook your dinner so come out, come out, when you're ready for a feast!'

If I tell him I want to be left alone, he'll take the piss or, worse, come in and ask why.

'I've already eaten, Niall.' (Untrue.) 'And Niall . . .'

'Yes, old man.'

'I'm going to have a bath shortly and I would love it if your sense of largesse this evening could extend to you not feeling compelled to join me in the bathroom.'

There's silence down the line.

'You don't want me to come in or you do want me to come in?'

'Don't want you to come in, Niall.'

By the time I am getting dressed after my bath, I know that it was a massive mistake claiming to have already eaten. I am very hungry indeed and the smell from the kitchen draws me to it. Predictably, irritatingly, the food looks fantastic.

'What you having?' I ask, with magnificent indifference.

'Just threw together some wild mushrooms on polenta with striplets of braised beef.'

'Uh-huh . . .'

Striplets? Is it even a word?

I use the tip of my tongue to force a soggy remnant of crisp out from my gums and wash it down with a siplet of lager.

'Why don't you try a bit, to make me happy?' he says.

'No, thanks, I'll try a bit to make me happy.'

'Good. I'll dish you up a small helping and you can have more if you're not too full.'

'Fine.' I spread out on the sofa and turn up the volume on the Channel 4 news.

Niall squeezes a drop of fresh lemon into a glass of water and brings it over to me. 'Swoosh that around your mouth and swallow it.'

'Swoosh it around your own mouth.'

'Get the taste of those crisps out of your mouth.' He shoves the glass in front of me. I can't be arsed to argue so I sigh like a teenager and do what I'm told.

Niall returns to the hob. 'I've had a brilliant idea today,' he says.

'Don't tell me . . .' I say.

He looks at me expectantly. I look away. I look back and he's still looking at me. 'Go on,' he says eagerly.

'Go on what?'

'You said, "Don't tell me," like you were going to guess what my idea is.'

'No. Don't tell me.'

This confuses him. It shouldn't. All he has to do is remember that I'm a grumpy prick in the midst of a crash-and-burn, and he'll know what to expect. He serves up two bowls of wild mushrooms, polenta and braised beef. It looks just about perfect.

'I'm going to tell you my idea.'

He waits until my mouth is full of food to say this. Bastard.

'Every day we should tell each other two things about ourselves.'

'We're not dating, Niall. Food's lovely, by the way.'

'Gradually, week by week, we'll get to know each other better. If people did it for a year, they'd learn seven hundred and thirty things!'

Niall kneels down at my feet, which is strange, and sticks one thumb in the air.

'My favourite place I have ever been to in the world is Machu Picchu. It felt very spiritual.'

He sticks up his index finger.

'My dad left when I was eight months old.'

I finish my mouthful. I really don't understand how he makes food taste so good. 'Niall, this is the sort of thing you

144

do when you are trying to get into bed with someone. This is relationship stuff. We are not doing this. There is no week-by-week for you and me. And Machu Picchu is so overrun with tourists that wankers like me send there, it's about as spiritual as a jockstrap.'

'You and I *are* in a relationship.'

'No, we're not. What sort of man leaves his own son at eight months old?'

Niall shrugs, wide-eyed.

'Do you know him?'

'Oh, God, yeah. He's a nice enough bloke these days, but he's always been useless, and he was horrible to my mum. I'll never forgive him that. He's just the clichéd shit dad who couldn't handle it. I found out, years later, that he paid eight quid a month child support, so I tap him up for cash over a pub lunch a few times a year and don't feel bad about it. Eight quid! What are your parents like?'

I look at him sympathetically, then scrunch up my face. 'Nah.'

'It's just a question.'

'Look, you and I are not . . . no, we're not doing this.'

Niall laughs at me. 'Not doing what? It's just a question – what are your parents like? It's not a trap.'

'Not doing it.'

'I mean, I know they're, like, dead. But what were they like before that?'

'Yeah, thanks for clearing that up, that you're not asking what they're like now, dead. I will say one thing about them, not anything deep, and I'm not doing this share-two-things thing, but even though I worked with them every day, when we went round to their house they were always waiting at the front door. They were always there to welcome us in, they weren't just finishing something else or preoccupied. Made it feel special. I loved that about them.'

145

'That's one thing. What's your second thing?'

'I'm not doing personal stuff.'

'Don't blame you, too dangerous.'

I have a think.

'My favourite album ever is *The Gift* by The Jam.' I get out my phone. 'Listen to this. A very underrated album. A very big part of my youth.'

'Yeah, I know it,' Niall says, and slouches back in his chair.

'Oh.' I smile and, inadvertently, smack my lips together. 'You "know" it?'

'Yeah.'

'What, all of it?'

Niall laughs. 'What does that even mean? Have I listened to this album? Yes. Is it the cornerstone of my existence and do I know every single lyric? No.'

'As I thought. Listen to this, "Ghosts". This track literally changed my life. It's—'

'From what to what?'

'What?'

'Changed your life from what to what?'

(I don't bloody know.) 'From what I was to what I am now? Let me play you—'

'When?'

'When what, you annoying tit?'

'When did it change your life?'

'In the early eighties.'

'From what you were to what you are?'

'Yes! Because Paul Weller is a genius.'

'So, you are still the same person you became in the early eighties? You haven't changed in getting on for forty years?'

'Just shut the fuck up and listen to this track. It's about being comfortable in your own skin, changing yourself to

146

fit in with the crowd. I was starting in the sixth form and it basically helped me navigate my adolescence.'

'Yeah. I know this track.'

'And?'

Niall shrugs. 'It's nice.'

'Nice? *Nice!*'

'Look. Your songs aren't my songs. I'm not living your life.'

'You're just living in my house. So show some respect.'

I walk out, leaving the best food in Woking behind. Soon enough, sure enough, there's a tap at my bedroom door.

'I do respect you,' Niall says, through the door. 'But you're not saying I need to pretend I'm into an album I'm not that into, just to show respect?'

'It wouldn't hurt.'

There's a long enough silence for me to hope he's gone.

'Okay, I'll give it a try. What other music should I pretend to like? Can you do one of your lists?'

'I've had a shitty day. Leave me alone.'

'Come and finish your dinner and don't be a moper.'

I take a deep breath. I'm sulking in my own home and being told to snap out of it by my daughter's ex-boyfriend who looks like Charles Manson and runs an ethical gardening business.

How – I said, how – did I get here?

It's eight-thirty in the morning. I am star-shaped on my back in bed, bathed in sweat. I woke at four, tearing at my chest, thinking that my heart had stopped beating, but it was my dry mouth making it difficult to swallow. The illusion of not being able to breathe: it is always the same when I wake this way.

In the early hours I reached for my phone and composed a text to Claire.

Claire – I feel like I'm disappearing. I don't want to. I can't see a way forward. I'm scared. I don't know what to do. Help. X

I deleted it.

Not fair on her.

And pathetic.

I got up and sat in the chair in the corner of my bedroom with my laptop. I opened the tab with an application to become a school governor. It was a quick process to fill it in. I don't fully understand what being a governor involves, or if I'll be snapped up or join a list of thousands waiting to offer their time. Are there lots of governors like me or is it weird to offer if you haven't got school-age children of your own? No idea but, fortunately, I was too tired to muster the finely tuned tools I possess to procrastinate. From the moment I hit 'send' on the application portal it gave me something new to think about. I got back into bed, shut my eyes and tried really hard to sleep. Which was, of course, a massive success.

I heard Niall's alarm at five to six. He went to the kitchen. I heard the kettle and then nothing. He is working, of course, diligently, reliably, crack of dawn every day, just like he's always said he does.

Just after nine, wide awake but feeling nauseous from lack of sleep, I hear the post land on the doormat and Niall humming beneath his breath as he picks it up. Then I watch him open my bedroom door and breeze in, reading a postcard as he plonks himself down on the side of my bed.

Un-be-lievable.

Momentarily, I wish I lived in a society where beating the shit out of him would be seen as acceptable, and that I possessed the strength to do it.

I pull the duvet up to my chin as if in fear of my chastity.

'Fuck off,' I mutter.

'Postcard from your ex-wife, from Norway – she flew straight there from Stockholm.' He paraphrases Claire's card as he reads it: 'Susie is well and looking forward to you going to stay with her. Fjords, blah blah blah, incredible light blah blah blah.' Niall suddenly leaps off the bed, ecstatic. 'She didn't meet Mark! He wasn't around! Yes!'

Not getting any comparable reaction from me, he sits back down and returns to the postcard. 'Norway stunning. Kayaking trip right now. Having a lovely time, wants the two of you to get better at talking regularly and being friends. Don't we all. Asks if there've been many viewings of the flat. Says Norway is stunning, again, uses exactly the same word to describe it, twice.'

Niall pulls a face at what he perceives to be my ex-wife's limited descriptive prose. I allow my mouth to hang open as I work out which of the many things wrong here I should explain to him first.

'I'm happy for her,' I say. 'And, to repeat, please fuck off out of my fucking bedroom.'

'Happy for her? I detect some subconscious sarcasm there.'

'Not really subconscious, is it, Niall? It's sarcasm.'

'A conflict of emotions then.'

'Wrong again, no conflict. I'm envious.'

'Of what?'

'Of her being in Norway, you tool.'

I snatch the card from him. Niall scratches his head theatrically. 'Because there's an embargo on *you* going to Norway?'

He snatches the postcard back and presents the photo of a dramatic Norwegian waterfall. 'The travel agent who doesn't go anywhere.'

'Says the gardener who doesn't leave the house. Go away. And . . .' I sigh. 'I don't even know how to explain to you

149

to not read my post and to stop just barging in on my private space.'

Niall looks startled and glances down at the bed.

'Oh, sorry! Were you having a . . . private moment?'

I sit up violently, tweaking a muscle in my lower back. 'No!'

Niall doesn't move. He looks at me with that one-size-fits-all smile of his.

'Why are you still here, sitting on my bed?'

'Actually, I have a slight problem too.'

I lie down and pull the duvet over my head. 'Best kept to yourself, in my experience, problems. Shut the door on your way out.'

'I might have had a few in the Pelham last night and given that Mrs Mellor character the impression I was up for helping her campaigning if there's an election thingy.'

I set him straight from beneath the duvet. 'You mean a general election thingy. She's going to stand for Parliament if they call another one so it's quite important to her. And she's called Miller, not Mellor. I imagine you said you'd help her because you want to sleep with her daughter even though you claim to be pining for my daughter.'

It's airless beneath the duvet and I feel faint, so I emerge from the cheap bedding I purchased when Claire took the White Company duvet covers and sheets with her and I finally, finally discovered why it's worth shelling out decent money on linen.

'Given that you were in the pub being led by your penis, you can see my angle on this vis-à-vis wanting to help you?'

'Full disclosure, I did think I wanted to sleep with Mrs Miller's daughter last night in the pub when looking at life through the distorted lens of reflecting tipsily on your daughter's infidelity. But in the cold light of day, I find myself incapable of looking at other women, such is the depth of my feelings for Susie.'

'Go away. And don't ever read my post again.'

'Okay, going, but on my way out can you address the problem in hand, which is that I might have offered to help Mrs Miller's daughter's mother—'

'Who we'll call Mrs Miller—'

'Without having realised that she objects to the Pelham's late-licence application and if I support her, I'll be barred. So, if you could possibly tell her I'm out when she comes round?'

'Mrs Miller was drinking in the Pelham and is trying to revoke its late licence?'

'All late licences. And she was drinking tonic water. Her daughter was drinking gin and tricked me into volunteering.'

'Will you leave me alone to read my book all day if I tell her you're out?'

'Absolutely. I mean, except for tea breaks, I'll probably chat to you without even realising I'm doing it whenever I come in to make a cuppa, if you're in the kitchen.'

'No tea breaks. No conversations with you. No sightings of you. No sounds of you. Wherever I am, you are not.'

'Okay. Just get rid of the Millers. I don't like politics.'

He leaves. I make a note in my iCal to buy a bolt for my bedroom door and, in a light-bulb moment that some might argue I should have had a few months ago, to get a bolt for the bathroom too. I don't know how to fix a proper door lock, but I can screw a bolt into a piece of wood as well as the next man, as long as the next man is a useless arse hat.

There's an email from Mary Blair in my inbox.

Good morning Peter,
    Thank you for your message. I can offer you an appointment at 5 p.m. today.
    Best wishes,
    Mary

I get a fuzzy recollection of emailing her, scroll down and see that I did so at ten past four this morning, asking for an appointment asap.

I email her back:

Thank you, Mary.

There's no hurry at all and I don't want you to alter your schedule on my account. If you'd prefer to book me in next week that'll be fine too.

Best,

Peter

She replies.

When someone asks for an asap appointment at 4.00 in the morning, I register a degree of urgency. I'm free at 5 p.m. and will leave it open for you to decide as and when you wish. No pressure.

Mary

Niall is as good as his word. I am left in peace and have a day of uninterrupted reading. Mid-afternoon, as I drift off to sleep on my bed, the doorbell rings. I put on my shoes and open the door to Mrs Miller and her daughter.

'How are you?' I say warmly.

The Millers have bought a holiday or two through me over the years and Mrs H has contributed office services and stationery to some of Mrs Miller's councillor work.

'Hello, Peter, very well. But not here to see you, you'll be relieved to hear.' Ruth Miller lets out a burst of laughter which her daughter replicates so exactly and fulsomely that it is clear she is very much a chip off the old block and firmly on message. Given Ruth Miller's record of public work, that has to be a good thing.

'You remember Sally, my eldest?'

'Of course. How are you, Sally?'

'Good, thanks,' Sally says confidently.

'What are you up to?' I ask her.

'Training to be a teacher, very happily.'

'Excellent.'

They are still on the doorstep, but I have no intention of allowing them to linger there for long. 'You've come to see Niall,' I say.

'We have,' says Ruth Miller, raising one foot off the mat in anticipation of being invited in.

'He's expecting you.'

I usher them in and point down the hall to Susie's bedroom door. 'He's right in there. I'm heading out but Niall will look after you. Good to see you both.'

I put on a jacket and head out, feeling deeply satisfied as I hear Niall greeting the Millers, his voice hitting a couple of high notes and his afternoon hitting the rocks.

I go for a walk, have a pint at the Pelham, sign their petition to keep late licences, browse Linked-fucking-In for some fresh sources of humiliation, google Norway, buy filled pasta shapes, pesto and parmesan from the Co-op and then head home to watch *Match of The Day* on catch-up.

The flat is quiet. I shut the kitchen door and settle down with a cup of tea to watch the football. As a Bristol Rovers fan, I can always enjoy *MOTD* because it doesn't pertain to me. I support Bristol Rovers because I saw them beaten 9–0 on the telly as a kid and thought it so unfair, so unkind, that I decided to follow them. It is the best possible way to be a football fan: no hope, no disappointment, and so little coverage on TV and radio that I can sometimes, blissfully, forget they exist.

An interview with José Mourinho begins so I mute the TV. I text Clare:

Thank you for my postcard. It sounds wonderful. I'm so glad Susie is settled in Sweden and that you saw her properly. Enjoy Norway, the geographical location of which I am fully aware of so don't waste valuable holiday time texting me hilariously to the contrary. Pete xx

I text Susie:

So pleased you saw Mum and had a great week together. She said she didn't meet Mark. If you and he have split up, please don't let Niall know until I have moved him out. I'm begging you. Miss you. Love you. You're the best. Have a wonderful time. Talk tomorrow? Xxxxx

The special one has left my screen, so I put the sound back on and watch the football whilst waiting to hear back from either my ex-wife or my daughter, preferably both, preferably instantly. I hear Niall and the Millers leave the living room and go to the front door. Another fifteen minutes elapses before I hear the front door shut.

The kitchen door opens and Niall takes a stance in the doorway and glares at me. I cast him a glance and then return to the football. Mark Chapman, he who presents *MOTD* these days, is busy trying to make football sound like quantum physics. I pretend to concentrate on what he is saying as Niall comes across and stands over me, presumably still glaring.

'Ruth Miller, prospective independent MP for Woking, and her daughter have left. Nearly two hours they were here. I've agreed to canvass for her. It isn't funny.'

'I disagree.' I keep my eyes on the TV. 'Do you think either of them will sleep with you?' I ask him.

'No.'

'Oh, dear, that's a wasted afternoon.'

Niall sits down next to me, in exactly the way that I find irritating. 'Think I'll watch too,' he says. He manages this for twenty seconds before fidgeting.

'Would you rather—' he starts.

'No talking during *Match of the Day*,' I say.

But he's not in the mood to play by my rules.

'Would you rather be good-looking like Jermaine Jenas but play for Tottenham and be a footballing failure and win nothing,' he asks, 'or have won everything like Martin Keown but look like Martin Keown?'

I don't respond, but I am thinking. I am thinking hard. I take a good look at Messrs Jenas and Keown. I take a deep breath and exhale slowly and loudly.

'That . . . is an excellent question. Get me a beer from the fridge and I'll address it.'

Niall goes to the fridge and gets a couple of beers.

'And some crisps,' I say

'Bollocks to crisps,' Niall says. 'They're shite and they're bad for you and they don't taste of anything real. I'll fix us something proper to eat.'

I am playing this man like a guitar.

It is not straightforward, the question posed. We discuss it, like adults. Jermaine Jenas is easy on the eye, it's true, and wealthier than a man of his abilities has the right to be. But he won nothing and played for perennial non-achievers and self-deluders in Tottenham and Newcastle.

You won't find Martin Keown fronting the next Hugo Boss perfume ad, but he lifted every domestic trophy the national sport offers, felt the adulation of a packed Wembley and Highbury victoriously singing his name, made Roy Keane look like a wind-blown poppy and is also wealthy.

'But for me,' I say, 'it has to be Jermaine Jenas. You are a footballer for only a few years, but you can be good-looking all your life.'

'That says a lot about you and me,' says Niall. 'I'm Keown, a winner, a battler, scarred and proud and victorious. Looks do fade, in time, but the medals are there and the memories of opponents vanquished.'

'Can I just remind you that you're a gardener in Surrey, not a gardener in *Game of Thrones*,' I say. 'Jenas, all day, but that's because I have experience of being good-looking and understand just how good it feels. You don't.'

'I love – no, I admire,' Niall says, 'that you've kept your sense of absurd humour even when every single facet of your life has ended in abject failure. I respect you for that.'

'If this helps you distract yourself from the reality that my daughter decided, rightly, that your people are not good enough for our people, then I don't want to stop you. You can further distract yourself by making me something nice to eat. Go now.'

I am beginning to like this man.

He must not find this out.

Chapter 12

It should not hurt to wake up.

There are so many good ways to gain consciousness: full of vim at the prospect of a day of adventure, replete with purpose at the dawning of another day fighting for social justice, making love with your partner, watching your shares rocket on the Nikkei. All of these are better than waking to the thought that since I told Ed everything, he hasn't sent me a single message.

We'll talk every day. I'll come see you next week. We'll work on a game plan.

I remember it vividly. And I remember now, also, that having turned instead to someone paid to listen, I forgot my five o'clock appointment with Mary Blair yesterday afternoon. For a second time, I transfer the fee into her account and email her an apology for not turning up. I immediately regret doing this at five in the morning. Still, this is an hour later than I asked for the appointment yesterday, so she'll see a sixty-minute improvement on the sleep and sanity front.

I have an email from LinkedIn suggesting I return to the fold. I delete it and switch off my phone. Around last Christmas I did spend a month on LinkedIn. (Does that mean I was digital?) My experience of it can be summarised thus: First week, I wrote a profile and sent out invitations to connect with five hundred people. Second week, I messaged the sixty people who had connected back to see if they were interested in giving me a job or buying my company. No one was. Weeks three and four, I applied for fifty jobs that had nothing to do with travel and for which I did not match the criteria. In a couple of cases, I didn't actually know what the job title meant. But the fifty rejections allowed me to cement my own view of myself as Uncle Wanker.

When you're desperate, someone accepting your invitation to connect on LinkedIn feels like the start of a beautiful friendship with a job offer thrown in, starting at sixty grand a year. Then, your new LinkedIn friends don't talk to you at all, and it leaves you feeling more stupid than ever. You sign up because you want something – a job – and you ignore common sense and all the evidence in front of you and kid yourself that everyone else on the site has signed up because they want to give you a job. It's only a day before the end of your thirty-day-free trial to premium that you realise they all want something and think they might get it from me. The idiots.

The bathroom door creaks, moved by a draught from an open window, and inspiration strikes. The shed door has two bolts on it. It only needs one.

I trudge out to the shed in my dressing gown, and on a shelf next to the box of TRX fitness ropes I bought and never opened is my drill and screwdriver set. I remove one bolt from the shed door and fit it to the bathroom door. It takes about ten minutes and makes me feel pretty good about myself. Maybe I'll build a seaworthy boat next.

My day gets even better when I am taking a hot bath and hear Niall come out of his room, whistle his way across the hallway towards the bathroom and face-butt the unyielding door which, for the first time, has not opened to his touch.

The door rattles, the bolt holds (which was not a given) and I hear a thud as Niall hits the deck. He groans as I grin.

'Please don't bleed on the floorboards,' I call out.

'K . . .' His voice wobbles.

'Me and Claire restored those floorboards ourselves.'

'You fixed the lock then.'

'I put on a bolt.'

'I didn't know that.'

'You do now.'

'Yeah. My head hurts.'

'Yeah.'

I can barely contain my pleasure at the thought of fitting an identical bolt to my bedroom door and being treated to a sequel.

Once I'm dressed, I make Niall a cup of tea and join him on the kitchen sofa.

'Look,' he says, showing me a microscopic spot of blood on the tissue he is holding to his nose.

'Did you kill one of those teeny red spiders, you bastard?'

'I'm actually bleeding. The bridge of my nose is stinging and I have a headache.'

'That's weird – it's not as if you walk fast,' I say.

'It is weird. Weird is the word.'

'Weird is a word,' I say, 'not necessarily *the* word.'

I fear that he is dragging me down into a Samuel Beckett play. 'I'm just pleased the bolt held under such a good test,' I say.

'Yeah,' he says, 'that is a result.'

We sit in silence for a while. I wonder if I should book in with Mary Blair again. It's not that I want to, but that I want to want to. Unsure, I tell myself instead to harness the momentum of my high-achieving start to the day by going in to work.

159

I am on the brink of seriously considering getting to my feet when Niall says, 'Do you want to play the fifty-paces game?'

'No. What is it?'

'Well, we both agree to spend the day chilling and we're each allowed to take fifty steps all day, no more. The fiftieth step has to be the one we take to get into bed.'

Niall explains this ridiculous game as if it exists in everyone's universe, not just his.

'Yeah, I'll play that game,' I say.

Of course I will – it's a licence to do nothing. I would email work to tell them something's come up and I can't come in but I never told them I was planning to show up in the first place.

And it would be a waste of steps.

'But once I'm in bed, that's it, end of the game?' I ask. 'I can go to the loo three or four times in the night, even though I get there and can't pee?'

'Will you promise to shoot me before I get old?'

'Willingly. It might be best if I do it now, in case I forget in the future.'

'How about it? Fifty steps. It's fun and it can lead to good chats.'

'Then, no, thanks.'

'You said you wanted to.'

'You hadn't said it would lead to conversation.'

'What are you going to do then?'

'Don't know.' I don't tell him that having watched the first episode of *Wormwood* on Netflix, I want to sit here on my own and watch the entire series in one sitting.

Or go in to work, of course.

'Going in to work?' Niall asks.

'Work looks after itself.'

'I think you're depressed.'

I look at him. He's being serious. He's trying to have a conversation with me, about me.

'I don't suffer from depression, Niall.'

'You may not have done in the past, but I think you're suffering from it now.'

'No, I'm not.'

'And it would serve you well to speak to someone.'

'Except that I haven't got it, so there'd be nothing to talk about. I might as well flush fifty quid down the toilet.'

I am able to use that figure with confidence, seeing as I know that's what Mary Blair charges to help people like me who are clearly suffering from depression.

'Or whatever these things cost,' I add. 'But there's nothing wrong with me, Niall.'

'There's nothing wrong with admitting you're unhappy.'

'I'm extremely happy.'

'Well, that's good news.'

'Really good news,' I agree.

'Epic.'

'Erland used to say "Epping" instead of "epic". It made us laugh, 'cause he tried to say epic a lot, like his sister, except he thought it was Epping. Claire and I wrote down the things they came out with as kids. I've kept them all.'

'I bet you have. Bet they're funny and you reread them.'

'They are and I do.'

'That's nice. Epping Forest is where my stepbrother beat me up the first time. Broke my arm and my nose. I was fifteen.'

I look at Niall. He shoots me a 'What can you do?' smile and takes a piece of paper towel away from his nose to look for blood. We remain side by side on the sofa in silence.

'How old was your stepbrother?'

'Twenty-two.'

Bloody hell, I think Niall has just said something important and real. I feel terrified.

'Have you watched *Wormwood* on Netflix?' I ask, like a brick.

'Yeah. Twice. You?'

'First episode so far.'

'Want me to tell you what happens?'

'Why would I possibly want that?'

'Save you the time watching it.'

'Watching it is the whole point.'

'I agree, but some people are strapped for time.'

'Do I give the impression I'm strapped for time?'

'Want to watch it now then, the whole series?'

'Yes, from episode two. On my own.'

'I'm not well enough to move with this head injury. I won't sue but watching a few episodes of *Wormwood* would go well with the fifty-paces game.'

I am not going to admit it, but I like the idea.

'The trick,' Niall says, 'is to divide chores so as not to waste steps. If you go to the fridge to get something, get me something at the same time, that sort of thing. And, basically, all our needs are tied up in the fridge.'

'Nearly all,' I say.

'Yeah, we should pee into a container until it's full, then one of us hop it to the loo.'

'That's not happening.'

'Because hopping counts as half a step.'

'Tell me you understand we are not peeing into a shared bottle in this kitchen.'

'I understand. Your reaction was entirely predictable.'

Niall gets up and takes two huge hops to get him to the hob.

'Need coffee,' he says. 'You want one?'

'Very much,' I say.

'That was two hops,' he says. 'One step.'

'I'm good at hopping.'

'We'll see if that's true,' he says, 'but bear in mind that you also think you're good at parenting and geography.'

'How about we play an alternative game, where I get fifty paces and you get fifty words?'

We spend the next six hours of our lives watching *Wormwood*. If you haven't done it, do it. For some of that time we multitask by simultaneously playing pétanque with rolled-up socks and a mop to retrieve them. My phone is in the bedroom and I can't afford the steps it would waste to retrieve it. The result is a prolonged period, the first since records began, of not checking my empty inbox. I feel better for it.

Between episodes three and four we stop to make food. I sit on the worktop, taking things from the fridge and passing them to Niall who stands pretty well on the spot whilst rustling up a large Spanish omelette, markedly better than the ones Claire and I used to make and which Erland and Susie called 'sick pie'.

'What did you put in your sick pie?' Niall asks.

'I dunno. Peas and carrots and stuff.'

'That's kind of retro for a Spanish omelette. This is the real deal – parsley, chorizo, potato and rosemary.'

'We have chorizo?'

'I have chorizo.'

'How can carrots or peas be retro?' I say. 'They're staples. And what does "retro" actually mean? Retro, vintage, classic, it's all blurred into one.'

Niall looks at me sympathetically. 'I feel your pain.' He points to my trainers. 'Those are retro,' he says. 'In a good way. Just. Borderline.' He points towards the living room. 'All your CDs in there. Vintage.' He points to my TV, 'Antique,' and then to my shirt, 'Awful.' And finally, as I smile warmly at him and remind him he won't be having to look at any of these things for much longer, he places the tip of his index finger against my temple. 'Medieval,' he says. 'But it's all forgivable at your grandfatherly age.'

'Bollocks am I old enough to be a grandfather.'

'Sorry, Pops, but empirically, mathematically, you so, so could be a grandad by now. In fact, I'm amazed you're not given my robust state of sexual health.'

'Why would your sexual health affect whether or not Susie and Mark have a baby?'

Niall's head drops. I am ever amazed by the speed at which his eyes well up.

'Sorry,' I say to him, for the first time ever. 'Too soon?'

'It will always be too soon.'

'Then I might as well take the piss now, 'cause I'm not holding back indefinitely.'

We eat and we watch more *Wormwood*. Niall sits forward and I slouch back and the side of his head is in my line of sight. I find myself watching his expression. It could be the intensity of the programme, but there's something wrong. He is facing the TV but not looking at it.

'Did you really have a stepbrother who bullied you?' I ask.

His next breath in is fractionally heavier than the previous ones, or perhaps I have simply gone deaf to the TV and can hear only him.

'Still do,' he says, without turning.

I press 'pause'. I sit forward and face him. I wait for him to look at me. When he does finally turn, he wears a hopeful almost-smile and I have no doubt that what he has just told me is true. And in the silence that I do not know what to do with, I say this:

'Do you really think this shirt is that bad?'

He takes the remote and plays the programme again, but I am still watching him, and he must know this. I step off the sofa and as soon as my right foot touches the floor, Niall mutters, 'One step,' without taking his attention from the screen. I get two bottles of beer out and then walk across to the drawer to get the bottle opener, with a carelessness that makes it clear the game is over. I put one bottle in Niall's hand and he glances at me and I chink his bottle. Then I switch the TV off. He sits back on the sofa and takes a swig. I take a drink too.

'I'm listening,' I say. And I do listen. And it grows dark.

Chapter 13

I've never had the heart to tell Erland I hate FaceTiming him. But I do sometimes hate it because I miss him so much afterwards. The WhatsApp group with him and Susie, on the other hand, I love. I love the photos he sends us and the abuse she sends him. This morning, I wake to this message from my son.

You guys around for an FT later? E x

Susie replies: It's what I live for.

Erland: Before we talk, remind me who you're sleeping with this week, so I'm up to speed.

Susie: Rude.

Me: I notice you don't ask me that question.

Erland: Who are you sleeping with this week, Dad?

Me: I'm having a week off.

Susie: You're having a life off.

Erland: Rude.

We agree to talk in an hour's time, by which time Erland will be home for the evening. Being the dark horse that he is, I've no idea if he'll be alone or not.

Over breakfast, I mention to Niall that I don't really like FaceTiming my son, and this is a mistake, because Niall has a theory on it.

'You know what your problem is, Pete?'

'Oh, goody.'

'You're living in the present.'

'Right, thanks for the advice. Now sod off.'

'You've got it all wrong.'

'Also helpful. You stay here, I'll sod off.'

Niall rubs his belly, always a sign he's enjoying himself and about to offer an opinion. 'Every FaceTime you have with him is time with him, seeing his face, knowing he is well, hearing his news, and when the call ends you should be ecstatic. You should be thinking, thanks to the brilliance of people inventing telecommunications tools, I have just seen my own son even though he is the other side of the world.'

I am silent for a very long time. Unusually, the runt of Hagrid's litter is too. There's only one reason for his silence: he knows he couldn't have said it better.

With what I now know about Niall and his family situation, I can't help but feel that his point of view when it comes to me appreciating the relationship I have with my son is something I should take on board.

He's right, I insist I hate FaceTimes with Erland because I want everyone to know how much I miss him, even though I am in the first generation of parents who can see their far-flung children every day. I know my son is safe and I could choose to enjoy FaceTimes as time spent with him.

I don't want to look at Niall right now because I know, I absolutely know, he's looking at me with a 'listen to your old

Uncle Nially' face. But I can't just stare at the floor for ever and I can't stand up and walk out staring at the floor because I'll bump into something. I sit back and look out the window. That too cannot be done indefinitely, so I turn to Niall. He is looking at me with a 'listen to your old Uncle Nially' face.

'Piss off, git.'

He laughs and leaves.

Erland joins the call last. He looks rugged and healthy. I have my phone propped against a pile of books and I sit on the chair in the corner of my bedroom. Erland holds his phone, sitting on the steps of his mobile home, and Susie is at work.

'Is that your office, Sooz?' my son asks.

'Yeah.'

'It looks like a toy shop.'

'Well, it's the café. *Dummkopf.*'

'Is it okay to just leave your desk and call your family?' I ask.

'Relax, Dad. Anyway, my brother lives the other side of the planet so I have no choice but to speak to him from work if I want to continue to witness his staggering success story first-hand.'

'The man knows how to stand on a grape,' I say.

'Standing on grapes is not learned overnight,' Erland says.

I ask him, 'Have you got a girlfriend or anything in that department to tell us about?'

'Subtle, Dad,' says Susie.

'Are you worried about me in that department, Dad?'

'No, I just don't want you to fall in love and never come back.'

''Cause falling in love is such a bad thing to happen to someone.'

'It's the best, but just do it in Woking not New Zealand.'

'Ooh, tempting . . .'

168

'Dad, you're safe,' Susie says. 'Curiously, Erl's interest in women waned the moment he arrived in the country with the highest sheep population in the world.'

Susie makes a baa-ing noise. Erland sinks his face into his hands. I shake my head.

'Dad, whilst your daughter humiliates herself at the office where she does the job she did not sleep with anyone to get, you might want to know that your son has now passed his vintner's certificate.'

I am delighted. 'That's fantastic, son. Well done. And don't forget, we have sheep here too, nice ones.'

Susie stops baa-ing. 'That's brilliant, bro.'

'Why, thank you, sis.'

'Is that a qualification that just applies only in New Zealand or internationally? Back home, say?' I can't stop myself asking.

'Just in his own imagination. Along with his friends.'

'Anywhere, Dad, UK included.'

'You've always been my favourite child, Erland. So that's welcome news.'

'Thanks, Dad. I know you find Sooz a disappointment, but she's qualified to talk shit about frocks in any country too.'

'Can we take the piss out of Dad now?' Susie says.

'No point,' Erland says. 'It's been devalued by Dad's actual real total failure in all fields.'

'Making me exempt,' I say.

'Then I think we're done here,' Susie says.

'Dad,' Erland says, 'Mum's coming to stay with me next week, for a month.'

I sit bolt upright and squeal with disgust. 'WHAT!'

My children laugh.

'Just joking. Sooz said how jealous you were of Mum going to Stockholm first.'

'Bastards. And I wasn't jealous at all.' Again, too high-pitched. We all take a breath.

'By the way, neither of you is mine.'

'Is that why you've adopted Niall, Dad?' Susie says.

'Yeah,' Erland says. 'Why are you living with Susie's ex-boyfriend?'

'He's living with me, not me with him. Anyway, he's going in a couple of days.'

'It's a bit weird,' Susie says.

'Not as weird as going out with him,' I say. 'Anyway, Sooz, he's got some options, and there's always the spare room at his ex-wife's place.'

I'm really pleased that I've not told Susie I know about the ex-wife until now, and that I've waited for a chance to mention it. All casual like.

'Cool,' my daughter says, equally casual.

'Niall was married, Erland, did you know that?'

'Yeah.'

'Bet you didn't know he was still living in her house.'

'How much?'

'All the time.'

'No, I mean, how much do you bet me?'

'You knew?'

'Yeah.'

'Why am I the only one who didn't know?'

'Because you're the only person on planet Earth who considers it an issue,' Susie says.

And the stupid thing is, I don't consider it an issue. Niall was married in his twenties before meeting my daughter. So what? But, I mean, really, really, actually, so what, Peter? I was born in 1968 not 1868 – of course it's not an issue. So why have I taken on that role here? Why am I taking positions that I don't even begin to believe? I write these

170

questions down on the back of a recently received and not yet opened letter from Royal Bank of Scotland's debt-recovery department.

'What else is happening, Dad?' Erland asks. 'Who have you seen, what are you up to?'

This and that, I tell them. All is good, I say. Seeing Ed and Peggs soon and making some changes at work. (Shutting it down counts as change, right?) I feel fired up about it, I say. They pretend to believe me, because they're nice. Erland tells us about a week's holiday he has planned in Te Kao Bay. Susie and I salivate over the details.

Later, when I saunter into my kitchen and see Niall in the garden, pruning some shrubs, bi-fold doors open and the cold sunshine flooding in, I spend a few minutes doing the washing-up; and there's a certain languid ease to Niall and me being in each other's company that ought to worry me but doesn't.

Until he talks.

'You know, Pete, I've got to say one thing to you. I know you're cash-strapped but with a tiny bit of ingenuity, you are actually free to go sailing in Te Kao Bay and hiking Cape Reinga and feeling equally excited about these places for yourself as you are for your son. This ought to be an amazing time of life for you.'

'So, basically, you were listening in on my family FaceTime?'

'Well, it depends on your definition. But, obviously, being a frail human being with a broken heart, I was keen to hear if Susie mentioned me at all. That's only natural.'

I take a deep breath. There's a silent version of him I could quite like. But it doesn't exist.

'Let's take a look at your list again later,' I say.

My phone rings in the distance. By the time I track it down to my bedroom, there is a voicemail message from a primary school outside Guildford who want to talk to me about a governor vacancy and am I free to pop in later?

It all feels familiar. It all feels good. The musty smell that has no one source, that cannot be expunged by cleaning or opening windows, the amalgam of plasticine caked in dust and chalk and crayon. The miniature chairs and tables. The class names. In this place, it is creatures of the sea. At Erland and Susie's school, it was colours. The children who stare at you as you wait in reception, the children who walk on the balls of their feet, the boys who lean into each other as they cruise the corridors. The kid whose parents, you instantly know, cannot afford to replace trousers that are too short or shoes that are worn out. The school's values, written in rainbow colours on the walls. The CCTV. The security gates onto the premises.

I was an active parent of my primary-school children. A member of the PTA, a volunteer storytime reader, one of those who turned up for playground tidy-ups, snow shovelling – although, not living in Lapland, that only happened once. I did it because I was my own boss and could choose to, and because Erland and Susie were the main project, and because being at their school was fun and seemed to mean something.

Petra has warned me by text that she's running late and when she arrives in reception she is full of clipped apology, hugging a stack of files. 'Peter, sorry about that, meeting went on and on across the road. You've got a lanyard, yes?'

I nod and she heads off. I walk behind her and she never gives me a chance to catch up and the tour of the school feels breathless and rushed. After a short while I stop even attempting to take in the information. The place feels disciplined yet ragged. An image comes to me, of Niall as a young boy walking these corridors, lost without a dad of his own, wandering in search of a new dad or a big brother and

172

oblivious to the bullying stepbrother that the future will bring him. It makes me sick with sadness.

We arrive at a large IT room, which is not being used. She shows me in and offers me a child's seat, which I take, like Gulliver in Lilliput, my knees offering themselves up as a chin rest as I listen to Petra talk me through the make-up of the governing body.

'We've parent governors and prospective ones coming out of our ears – it's co-opted ones like you that we need to strengthen on. It's six meetings per year plus a couple of smaller team meetings depending on the role you have, and what we really need now is fundraising expertise and health and safety like yourself.'

I clearly look confused.

'You're in health and safety, right?' she says.

I shake my head. She looks confused and irritated and sifts through her papers.

'I own a clipboard, if that counts.'

She doesn't respond to that at all. Not a breath, let alone a laugh or a smile. I'm not saying I could sell the line to Josie, but at least acknowledge that I'm here, on the brink of hitting the new low for me of being turned down for a voluntary position.

I sit in my car for a few moments before driving away. She couldn't get me out of there quick enough once she'd realised they'd given her the wrong person to meet. I've no problem with that: they need certain skills and I don't have them. They misread the papers and got the wrong guy in, no worries. But bloody hell! Ask me one thing about what I can do. Thank me for offering to give my time to their school. Is it so hard to take ten seconds off from her overworked, probably underpaid, job to say the very few words that stop the other person feeling like a useless bag of crap?

I drive home in a daze. I watch people on pavements and in their cars as if they belong to a place I don't know about. What does it take to feel that you belong somewhere? What does it take to feel like you always did, for decades, which is to say, happy?

When she was eight or nine, Susie could not stop herself ambushing me and Claire when either of us returned from work. She would run up to us and get under us as we came through the front door, removed coats, tried to carry in shopping, and she'd tell us about her day or something she wanted to get or an idea she'd had. She seemed not to draw breath when she was talking. We once had a word with her about giving us five minutes to get in and then catch up on her news, and we immediately felt guilty for having done so. She didn't really get what she was being asked but she got that something she did was not right. Either way, she never stopped doing it until she grew out of doing it and we then missed her doing it.

Niall does it too. At thirty-one years of age, Niall comes out into the hallway when he hears me getting home, and he starts talking to me before I've stepped into the house.

'I have a proposition for you. Well, for us, really.'

Fortunately, I don't have to handle an uninvited lodger the same way as one's own child.

'Not remotely interested,' I say, stepping straight into my bedroom and shutting the door. But this rudeness towards Niall, though heartfelt, has become a game.

And when I have changed out of the collared shirt and jacket that I thought would be school-governorish and I amble into my kitchen to make myself a cup of tea and turn on *PM* so I can have an argument with Shaun Ley, Niall continues the sentence he started ten minutes earlier.

174

'I propose a phone-free evening, cut off from all social media. It will do us good.'

'Sounds really fun, Niall. Cut ourselves off from civilisation. Goody. Anyway, shouldn't this be the other way around?'

'How so?'

'Isn't it me, farty old bastard, who's meant to say your generation are too obsessed with your phones and let's see if you can manage without it? Isn't it my job to have a go at you for constantly being on Facebook and TikTok?'

'I'm thirty-one, not thirteen.'

'Anyway, a night off from what? I'm never on social media.'

'But you're on your phone every five minutes, tapping the screen, checking in.'

'Rubbish!'

'Right. Yet, at the same time, accurate and not rubbish.'

I struggle for a response. Bang to rights. I rarely carry my phone around with me but I do have it placed strategically all day – on the kitchen counter, my bedroom table, the arm of the kitchen sofa – so I can tap it every few minutes to see if either Susie or Erland has messaged me or called. But, mainly, to see if Claire has.

Niall has noticed this habit and is trying to help.

'Niall,' I say.

'Yes, Pete.'

'You are a colossal wanker.'

He nods and smiles victoriously to himself.

Isn't it unfair that I can be described as low mood and negative these days and yet every five minutes of my life, I carry the belief that waiting for me on my phone there could be a message from my wife saying she wants me back or an email from a complete stranger offering me a job. I'm the king of bloody optimism, me.

Brave and brilliant.

'An evening without the phone on would be liberating for you,' Niall says. 'Your phone is one of the main things contributing to you feeling down about yourself.'

'I don't feel down about myself, because I'm fabulous.'

'Because every time you check it and there's nothing, you're delivered a small blow.'

'It's a no to your suggestion, Niall, even though it's a good idea, because the truth is that once you have children you never switch your phone off. It doesn't matter how old they are. You'll find that out, at least I hope you will, 'cause you'll make a fine dad.'

He is taken aback by this. 'Thank you,' he mumbles.

'And the first step for you being that is to move out, so you can meet someone. So, let's get that list of yours out again and help you make a decision.'

He looks pissed off. And I guess I have, without planning to, hijacked the first compliment I have ever paid him to get back onto the subject of evicting him.

'No need,' he says sulkily. 'I'll go out and have an evening not watching you look desperately for answers on your phone. And I don't need your help with the list. I'll take care of it myself.'

I don't see Niall for the next two days. When I speak to Susie I ask her if she's heard from him. She hasn't, so I text him and ask if he's okay. He replies the next morning, at six, which is fine. I'm awake of course. His message says that he's looking at flats.

On the third day, he gets back in the evening with a load of shopping and offers to cook dinner for us both, but he is monotone with me.

'I've found a place. Pretty good, larger than I'd hoped and affordable. It's a result.'

He shows me pictures on his phone. It's a one-bedroom basement that is part of a house and he has to use a shared bathroom and kitchen upstairs. It looks a bit depressing to me and I don't feel great about it, but he seems keen.

'But there's a thing,' he says.

'What thing?'

'I can't move in for a month. If you're really desperate to have your own space, I could go to my mum's. If you're not, I could stay here and try not to be so in your face.'

'What's different?' I ask him. 'You're not yourself, which is fine, obviously, 'cause you're an idiot, but you're subdued. Something's different. What's going on?'

He turns away and gets down to chopping up vegetables and producing a piece of topside so large and red my mouth begins to water.

'The beef is from my stepdad. He's a butcher.'

'Looks good. Where have you been?'

'Nowhere much. Stayed at my mum's.'

'How was that?'

'A dream, as ever. She lent me the deposit, as long as I keep it secret. My stepbrother is coming over from France on business and wants to meet up with me.'

'Just don't,' I say.

Niall shrugs and waves me away. He starts preparing our dinner.

'Don't see him, Niall.'

I have never seen this man shut down – he's the most open-faced, wide-eyed adult I've met – but that's what happens now, momentarily. His head goes down and his entire body becomes a single, unassailable *Keep Out* sign, from behind which he says, 'He called the house when I was with Mum and Ian. I got roped in and it's easier to just do it and not upset them. Ian thinks the sun shines out of his son's arse. I'll never come out of it in one piece if I tell them the truth.'

I open my mouth to say something about this, but he raises a hand, signalling not to bother. He gets a bottle of red wine from one of the shopping bags and hands it to me.

'Open that and get us both started on it. It's Argentinian.'

As I pour, he talks. 'It's easier if I see him, better than a barrage of abuse about not putting any effort into the family. He asked to go on speaker and said in front of them that he'd come and visit me and I can see they're thinking, That's nice, and then my stepbro started talking about his new motorbike and that's partly why he's coming over, to give the Beast – that's what he called it – a good run out, and he'll come over here and be a wanker for an hour or so and then leave because he's bored.'

'And don't tell me, he'll offer to take you out on it?'

Niall nods.

'It's a game. He's trying to control you.'

'Yes, but after fifteen years I know how to live with it pain-free. Mostly pain-free. When I see him, at some point he'll say something like, 'If you or your mum try to take anything of Dad's when he dies, I'll kill you, no question.' He's been on about that for ten years and Ian's fit as a fiddle. I just let him talk and then say goodbye.'

'And he calls his motorbike "the Beast"?'

'This one, yes.'

I roll my eyes. 'Invite him here,' I say. 'Not out somewhere, and don't even try talking me out of being here. He's not treating you that way under my roof.'

I take a sip of the wine and it's really good but I'm too angry to enjoy it. The anger we feel for other people is often stronger than they feel for themselves. They're inside the situation and accustomed to it, they've found a way of absorbing the abuse and just want to sleep easy. An outsider sees it for what it is and wants to solve the situation, deliver moral justice. The weapon of bullies is that people try to appease them, avoid antagonising them. This is their bread and butter.

'Stop thinking about it and enjoy the wine,' Niall says. 'It's a good one. Strictly speaking, my mum bought it for us as I slightly miscalculated the cost of the deposit and had some change. Sit down and drink the finest Malbec Essex will ever provide. And, believe me, I am trying to control the situation the way I know how. Susie doesn't know about him. No one does. That's the best way for me. Truth is I hate him, but I don't feel comfortable feeling like that about anyone. He's the only person in the world I hate, but he doesn't make too many appearances in my life.'

'He's the only person in the world you hate?'

'Yeah. I would say so.'

'I hate most of my friends a lot of the time. What's wrong with you?'

'You might want to look at that.'

We drink whilst the beef roasts in rosemary butter and I contemplate a return to my pre-Niall diet in a month's time. It is not going to be pretty. My taste buds will enter a period of mourning.

'I once agreed to meet up with him in Paris,' Niall says, pouring us both more wine.

'Your stepbrother?'

'Yup. I'd always wanted to go there and to go on the Eurostar and I saved up and did it. My stepbro didn't turn up. I waited on a street corner in Paris for hours, and he never showed. I called him. I left a message. He texted next day, "Sorry, was impossible to get away from the kids, family life you know, Nially." He lives in Grenoble. It's a four-hour journey to Paris. He said he was going to be there on business. He had hours to tell me he wasn't going, days probably.'

'He never intended to be there.'

'No shit. But he did me a favour. Know how?'

I shake my head.

'I wandered over the river and into a place called the Sainte-Chapelle.'

'I know it,' I say. And I do know it, very well. It's where I proposed to Claire. I do not share this fact with Niall, and it makes me sad that the place of one of my happiest moments is the setting for one of his lowest.

Chapter 14

Three days later I do something I have never done before. Whilst Niall is taking a shower, I disconnect the doorbell. That's not the thing I've never done before, although it is true that I have never done it. I disconnect the doorbell and stand at my bedroom window until I see a motorbike pull up on the street. I check that Niall is still in his bedroom, listening to 6 Music, and I step out of the front door, shut it behind me and approach the man in leathers coming towards me, as he removes his helmet.

'You must be Owen.'

'Yeah, must be.'

'Niall's away.'

Owen stops and glares at me. 'What do you mean?'

And then I do the thing I have never done before. I say something I've never said to another person face to face other than jokingly to a friend.

'Fuck off.'

Owen laughs and power-stances.

'Niall isn't here, so now you know what it feels like and now you can fuck off.'

I do this because I want to and because I think it is the best thing for Niall and because it turns out Owen is shorter than me. When you're pissed off with a lot of things in life, finding someone smaller than you whom you dislike and telling them to fuck off is a therapeutic thing to do. And you know what he says to me?

'Can I use your bog? I'm busting.'

That's his response to the Batman of Beaconsfield Road. A request to use my lav? Nothing in life goes the way I imagine it will any more.

'There's a pub around the corner,' I say.

He shrugs and leaves.

'Don't ever come back here.'

He makes a 'whoooo!' sound, right out of the playground.

For Niall, given that I do not tell him what I've done, it is another no-show from his stepbrother (I hadn't totally thought this through) but one which has not cost him two hundred quid on the Eurostar, and one about which he is visibly relieved.

'This time don't message him,' I say. 'Don't ask him where he got to. Don't give him the satisfaction. Starve him of oxygen.'

Niall nods thoughtfully. 'I like that,' he says. 'Starve him of oxygen. Thanks.'

'You're welcome. Do you want to show your appreciation by cooking supper?'

'No, thanks,' Niall says. 'Just saying "thanks" was scale.'

'Bastard.'

'I could teach you to cook before I move out. You could learn a lot in a month.'

I think about this. 'Mmm-nah, it would only be you talking a lot. I can't see past that. Can't you just keep cooking for me after you move out and drop the food off, same time you do my gardening?'

Niall smiles and goes to Susie's room. He seems subdued and, sure enough, I hear classical music come on. I could name it – 'The Swan of Tuonela' by Sibelius – but I won't because I really am trying to feel younger and get my mojo back and neither Inspector Morse nor Alan Titchmarsh is the vibe I'm after.

I miss Susie. In the same way that I don't analyse bad stuff, just absorb it and hope it'll go away, I am unconditional in my enjoyment of the good times. A part of me persuaded all of me to believe that Susie being back would be the next huge chunk of my life. Piece by piece, life would return to its natural state. First Susie, then Erland, finally their mum. And then, oh, how we'd regret not keeping that staircase.

I watch a *Queer Eye* and eat Revels. I'm not sure if it makes me feel better or worse, but I feel that calm stillness that is a comfort when you don't know what you're feeling. A second episode is starting as Niall comes in.

'What are you watching?'

'*Queer Eye*. It's brilliant.'

'Ugh,' he says. 'No, thanks.'

He stands at the end of the sofa, leans against the wall and watches.

'Take a seat. You might learn something about personal grooming.'

I hold out the bag of Revels towards him.

'Ugh,' he says again.

'"Thank you, Mr Smith, but they are not to my taste,"' I say.

'Thank you, Mr Smith, but they are not to my taste,' he says.

'See you later,' I say.

Niall doesn't move. He keeps watching and tuts from time to time. Then he watches some more.

'So not into reality TV rubbish,' he says.

'See you later, then.'

We watch the Fab 5 visit a roadside barbeque shack run by two overworked, exhausted sisters.

'I mean,' he says, 'every episode is basically the same.' But he hovers where he is and keeps watching. 'It's just rubbish. Just a bunch of saddos patronising poor people. I bet they hate each other off-camera.'

'See you later, then.'

I realise that I have reached that nirvana with Niall where I can totally zone out of hearing him, the same way Claire and I did with the kids' CDs in the car when they were little. There was a time I thought that hearing the teenybop version of 'Ten Green Bottles' just once more would turn me into a mass murderer. I could not have believed then that the day would come when the songs would play and I wouldn't hear them, and I could chat to Claire or enjoy the drive as if in silence. I've reached that point with Niall. He is talking but I'm not hearing. Happy days.

The Queer Eyes help the barbeque sisters turn their own recipe sauce into a properly produced branded product, transform the joint and replace their oversized T-shirts with clothes that take a couple of decades off both of them.

'Basically,' Niall says, 'it's people starting from rock bottom so I can see why you're drawn to it.'

'Sure,' I say.

'Utter rubbish though,' he confirms.

'See you later, then.'

One of the sisters, Deborah, gets new teeth and we discover that the reason she constantly covers her face with one hand is the shame she feels at the state of her smile. Suddenly, she is laughing and smiling again, and beautiful. These women's lives are going to be different, not just because they look and feel better but because they are going to earn more and shift a little away from the hard-slog minimum-wage existence they've laboured under for so many years.

The episode ends and I notice that Niall is still there, slouching against a wall. (There is no surface, no matter the angle or gravitational forces at work, that this man cannot slouch against.) There are tears streaming down his face.

'That was beautiful,' he whispers, and walks out.

Aware of my lethargy, I summon the mental and physical strength to switch off the telly and go to my bedroom. I get a pen and paper and write across the top of the page, *Assets and Ideas Going Forward*. I look out of the window onto the street, chew my pen, lie down on my bed and have this overwhelming wish to be in contact with Claire and the kids. It's not that I feel low. I just want to share with them something of what I am feeling. It will sound immodest, and it's not something that would make sense if I tried to talk about it, but it is something about telling Niall's horrible little stepbrother to take a running jump. Today I can remember what it felt like to fall in love with Claire, because apart from being exciting and breath-taking, it felt strong. I felt determined not to lose this person. I had purpose. And I'm grateful to Niall's abhorrent little stepbro for reminding me what that feels like.

Now that I've met him, Owen the biker feels like a different animal to the one I pictured when Niall talked about him. What I saw standing on my path was pathetic, and not all of that was down his creaking leather trousers. But if one human being decides to bully and control another, and if they have traction because the other person doesn't want to upset his mother's second marriage – in Niall's case – or a bullied mother has to allow an aggressive ex-husband time with their kids, or a person fears the sack if they speak out, then even the most pathetic of people can have a hold over you. I have a perspective on Niall's stepbrother that can help Niall. It is easier to see a bully from the wings than head on.

Niall didn't say anything at first, on that day which started with him head-banging the bathroom door (still makes me smile) and led to us camping out on the sofa with a limit of fifty steps to get us to bedtime. After I turned the TV off, we drank a bottle of beer each, in silence. A couple of times he shifted on the sofa and I thought he was about to speak, but he didn't. His breathing grew heavy sometimes. At one point, he opened his mouth and a small noise came out but nothing more.

In the end, I got us another beer and when he took his from me, I laid a hand on his shoulder and said, 'I never thought I'd say this to you. Talk to me.'

He smiled. Looked at me, looked at his feet.

'Epping Forest,' I said. 'Start there.'

And he put down his beer, took a breath and talked.

'March the twenty-ninth 2003. I was fifteen and my mum and Ian had just got together. He's got two daughters who are way older than me, and his son, Owen, who was twenty-two and still living at home. Kim and Lou, my stepsisters, were never bothered by me or Mum. They have their husband in one case, and wife in the other, and children, and back then it was easier for them if their dad was with someone. They'd done a lot of looking after him after their mum died. They were nice to me, but they didn't do anything with me. Owen was unhappy about Ian being with someone. We met the first time and he was openly hostile to me and he got away with it – his dad pretended it wasn't happening and my mum was polite. She told me he'd come round. So they were both happy when me and Mum spent a weekend there and Owen comes downstairs on the Sunday morning, having ignored us the day before, and is really nice to me and makes this big thing of handing me a helmet.

'He said, "I borrowed this off a mate. I'll take you out on my bike."

'I was delirious, Pete. Couldn't wait. My mum thought Christmas had come early. It was just what she'd hoped for,

Owen's nose was out of joint and he'd come round. Things were going to be great. She had every reason to want to believe things would be okay – she'd been alone for years and years.

'Owen said, "Chance for us to get to know each other a bit," and he jammed the helmet on my head and then sat down for breakfast. He said, "If you like it, maybe we can find you a second-hand moped or something. I'll learn you. When are you sixteen?"

'I answered from inside the helmet, my cheeks squeezed tight against the inside. I wanted to take it off, but I didn't want to seem ungrateful, so I kept it on whilst he had his breakfast. It was really sweaty and unpleasant.'

I say, 'I bet your mum and stepdad thought, Oh, look, he wants to wear that helmet everywhere!'

'Honestly, Pete, I'm sure that's what they said as soon as we left the house.'

'What happened?'

'Owen rode the bike so fast on the A12 that I was nearly sick with fear. I was fifteen. I clung on tight to him and when we stopped at a small tea bar in Epping Forest I was shaking and thinking up excuses to go home on the train. Owen asked me if I was queer. I mean, one of his sisters is married to a woman and he used a word like that, and then he said, "Is that why you were cuddling me on the bike like a fucking gay?"

'"I was scared," I said.

'"Let's look at some trees," he said, and marched off.

'I followed him into the woods and he yanked me by the arm and rammed my face up against the bark of a big old oak tree.

'Then he said, "If you think I'm letting that rancid old tart replace my mum you're fucking stupid. I'll kill her if she's still with my dad in a year's time." Something like that – that's almost word for word.

187

'I knew my nose was broken. I couldn't feel it – I couldn't feel anything – but I could hear it, the squelching of tissue and the clicking of the bone. I didn't discover my arm was broken until the pain of it got too much at school on the Monday.

'When people asked how it happened, I said, "Me and my stepbrother came off his bike." Even in my teacher and the school nurse, let alone my classmates, I saw their expression that said, How cool to have a stepbrother who takes you out on his bike. The war wounds were cool too. And wasn't it nice that Niall Drewid's mum had met a new chap, after Niall's father being such a wrong 'un. Everyone thought so back then, and they still do.'

We sat in silence for a long time. Then I asked him how much of this Susie knew and he told me, 'None of it.'

'Why?'

'Being bullied is humiliating.'

He smiled and looked away. I felt an anger rise in me like nothing I have ever known.

I hear a knocking at the door. A man of my age stands there and immediately steps back, looks confused, and checks the number on the front door.

'Oh,' he says. 'I'm here to view the flat.'

I glare at him, which is monumentally unfair, and direct him to the side door.

'Your doorbell's not working,' he says as he goes.

I phone Matthew, who answers from thirty feet away, down the side of my house, as he lets the man into the flat upstairs.

'It's Peter Smith.'

'Yes.'

'I was meant to be aware of any viewings and to meet the viewer.'

'Your ex-wife controls how viewings work, and this was arranged last minute.'

'You could have tried my door. He did.'

'I presumed you were at work.'

Now he's just being silly.

I return to my bedroom and the blank sheet of paper detailing my *Assets and Ideas Going Forward*. I'll take you through them another time, when I've thought of any. I listen to Niall sing *The Champions League* theme in his room. Moments later, with my ideas for business rejuvenation still safely locked away inside my subconscious, Niall joins me, holding an old football.

'Keepy-uppy in the garden?'

I'm in a shit mood about the viewing and from thinking about what that evil little bastard did to fifteen-year-old Niall. So, naturally, I take it out on Niall.

'It's Tuesday afternoon, it's a work day.'

'You've just been watching *Queer Eye*.'

'Yes, well, whatever, it's good you think you've got time for keepy-uppy.'

'You're right . . .' Niall says. He peers over my shoulder at my 'work'. 'It is good. In fact, it's great. Keepy-uppy makes me happy-wappy and gets me outsidey-widey and is excellent for motor skills.'

'You haven't got work and stuff to do?'

'I've done it.'

I laugh disdainfully, and regret it as it never ends well.

'Are you the sort of person,' Niall says, 'that makes a list of things they need to get done every day?'

'Yes, I bloody well am.'

'So am I. And I've done them. I bet that your list is always about one hundred and thirty per cent of what's achievable, so you're always feeling you've not done enough. I have a small list every day and I nail it every day, and then have time off. For keepy-uppy.'

I get up abruptly (I don't know why) and flap my hand to demand he gets up too (I don't know why) and say angrily (I do know why – money, work and Owen), 'Come on then, let's play keepy-uppy.'

I march into the garden and Niall follows. He throws the football against the wall of next door's house, traps it when it comes back to him, and does a few keepy-uppies before he lobs the ball to me. I coolly execute a couple more keepy-uppies and then punt the ball high out of the garden. I watch the ball sail away, then look at a bemused Niall. 'Now I'm werry, werry happy-wappy,' I tell him calmly.

I knew I was going to kick the ball as far as I could at least a few moments before I did it, but it takes me by surprise when, as I return to the kitchen, I look up at what used to be my son's bedroom window and let out a loud, angry roar at the middle-aged man looking down on me.

'RAAAAAAAAAAAAAAAAAAARRRGH!'

I take my seat in the kitchen and watch as Niall shrugs up at the man in Erland's room and calls out, 'He's just unconventional.' He smiles at the man, does his weird, bouncy, balls-of-the-feet Keanu Reeves walk across the garden and yells out over the back gardens, 'CAN I HAVE MY BALL BACK, PLEASE?! NUMBER SIXTY-ONE BEACONSFIELD ROAD!'

This delights me. Moments later, I hear the viewing upstairs end. Niall ambles in. 'Another buyer bites the dust,' he says.

I put my arm out and stop him in his tracks. He looks down at me in my chair. I look up at him gravely.

'Every single viewing. If you let one slip past, we're buggered.'

'I tend to be thorough when I turn my mind to something,' he says.

We nod at each other.

Chapter 15

What I said to Niall last night was, 'I've got my two best friends coming round for breakfast tomorrow morning, so make yourself scarce.'

What Niall heard was, 'I've got a couple of friends coming round for breakfast tomorrow and I'd love it if you could join us.'

Once a month Peggs, Ed and myself meet for breakfast. Occasionally, it runs into lunch. There was a time when it ran into the following morning's breakfast, in New York, but that was a long time ago. Peggs lives twenty minutes away. Ed, as you know, lives in the Cotswolds and has a flat in town. We take it in turns to either host or foot the bill in a café in London.

Ed and Peggs met at senior school, through me. We all attended the Bishop Wand secondary school and devoted seven years of our lives to propagating the pun potential of our school's name. There's a lot you can do with 'wand', none of it impressive. The word 'throbbing' was a recurring feature.

I had been at primary school with Ed, best friends since the age of four. Ed's parents sent him off to boarding school at eleven whilst I went to the local state secondary and made friends with Michael Peggson. Michael was called Pegleg from day one, what with eleven-year-old boys and girls being all hilarious and everything, and this matured into a nickname of Peggs by the time he was completing his Masters in Social Development. At the age of thirteen, after two years of their son begging, Ed's parents realised that they had made a pretentious educational mistake and re-called their son, installing him in the local comp and the warm embrace of me, his best friend. Ed and Peggs and I have been pretty well inseparable for the forty years since.

Ed and Peggs find themselves at polar-opposite points in their lives right now, and I am situated in a muddy area between them. Ed is on the cusp of retiring at the age of fifty-three. The utter bastard. Peggs is, at the same tender age, the father of a ten-month-old son, his first child. It's fair to say that Ed and Peggs have different things on their minds. And, with Ed being rich and Peggs being solvent, I have something different to either of them on my mind: possession of no money.

The boys are due here in twenty minutes and I thought that Niall had gone out for the morning, as instructed. If you can run a gardening empire from my sofa you can run it from Costa. But I hear the front door open, and the live-action version of Animal in *The Muppets* walks into the kitchen and unpacks a pile of fresh produce, all of which looks better than the limp croissants I went out for earlier.

'You won't even know I'm here,' he says. 'Apart from the aroma of artisan unsmoked back bacon mixing with the oregano-dusted scrambled eggs on seeded sourdough and grilled buttery mushrooms.'

He ties back his hair, washes his face in the sink, and appears instantly functional and handsome.

'I've even taken the liberty of buying some organic black pudding from the butcher and a cheeky chipolata.'

'You bought one chipolata?'

'I bought many.'

'And one of them is cheeky or all of them?'

'Is this pithy dialogue your way of saying I can stay or a prelude to kicking me out? I really can't tell any more. I preferred the old days when I knew it was heading towards you swearing at me and telling me to sod off.'

'I've already asked you to sod off for the morning. But you haven't and you know I want the food.'

'So I can stay and hang out with your friends?'

'No, you can cook us breakfast and then sod off.'

'I want to stay, though.' Niall goes all puppy. 'I like you and I can't imagine you having friends so I'm curious.'

I sigh. 'I haven't got the energy to abuse you or reason with you. Stay. Cook. But don't hog the conversation.'

'Absolutely, won't say a word. I just want to watch.'

'Well, that's going to be weird.'

'Then I'll hog the conversation. Make up your mind.'

'How about something in the middle ground? Don't hog, don't stand like a mental case watching a conversation, just occupy the middle ground of normality.'

'Fine. I'm just interested to see you mix.'

Peggs texts to say he's at the front door and his boy is asleep. I open the door gently and find the little one strapped to his dad's chest. I usher them into my bedroom where, in advance, I have removed the duvet, laid out a blanket and positioned three pillows on it in a U-shape, for just this eventuality. Peggs lays the baby down, puts a small blanket from his backpack over him and we tiptoe out.

I leave the front door open so that Ed doesn't need to ring the doorbell. We go into the kitchen as Peggs tells me that Summer, his wife, has gone in to work for a few hours. 'It's her first time back in since the baby was born. She's just putting in an appearance to make sure they're not shafting her behind her back.'

I introduce Peggs to Niall. 'This is Niall. He's staying, short-term. His presence here is inexplicable so I'm not going to try.'

Niall steps forward and shakes Peggs's hand warmly. 'Hello,' he says.

'Good to meet you,' Peggs says. Unnecessarily, I feel.

'It's really easy to explain my presence here, Peggs,' Niall says.

'I'm all ears,' Peggs gushes.

'I used to go out with Susie and Peter very kindly allowed me to cohabit with her here, under his roof. Susie then went to Sweden to work and met someone else and Peter has allowed me to stay on until I find suitable accommodation – and partly, if he's honest, because he dreams of Susie and me getting back together again.'

'They're nightmares,' I say. 'And it's not going to happen.'

'How can you be sure?' asks Peggs.

'Because her new boyfriend has been after her for about five years and is better-looking than Niall, better turned out, more interesting and more attractive.'

Peggs smiles at Niall. 'Bummer. You messed up there, Niall. Susie's brilliant.'

'It was unfinished business,' I add.

Peggs grimaces at Niall. 'Then you're fucked.'

That's more like it.

I feel nervous about Ed's arrival, which is a strange thing to feel about your best friend. I'm upset about his radio silence since Birmingham and I don't want it to show. I want to rise above it, forget it, but I'm struggling to. When he arrives, any awkwardness is sidestepped by the fact that he's on a call. He smiles apologetically as he marches through the flat into the garden to conduct his business out there.

I see that Niall is hovering, watching Peggs and me, waiting to witness me mixing with a friend.

194

'Cook,' I say. 'Cook or leave.'

Niall gets to it. I hold up the coffee pot to Ed and he does a thumbs-up from the garden. He mouths 'Sorry' to me, about the call, and it tips my mood, makes me feel calm. Having these two in my house is as good as it gets for me right now. I love them both. I take Ed's coffee out and stand three feet from him and send him a text, asking him to stay behind after Peggs & Son have gone, so we can have a chat. He glances at his phone mid-conversation and gives me a thumbs-up.

Ed is a softly spoken man whose conversation has no frills or fat. He is direct, yes, but he is not sharp. He always wears a suit. They are loose and easy and never make him look like he's in love with himself, which is ironic because he's infatuated with himself. He is more comfortable in his own skin than anyone I know. He's good with people and he's a thinker, not about emotional stuff but about ideas and connections. I should have asked him years ago how to stay ahead in travel, but I was too proud. I liked being his equal, or the appearance of it I achieved by being successful enough not to need anything.

There is one thing Ed and I have talked about and that is the name Peggs and Summer have given their son.

Mick.

Not Michael.

Mick.

That's the name on the birth certificate and it's a crap name for the twenty-first century. Not if you're born into a working-class neighbourhood in the 1970s. Under those circumstances, Mick works fine. If you live in the shadow of Deptford power station and support Millwall in 1972, Mick is golden, Mick is mustard. But now? Here? Mick? Awful name, don't want to talk about it, hope it doesn't come up this morning – and it needn't, given that the baby is so young we don't talk to him, we only talk about him, so can refer to him as 'your boy' or 'the baby'. By the time he's an actual person he'll hopefully have a nickname that has taken over. That does happen; it's certainly something to hope for. Bodger or Psychic would be fine.

The baby wakes and cries out but is easily soothed. I go and pick him up from the bed, give him a cuddle and a kiss and then Peggs straps him back into his carrier so Mick can see us and so that Peggs does not spend the next hour running after him as he bum-shuffles all over the place.

Ed joins us, his call over.

'Sorry about that. Stuff, you know.'

He gives me a hug and a slap on the back. 'Hello, mate.'

He gives Peggs a one-sided embrace, to avoid crushing the boy (see what I mean, he's always been good with people). 'Lovely to see you, mate . . .' Then he stoops down to the baby's eye level. 'And you, you rascal, how lovely to see you, how lovely, yes, it is! Yes, it is!' Predictably, the baby starts laughing and bubbling at the mouth and kicking his legs. I'm not sure Ed has ever missed a target.

'Ed Lewis,' he says to Niall, then looks at me as he shakes hands with him. 'Strictly against the rules of breakfast, this, having a third party present.'

'I'm just the cook,' Niall says, before I can.

'And the arse who let the most wonderful young woman on the planet slip through your fingers,' Peggs says.

This makes me smile.

'Well,' Niall says, without looking up, 'I didn't really let her. Given the choice we'd be together now. I'd spend the rest of my life with her.'

'Even as a hypothetical idea that makes me feel nauseous,' I say.

Long after I have unstrapped the baby from his carrier (Peggs calls it a Björn Borg – it is, in fact, a BabyBjörn) so I can play with him, Peggs keeps swaying from side to side. We feel obliged to take the piss out of him for this. Peggs gives not a shit, so happy is he with his life these days. He and I ask Ed about his retirement plans and continue to master the art of appearing pleased for him. Ed does not talk about this unless asked. He may not be the most emotionally intelligent of human beings, but he does know that being extremely well off in the company of a man who is fine but will need to work for ever due to his late fatherhood, and a man who is in desperate financial straits, is a no-no.

From a culinary point of view, breakfast is shaping up on the hobs to look mind-blowingly perfect. Conversationally, it's less of a hit for me as I realise how much I wanted to speak to these guys in private, to ask them to help me work out a way to get out of this trough. I might even have plucked up the courage to admit that I am feeling very . . . low. Although Ed is aware of that and it hasn't sparked much interest in him.

But, instead, it is me who watches a conversation. Ed, intrigued by the way Niall runs his gardening business, is more engaged with my hairy, potbellied lodger than he has been with me for some time. I am jealous.

'That's an absolute, is it? You pay your staff—'

Niall interrupts Ed, which is no mean feat. 'They're colleagues, not staff.'

'You pay your colleagues at least double what you're obliged to because you have that fixed as what the minimum wage should be—'

'I haven't fixed that price, I've observed it. That is what's needed for someone to have a hope of a decent standard of living.'

'And you take on fifty per cent pro-bono or at-cost work whatever the state of the market?'

Niall nods. 'Yes. Every business needs its moral compass. You start with that and go from there.'

Ed laughs. 'Moral compass, that's brilliant.'

'You do realise he's serious about that, Ed?' I say.

'And, what, you're all druids?' Peggs asks.

Bless you, Pegleg.

Niall relieves him of this misconception. To be fair to Peggs, every time I phone-moan about Niall I describe him disdainfully as a druid gardener, so there's no reason Peggs would know any better.

'You,' Ed says, jabbing a finger at Niall, 'are doing exactly what big business needs to learn to do a version of. You're coming at things from a customer-centric perspective. "What do my clients need and value?" And a motivated, loyal, decently treated workforce is one of those things. Transparency.'

'The question,' Niall says, making a steeple of his fingers in a way I have never seen him do before, 'is, "What next?"'

'What is next?' Ed is blunt, direct, fierce and obscenely confident. No wonder he's so good at what he does, even though I've never been sure exactly what that is.

'Next for me,' Niall says, getting his tablet from the sofa and removing a browning apple core from it, 'is a tech investment so that every one of my team is interconnected on the same tablet system, viewing shared schedules and job specs in real time – an upfront cost but it will allow me to train up a manager to run things whilst I focus on new business amongst the non-pro-bono client community so that my profits go up and I am out face-to-facing it with customers, as a part of which I'm going to livery all vehicles used by colleagues to build brand awareness and word of mouth so I can also hopefully earn more.'

'So it isn't a charity after all – you do want to make more money?' I say.

'Never said it was a charity. And, yes, I want to earn way more money so I can buy a home and have holidays and marry your daughter.'

'That'd mean my daughter growing to like you again more than her really excellent new boyfriend.'

'Women like powerful men,' Ed says.

'Powerful!' I hate it when my voice breaks upwards.

'There's nothing more potent than a man who knows his company ethos and is prepared to stick to it and work his bollocks off.'

I am now coming to the boil nicely. 'Working his bollocks off? Are you kidding? He doesn't leave the house.'

'More of a flat now,' Peggs says.

I glare at him. '*Et tu, Brute?*'

'We were thinking of calling the baby Brutus,' Peggs says. He sees our jaws drop. 'I mean, only for a moment. But we both loved Shakespeare at school and thought it might set him up well in a don't-mess-with-me way.'

'You didn't see the potential for an are-you-the-prick-called–Brutus? situation at school?' Ed says.

'How do you get from Brutus to Mick?' I say.

'To be fair,' Niall says, 'they're both terrible names so it's not such a stretch.'

We all fall silent.

Excellent. Golden balls has finally messed up in front of my mates.

'You think Mick is a bad name?' Peggs asks.

Within his rights.

'No.' Niall stays unflustered. 'I actually don't because, one, I love that name and, two, to be honest, I think that the moment a name is given it's perfect because that baby is perfect, and that perfection is bestowed, in turn, on the name.'

This is the first time the word 'bestowed' has been used at one of our breakfasts. Peggs looks confused, so Niall clears it all up for him.

199

'But Pete hates Mick as a name, says it reminds him of Ford Cortinas and Brylcreem.'

Ed, still distracted by the sun shining out of Niall's hairy (I know) arse, leans forward and speaks with the kind of purr that only a man that wealthy can.

'How much?'

'How much what?' asks Niall.

'Investment.'

Niall hands his tablet to Ed and points to something on it. 'Fifty thousand for a fifteen per cent stake.'

'I'm sorry that I forgot to ask Evan Davis to join us this morning,' I say. 'Remiss of me. Won't happen again.'

Peggs turns to me. 'Do you hate Mick's name?'

Mick, until now wriggling and laughing as I bump him up and down on my knee, turns and looks at me too. 'I did say the thing about Cortinas and stuff but purely as a joke. I absolutely love this little chap and his name, love it, love-love-love it, and I want to see him all the time.'

Peggs is thoroughly satisfied with this, and grateful that his son is off his hands for a few minutes. I am suddenly aware of only one thing – that it feels like a state of grace to be holding a baby – and it feels like yesterday that I held my own. It's like a rapture.

'I might invest, subject to checking you out,' Ed says.

'WHAT!' I shout, disgusted, and jolt forward. Mick bursts into tears. Peggs lurches at me, as if I'm going to drop his son.

'Sorry,' I say, and cuddle Mick, who starts laughing mid-cry. I carry him out of the room because I can't listen to any more of my oldest, closest friend throwing a fortune at Niall. Peggs follows me into my bedroom.

'Sorry for making Mick cry,' I say.

'It's okay,' Peggs says. 'Babies cry all the time.'

'Shouldn't have raised my voice.'

'Look how good you are with him,' Peggs says. I hold the baby up and nuzzle my head against his tummy. 'You were always a natural with kids.'

'It's the one thing I loved doing,' I say.

I hadn't realised this was true until now.

We return to the kitchen where Niall is setting down three plates of breakfast whilst giving his contact details to Ed. Ed takes off his jacket and tucks into his food.

'Brown sauce, Niall?' he says.

Niall shakes his head. 'I don't believe in it.'

Ed stops him. 'Well, it exists, believe me, in the fridge. Don't even think about denying me.'

Niall gets the sauce and puts it down on the table. Peggs and I take our seats. Peggs takes Mick from me and puts him on his knee.

'This looks incredible,' says Peggs. 'Thank you, Niall. You can come again.'

'Amazing, Niall,' I say. 'Where's yours?'

'Mine,' Niall says, taking the baby from Peggs and wrapping his hoodie around him, 'is a bacon roll and I'm going to have it in the garden with this little one, so you guys can enjoy your breakfast together.'

As the Second Coming slides the doors to the garden open, Mick looks up at him adoringly and pulls on his facial hair. Peggs looks approvingly at Niall and Ed groans with pleasure at his first taste of the food.

'He's great with Mick,' Peggs says.

'He's a fantastic cook,' Ed says, through a mouthful.

He's a total wanker.

We talk about the food and they talk about the chef and then, all of a sudden, it is over when Ed puts the last bit of food in his mouth, takes a sip of coffee and puts on his jacket. Standing over us, he says, 'Guys, my bad but I gotta go. Selling a business is way more time-consuming than running one. Sorry, and I mean that. It's been sensational, as always. My turn next.'

Ed is nearly perfect in an anthropological sense. If you're going to evolve, evolving into Ed would be good for your species. But a man in his fifties using the phrase 'my bad' does not do him any favours.

'You off?' Peggs asks; a redundant question to someone putting on their coat.

'I'll see you out,' I say.

Ed goes into the garden and kisses Mick tenderly on the head. He shakes Niall's hand and says something to him and Niall nods.

'So happy for you, mate,' Ed says to Peggs as he comes back through the kitchen, hugging him.

'Cheers.' Peggs has that soft, wrinkled look on his face, the one that tells us how happy he is and how exhausted.

Ed and I walk down the path. He wraps his arms around me and slaps my back. 'Great to see you. Sorry it was brief. For God's sake, keep hold of your chef.'

I find some old off-the-shelf smile for him and exhale, loud and slow. It sounds melodramatic and I had not intended it to. I look at him and wait; it's an invitation to him to talk to me about all the things I poured my heart out about.

Ed winks at me and goes. I'm fifty-three and I think I'm about to burst into tears.

'Ed.'

He stops and turns. 'Yes, mate.'

'You know my business is in trouble and you're throwing money at the druid.'

'He's not a druid. That line is only funny if it's true. And he's got a business plan. You haven't.'

'Great, slag off my business and my sense of humour.'

'You've got a brilliant sense of humour, mate, always have had, although it's a bit brittle at the moment. But you haven't got a brilliant business. If you had a new start for it, a new idea, I'd invest in it if you'd let me, which I doubt you would.'

I do a thumbs-up. 'Cheers, mate, good to know,' I say, through gritted teeth.

Ed turns away from me and marches off, muttering, 'For fuck's sake, Peter.' He takes his phone from his pocket, makes a call and returns to his real life.

I watch him go and I feel shaken — by the feeling that I'm an annoyance to him right now, by not being my usual self. I turn to check that Peggs and Niall have not witnessed Ed walking off. The front door is open but, thankfully, they are not there. My heart is racing. I look down at the hill I used to be able to run up, with a child on my shoulders. I need to get fit. I need to get busy, as busy as Ed, so I can shake off moments like this, so I don't have the time to spare for feelings like this to get a hold of me. I step back into the front garden and sit for a few moments on the small, raised wall by the beds. I shut my eyes and listen to the sounds in the air. I take slower, fuller breaths and calm my heart. I hear Mick giggle. Peggs, the boy and the eternal lodger appear in the doorway.

'You okay?' Peggs asks.

I smile and nod. 'Just enjoying the fresh air. More coffee, anyone?'

Peggs nods. Niall pats his belly and sighs happily at the sky. 'Shall I make it?' he suggests.

'Obviously,' I say.

'Oh, FYI,' Niall says, 'your ex-wife just texted you and said she wants to come and see you. Exciting.'

'*What!*'

'Claire just texted you and said she wants to see you.'

'Niall! Stop reading my fucking fucking fucking messages!'

203

'It was there on the counter! It pinged. I literally just glanced at it.'

'Thanks for limiting it to three f-words in front of Mick,' Peggs says.

'Sorry. Sorry, Peggs. Sorry, Mick.'

Shit name for a baby, shit name for an apology.

We all go inside. Peggs stops to let Niall through the doorway first and puts his spare hand on Niall's shoulder. 'Don't read his messages, Niall, for Christ's sake. Privacy, man, privacy.'

Chapter 16

I haven't driven into central London in years. At five on a late winter's morning, the streets of south-west London are a painting of a less populated past. I spend a week's income parking underneath Cavendish Square and walk through the waking streets to Ed and Debs's flat.

It is ten past six when I ring on their buzzer. I know he's here because at breakfast he said he was in town for a couple of days. What I have forgotten to consider until I take my finger off the button is that Deborah is here too. But what sort of man sends his wife down to open the door to God knows who at six in the morning?

Well, nobody does that because they have an intercom, obviously.

'Who is it?' a voice says to me above static that suggests that even when you have a two-million-pound pied-à-terre in Marylebone, the intercom still sounds like crud. There's some comfort in that.

I'm relieved it's Ed's voice I hear, not Deborah's.

'Peter. Can you come down?'

There's a moment's hesitation. 'Come up, mate, please.'

'No.'

I step away from the door. Up the street I see a café, its blue canopy out and lights on inside. I stroll up to it. The door is open, there are people inside. A smell of cinnamon makes me feel like a child in search of safety. I almost swoon at it.

I text Ed. *I'm in the Nordic Bakery. You have a coffee waiting.*

I go to the counter and order, then step back to the window and look down the street to Ed's building. I see the door open and Ed peer out. He's in his dressing gown. He digs into his pocket and looks at his phone, and his body language suggests a roll of the eyes. He goes back inside. I get a message back.

C u in 5. Their cinnamon buns amazing.

There's a coffee and a bun waiting for him when he arrives. He is in his suit and looks impeccable. He sits down opposite me, reaches across and lays a hand on my shoulder.

'Morning,' he says. He takes a sip of his coffee. 'So, either you were clubbing all night, or you woke early and jumped on a train to come and see me.'

'I woke at the same time as usual and drove up to speak to you. Or listen to you.'

'Well, it's good to see you,' he says.

He takes a bite of his bun and groans. 'Pretty incredible, huh?' I don't react so he pushes the bun aside and leans across. 'Listen to me say what?'

I look right at him. '"I know exactly what's worrying you, Pete. I know you can't sleep, you're scared of dropping dead from stress, scared of your children not respecting you. I know you feel very low indeed because you told me, and I'm here for you."'

He says, 'I know, mate, I should have rung.' But when he looks at me it's a neutral look, neither apologetic nor angry, and that unnerves me. The apology that isn't sorry for anything. 'It's all a bit crazy, you can't imagine.'

'All I wanted was for you to put your arm around me and say, "There's no way I'm letting you go under, Pete. I'm gonna help you get back to how things need to be."'

'What do you want me to do? You wouldn't accept money from me if I offered. I can't give you a job. I don't have a list of people who can give you a job.'

'Why not? What's wrong with me? I can do anything I'm asked to do. I just need to go to work and be paid.'

He folds his arms. 'How can I make that happen? I don't understand. I don't know anything about travel.'

'Not in travel!'

'Don't get shirty with me.'

'I've applied for jobs in travel. They're not interested. I'm fifty-three years old. I just need a job and some dignity and to stop feeling like a piece of dirt.'

Ed shuts his eyes and draws in a deep breath. He opens his eyes again and stares at the ceiling. 'I don't want this to be happening to you but from the bottom of my heart I have no idea what I am meant to do.'

'You said you'd call every day. We've known each other fifty years. We're best friends.'

Ed sits back and drinks his coffee as far from me as possible. 'You're not my best friend. You're my oldest friend.'

I don't allow myself to show any outward sign of the winding blow this has landed. Half a century with this man has brought us to one of the saddest moments of my life. My throat has gone dry and I cannot speak. But Ed can.

'I've been making other friends for the past couple of decades. You haven't.'

'I had Claire,' I say. The words limp out of my mouth, barely a whisper.

'That's too much to put on her shoulders. Maybe that's why you lost her.'

207

I clear my throat and take a sip of my coffee. 'I didn't come here for marriage guidance and if you wanted to give it, two or three years ago might have been more useful. Why don't you stick to the subject of you dumping me after fifty years, not my wife dumping me after thirty?'

'Poor you, always the victim of other people not standing still. I have let you down, Pete, and I apologise. I've always been too absorbed with work and I'm sorry. After you turned to me, every day I've had "Call Pete" in my iCal and it gets bumped to tomorrow by everything I've got on my plate.'

'Brilliant,' I say. 'For a moment there I was worried you had your priorities wrong.'

'But it is, like it or not, also because Debs and I have quite an active social life with friends who happen not to know you and I'm not apologising for that, Pete. It's taken me a long time to realise you weren't into making new friends.'

'But now you know all about that?'

'Claire talked to me when you guys separated about how little you socialised outside of being with her. She was concerned about that.'

The idea of such a conversation taking place turns my stomach.

'I meet you and Peggs for breakfast every month.'

'Yeah, same old arrangement. Sometimes we really bust a gut to make that.'

'Fuck you.'

'In a couple of months when I'm out of the firm I'll have a lot more time for you.'

'Thank you. I apologise for not scheduling my unhappiness around your obscenely early retirement.'

'Don't be jealous, you're not that person. You are so not that person, Pete. You've always had it just right when it comes to values and being happy with what you've got.'

'I haven't got any of it any more.'

'You cannot afford to think like that. All our kids grow up and leave home – what the hell did you expect? You're divorced but you are not banned from being with someone else and having a great time with them. Your business is struggling but you are not forbidden from trying to revamp it, starting a new one or doing something different.'

'You and Debs are going sailing for six months as soon as you're out. She's taking a sabbatical.'

'True. Shall I postpone that, so as to be there for you?'

'If you would, thanks, that's what friends are for. I'm fucked right now but you can sail any time.'

Ed folds his arms and shakes his head. He looks at me one more time then gets up and walks out.

As I drive home, I get a text message. I glance down and see that it's from Claire. Cool and nonchalant, I cut across the traffic on the A3 into the first lay-by I see, almost causing a pile-up. Her text is to suggest again that we meet up. Obviously, with Claire being the person I most want to see, I haven't replied to her first text suggesting we see each other. It is this intelligence that has taken me to the top.

I drive off and start composing a cool, detached reply in my mind – even though a yes would work – when it occurs to me that she might be doing this at Ed's suggestion. She texted me after Ed and I argued outside my house yesterday, and now she's texted me again after he and I have had another row.

I have no idea if Ed has spoken to Claire, but I get another message from her later that day suggesting she pops round 'to say hi'. I say 'yes' but set it up for four days later so that if she has any thoughts of getting involved in my and Ed's stuff, she can forget it.

The nearer Claire's visit gets, the less likely I think it is that, one, Ed would talk to her about him and me having a disagreement or, two, Claire would offer to get involved. She really has got better things to do. They both have. I need to have.

I am so distracted by the prospect of her visiting that I spend an entire day at work, thinking about it there. Something about getting out of the flat and walking to the shop and being in the company of others focuses my feelings about her coming and I find myself looking forward to it more and more, to simply seeing her in the flesh and spending a bit of time with her. I keep waiting for this feeling to implode into anger and hurt but it doesn't. She's been my best friend for thirty years and I'm looking forward to seeing her. For a moment, I glimpse a way forward that looks deceptively easy. I try not to complicate things and to enjoy my anticipation at face value.

That works until the morning of her visit, when I compose a list of possible reasons why she wants to see me. There are some I can dismiss. I've signed all legal and financial paperwork, given up on having any control over the flat-viewing process (big of me), and I'm sure she's not here to referee my friendship with Ed. It might be that she's worried about me. It might be that she wants to get back together with me despite all evidence to the contrary in every single thing she has said and done for the past year.

Or, radical idea I know, it might be that she thinks it would nice, and healthy, and mature, for two people who have thirty years and two children under their belt to spend a pleasant few hours together like adults.

Or she's sleeping with another man.

I'm not going to use the phrase 'she's met someone' because, clearly, that would not be what I mean. She can meet a thousand men for all I care, attend men-only rallies, move to Man City, where all the inhabitants look like Pep Guardiola and bounce up and down with their back to you, as long as she doesn't sleep with any of them.

Or watch *Crazy, Stupid, Love* with any of them.

And doing both these things with one of them would be the end of me.

I have trimmed my pubes and sent my electric razor up into my nostrils ahead of Claire's visit. Of all the futile acts for a human being to perform, this is at the top of the list. I have more chance of sleeping with Zoe Ball this afternoon than with my ex-wife. That is not meant to be a slur on Zoe, who I admire and find brilliant, talented and beautiful, though it probably is one.

I've had my hair cut short because that is what makes thinning hair look fullest, according to an article in *GQ* magazine I found after a Google search on the subject. But in contrast to the clear implications of said article, I did not emerge from Youssef's barber's shop yesterday looking remotely like Jude Law.

I am in my bedroom, going through my clothes, laying out a few shirt options on the bed when, inevitably, the bearded one walks in without knocking.

'I've got this theory,' he says.

'Which I expressly do not want to hear.'

'It's quite a cunning one.'

'But you're not Baldrick and I'm not listening.'

'It pertains to you and your ex-wife.'

I carry on taking the shirts out. 'Go on then.'

'Looking at your wardrobe, I'm going to take a guess that you and your ex-wife met in . . . ooh . . . 1988?'

'Can you call her Claire, not my ex-wife?'

'You and Claire met in '88 or '89?'

'1988. Well done, but Susie probably told you that.'

'Yeah, her parents' courtship was all we ever talked about.'

'What's your theory?'

He steeples his fingers again, presses the tips of them to his lips like he's presenting jazz on BBC 2 in 1978. 'A man's sense of fashion is locked into the point at which he first became sexually successful, and he never really moves on from it because subconsciously he knows it worked for him.'

I fan my hand across the clothes on my bed. 'Evidently not true in my case.'

Niall laughs mockingly. 'You card.'

'I dress fine,' I say. 'Please vacate the room. And, by the way, Claire was not when I *first* became sexually active.'

'Can I ask you something else?'

'If you absolutely have to.'

'Well, I think I kind of do. Is it at all possible that my stepbrother did in fact come to see me and you told him to go away, by any chance?'

My reaction is all the answer he needs, and he didn't even need that.

'He's been in touch?' I ask.

'Yeah . . .' Niall says, sitting on the bed. 'Got a charming email.'

'I'm sorry, I shouldn't have—'

He waves my apology away. 'No,' he says, 'I appreciate it.'

We're silent. The possibility of a hug hangs over the room like a threat, so I talk.

'I just . . .'

'Just what . . .'

'Whilst going full steam ahead with your firm commitment to move out in two weeks and five days, I just want you to realise that . . .' I sigh.

'Realise what? Apart from the fact that I'm a git and I'm moving out and I'm not good enough for your daughter, blah blah, all of which I know. Realise what?'

'That the way he treats you . . . it's got to change.'

'You think you telling him to fuck off will change him?'

I shake my head. 'Again, I'm sorry.'

'Don't be. I love that you did that, I love that I didn't have to see him.'

He looks at me, a bit too long for comfort. What's more, he's looking at my nipples, not at my face. What's even more, he's looking at them with a frown.

'Wait there a minute,' he says, jumping up and leaving the room.

He returns holding a plastic bag. 'What time is Claire getting here?' he asks, holding the bag out to me.

'Any minute. You think I should suffocate myself before she does?'

'Try that on.'

I take a T-shirt from the bag. It's pale blue with a very cool, minimalist graphic on it: three vertical dark blue stripes down the right-hand side.

'Susie gave it to me. It was a free sample at one of her internships. But it's too small for me. It's classy and it's retro in a good way, not in a had-it-so-long-it's-back-in-fashion way. It's also something Claire won't have seen you wearing.'

I put it on. Fits like a glove and looks markedly better than the clothes spread out on my bed. I nod at him. He gives me a once-over and nods back.

'Yeah,' he says, and leaves the room without being forced to.

When she's not at work, Claire wears skinny jeans and cashmere jumpers, or just a shirt if it's warm. She never wasted time deciding what to wear, always looked elegant and relaxed, always looked as if she could leap to her feet and run after her children or step straight into a meeting. Today, she is wearing a raspberry-coloured turtleneck sweater that softly engulfs her.

I still love what she wears. I look similarly exquisite in Niall's T-shirt, but I'm cold. I grab my cashmere cardigan from my room and put it on.

Claire teases me. 'You putting that on just to be nice?'

'I'm not nice. I love this cardi.'

She leans forward and peers at me. 'It's torn.'

'Brambles,' I say.

'That was two hundred quid in Selfridges. You're not meant to be gardening in it.'

'Two hundred quid on a cardigan!' I squeak.

'I was feeling guilty for leaving you and all that.'

'Two hundred quid for ending our marriage?'

She shrugs. 'I let you keep the car.'

I weigh this up. 'Hmmm, still . . .'

'And supported you financially for the last two years of it.'

'Well, if you're going to obsess about detail.'

I make some tea and take the opportunity to stand back and relish the moment. Claire is sitting in my kitchen. She is slouched on the sofa and her legs stretch out into the room.

It's wonderful.

When people meet her, many of them think of Sigourney Weaver. To those who mention it, Claire tends to mention the twenty-year age difference. They could settle instead for the simple fact that she is tall. Willowy. Elegant. Kind-hearted. Curious without end. Not merely fiercely intelligent but something much more: highly intelligent. Well read. Informed. A thinker.

She looks beautiful, content, as she cradles a mug of tea on her lap. She is not wearing her wedding ring. She's not wearing any rings.

'It's crazy how long it is since we were just in the same room as each other,' she says. 'So surreal.'

But she can do this and leave, whereas my dread of her going means I can't truly enjoy her being here.

'Not really, we got divorced because you no longer wanted to be in the same room as me. Never being together follows on naturally.'

She lowers her head and stares at her tea. When she looks up there is a sadness in her eyes that I know I am responsible for. She whispers, 'Don't say things like that.'

I see how easy, how tempting it must be, for people to abandon reason and become hateful when they feel wronged. I'm not a creative man but I could write a whole new narrative for myself right now: I see it all laid out in front of me and it looks never-ending, self-fulfilling, even appealing in parts.

Once upon a time I was the victim of a sad thing (my wife left me) and I've been the victim ever since and poor me and she's to blame and poor me. The End.

Except it never ends, that story, and in time it begins to revise your working life and your upbringing and your friendships, and in all these subplots you are also the casualty, a lovable person among people who let you down eventually. That's an easy story to write and star in. It's a cliché and clichés are effortless. They fit your purpose as perfectly as this T-shirt fits me.

Men who are to blame for the failure of their marriages portraying themselves as the victim is one of the biggest clichés known to mediators and family courts, and they can be smelled a mile off. My divorce lawyer told me that. I sit next to my ex-wife and hold her hand. She presses her head against me. 'Sorry,' I say. 'Won't do that again.'

She smells of bergamot.

I am uncouth in some ways – getting potty-mouthed in my bitter middle age, on the brink of getting stuck into the Tinder account the early man gifted me, no longer a total stranger to soft porn, and once got arrested at a football match in 1991 – but I know the smell of bergamot on Claire's skin when it's there and I still love it.

And suddenly, I find myself shaking and I am sure she is about to tell me she has met another man and I am listening for the infinitesimal sound of her lips moving to begin to tell me. And I want to be put out of my misery. I want to hear it and pile it on to everything else and get on with living with it. The anticipation is the worst bit.

'Anything you need to talk about?' I say.

'Yes,' she says. 'That's why I'm here. How are you? What you up to? How are you managing divorced life? Shall we talk about Susie and Erland? We should hang out. Be normal, even if it is hard and feels weird and sad.'

'That's all?' I say.

'That's quite a lot.'

We sit shoulder to shoulder on the little sofa, both slouching, no longer touching. And I could gladly stay like this all day but the creaking of floorboards from my should-be-spare bedroom reminds me that there's a third person in this flat and it is only a matter of time until I am not alone with Claire.

Fifteen seconds, to be exact. In the last few of which I ask Claire, 'Have you already met Niall?'

'Of course. Susie brought him round a couple of times.'

The door opens and a presentable, well-groomed, freshly shaved male resembling Niall enters.

'Hi, Claire,' it says.

'You all right, Niall?'

'Never better.'

'Pete asked me if we'd met!'

Niall pulls a face that registers how stupid of me that was.

'Mind you,' he says, 'not that often. You're always working or going out with friends or off on some holiday.'

I smile bravely at this and rub my belly soothingly at the point where I felt the knife go in. Niall and Claire cheek-kiss like they're at the Ambassador's Ball. How does he appear instantly sophisticated? It baffles me. He's even wearing shoes.

'Given that you're away so much,' I say to Claire, 'would you like Niall to be your lodger, keep an eye on the place?'

Niall's face lights up.

'Down, boy,' Claire says to him. 'Not gonna happen.'

Niall slumps and pulls a pouty face. It makes Claire laugh.

'Can I make you both tea?' he says.

'Got one, thanks,' says Claire.

'Bye, Niall,' I say.

'I'll just make myself one and be out of your way,' he says, but that seems unlikely to me.

We all watch the kettle boil. Niall taps his fingers on the worktop and repositions the milk an inch nearer his mug. 'Should I remove any sharp objects or vases?' he says. 'Or are you getting on fine?'

Claire smiles politely.

'Perhaps you should,' I say, 'for your own safety.'

Niall pours hot water into his mug. 'Only joshing, you two seem to get on so well. Never hear you tearing strips off each other on the phone like some exes.'

'He never calls,' Claire says.

'We should argue more,' I say. 'Why don't we?'

'Because we never argued about small stuff and you're a feminist, so there wasn't any big stuff.'

'How can two people who argue so little break up?' Niall says.

'Go away, Niall,' I say.

''Cause I wanna argue,' Claire says. 'Look at the world, Niall. I've got issues with it and I want to slog it out. He doesn't.'

217

'Couldn't agree more,' Niall says.

'Slog it out and be home in time for dinner,' I say.

She turns to me. 'Do something totally new, that you've never done before.'

'Yeah,' Niall says, stirring his teabag and smiling to himself in a way that ought, by now, to trigger alarm bells in me about what's coming next. 'Something totally new like going an entire day without mentioning your ex-wife.'

Silence falls upon us. I glare at Niall but he's not looking. Claire smiles to herself.

'Enjoying this conversation?' she says, digging me gently in the ribs.

I sigh and pull a face. 'His tea has to finish brewing some time.'

We sit in silence some more.

'Watching much porn?' Claire asks. It's an old family joke, it's how we used to break awkward silences or end arguments. Susie was the first to use it, to Erland when he grew a bum-fluff moustache and got acne in his mid-teens. 'Off for a wank?' she once said to her brother when he left the living room, in front of me and Claire. She was thirteen. No wonder my son lives in New Zealand.

I scrunch up my face and shake my head. 'No. You?'

'A bit.'

'What!'

'You should be pleased.'

It takes me a moment to work this out, and she waits patiently.

'Oh, yeah,' I smile. 'Yeah, well, me too.'

Niall uses his spoon to catapult his teabag into the bin. He stirs his tea but doesn't yet show signs of picking it up and heading for the door.

'Susie mention me at all when you were in Stockholm?' he asks Claire.

Claire looks at Niall warmly and waits a beat, like a true pro. 'Nope.' Emphasis on the 'p'.

Makes me want her.

'Did you see much of Mark? I heard you didn't.'

'No, didn't see him, wasn't around.'

'Really?' Niall likes this and gets that energetic, balls-of-his-feetness about him. 'But presumably,' he ploughs blindly on, 'when you went back to your hotel at night Susie went round to his place or he came round or whatever?'

'No. I stayed with Susie, in her bed with her. I would have noticed if she and Mark were having sex.'

Niall's eyes light up. 'A whole week and you didn't see Mark.'

'Not once . . .' Claire says.

Niall looks at me and raises his eyebrows excitedly, as if we are together in a Machiavellian pact to eradicate Mark.

'Mark was on the Aeolian Islands looking at buying a villa, probably on Salina,' Claire says.

I smirk. Niall's face drops.

Claire rubs my arm and says, confidingly, 'It's in Italy.'

I ignore this at first, because there is goading-of-Niall to be done, but then decide to kill two birds.

'Lucky Susie,' I say. 'Boyfriend with a villa on Salina, very nice. An exquisite place to go for weekends with your gentleman lover and a great location for a wedding, one day. Salina, the second biggest of the Aeolian Islands and a UNESCO World Heritage site. Flights to Catania, Calabria and Palermo offer connection to the islands by helicopter, hydrofoil and ferry.'

Niall looks crestfallen. 'Bollocks,' he says.

Claire and I laugh at Niall, proper belly laughter. There is no better sound than Claire laughing like this, right next to me.

'Niall,' Claire says softly. 'Mark was in Denmark on some boring management training course. He wasn't there but he's still on the scene.'

Niall looks bemused. 'Not buying a villa on an island?'

Claire shakes her head. Niall beams at me. My face drops.

'So, what, wait a minute,' I say, 'no free holidays on Salina for me then?'

Niall laughs, and says, 'Nerr nerr ner-ner nerr.'

'Bollocks,' I say. 'I nearly felt really happy for a moment there.'

Claire looks down her nose (lovely nose) at me. 'If you go to that travel agent on the high street, you could get them to book you a holiday to Salina and go there anyway.'

'That would mean leaving the house, though, Pete,' Niall says.

'It's a flat, not a house,' Claire says.

'Sod off, Niall,' I say.

'He'll miss me when I'm gone,' Niall mutters.

'Why are you moving out?' Claire asks.

'What do you mean, why?' I say. 'Why is he still here, more like?'

Niall laughs disdainfully. 'Why am I still here? Er . . . probably because you rely on me making it impossible for the estate agent to sell the flat upstairs so that your ex-wife can't fully move on because you're, er . . . jealous and stuck in a rut.'

I stare at him, speechless.

Claire looks at me accusingly. She shakes her head and says beneath her breath, 'Jesus! That's probably true.'

'Niall . . .' I say.

'What?'

'It just pours out of your mouth, doesn't it?'

'What does?'

'Just . . . just . . .' I splutter.

'The truth does,' Claire says.

'Brilliant! Anything else you'd like to say, Niall, in the name of fucking truth?'

He shrugs. 'Sorry.'

I sigh, already regretting swearing and using that tone with him.

He shrugs again. 'Just . . . I guess, that you're still in love with her, I suppose.'

I throw my head back. Turns out saying 'sorry' was a holding tactic, whilst he racked his brains for more truth.

'You know what he's like,' Niall says to her. For which, he'll later be killed slowly.

'I do,' Claire says softly.

I cross my arms and stare at the floor. 'I'm not *like* anything,' I mutter.

Niall smiles knowingly at Claire. She does the same in return and he leaves the room. Except, being Niall, he doesn't simply leave the room. He goes to the door, which is enough to raise my hopes that he is finally going to fuck off, but then, inevitably, he stops and decides that what this moment needs is more Niall.

'He's kind and loving and he believes love is for ever, no matter what,' he tells Claire. Presumably he's talking about me, the bloke sitting right there, a generation older than him who'd love not to be patronised by him in front of his ex-wife. 'That's what I admire about him.'

And he leaves, finally, two minutes too late.

'Me too,' Claire says.

I don't look at her. If you admire that about me, then love me too. Don't say sweet things to me and leave.

This atmosphere needs changing before I look my ex-wife, who admires me, in the eye.

'NIALL!' I yell.

He returns, peering around the door.

'What's for lunch?'

'I don't know,' he says. 'What *is* for lunch?'

'*What?!*' Again, that annoying high-pitched thing just when I want to sound like Darth Vader. 'You knew Claire was coming for lunch.'

'Why should he cook lunch?' Claire asks.

'He makes the food when humans visit.'

Claire frowns at me. 'Peter Smith, you have to learn to cook again, you lazy sod. You are a perfectly adequate cook.'

'You're right, Claire,' Niall says, 'he *can* cook.'

'I know I can! I cooked for my family for twenty years.'

'At times,' Claire says. 'On occasions. I mean, I wouldn't say that when searching for you the first place I would look would be by the oven.'

Niall nods his agreement.

'No, it would be at Erland's football or swimming, or at Susie's swimming or gymnastics, or decorating the house or gradually replacing all the rotten wood on the windows one window at a time because the fifteen-grand bill to have them done professionally was beyond us.'

'Yes . . .' Claire says affectionately. 'All true.'

'You can do all that?' Niall says. 'Why did it take you a year to put a lock on a door?'

'Because I don't fucking care now,' I say sulkily.

I'm not angry when I say it, and I don't say it angrily, but when I hear myself, I realise how true this is. Niall and Claire are both quiet and looking at me. I open the bi-fold doors, to avoid them and have something to do. Claire steps out gratefully into the garden. I follow her. She makes a couple of comments about how good the garden looks and leaves open the possibility that I could be responsible for it.

Then, she says with a sigh, 'Look . . .'

Oh, God. That tone of voice. This is news. And I don't want Claire to have news. It can only mean terminal or sexual. Oh, God, no. Oh, God, oh, God.

'There is something I wanted to say . . .'

It's too soon. You can't be in love, there can't be a man you're loving and laughing with and introducing to my children. Oh, God, oh, God, oh, God.

'This isn't going to go down well but please don't react.'

I walk inside, into the kitchen. I stand by the oven and stare at it. Claire comes in too and stands a few feet from me, arms folded.

'Pete. I want to help you out, with your business, with money.'

I turn and look at her. We both fall silent. My brain is rewinding and playing what she just said, like Gene Hackman in *The Conversation*, and equally insane. As I replay her words, my brain (if I can call it that) searches for the words 'met someone', 'man', 'love', 'moving in', 'huge penis'. But nothing comes up, apart from the undeniable fact that I am, indeed, a huge penis.

I peer round the kitchen door into the hallway to check that Niall has not heard Claire's offer. I shut the door.

'I can still be there for you in that way. I can help you with a strategy and back you, long-term, zero interest.'

Zero interest. That's what I have in this idea, and what Claire has in waking up to me every day.

'Our job,' I say, 'is to be great parents in divorce. Separate to that, I need what you're offering, I need advice, but I need it from anywhere but you.'

She sighs and shakes her head. 'And if our situations were reversed and I turned down your help?'

'You'd be congratulated for being empowered and independent just like you are already congratulated by all your friends and most of mine for leaving a boring marriage.'

'That's paranoid,' she says. 'But kind of true.'

'I'm doing the same thing here, trying to claw back a little of my own identity, but I will now be accused by you of being pig-headed which is no more than a lazy male stereotype, when in truth being free of relying on you is what I need more than anything. I am totally emotionally dependent on you. Not turning to you for this is essential for me and it's got nothing to do with me being a man and you being a woman – I will happily take advice on this from a woman or from anyone qualified, but not from the person who has broken my heart and over whom I now need to get.'

She grimaces and throws her arms in the air. 'Oh, no! That was such a great speech, darling, until the very last moment you train-wreck it with "over whom I now need to get". So close, babe!'

She's smiling patronisingly and it makes me laugh.

'Fucking gutted,' I say.

'But,' she says, putting her hands on her hips the way she always did when she made a decision, 'point taken. You're right and I apologise for the male stereotyping. Naughty.'

'That's okay, blossom, don't worry your pretty little head about it.'

'Might kill you a bit now,' she says.

'Do it softly,' I say.

'You can stop staring at the hob, I'm not hungry.'

'Excellent.'

We sit in silence for a while. Each time our eyes meet we smile, and each time we do it the smiles become more strained, because when it's good between us it's so good, and then we have to come back down. I want to make love with her so, so much, it's all I can think about.

'Better get going,' she says.

224

'I was thinking that.'

We hug on the doorstep.

'You take care, darling,' she says.

'You too,' I say.

She looks at me. 'I presume the state of the garden is down to Niall.'

I am outraged. 'How dare you? Yes.'

She smiles and kisses my cheek. The only thing that has felt really good today is making her smile and laugh.

'Speak soon, yeah?' I say.

'Yeah. Please.'

I watch her go to her car. She gets in and belts up and gets her phone out and starts doing something on it. I remain there to wave her off, but she doesn't look up and eventually I close the door. I shut myself in my bedroom and lie on the bed.

I get a text from her:

Hi Peter, this is Zoe Ball. I'm using Claire's phone to text you but this message is actually coming from me, not the daft old twat who divorced you. You probably know I've always been a big fan of yours and admired you and I've decided I'd like to share some thoughts with you from time to time. The first is, don't be scared to ask questions about all the things you feel you no longer understand – the average age of my team here at Radio 2 is twenty-seven. I ask them stuff all the time and it always makes me less scared of my own opinions and prouder of my experiences. Also, speaking as someone who has made mistakes in life, don't beat yourself up. Remember you're a brilliant human being. Zx

I hear Claire drive away. She's been here. It wasn't easy but she was here. The place is quiet now and I am left only with the fact of it, that Claire has been here in my flat, in our old place, and I want to hang on to the feeling the same way I have to leave my cinema seat but don't want to leave the film. Not that I'm going to go back to spraying bergamot around the place. I was doing that ten months ago and it didn't help.

Chapter 17

I am staring at the ceiling above my bed. I've been doing this a lot since Claire's visit. I'm pretty sure that I feel neither more nor less sad about being divorced than I did before seeing her. I won't ever quite believe that I am not with her but the fact of it is established nowadays in my frontal lobe. It's like a bereavement without a death. This might be a good way to see it; I've lost her, but no harm has come to her. Quite the opposite: she's thriving and looks amazing, which I'm totally fine with, obviously.

I know that comparing the situation favourably to a death is setting the bar low, but there's something in it. My children haven't lost their mum and I can still see her. I would celebrate all this if I was standing next to a man whose wife had died. But, there again, that widower would have carte blanche to not get over it, he'd have permission to feel sorry for himself, to rattle about in a house that's too big for him because the life policy paid off the mortgage. Whatever he did, people would say, 'Poor guy, he's lonely.' I have none of that. He'd get sympathy sex at the deluxe widower level whilst if I were to even go on a date, I'd have to navigate the why-are-you-divorced/what's-wrong-with you? vibe.

And any latent paranoia I might possibly possess.

I realise Niall is in the room, just inside the doorway. I have no idea how long he's been here.

'Not a communal space, Niall. Told you a thousand times.'

'You've been kind of quiet since Claire came and I wanted to ask you how you're feeling about it and how it went and everything, 'cause you basically haven't said a word for a day since she was here. Which is quite a long time to not talk.'

I keep my eyes on the ceiling and take a deep breath.

'You don't have to talk about it if you don't want to.'

'Witness me not talking about it right now.'

'But it made me think, you might well be wondering how I'm feeling about Susie.'

'I'm not.'

'Because it's not something I talk to you about.'

'It must be the only thing you *don't* talk to me about.'

'And I thought it would be good to clue you in on my thoughts as you and I are in the same boat.'

'Yeah, your ten months with my daughter and my thirty-year relationship, they're the same.'

'And the thing is, basically, the way I see it, I think, for me and Susie, our time has not yet come.'

'It's been and gone.'

'For now, she's moved on.'

'She's moved on up.'

'All I want to say is, I realise I have to let go and trust life, trust the world, believe in myself and want her to be happy. The opportunity I am being given is to love her by wanting her to be happy.'

There endeth Niall's thinly veiled lesson. I sit up on the side of the bed.

'If Susie told you she was deeply in love with Mark and realises she has been since she was nineteen, would you be happy?'

228

Niall tries to disguise swallowing hard at the thought.

'Happy for her, yes,' he says. 'Technically.'

'If she told you they're having a baby, would you be happy for her?'

He pulls the hem of his T-shirt away from his neck and looks over me to the window.

'Absolutely. I would. Try. Yes.'

'Then you were never in love with her. Shut the door behind you.'

'But I wanted to see if you're okay.'

'Worse off than a widower, is my current train of thought.'

'Impressive,' Niall says. 'Even by your standards.'

He has a point. I might well have reached a place of self-pity not previously discovered by male explorers.

'The problem for you is you need to talk about your loss but you're too proud to, whereas a widower is universally understood.'

'Niall, just because you look like a genie doesn't mean you're wise. Although, yes, that's exactly my thinking.'

'Look, the thing is, I am genuinely worried about you being alone and as a result of this, I'm having serious doubts about this flat-share of mine.'

I laugh. 'Brilliant, I've heard it all.'

He sits down on the edge of my bed and adopts his gravest tone. 'The kitchen is the size of a cupboard and I like to cook, one of the three of them has whatsapped me to say the other two have just got together as a couple and are being a nightmare to live with, and the guy from the couple texted me to invite me to come along with him to the Dante or Die theatre group before moving in, as an ice-breaker.'

'None of which involves you worrying about me being alone.'

'I've already said that was my main reason.'

I get up and gesture that I want him to do so too. He follows me into the kitchen.

'I've got my own shit to sort out and I need to do it alone,' I say.

'And you will sort it out,' he says earnestly. 'You already are doing, brilliantly. You're going to be okay because kindness doesn't go out of fashion and you are in the top five kindest men I've ever known, you really are.'

'Oh, thanks. But you're still moving out in two weeks.'

He pouts.

'Wait,' I say. 'Top *five* kindest men?'

'Possibly top four.'

'Your dad abandoned you when you were in nappies, you don't like your stepfather, you hate your stepbrother. I've never met a single male friend of yours. How am I struggling to get in your top four men?'

'I hardly know you.'

'You think there's more to me?'

'There isn't?' He sounds horrified.

'No. This is me.'

'Shit. Then you're fucked. I thought you were withholding the interesting bits.'

'Nope. Can you make me a nice coffee to help ease my pain at being me?'

He agrees to and I follow him into the kitchen and claim the sofa. 'Nope. I have no hidden qualities, Niall. No hidden talents. No hidden cash, vices or social life. No friends I've not mentioned.'

'Blank canvas is good,' he says.

'In fact, I have less friends now than at any point in my life since I was three years old. A widower who was widowed when an earthquake hit his wedding reception, dragging everyone he's ever known and liked down into

230

the molten core of the Earth, would have more friends than me.'

'But they wouldn't be real friends. They'd be sympathisers. Anyway, it might be good to stop this life-would-be-better-if-I-was-a-widower thing, it's a bit dark.'

'You're right. I will stop that.'

I dig the remote out from between the cushions and under Niall's tablet and switch the TV on. I mute it whilst I look at the guide.

Switching the TV on is the universal language for ending a conversation. However, muting the screen keeps the conversational door ajar.

'Can I ask you something?' Niall says.

'No, I am busy watching TV now.'

'Do you ever think about your effect?' Niall asks.

A text comes in from Claire.

'Shh, you don't exist,' I say, unlocking my phone. 'Other than to bring coffee.'

As I look at the text, Niall places a shot glass beside me on the arm of the sofa. It has water, gin or vodka in it.

'Coffee's coming,' he says.

'What's that?'

'One of the best vodkas money can buy.'

I look at it like it's landed from Mars, given that it's lunchtime.

'Whatever,' I mutter, and down it as I read my text.

Hi Pete, Zoe here. You free for a text chat? X

Nah. Kind of busy.

I'm texting from my bubble bath x

Go on then.

You okay?

Not sure, drinking vodka at one in the afternoon, whatever that tells you.

Why don't you use your contacts to book yourself a diving holiday and let your ex-wife treat you? X

Zoe, if you want to offer advice it needs to be better than that.

I put my phone down. Niall hands me my coffee.
'Thank you.'
'You're welcome.'
He looks at me, like he's studying me. He smiles affectionately. I grimace at him and look away. My phone pings.

Okay, fair enough. This is what I'd like to say to you today, Pete . . . us girls were denied a lot of stuff for a long time vis-à-vis, like, fundamental rights and stuff, so someone as lucky as me has made some advances whilst you guys have just all the confusion of, you know, the feminism and not being allowed to quote Louis C.K. any more. But you, Pete, have always thought of others and put others first and been bewildered by anything unfair. And now you're stuck and don't know what to do – the solution is to put yourself first for once but it's not in your nature and you keep losing out. Put yourself first, from right now. Zoe x

Given that this text has come with no detailed user instructions, I ignore it and start a five-part documentary about Thatcher on the iPlayer and turn the volume up. Niall puts another shot of vodka next to my coffee and leaves the room.

You know those toxic relationships that are screwed and full of arguments and recriminations that serve no purpose, but the couple just can't stop? They're addicted to the catfight. Listening to Niall is like that for me, without any of the poison. I want him to shut up and go away, but whilst he is here and, inevitably, talking, I don't want to miss any of it.

I pause the TV and call out, 'What do you mean, have I thought about my effect?'

The door opens and he returns with a supercilious smile on his face and takes up position, using the kitchen island as a lectern.

'I mean, where are all your friends? What do you fall out with them over?'

'I don't fall out with them. I just lose contact. It happens. Jay is the only mate I ever actually fell out with.'

'Apart from your wife, and there's obviously some sort of tension between you and your best friend.'

'I'm his oldest friend, not his best friend, apparently. And Claire and I care for each other hugely – we didn't fall out.'

'You're right, the two of you are still happily married. She's upstairs right now.'

'Getting divorced is not total proof of falling out.'

'It's a pointer. Tell me all about Jay, the only person in the history of the world you have ever fallen out with. I've never heard of him.'

Niall pulls a chair up beside me on the sofa.

'Not sure if we were ever really friends,' I say. 'Considered him a mate, through work. He had an affair. He was married, still is, with three daughters and he worked all the time and for years he had been telling me that his wife was really unhappy about having turned into a full-time mum with no career.'

Niall nods as I talk and removes his socks and rolls them up into a ball.

'And Jay was always sounding so concerned about her, that it took me years to realise he never did anything about it. He loved working late every day with his team and was happy just having weekends with his family. He didn't want his wife to have a life and to have to raise his own children.'

Niall lobs his sock-ball into the empty Amazon box on the floor.

'Three points!'

I remove my socks and ball them up.

'But I went along with his version of what was going on for years. He complained about her not understanding how busy he was and that they had a great lifestyle thanks to him and then he slept with someone on a work trip to New York and he moved out into a flat and he said all the right things, that he was in the wrong, that he was sorry, that he loved her and wanted her to be happy but, you know . . .'

I lob my sock-ball into the box.

'*Trois points.*'

Niall retrieves our socks. No money in the world would encourage me to pick up his socks, but he seems squeam-free about touching mine. If 'squeamish' is a word, then 'squeam' is one too.

'He never made any attempt to move back in. He loved a bachelor-lifestyle approach to parenting.'

'And were you a tiny bit jealous?' Niall says, throwing and missing.

I look at him. 'I love it when you get something totally wrong, Niall. You don't do it often. It's such a relief.'

'You weren't jealous?'

'What he wants and what I want couldn't be more different. One evening we met for a drink and I finally said what I really thought – "You should move back in and spend less time at work, even think of selling your business, and do something that means you are a proper family and you have a proper marriage."'

I shoot and score.

'This is a rubbish game,' Niall mutters.

'And Jay said to me, "You don't get it, the girls have got these hamsters in the kitchen and it drives me insane – you try to sit down for breakfast on a Saturday morning and it's all noise and the smell of straw." So I told him what I thought of him . . .'

Niall retrieves the socks and hands me mine.

'. . . that he had no idea what family or marriage takes, that the bedlam is what it's all about, and that he didn't need to tell me he was sleeping with other women because it was obvious.'

'What did he say?'

'He said it was none of my business and it was one woman, not a line of them. And he never spoke to me again. Not a word in five years.'

Niall puts his socks back on. He can balance steadily on one foot whilst socking-up on the other. I can't. I need a wall to lean against. What's more, he can talk whilst standing on one leg. He's got so much talent that I no longer have.

'So,' he says, 'why are we talking about him?'

'Because you asked about effects on others. Why did I pretend for so long that I understood what he was doing? Why didn't I say earlier how I hated the way he treated his family?'

'Maybe you're too accommodating.'

'Kicking you out would buck the trend.'

He double-takes. 'What?'

Instinctively, in response to the threat to move him out, Niall gets up and starts preparing me a snack.

'All I know,' he says, 'is that when things go wrong between people it's often because they aren't thinking about the effect they are having on the other person.'

'Where did you read that?'

'I don't know, probably on a blackboard outside a coffee shop. Or on Instagram.'

'So, when you moved your new girlfriend, my daughter, into your ex-wife's flat—'

'It's a house, not a flat.'

'You were really imagining what that was like from your ex-wife's perspective?'

'Exactly. Prime example. I wasn't. Total failure, except that I knew I was messing up but simply didn't have the mental strength to stop myself.'

'That's all right then.'

'The point is, what was Claire experiencing these last few years? What was it like for her being on the receiving end of you?'

'Not that I'm getting into this with you, but I would say, without particularly getting into it, that I wanted to do everything with her, wanted to visit the children at college a lot and neither Claire nor the kids wanted that. I ran out of ideas and her mind is exploding with them. I thought that the kids growing up would mean I'd stop worrying about something happening to them, but it never does.'

And as I speak, I am aware that I am zoning out, drifting away from myself, talking on autopilot. These words are noise that I've produced before. The only interesting thing I've done lately is make Claire laugh, yesterday.

Niall gets the vodka from the freezer. He fills my glass and pours one for himself.

'*Na zdrowie.*'

'Cheers.'

'No wonder she left you. But all you have to do is not be like that any more.'

'Not be like me? That's technically impossible.'

'Change what you're like.'

'You change what you're bloody like, there's nothing wrong with me.'

Niall pulls a confused face. 'Apart from everything you've just outlined.'

'What, change and she'll take me back?'

He shakes his head. 'She's not coming back.'

'Then what's the point?'

'You are the point. Not Claire. You. Your own life, that, by the way, you are not living.' He gets up.

'Do not put the bottle away,' I warn him.

I am aware, although I will never, ever, admit it to him, that Niall sees things I don't. The bottle is not to lubricate his wisdom. He doesn't need help. As a member of the there-are-no-words generation, he doesn't blend. The bottle is to ease me into being able to admit that I am listening. The bottle is my preparation for insight.

But to the same extent that one should never underestimate Niall, one should never overestimate him either, for what he says to me as he pours our next shot of vodka is, 'If *Queer Eye* was in England, and I nominated you, would you go on it?'

I knock back the shot and, given my lowish tolerance, begin to feel a bit drunk. The booze is mind-blowingly good but I don't say so because I don't want Niall going off on some long-winded lecture about Russian vodka and pure taste and whatever the hell else he's got inside his hairy head.

'Hypothetically?' I ask.

'Obviously.'

'Not obviously. I have to check because if I thought there was any chance of you nominating me, I'd just say a straight "no" and not get into this conversation.'

'But what with us not being in Texas, you're not going to get queer-eyed.'

'Yeah, but you're so . . . I have to check.'

'I'm so . . . what?'

'You talk in tongues.'

237

'You think anyone who doesn't keep their conversation to "I'm fine" is talking in tongues. Would you go on *Queer Eye* to make a new start?'

'Absolutely not.'

'Why do I bother?'

'Sorry, was that not the script? Tell me what to say so you can have the chat with me you've planned and cover all the points you want to.'

'They'd help you move on, maybe have that first date, shake off the old.'

'What, evict you?'

'I'll be gone way before the Fab Five get here.'

I stuff my knuckles in my mouth. 'Oh, no! Please don't go!'

Niall cocks his head to one side and looks at me, unimpressed. 'They might make over your sense of humour.'

I get up and take control of the bottle myself. I chink Niall's glass and we both throw another shot down our throats. I pour another for each of us and settle back.

'No more shots. I just want to sip this one. It's beautiful stuff and I'm getting too pissed.'

'It's bison grass vodka. They make it—'

'Don't care. I don't want to understand the vodka, I just want to drink it. But you understand this, I don't want to shake off the old. I don't want to move too far on, because then I'll really be lost. If I didn't have losing Claire, I would have nothing. It won't last for ever, but an entire lifetime doesn't get washed out of your hair in a year. If this gets rushed, then one day I really will crash.'

He nods and, extraordinarily, says nothing.

I return to the remote control. I sit on one side of the sofa, leaving room for Niall if he wants it. I look at the freeze-frame of Maggie Thatcher and have no desire to press 'play'. I know exactly what I want to watch: fantasy politics, not the real thing.

It came to me a few minutes ago and I'm like a pig in shit at the thought of watching it for the first time in twenty years.

'You ever watched *The West Wing?*' I ask the hairy one.

'Nope.'

'My plan is to watch four or five hours of it right now, with vodka, giving way to a cleansing lager later and then, probably, takeaway pizza. You are welcome to join me. No more talking, though.'

Niall smiles and seems genuinely moved by the invitation. He takes the bottle of vodka by the neck and sits next to me.

'There's one thing I want to negotiate,' he says.

Like taking candy from a baby . . .

'Sure . . .' I say.

'Later, when it's time, let me knock some food up, instead of the pizza.'

I press 'play' and take a sip. 'If you insist.'

I fall asleep during the third episode and wake up with a sleepy aeroplane erection (it's a thing, don't pretend it's not, chaps) that is only encouraged by the sight of Allison Janney.

Allison – Sigourney – Zoe – Claire. It's an axis. A tall one.

I am sleepy, drunk and aroused.

'Niall, go and sit somewhere else.'

'No!'

'Seriously, get a chair and sit over there. You can't sit next to me right now.'

I lie out on the sofa and kick him off. He jumps up.

'I was really comfy,' he whines.

I write a text for Claire. It flows, which should always be a danger sign. I hesitate before sending it, aware that feeling drunk and horny creates unfavourable conditions for divorce-text. I reread it. It still seems humorous to me. And it still appears to me that there is a 0.0001 per cent chance of what I am suggesting being granted, which is more than no chance. Beyond the maths, deep down beneath the swaying of the bison grass, I do doubt the wisdom of this text. Here, my thinking on it slides into uncertainty, a lack of clarity inevitable given the cocktail of drinking, sleep and general not-knowing-what-the-hell-is-happening in my life on a daily basis. As my finger hovers over the 'send' arrow the bison leans close and whispers in my ear, '*You've nothing to lose.*'

I send, just on the off chance Claire has taken the day off work and been drinking since lunchtime too.

> Zoe, vis-à-vis putting myself first after years of self-sacrifice, I wondered if you'd like to pop round for one-off meaningless sex. Or I could come to you. It might seem like an outrageous idea, but truth be told, for most of my marriage when I was in bed with my wife, I was thinking of you anyway, so for me it would be business-as-usual. Pxx

Claire replies a few minutes later, minutes during which time I have imagined her thinking, What the heck, a shag would be nice and he's so funny, and getting her coat.

> That will never be funny. C

And that is not the accidental 'C' of someone meaning to send a kiss and fat-fingering a 'C'. That is 'C' for Claire. Zoe is off the table. But I plough on, because it is a truth universally acknowledged, that a single man in possession of a good bottle of vodka is a comedy genius.

> Then maybe you're not the gal for me cos I am wetting myself.

> I'm not the gal for you. We're divorced.

> That will never be funny. P

Two further episodes of *West Wing* later, I am drifting in and out of sleep again and the kitchen is filling with the smell of something delicious. I go to the bathroom and take a shower and when I'm ready to get out I follow the advice of some Scandinavian lunatic I heard on the radio yesterday by turning the shower to cold. I scream, repeatedly, but stick with it and keep myself under the ice-cold water for a couple of minutes. It must be good for me because it's a miserable experience, and a sobering one.

I dress and am being led by my nose towards the kitchen when I hear noise from the flat upstairs. Too nervous to venture up there, I go into the back garden and look up.

I call out, 'Is that you, Matthew?'

A window opens and Dennis appears. 'Hi, Pete.'

'Dennis . . . everything okay?'

'Yeah, just helping Claire put some bits of furniture in.'

Another window opens. Claire appears. 'Hello.' She winks at me mischievously. I smile back defensively.

'Thought the place might need something in it to soften it up. Such a mystery it's not had an offer.'

'Cool,' I say.

Dennis disappears. Claire smiles at me again and I feel a foreboding that she's about to win at a game I have no idea we're playing.

'Well, better get on,' she says.

Phew.

'See you,' I say nonchalantly.

'By the way . . .' she says.

'Yeah?' Here's my 0.0001 per cent chance. She does fancy a shag. She is desperate.

'Alan Rickman . . .' she says.

'What about him, God rest his soul?' Love that man. Love Severus Snape.

'That's who I thought about.'

'When we were having sex?'

She shrugs. 'Yeah, then, and . . . often.'

'Fair enough,' I say, as she shuts the window.

I go inside. A minute later the doorbell rings and Claire stands on the front step in her coat, with her bag slung across her shoulder.

'You can go upstairs and help Dennis with flat-pack furniture or take me for a drink.'

'Sounds good,' I say. 'Be nice to spend some time with Dennis.'

'Buy me a pint, you cock.'

I get my coat and we head for the Pelham, a five-minute walk we've done hundreds of times: after making love, before the cinema, on summer evenings with the children. They would run back and forth between the swings in the garden and their crisp packets on the trestle tables.

'To be a hundred per cent honest,' I say, as we walk these familiar pavements, 'cause we've always been big on truth, 'the only time I ever fantasised about getting with Zoe Ball was when having the perfectly natural, standard, run-of-the-mill fantasy of being abandoned by you to raise the children on my own and many women seeing me as dad-of-the-century despite my heartbreak and them all wanting to sleep with me.'

'Including Zoe?'

'I bump into her in the supermarket and we get talking. She believes I'm a standout human being who needs to be left alone to his heroic parenting but deserves no-strings physical happiness and can't believe what a tiger I am between the sheets, able to go at it until the early hours bringing her pleasure she never knew possible, and yet when she wakes each morning with a lusty satisfied smile on her face, she finds me up and dressed and good-looking and giving my kids breakfast.'

'Not that you ever thought about it.'

'Not when you and I were making love, I didn't.'

'Anything else?'

'That's it.'

The Pelham Arms was my and Claire's local for a quarter of a century. I have hardly stepped inside since my divorce. I hold the door open for Claire and we go to the bar. The landlord beams at seeing us together.

'Hello, you two!'

I cast him the it's-not-what-you-think look.

'Pint of Stella and a pint of Tim Taylor, please, Mark,' Claire says, without conferring with me. Which I love.

We sit down. I elect for side by side rather than opposite and it feels wrong the moment I've done it.

'You do know we are not going to bed with each other?' she asks, shuffling a few inches away from me.

'Hundred per cent,' I say, which is 99.999 per cent true.

'Cheers,' she says, and gets stuck into her pint.

'There is one other detail, seeing as you were asking,' I say. Well, I've nothing to lose now. 'Zoe is clubbing and DJing with all her mates from that side of her life but finds it no longer has meaning or brings her pleasure, compared to being with me, so she gives all that up to be with me as much as possible, as and when I can fit her in.'

'Zoe Ball gives up music because of you?'

'Yup.'

'That would be very you.'

'Thank you.'

'Wasn't a compliment. And does she give up her children too?'

'Has she got children?'

'Yup.'

'Oh.'

'Oh.'

'Well, she leaves them, just like you left yours at the start of this fantasy.'

She reaches for her drink and her fingers tap the table as she thinks. 'Pete,' she says, 'Peter darling, you need to be much busier.'

We fall silent for a few moments.

'The thing is,' I say, 'I'm just not up for being given advice by the person who ruined my happiness.'

'How can I possibly argue with that? I'm sorry.'

'You don't owe me an apology. But you can't fix me.'

'Okay.' She nods. 'Thanks for not killing me off in your fantasy, like most men do.'

'I could never do that.'

'You're a good man.'

'You're welcome.'

Then I tell her, randomly, that I burst into tears listening to Simon and Garfunkel's 'The Boxer' yesterday.

She thinks about this and nods. 'That makes sense,' she says. 'Great song.'

'Great song.'

After that we enjoy being together but we don't speak much, until I guide us to the conversational safety zone of Erland and Susie.

'We're so lucky with those two,' I say. 'And how well they get on. They're nice adults and they were wonderful kids.'

'They were wonderful, you're right . . .' Claire says.

'I miss them,' I say. 'So much.'

'. . . but they were also absolute arseholes at times. Erland was a total dickhead from the age of nine to thirteen, if you remember. He was actually nicer when he became a teenager, which tells you something.'

'I don't remember any of that.'

She looks at me and, for a fraction of a second, digs her elbow into me. 'I miss them desperately, but I prefer not to think about it too much.'

I nod and I hope it conveys how much I admire the way she faces up to things. We walk back home and say goodnight to each other on my doorstep. She kisses me on the cheek.

'Thanks for the drink,' she says.

'Thanks for ruining Alan Rickman for me, for ever,' I say.

She goes upstairs and soon she leaves and I hear her, but I don't rush to my bedroom window to watch her go and I don't miss her like hell after not doing so.

Lie–la–lie

[Boom]

Lie–la–lie–lie–lie–lie–lie

Lie–la–lie

[Boom]

Lie–la–lie–lie–lie–la–lie, la–la–la–lie . . .

Chapter 18

My shoes leave prints in the dew on the golf course as I walk towards Pyrford. A golf ball bounces near to me. I turn and see an elderly man raising his arm, and wave back. I continue on but as the man crosses the tracks I have left, I turn and watch him take a club from his bag, quickly address the ball, hit it, swear and march off. He seems to be playing alone, furiously. He takes a call on his mobile and his voice lights up, 'Morning, darling! You having breakfast? Lovely! No, I'm being totally shit as usual!' and he laughs.

I watch him go, take in the view. It's a beautiful morning and I text Claire.

Going back to school, wish me luck

Whatty whatty what what?

Got an interview about being a governor at a primary school

An interview!!! They should be begging you to help them out x

That's nice.

I'll mention that to them x

Be sure to.

Then she sends another.

Great thing to be doing. Best dad in the world should make a great
governor x

You'd think x

Thanks to my ex-wife, I head to the school with a smile on
my face and an ounce or two of self-belief. And, as I wait in
reception, I get one last text from her:

And forget what I said in the pub about children being arseholes. Cx

The Grove is a primary school of RI status – Requires
Improvement – and it's been plummeting for a decade.
The head who oversaw that decline was moved on a year
ago and the school is being turned around by an interim
head.

This much I was told on the phone by the chair of
governors, who meets me in the school reception and signs
me in and gives me a purple lanyard. Grove is a large, single-
storey, 1960s school with a huge Millennium-era sports hall.
The children who attend it come mostly from the terraced
streets and estates either side of the industrial-estate-lined main
road that splits this part of town. The corridors and classrooms
are light-filled and messy. The atmosphere makes my heart
lift. Young voices, far-off screams of play, teachers trying to
get heard. It's wonderful. But it is chaos.

A girl from, I would guess, Year 5, comes up to me and
stands immediately in front of me. We're toe to toe.

'Who are you?' she demands.

I'm terrified. She actually crosses her arms waiting for an
answer. The chair of governors, Sharon Meek, doesn't help me

247

out with an introduction and my mind goes blank. I sense that whatever I say isn't going to impress this girl, that she's staring not at me but through me. She's nine or ten and instinctively knows I'm divorced, broke, clueless, lonely and not going to be accepted here as a governor.

'I'm Peter, I might be getting involved here, I've got two children of my own and I go deep-sea diving all over the world.'

She smiles and cocks her head to one side. 'That's quite good,' she says, and leaves.

Later, after I have been introduced in passing to the Safeguarding officer and told about the higher-than-average SEN and Pupil Premium numbers at Grove (I will look all this up later, but nod through it for now) a much smaller boy comes up to us, his eyeballs bulging through Mr Magoo specs that are held on by an elasticated headband. He says hello to me and wraps his arms around me, around my legs. Tentatively, I let out a little laugh and pat his head, unsure as to what's acceptable. And I do mean what's *acceptable*, not what's appropriate; what's appropriate is to kneel down to his height and hug him back. But that's not acceptable.

'Hello, Albee,' Sharon says.

'Hello, miss,' he replies, with a trace of the drone with which children greet their teacher each morning (or did, in the 1970s).

Albee lets go of me and walks off and we watch as a girl of his age crosses his path and he smacks her bum and runs off. She gives chase and as they disappear around a corner. I have no doubt that the girl is about to beat five shades of crap out of Albee.

'What can you bring to us?'

Sharon has turned to face me. The corridor has fallen quiet. There's a bell sounding somewhere outside.

'Time and . . .' I scroll the blank pages in my mind. 'I'm a nice bloke.'

She hugs her stash of files a bit closer to her. A tired-looking woman walks past us.

'Morning, Sharon.'

'Morning, Jo. Stuart Case wants a conference call about the MASH proposals.'

'Me and you?'

'Please.'

'Okay.'

By the end of this exchange, Jo, who has not stopped walking, is almost out of sight.

'Perfect,' Sharon says to me.

She takes me to a large empty room.

'I'll get Helen,' she says, and leaves.

She returns with the school's interim head. She is in her sixties, I would say. She looks tired but her eyes are a translucent pale blue and when she starts to speak, there is a music to her gravelly voice that suggests huge resources of energy and hope. Perhaps that is a minimum requirement for a school with, as she puts it, 'a few little challenges at the moment'.

'I was about to retire, but I had always wanted to be head of this school, all my career. I've been a headteacher twenty years and I love this school like no other. The governing body has nearly all been replaced since I arrived. The couple remaining are still here because we want them here. We want some non-educationalists. I'm enormously grateful to people like you, prepared to do this for our young people. People like you are amazing. What do you think of the school? Would you like to be a governor here?'

She stops talking. And that's a shame – firstly, because I could listen to her for hours and, secondly, because it means I'm up.

'I think', I say, 'it's a matter of whether I can add anything. But I am drawn to a place that isn't ticking along perfectly well. Where there is work to be done.'

'That's handy,' Sharon says.

'And what can you bring to us?' the head says.

'He's got time and he's a nice bloke,' Sharon says, with the slightest hint of a giggle in her voice that makes me wonder if being a school governor might possibly, somewhere down the line, get me laid.

'That's more than enough,' Helen says. 'Anything else?'

I say, 'Yes,' immediately, just to stop Sharon answering for me. And I do have a pretty good idea of what I want to say, but I take a moment to think, given that these days I no longer have any confidence about what I think let alone what I say.

'Look,' I say, 'I could list the things I don't know, like how to be a governor—'

'We teach that,' Helen says. 'We're good at teaching stuff.'

'But raising school-age children is the thing I was best at in my entire life. And I miss it. And the combination of those two things might make me okay at this.'

'The key', Sharon says, 'is to ask questions and not to worry if they might be wrong. We're here to support and challenge the teachers and to get the children the best school life they could possibly have.'

Helen smiles at me. She shakes my hand. 'We'd love to have you if you decide to join us. Let Sharon know.' And she checks her watch and is gone.

I turn to Sharon, glance at her ring finger (it's occupied) and say, 'I want to join.'

Sharon gets her iPad out and types some notes. 'Our next job is replacing Helen. And that is not going to be easy. We won't find another Helen. You should put yourself forward to be on the head recruitment panel. You'll learn a lot about the school and the LA on that. There's governor training courses available, if you can find the time.'

250

I nod and smile; it's more dignified than revealing how much time I have.

'I'll send you a link. Okay, good, I'll write to the governing body about you and let you know when you've been ratified.'

And that's it. I have put myself forward and received a 'yes' in reply and the shock is so great that I walk home gripped by the ridiculous idea that I can sort my life out, and that all I need is a little time alone in my flat to get my head straight (because sorting your life out is something you do in an evening) and I develop a craving for the sort of celebratory tenth-rate takeaway curry that Niall has banned from the flat.

Niall is working on his tablet when I get back. Not slouched-on-the-sofa working, but seated-upright-at-the-table, with-a-mini-keyboard, wearing-clothes working.

'That looks serious,' I say.

'It is.'

'Can I make you a cup of tea?'

I'm hoping he'll make me dinner later in return for this.

'Yes, please.'

'What are you doing?'

'Extracting fifty thousand pounds from your best friend, if I get all this right.'

'So glad he's there for you, that's just Ed all over. I've got a favour to ask.'

'If I can, I will.'

'I need to get some things done tomorrow and I realise that I need some headspace. So, tomorrow, I want you to go out first thing and do your work wherever – hey, you could even do it in a garden – and stay out. I need a day to work and an evening to unwind with no one and no chit-chat to navigate. I just need space.'

Niall looks hurt. I think he even toys with the idea of doing his tears thing but realises it would be overkill. He quietly packs up his stuff and vacates the table.

'I'll go and work in my room.'

'You having a sulk, Niall?'

'A little one, yes. If I was paying rent you couldn't do this.'

'That's a pretty hefty "if", isn't it? Here's your tea.'

'No, thanks, I can make my own tea.'

I guess dinner is off the table. Niall goes to his room. I sit on the sofa and start a list.

Tomorrow: Governor research. Job for Josie. Re-book Mary Blair.

That's my list finished. I'm going to devote nine in the morning to six in the evening to accomplishing this list and then I'm going to have a curry with a movie: *Inception* is the current front-runner, but *Trainwreck* could come up on the rails, so could *Jaws*, so could *The Deer Hunter* and so could *Short Cuts*. Let's say I'm undecided. A few episodes of *The West Wing* is always a possibility. I once got so drunk with Claire after we'd had sex that I convinced myself I looked a bit like Rob Lowe.

That was good and drunk.

When Niall says goodnight he's still pouting. In fact, he only says goodnight so that I can see he is pouting.

'Not that it's any of my business,' he says, 'but what's happening? Why don't you want me here for an entire day?'

'Exactly what I said and nothing more. I need a little thinking time.'

'Sure . . . course . . . I get it . . .' Niall says, and leaves.

He's back within seconds. 'But—'

'I've a list of things I need to get done, Niall. That's all.'

'I've got a list too,' he says. 'My list is of the three possible things you're up to.'

'I'm not "up to" anything. This is my house and I'm having it to myself tomorrow.'

'One, you have a date. Two, linked but different, you're having a porn day. Three, you're showing my room to a potential lodger because you need the rent but you don't want it to be me.'

'Or, four, I'm signing you up to the Royal Paranoia Society.'

'You don't need to keep a date secret, for starters. Youthful people like me, in their prime, understand that old people like company.'

'Gee.'

'And you don't have to be alone to watch porn. I don't mean I'd watch it with you on the sofa – I would not – but it's perfectly normal to watch it in one room when a flatmate or family member is home too.'

'I can't even begin to explain to you how wrong you are about that. But no, that's not the thing, I'm not watching porn.'

'So, it's a lodger or a date then.'

'And bravo by the way, if you devote whole days to watching porn.'

'Is it a lodger or a date?'

'Neither. Goodnight.'

'Which?'

'Still neither. If I had a date, would you understand that and leave me alone?'

'Of course.'

'Then, yes, I have a date. Goodnight.'

'Who is she?'

I stare at him. Given that I know he isn't stupid, he has to be the most stubborn man I know. Along with every other man I know. And myself.

'Who is she?' I say. 'She's a fiction invented right in front of you just now to give you an answer that ends this conversation. Go to bed.'

It is, of course, not enough to label Niall stupid or stubborn. He's neither. He gets an idea in his head and allows it a good and full life. He knows I don't have a date – he has seen me choose it as an answer to end the conversation – but he also wants to know who that date might be, if it existed. And he wants to keep the conversation going. Whether this is to annoy me or because he likes company, I still couldn't tell you.

The most stubborn man or the most open? Niall thinks like this: Maybe Pete does have a date? Why not? Stranger things have happened (although I can't think of any). Who would she be? What if I ask him? What if I bring my new girlfriend back to my ex-wife's house for the night? Maybe she won't mind. What if I run my own business on totally ethical grounds? What if I charge people what they can afford and pay people what they deserve, not the minimum I'm obliged to pay? I'll do these things and see how it pans out. Even if it leaves me broke and couch-surfing in my thirties.

I get it now. Open-minded. Good-hearted. Stubborn. And a tiny, tiny bit stupid.

I hear Niall leave the next morning before six. I make coffee and open the doors and the breeze is less biting, with a promise of spring. I have been awake since a quarter to five, convinced that I can't be any good as a governor and plotting ways out. Then I imagined being governor of the century and Sharon turning up on my doorstep unable to keep her feelings for me a secret any longer. It's feast or famine up there in my head. A character in *The West Wing* in the early stages of dementia said he had a 'demolition derby' going on in his brain. I've not forgotten that line, proof perhaps that I both fear senility and don't yet suffer from it.

Sunrise brings hope lacking a plan. It's the most basic package of hope available on the market but it's better than nothing. I shower, dress and place my laptop on the kitchen table. I work through the information sent to me by the school and by the Local Authority about being a governor. I complete the forms, activate my email address and my account with the Virtual Governance Office, sweat profusely at the sight of the word 'virtual' and spend half an hour writing and rewriting the fifty-word biography Sharon has requested for the school website. I sign up to do three courses: Effective Governance, Introduction to Safeguarding and Introduction to Growth Mindset. I commit to them before I can talk myself out of it.

It's 8 a.m. That was all meant to take until midday. I walk into town, opting for a coffee in the place Susie took me to so that I don't go too near the shop. This place is on trend. I wonder if Claire ever comes here. I write her a text:

Am having a coffee in the Boatshed coffee shop if you happen to be in town and fancy a coffee. X

I don't send it.
I plan another text in my head:

I'm concerned I didn't use the word coffee enough in my previous message.

I don't want to send the first one, not without a guarantee of her responding to say that she's free and would love to come and join me, but I do want to send the second one because it will make her laugh. But to send the second one I have to send the first one. Life's a conundrum. And she's probably at work anyway, like a normal person.

I get home shortly before ten which means I can set about the second item on my list: Josie. I have four calls to make, four people I feel I can call on, after a quarter of a century in the business. That means I have made one meaningful professional connection every six years. I'm such a people person.

I leave a message on Jack Kinney's voicemail: 'Jack, this is Peter Smith at Smith's Holidays in Woking. Good seeing you in Birmingham last month, I hope all's well with you. Listen, I have someone working for me here, nineteen, bright, trustworthy. I want to find her something in the area, somewhere better. She's not learning enough with me, we're too quiet. I can't think of anyone better than you for someone like her. If you did have room for her, I'd be so grateful to you now and you would be to me in a year's time. That sounds like a line, but it's not meant to be. If you can help, I'd appreciate it hugely. Sorry for the long message. Cheers.'

I can't in all honesty rave about Si, and Mrs H does not want or need my help, but I am determined not to let Josie down. I call William Cottrell and leave a shorter version of the same message with him. I slump at the thought that Claire has not replied to my earlier text, then remember that I didn't send her one. I'm geared for disappointment. It's as if I want it.

Third on my list is Bill Peet. He is friendly, sounds pleased to hear from me, and listens attentively to my pitch about Josie as the potential jewel-in-the-crown of his travel business.

'Peter,' Bill says, when I finish, 'if I'm still here in two years' time it will be because I have cut my staff from two, including me, to one, including me. I have already reduced from eight to two in the last three years.'

He then says some lovely things about me and my parents and I apologise for troubling him when he's struggling himself.

'It's not that I'm struggling, it's just that to not struggle I've got to work hard and do it all myself. You are obviously finding the same thing.'

'Yes,' I say. I ought to be honest and tell him I'm just giving up.

Call number four. Oliver Wallace. I can't remember if it's Oli or Oliver. But that, it turns out, is the least of this phone call's problems.

'Peter, I'm sorry to interrupt you and your employee sounds faultless, but I am really struggling to place you.'

'Oh.'

That's weird because I'm not struggling to recall the numerous times he and I have met, not to mention his offer to buy me out eight years ago which I turned down because I am a dick.

'Peter?'

'Peter Smith. Smith's Holidays. We've spoken many times.'

'Okay, if you say so, let's pretend we know each other and continue, I'm perfectly happy to do that.'

I find myself tongue-tied that he could blank me like this. What a prick. I hang up.

Fuck!

It was Oliver Ford who I know. Who the fuck is Oliver Wallace? Now, a virtual stranger in my industry knows that I am probably closing down and that I'm an idiot. One of those two things is news. I step into the garden to calm myself down and write Claire a text.

Josie who works for me . . . I want to find her a better job. She can't develop in her job here and she deserves a better job. Can you or anyone you know give her a job? She'd be good at any job she did, but I want to her to have a really good job. She's bright and hard-working, but you've heard me say that before. I want to find her a great job. Any thoughts?

I send it without rereading it.
I send her another text:

I'm concerned I didn't use the word job enough in my previous message.

If it's funny with 'coffee', then it's funny with 'job'. But now that I've sent it, that feels like a big 'if'.

It's time to call Mary Blair but I must check something first. I knock on Niall's door. There's no reply. I open the door and peer in.

'You are out, aren't you? Not in the cupboard or under your bed? Good. Thank you.'

Talking to an empty room. The latest in a line of personal triumphs.

I lie on the kitchen sofa but that doesn't feel right. I stand by the kitchen windows and look out on the garden. That feels better, so I make the call. (I'm calling because I know it will be harder to chicken out having spoken to her).

Mary answers immediately and is upbeat.

'Hello, Peter. How are you?'

'Apologetic for two no-shows.'

'No-shows are not uncommon.'

'But really, I am sorry. And calling to book in again if you'll entertain the idea.'

'You'll find it harder to no-show now that we've spoken. Well done, you. We're looking at next week.'

'That's fine. Just tell me the best slot for you. I can do it.'

We book it in, and she offers me some advice in closing.

'Peter, whatever you're unsure about or even scared of, however much it feels like something you don't want to do, just turn up and see. I can't guarantee it will help or that you'll love it, but I promise you it won't be like what you're fearing when you—'

'Chicken out.'

'Yeah.'

'Opening up is pretty scary.'

'I'll help.'

'I really do want to turn up.'

'If you're wavering on the day, call me.'

'Okay.'

'It will be as easy as this conversation we're having now.'

'This isn't easy,' I say.

Chapter 19

It is eleven in the morning on my day to myself and I have done everything on my list. Nothing and no one stands before me and I am enjoying the longed-for luxury of my own company in the peace and quiet of my own home.

Shit.

I check my phone but my ex-wife hasn't replied to my text and no one else has emailed me, whatsapped me or texted me today.

This is the perfect opportunity to start a DIY project or to tick off some chores like buying new underwear or closing down a half-century-old family-run business. But the latter would take balls so I settle for buying some cotton briefs to put mine in. I rule out anything DIY because it would inevitably lead to partial success (at the very best), meaning I don't get the job finished and instead of a day of sorting things out I will have created another unfinished thing. Better to have an un-started project than an unfinished one. Put that on my plaque.

It's three minutes past eleven.

I could drive down to the coast or up to Richmond Park. But that's a waste of an empty flat. No, this is the perfect opportunity to start *The Cicero Trilogy*. I get the first volume from my bedside table and before I know it, I'm a hundred pages in and gripped. It's lunchtime and I'm hungry but I can't be arsed to move from the kitchen sofa let alone prepare food and I want to be really hungry for my curry tonight.

I compromise and make a cup of tea and relocate to my bed where I read until a few hundred nights of curtailed sleep drag me into slumber and the next thing I know it is dark outside and I am shivering, waking from a sleep so deep, long and disorientating that the need for it seems, in retrospect, primordial. It is five-fifty in the afternoon. The day has gone, consumed by sleep. I fold the duvet across me. I am bewildered and cold and I begin to cry from the realisation that I am all alone. The ransom of good sleep is that in the waking, when my mind is not yet fully operational enough to wrap a protective shield around me, I miss my parents so deeply that I weep. Is there a child in the world who could ever imagine that in your middle age and, I dare say, your old age too, you remain someone's child inside, capable of being orphaned anew every time you feel lost and alone?

I lie curled on my side in the gloom. I sit on the side of the bed for a while then wash my face with cold water. I put a few lamps on in the place and even venture into the living room in which I do so very little living, and switch on a lamp. I look at the woodburner I installed as a surprise for Claire when she was pregnant with Erland.

'*I'd forgotten you were here,*' I tell it.

'*I'd noticed. Why don't you light me? There's kindling under the stairs still.*'

'*Is there?*'

'*Yeah.*'

I discover there are some old newspapers too. I get an armful of cobweb-strewn logs from the garden and light a fire. I watch the flames and feel the flat grow warm and lonely. There is no text from Claire. I am deeply unimpressed that she can't conjure up a job for a nineteen-year-old she hardly knows.

There's a noise at the front door. I sit up and put the TV on, so as not to look pathetic when Niall walks in. In the silence, I realise it was the letter-box. I order my curry but my heart's not in it and when it arrives it sits in the bag slowly going cold whilst I lie on the kitchen sofa wondering who needs me. I send a message to Erland and Susie on our WhatsApp group, 'GirlBoyGrouch.'

How are you guys? FaceTime tomorrow? All good here. Love you both loads xx

Erland replies immediately: Your tomorrow or my tomorrow?

Susie is fast behind him: Don't even think about starting that my tomorrow/your tomorrow shit again. Anyway, no thanks, I've nothing to say to either of you.

Give me a moment to get over that. (Erland.)

Having adult children is better than Netflix. Better than Robert Harris, although less well structured. I find myself staring vacantly at the floor imagining Susie having a baby with Mark, then Mark deserting her or dying, and Susie bringing the baby home for me to help raise it. In the movie *Jerry Maguire*, there is one of the crudest of plot points, where Tom Cruise falls for Renée Zellweger and child and Renée tells us, conveniently, that not only is the child's father dead but that he was a bastard. So he's not in the way and he's not to be mourned. Nice and easy. That's how my fantasies go. People like Mark get killed off or shipped off, so I can have things just how I want them. My own children producing kids in a manner that leaves me as the main carer. Take me to Hollywood.

A FaceTime is arranged for tomorrow. I open the lid of my curry carton, breathe in the smell and feel no inclination to eat anything. I make a call.

'Where are you?'

'Out and about,' Niall says. 'Have you had a productive day?'

'Very,' I say. 'Very, very productive.' Using the word 'very' makes my case watertight.

There's silence down the line, the polite form of '*Why are you calling?*'

'Everything okay?' Niall asks.

'Oh . . . yes, totally fine.' I reply far too loudly and quickly. 'Just didn't know where you were that's all or exactly what time you were coming back but the only reason I rang was just to mention that I've got all I needed to do done, I've had an excellent day, so if you are desperate to head home then that's fine.'

'No, it's okay. I'm out for the night, don't worry.'

'Fine. Sounds good. I've got loads else to enjoy getting on with, it was purely just so you know it is okay to come back if you were, you know, wanting to, at a loose end. I'm easy.'

'Okay. Cheers. I'll see you tomorrow.'

'That's perfect, yes. Okay, really gotta go.'

I end the call and feel manacled to the kitchen sofa by a lack of ideas. The day is ending and I have not found Josie a job and there is no guarantee I will show up for the governor's training courses or my appointment with Mary. I feel half-asleep, lethargic, crumpled. My mind is crammed full but a blank. I am the complete opposite of what I wanted to be by this time.

So, like a man of true wisdom, I decide to top up my good spirits by watching the news. I grab the remote, sling my legs over the sofa arm and settle back. Niall's tablet digs into my lower back. I swear at it, remove it from between the cushions and as I place it down on the floor (the table is out of reach and I'm me) the screen comes to life and I see an email on it that I can't, or don't, ignore. There's a photo of a French newspaper article in the email. On the page of the newspaper is a black-and-white image of a large bear of a man in handcuffs. He has long greasy hair, is unshaven, and wears a baggy T-shirt. If I passed him on the street, I might possibly think this is how Niall could look in twenty years' time if he spends the intervening years eating and smoking and drinking and not sleeping. But I would not mistake the man on the front page of what looks like a regional French newspaper for Niall. Nor would I mistake the headline – *PÉDOPHILE* – for anything other than the French word for a child abuser. There is nothing else in the email, just this photo of a front page, but in the subject line above are the words *The likeness is uncanny* followed by laughing-face emojis. It is no surprise to me at all to see the sender's name is Owen Mankalow, Niall's stepbrother.

I sit forward on the sofa. The tablet goes to sleep. I pick it up and bring it back to life.

Wakey, wakey. I'm going to ask you some questions.

Beneath Niall's inbox I see a folder entitled 'Owen' and I open it. It has thirty or forty emails in it, sent over the last ten years. I open the oldest one first, the subject line of which reads *Happy 21st*. It's a long email and I allow my eyes to land in the middle of it and to scan, as if I don't really want to know what it says.

. . . A LONG COSY CHAT WITH YOUR MUM YESTERDAY EVENING OVER A FEW BOTTLES OF WINE. THE LIGHT WAS LOW AND SHE WAS IN A DRESS AND LOOKED HALF DECENT, COULD ALMOST UNDERSTAND WHAT DAD SEES IN HER. NICE PAIR OF LEGS ON HER YOUR MUM. TAKE A JOKE. I ASKED HER ALL ABOUT YOUR DADDY, AND SHE SPILLED THE BEANS, HOW HE FUCKED OFF AS SOON AS HE MET YOU, HEARD YOU CRYING YOUR FUCKING EYES OUT AND DECIDED 'NAH, NOT FOR ME.' THAT MAN WAS

A FUCKING NOSTRADAMUS, DECIDING HE DIDN'T WANT TO BE YOUR DAD. OH, COME ON, NIALLY BOY, TAKE A JOKE, JUST TEASING. LOVELY WOMAN YOUR MUM AND VERY CHATTY WHEN SHE'S HAD A FEW. SHE AND MY DAD RETIRED TO THE BOUDOIR EARLY AND I HAD TO TURN THE TELLY UP. HAPPY BIRTHDAY YOU MASSIVE HOMO. ATB, OWEN.

I open another with a subject line of *Visit*. There's a chain of emails, starting with Owen who, it seems, only writes to Niall in capital letters.

NIALL – NEED TO BOOK YOU AND YOUR MUM'S TRIP OUT HERE IN THE NEXT HOUR. THERE'S AN OFFER ON EUROSTAR AND I CAN GET TICKETS TO POITIERS RIDICULOUS CHEAP. SHE TALKED ABOUT 12 DAYS FROM AUGUST 17TH. THAT WORK FOR YOU? CONFIRM ASAP AND I'LL BOOK AND YOU CAN PAY ME LATER. O.

Hi Owen – Mum and I always talked about a 5-day trip. There's no way I can take 12 days off work and not at a few weeks' notice. Also, this was always planned for September. Don't worry about rushing it, I'll pay full price, more important Mum and I get the dates straight, but I can only take 5 days off.

NIALL – ALTERNATIVELY, THINK ABOUT YOUR POOR FUCKING MOTHER AND DO THE DATES I'M TALKING ABOUT. REAL WORLD TIME FELLA, GOTTA BOOK NOW, SO CONFIRM.

Owen – relax, I've just spoken to Mum and she understands I can't drop everything at short notice, that was never the plan. She sounded quite stressed about it. Whole point is for her to have a break and get some rest after your dad's shenanigans this year. We'll get back to you about September.

NIALL – HAVE BOOKED YOUR TRIP FOR AUGUST 17TH AS PER MY FUCKING CONVERSATION WITH YOUR MUM. HAVE JUST CALLED HER AND SHE'S LOOKING FORWARD TO IT. I'LL SEND YOU PAYMENT DETAILS.

I won't be coming, Owen, which means that because of you Mum will have to travel alone. Do it in September as we all discussed and I can take 5 days off from work to accompany her.

NIALL, YOUR MUM IS IN TEARS, YOU'RE A PIECE OF SHIT. I'LL COME OVER AND ESCORT HER IF SHE'S TOO NERVOUS ON HER OWN. WELL DONE ON RUINING EVERYTHING. PRICK.

I read an email Niall sent to his stepbrother from a Paris street asking where he is. I read another from a few years ago when Owen writes, *IT'S NOT HARD TO SEE WHY NO ONE TAKES YOU SERIOUSLY AND YOUR MOTHER IS EMBARRASSED BY YOU.* In another, the subject line is *Marriage failure* and Owen invites Niall to spend some time in France with him and his family getting over the ending of his marriage. *I'VE GOT TEN YEARS OF MARRIAGE TO A BEAUTIFUL FRENCH WOMAN WITH CHRISTIAN VALUES BINDING US TOGETHER, IF YOU WANT TO COME AND WATCH AND LEARN SOMETHING YOU'D BE VERY WELCOME.*

There are a couple of very short ones, seemingly sent in isolation, not in reply to anything from Niall.

TAKE RESPONSIBILITY FOR WHAT A SARCASTIC HORRIBLE HUMAN BEING YOU ARE, YOUR TOTAL DISINTEREST IN MY CHILDREN AND WHY YOUR MUM IS

EMBARASSED BY YOU. YOU MUST BE THE LONELIEST FUCKER IN THE WORLD, THE WAY PEOPLE FEEL ABOUT YOU.

IF I EVER HEAR ANOTHER REPORT FROM MY DAD OF YOU DISRESPECTING HIM OR ACCUSING HIM OF ANYTHING I WILL GOUGE YOUR EYES OUT YOU FUCKING BENDER.

I've read enough. I put Niall's tablet on the sofa and stand up. I stretch and let out a loud, rasping breath. And then, without meaning to or planning to, I roar. I just roar with anger, as loud as I can. I look at the tablet and consider closing the inbox and wedging the thing back between the sofa cushions but realise I don't want to pretend I haven't read all this.

I'm hungry. Suddenly, I'm hungry. I turn on the oven and shove the foil containers in. Chances of food poisoning, even higher than if I'd eaten it first time around. Chances of caring, nil. I sit and eat and with Niall's tablet propped up in front of me I forward all his stepbrother's emails to myself. On my laptop I edit them into one document of highlights. Then I email Deborah, Ed's wife.

I'm in town tomorrow for a meeting, very near you. Can I pop in and see you for ten minutes to ask you something?

I finish my curry and get my coat and keys. Outside, there is the lightest of rains, a slow-motion mist caught in the streetlight. It doesn't put me off. The need to walk off my curry is great. I can also decide what my fake meeting in London is about, before Deborah asks me.

I sleep later than usual and when I look at my phone at seven there is an email from Deborah.

Be lovely to see you, Pete. My only free slot is 10.15 to 10.35.
Shame Ed not in town today. Do come by if timing works. Hug xx

I reply, saying, *As it happens, timing is perfect.*

I wear my suit. It feels good to have it on. No tie. I polish my shoes. I have an answer lined up if Debs asks me about my meeting: 'Just a bit of business, might not come to anything.' Brilliant, huh?

I take the train to Blackfriars and walk along Fleet Street to Chancery Lane. Deborah's building overlooks Lincoln's Inn. It's an old building with a modern extension at the back. As I walk two flights up to her office I am warmed by the sun through the glass and by the quality of the rooftops view. This is old London; it reminds me that dense population and fast living and commerce and law and conflict are not a modern invention.

She hugs me and we hold tight for a moment. She sticks her index finger into my chest: 'I want to see you properly, for a drink, with Eddie, and grill you about your life and ask all the questions my useless husband will never ask, until you are very uneasy. But today we've only got a few minutes, so shoot.'

She returns to her desk and I sit the other side of it.

'I need your advice, your reaction to something.'

'Sure.'

I take an envelope from my inside pocket, take out two pages of A4 and slide them across her desk. They contain the worst emails from Niall's stepbrother, and my summary of what he did to Niall in Epping Forest when Niall was fifteen.

I tell her, 'Niall@DrewidGardening is Susie's ex-boyfriend. He's a good guy. Ownman@Gmail is his stepbrother, Owen Mankalow. Is this a hate crime? Can you get an injunction against this sort of thing? What can we do?'

When Debs has finished reading the pages, she sits back and looks out of the window. 'You're not going to change someone like this.'

'All the more reason.'

She looks dubious. 'So, who's married to whom for them to be stepbrothers?'

'Niall's mum married that bully's dad when Niall was fifteen. He beat him up then, and physically threatened him since a few times until Niall grew to be twice his size.'

'Pete, just call the man by his name. Calling him a bully or a bastard or anything like that doesn't strengthen the idea. What do his mother and stepfather know?'

'Nothing.'

'Why hasn't he told his mother or both of them?'

'I can't claim to know, and he has barely talked about this, but I'd guess he is scared of his stepfather and that he's worried it would spoil his mum's happiness. He shrugs it off, says the man's in France, it's once or twice a year, he can live with it.'

'So, why are you . . .' She gestures aimlessly. 'Why this?'

I feel agitated. 'This is not okay, is it?'

'Niall asked you to show me this?'

'Yes.'

She smiles at me. 'Liar,' she says sweetly.

'Yes.'

She looks at me. My turn to find a window to look out of. I've always wanted to be liked by people like Deborah, established, solid, strong, confident people. And yet Claire, who I want to be loved by, found people like Deborah dull and their professional lives unimaginative and she included herself in the description of people she found tiring. She even used to tell me why she saw me as different to that, as more individual. She once said to me, very seriously, that my work

269

life was small but perfectly formed and I helped people find happiness and pleasure with what I knew. Where did that go? Why did she stop thinking that way about me?

I look at Deborah again. This woman could stop working today. She could retire with the man she has been married to for more than half her life and choose what to do every day of her life. She chooses to work strenuously with other people's lives and happiness in the balance, and to spend half her week separated from her husband. All of which only goes to show me that I hardly know or understand Debs and Ed. In friendships, longevity is no guarantee of insight. Relationships need to be nurtured and worked on, fed regularly with new stimuli. I have known this woman for a quarter of a century and I have no clue what really makes her tick. I don't know if and how much she loves Ed. I don't know if she loves work or money or neither in particular. I admire her. I look up to her. I like her. I trust her. But I don't know her well.

But I do know Claire, I really do. And that is something great. That is a privilege but it's not a right. I am going to have to establish my own rights and my own life in order to stop dwelling on being ejected from Claire's. She's done nothing wrong. She didn't stop admiring me and finding me interesting for no reason, or out of spite. She stopped because I stopped doing that thing, being that man. I stopped brightening people's lives, going to any lengths and into great detail to find something perfect for them, creating holidays that would bring them joy, exploring possibilities they hadn't thought of, introducing them to places they didn't know existed, spending hours on sorting out a problem for them that had arisen. I stopped. I just wanted to go home. There was less and less for her to admire.

'You're wasted, Pete. I get the impression that business isn't great for you but even if it was, there's so much about you that doesn't get put to good use.'

270

'That's an incredibly kind thing of you to say.'

She leans forward. 'Cheer up, chicken,' she whispers.

We both smile at the words.

'Your dad always said that to me if I looked serious,' she says.

I don't need reminding. It was one of his phrases.

'Such a lovely man. You must miss him.'

'Nah.'

She laughs. 'I didn't say it to be kind, Pete. I said it because it's true. You could do more. You have so much to give.'

'But, what to do, Debs?'

She comes round from her desk and takes my hand and leads me over to the uninviting, extraordinarily uncomfortable Chesterfield. We sit together.

'I am totally ignorant on that front,' she says. 'I've had one job and I've never had the guts to leave it. I don't know what you do in your situation.'

I immediately hate sounding like a charity case.

'What about Niall?'

She sighs and shrugs. 'Let me talk to someone who knows this kind of thing better than me, but you have to talk to him about asking me, see if he wants any help.' She taps her finger gently on my temple. 'Kind man, he might not.'

I smile at her. 'It's just not okay what that man does and says.'

She nods and shuffles closer and takes hold of my hand, grips it tight to give me strength. 'It's not okay. But the law doesn't change what people are like. The law is bruising, it gives a bully the stage. And it's expensive. We're . . . expensive. The problem with the law is that lawyers think if they can argue a point, they've got a point.'

I nod. I haven't been in a fight since I was a schoolboy. I wouldn't know how to land a proper punch and yet I want to kill Niall's stepbrother right now with my bare hands, out there on the lawns of Lincoln's Inn. Good a place as any to get arrested.

'You want me to set you up with attractive, interesting, lovely, divorced women of our age?' Debs says.

I look at her, and, not knowing whether to laugh or cry, I do nothing other than stare at her blankly. 'No,' I say. 'I honestly don't know.'

'Including my sister, who is gorgeous.'

'I don't think progressing to being Ed's brother-in-law is a great idea.'

'You do know that before and quite possibly instead of the marrying-someone-else bit is the having-a-laugh, going-out, dating, doing-nice-stuff and shagging bit? You don't have to marry her, Pete. She might not want to marry you.'

'Sex, laughs and company? Sounds awful. Ed probably told you he and I had a bust-up.'

She looks horrified. 'No, he didn't mention anything.'

'Really?'

Why the hell hasn't he mentioned a bust-up with his oldest friend? It should be eating him alive.

'Man fails to tell wife details of his male friendships – shocker,' Debs says.

She has a point.

Something good happens after my meeting with Deborah as I stroll aimlessly and get myself a coffee in a bright, modern, concrete square which is towered over by ugly modern office blocks. I watch thousands of people passing me, coming out of the dense shadows of the buildings into the blinding light. Others march through swing-door security, lanyards around their necks, most of them rushing, most of them with phones to their ears, bags under their eyes. And I feel lucky not to have their jobs.

I know none of them would want to swap places with me, take on my salary, or absence of, and lifestyle, the lack of. But I wouldn't swap with them either. And if getting the last twenty years back, and along with them the chance to never lose Claire, meant coming to work in a place like this, at a pace like this, and being on a train every evening when my children were being read to and tucked in, I wouldn't take it. I would take what I had and start from this point on with what I've got. And that is a very good thing for me to realise.

I let the sunshine beat down on my face. With eyes closed, I listen to the buzz of the square, the voices passing close by, heels tapping the paving, men laughing under their breaths, exasperation pouring into phones, the milk frother in the rickshaw I got my coffee from. Somewhere distant, a lorry rattles over a bump in the road.

I have the rest of the day ahead of me and London at my disposal, but I am itching to go home. I'm not sure if this is a good thing or not but I am going to trust myself. I leave the square, which has been good to me for ten minutes, done me a favour, and head towards the river and the station that these days sits across it. At Blackfriars, on the platform, another good thing happens. Erland and Susie FaceTime me, as planned. I had forgotten and that is unheard of. If I had been at home today, I would have been waiting all morning for this call and realising that makes me shudder. Erland is in bed, Susie is outside her office. I am a hundred feet above the River Thames, in a suit, returning from a meeting, doing a good impression in front of my kids of having a life.

Imagine if I really actually did have stuff to do, work to occupy me, money enough to stop waking up in the middle of the night in the arms of fear. Wouldn't that be good?

I remind myself that this is possible, essential, that one day I will sleep soundly again, wake up excited. From that, who knows what might happen?

My children express their amazement that I am not in my flat. Erland asks me, 'Work or pleasure?'

'Work,' I lie.

They seem lost for words.

Back home, as I turn the corner on to my street, I realise I am not quite ready for company yet. I go back up the hill to the bus stop and wait for a 737. I sit there for twenty minutes, happily; I am, after all, trying to elongate the day. I feel content waiting there. Life has a momentary calm and I've always been a sucker for that. I feel blank. That's why I feel good, because I do not feel scared or sad or angry or self-pitying. Neither do I feel confident or clear or robust. I feel blank. This could be the emotional equivalent of neutral buoyancy under the water.

The 737 takes me to a lookout across the Surrey Hills that Claire and I used to go to often, especially when we were first married. We came up here with boozy picnics after we discovered that a bus went from the end of our road to the summit. We came here to talk about starting a family. We came here when Claire was heavily pregnant with Erland and I had to stand behind her and push her back up the hill after we had strolled down into the valley. There really is an angle of slope which is impossible for a heavily pregnant person to walk up. Not everyone knows that.

It's good to be back at this spot. I'm going to catch the sunset. A lot of my life is beneath me here, scattered amongst the roads, fields and urban sprawl. I wonder about living somewhere else. I don't have anywhere in mind. I don't have anything in mind. But the mere idea sits with me as I look at the view.

I could. That's all.

I am not obliged to live here for the rest of my life.

That is all, for now.

When I get home at six, I've been in my own company and headspace (save for twenty minutes with Deborah and a ten-minute FaceTime with the kids) for nearly two days and it's been good for me. Lonely at times, empty in parts, but that is exactly what I must get through. Today I have made a start.

When I woke shivering on my bed twenty-four hours ago, I knew, for a few vivid moments before the tears came, that I did not want to be alone. More than anything, I do not want that. More than keeping things as unchanged as possible for Susie and Erland, and being there for them whenever they come back, more than being available for Claire if she has a change of heart, because being devoted to her is the one significant thing I can think of doing with my life without breaking sweat – more than those things, I do not want to be alone. And that means that the first thing I need is to be living by myself.

Niall is in the kitchen, slumped on the sofa, drinking tea and watching *Countdown*. The warmth of the smile he gives me suggests he is over his sulk at being evicted for a day. Perhaps, then, he is ready to try it full-time.

'Hello,' he says.

'More tea?' I say.

'Yes, please.'

There's a meekness to his voice, as if he knows what's coming. It immediately makes the job in hand harder. But something is different now, because sitting in that sunny square in London surrounded by the powerful and the haunted of Deloitte and Goldman Sachs (I looked the place and its tenants up on Google Maps on the train home, which I thought was quite digital of me), I understood that I am clinging on and that if I do not change something now, I might never recover. It is not a given that we remain at or even close to the best version of ourselves.

He gets up from the sofa, punches the cushions into shape, puts his tablet aside and joins me at the kitchen counter. He pours the dregs of his last tea into the sink and hands me the mug.

'Sit down,' I say. 'I'll bring it over.'

I had planned to come clean with Niall about reading all his stepbrother's emails, before he works it out for himself. Like any man half-wanting to get caught, I didn't cover my tracks. But as I look at him now, I wonder if he would find it embarrassing to acknowledge that I know the detail of how he is treated by that man. Does Niall live in fear of him? I doubt it. But it is humiliating to be singled out and bullied, and who wants to admit to humiliation? Owen Mankalow is a father and husband with friends and colleagues, which suggests he is nice to most people. So why isn't he nice to Niall? This must be a side to being bullied that you don't want to share, the fact that you've been singled out.

I give Niall his tea and sit beside him on the sofa. He thanks me. I switch off the TV and turn to him.

'Uh-oh,' he says.

'Your stepbrother,' I say. 'You do know . . . it is not okay what he does.'

He doesn't ask me how I would know. He doesn't tell me he knows how I would know. He just nods. 'I know,' he says.

'It's not okay.' I swallow and my words get trapped in my throat. 'Ed's wife can help you. If you want . . . She can advise you if you ever want to take action.'

Niall looks at me. I have no idea what he is thinking. He is quiet today, outside and inside. His eyes search me for a moment. 'I don't need it,' he says. 'Thank you.'

He takes a sip of his tea and switches the telly on again.

'Can't believe I switched *Countdown* off for that,' he says.

'It's not okay, what he does,' I repeat.

He mutes the TV, sighs theatrically and smiles at me. 'I'm glad I told you about it. It reminded me how pathetic he is. He won't change. Thanks for talking to her. It feels good. He is pathetic. I'll ask for help if anything changes.'

'Okay.'

Niall gets up and goes to the fridge. 'I feel like cooking something.'

From the sofa, sitting on the edge of it, I turn and watch him. 'Niall . . .'

'Yeah . . .'

I feel sad. I feel bad. I feel blank.

'Niall, I'm going to have this place to myself now. I need to find out what it is I'm thinking and going to do.'

He smiles at me and nods. 'You've been so kind to me, for a miserable old loser like yourself. It's been great. Thanks.'

'Welcome.'

'Go and have one of your vaudeville baths and I'll cook something tremendous.'

'You ever watched *Inception*?'

'Probably fifteen times. Gladly watch it again, though. Really. I love that movie.'

'Can you explain it to me as we go?'

'Afraid not. I've no idea what it's about.'

Chapter 20

I march in to work. I catch myself doing it, make myself slow down, and the next thing I know I am marching again. It's like finally plucking up the courage to jump from the high board and knowing that if you don't take a run at it now, you never will. And it is this fingers–in–the–ears–singing–'la–la–la' approach to a grave job in hand that allows me to mess it up so badly.

I position three chairs around my desk, push my computer to one side so that we can all see each other and ask Mrs H, Silent Si and Josie to gather round for a meeting. I notice Si smile knowingly to himself, it's almost a chuckle.

'Look,' I say, and my mouth dries up at the fact that this is happening, no longer an abstract idea hanging over me, but real and about to become so to these three people whose reactions I have not stopped to guess at, predict or think how to handle.

'Look. There is no easy way to tell you that I have decided to close the business immediately. It's losing money and if I don't take action now, it'll kill me. None of which is fair on any of you.'

Si nods his head and his expression seems almost affectionate, which is kind of disturbing. Josie is listening intently, her face set rigid in a soft kind smile. Mrs H has bowed her head slightly and I can't see her face. I am shaking but already feeling the adrenaline of liberation at sharing – at offloading – this news.

'I've let you down. I feel terrible and . . . I'm sorry. I really am.'

I hear Josie's voice first. It's faint and warm. 'It's okay,' she says, to assure me.

'Yeah,' Si says, backing her up in a way that I am staggered by. 'You have to, Pete, it's ridiculous to carry on.'

'I've loved it,' Josie says, and a tear escapes onto her cheek. 'Sorry.'

'You don't owe me anything,' Si says. 'Except some money, obviously.' He laughs. I laugh too, with relief.

We all look to Mrs H as she looks up at me, with a face, as my mum used to say, of thunder. Her jaw is clenched, and she grinds the words out through her teeth.

'You owe me not doing it like this,' she says, and goes back to her desk.

I look at Si and Josie and all of us show our unease. It suddenly feels like we're working in a funeral parlour. Although, I guess we've been doing a pretty good impression of that for a while now. I whisper to them, 'Business as usual for now and I'll . . .' I stop whispering and mouth the words, 'talk to Mrs H.'

They both nod.

'I'm sorry,' I say again.

They go back to their desks. Josie has a little cry, with her back turned to the room. When she swivels round again and taps her keyboard, she is calm and dry-eyed.

I spend a bit of time in the back office to allow Mrs H the opportunity to come and talk and I curse myself for not telling her first and separately. That is, of course, what I should have done; she's been here for ever. I presumed I'd have her instant support because she knew it was coming, but how insensitive

279

and stupid of me not to have talked to her first. I was just so desperate to get it done, having finally located the balls to do it, and as a result I have bulldozed this elderly woman into a retirement that is due by tradition but not her choice.

When I glance up, my heart sinks at seeing Mrs H putting her coat on, standing by her tidied desk – cleared, some might say – and with a carrier bag of her stuff on the chair. She moves quietly so as not to draw attention to herself and is at the door by the time I have run across the shop floor to stop her. She opens the door and I take hold of it, shut it a little so that she has to remain on the threshold with me. She is angry, I can tell, but before I can apologise for getting this so wrong, she says something to me that is like a punch in the stomach.

'Thank God your parents can't see this.'

The words rock me backwards. I feel sick with shock. Her face is tight and mean and she won't look me in the eye. Instantly, I see this person, who I have known for fifty years, differently.

'Yes,' I say, opening the door wide for her to leave. 'Thank God both my mum and my dad are dead and I and my children will never see them ever again.' I usher her out and close the door gently behind her, stealing the time as I do so to gather myself and put on a smile for the others. I return to my desk depressed by the encounter.

Si has watched the whole thing. 'She's not coming back.'

'Don't say that,' Josie says.

'She'll be here in the morning,' I say. 'She's angry and she has every right.'

I get down to work, checking Si and Josie's contracts and transferring a severance pay into their accounts. Si seems unsure as to what to do and, after a while, sits back from his desk, swivels his chair to look out onto the high street and chews on his pencil. Josie answers the phone and, sensibly, takes down numbers and says an agent will get back to them. I am referring here to the three calls that we receive all morning.

The clock given to my grandfather when he retired from the Prudential chimes for noon. He worked for them as a caretaker, for forty-nine years, except for five when he served in the Second World War. I have done nothing for the last hour but delete old emails and now I simply want to close this place down as quickly as possible. You spend a few years avoiding something and then want it done by teatime.

'Guys . . .' I say.

Si and Josie look up.

'Tell me something. I've paid you both three months' salary. It's in your accounts. What I really want to do now is pack this place up, right now. I just want to get on with it. It's not in your job description but, would you mind?'

'It's one month's pay, my contract,' Si says.

'I know, but you're both getting three.'

'Thanks,' Si says. 'Are you sure, I mean . . .'

'I couldn't be more sure.'

'Thank you so much,' Josie says.

'Let's get stuck in then,' Si says.

He's like a different person. And it strikes me that he's grateful. He might be the only person on planet Earth less motivated than me, or less capable of change. Perhaps he's been wanting me to force his hand for years.

'I've made a little list,' I say. 'Over the next day or two I'll need you both to delete any personal emails from your inbox and change your password to something unconnected to you so I can have access to your client emails. But today, I actually want to shut this place down, physically. I want to tidy it up, send things to the tip for recycling or trashing, get anything we can sell up on Gumtree.'

'Cool,' Josie says.

'I don't know how to do that, by the way,' I say.

Josie nods, in a way that confirms no one thinks I would know how to sell anything on Gumtree. 'I can do all that,' she says.

'I wish we had blinds,' I say.

We get down to it. I box up all the paperwork in the back office alongside a few boxes from my parents' era that I have never thrown out. I make a pact with myself that if I haven't needed to go into any of these boxes by the time someone else moves into the shop, I'll bin them. Yes, deep down in one of them might be some photos of a trip, or a note to me from Dad or Mum, but I'm replete with good memories and even if I live to be a hundred, I shouldn't make time to trawl through twenty boxes of the past.

Whilst Josie and Si are out getting a sandwich, I record an answerphone message.

'Hello. This is Peter Smith. Smith's Holidays has ceased trading and the shop is now closed for business. I have loved serving my community's travel needs for many years but now is the time for me to begin an exciting new venture. My best wishes to you all and my sincere thanks to you for your custom over the years.'

I sound about seventy-eight years old.

The three of us work all afternoon at packing up. We get into a rhythm and, personally, I have not felt this good for a long time. I call Si into the back office at one point and apologise again. And I thank him for his attitude. His body language has changed slightly. It's a subtle shift but it's as if he is free to be himself and to like me a bit. He's never said a rude word to me, never disagreed with anything, but neither has he ever said a kind word or looked happy to be here. My first thought is that it's sympathy that is the difference, that you've just got to feel a little sympathy for a man closing down his family business, but then I suspect that what's changed is that he's let go of the resentment he brought with him to work every day, for me having him in this shitty job which, whilst it was still on offer, he dared not leave.

'I've been thinking about this for ages,' he says, 'the fact that I don't particularly like working with people, so I might go back to painting and decorating, my first job. I think I'd get loads of custom from my parents' friends, and I like the idea of being on my own listening to podcasts, not being at a desk. People appreciate a job well done if you have a trade. I could learn a language whilst I'm working, which is pretty awesome.'

'Sounds good,' I say.

I'm smiling at him having said so casually that he doesn't like working with people.

Later, I steal a moment with Josie too. 'I'm sorry I can't set you up in a new job.'

She shrugs, smiles and shakes her head to tell me it's not my fault. (It is actually.)

'I did wonder . . .' she says. 'Thing is, I think I do like selling holidays and stuff. And I suppose I wondered if you could recommend me to other travel agents, people you know really well, and you can influence.'

I can do one of two things here: promise her I will and get her hopes up, knowing already I can't, or come clean.

'Josie, I already have. I called my contacts and none of them are looking for people.'

'Oh.' She smiles bravely. 'That's so kind of you to do that.'

I watch her taking the display panels off the walls. I ought to be able to send that woman into three or four meetings with exciting travel companies, but I have not kept those professional ties watered and fed, I have not nurtured and re-booted them with new information and fresh ideas. What if I am failing to do that with Susie and Erland too? The thought of stagnating with them terrifies me. I write the letters E and S on the back of my left hand, the sort of temporary tattoo that teens use to remind themselves to do their homework reminding me not to mess up with my children.

We get into a rhythm and get a lot done. Maybe I could shut down family businesses for a living. I order pizza, beer and wine, and we work late.

'Are you going to write about this?' Si asks Josie. (He's initiating conversation now; the world's gone mad.) 'Are you going to do stand-up about us, the sad old bastards at the firm that closed down?'

'Thanks for that, Si,' I say.

'Um . . .' Josie says, looking confused. 'Say something funny about you? I'm a stand-up, Si, not a magician.'

I walk home at nine in the evening, feeling tired and slightly drunk. I call Mrs H and am relieved when I hear it go to voicemail. 'It's Pete. I got things badly wrong today, should have talked to you about it first and given you time to get used to the idea and to help me if you wanted to. I apologise, I'm really sorry.'

Having left the message, I don't feel concerned about how she responds. After what she said to me earlier, she's a different person to me. I'll find it easy to get on with her if she turns up tomorrow, and I'll not lose sleep if she doesn't.

I'm pleased Niall is home when I get back. I'm pleased he notices that I look worn out and I like that he gets up off the kitchen sofa and offers to make me tea. I wash my face with cold water. I light the fire. I sit there and wait for Niall. He enters the living room like a cat tentatively checking out a new home.

'You've got a living room,' he says.

'I know! Nice, isn't it?'

I tell him about closing down the business. He listens without interrupting and doesn't seem to consider it big news.

'Good idea,' he says, throwing his legs up over the arm of the sofa he is on.

I am sitting on the rug, my back against the other sofa, watching the fire and drinking my tea.

'Why would you possibly need a premises or staff to sort people's holidays out for them?'

I nod, my way of defending how I've done things up until today whilst implying that I agree.

Niall sits forward, goes as far as to put his cup of tea down, such is the importance of what he wants to say to me. And he does that weird thing of his where he stares at me and waits for me to see him. I'm wise to it, though still slightly unnerved by it, and enjoy avoiding eye contact for as long as possible.

'So, you are in this amazing position now,' he says. 'Your master plan can be to use all your travel contacts to create a world trip, a silver-top gap year—'

'I'm not grey – my hair's not bad for someone of my age.'

'An environmentally friendly mega-trip, over land and sea where possible, but some flying, fuck it, life's too short, writing a blog with all your experience and knowledge about the trip and setting yourself up as a very experienced travel guru for elite clients. Get followers and start trending.'

'Yeah . . . I could pretend I was trying out places for a new venture, use all the air miles I've got and get loads of discounted travel and accommodation if I made out that it was a blog for a new travel company, ethically sound scuba or something like that.'

'Yeah,' Niall sighs and throws himself back on the sofa, 'you could pretend you were doing this as part of setting up an ethically sound scuba travel company, or . . .'

He stands up.

'YOU COULD ACTUALLY FUCKING SET UP AN ETHICALLY SOUND SCUBA HOLIDAY COMPANY!'

'Keep your hair on,' I say, what with it being 1950 and everything.

'And have, you know, the coolest job in the world!'

'Sit down, Niall.'

'And if you still don't get any sex even with a job like that, you'll finally just know that you are primordially unattractive.'

'It'll be nice to have that confirmed.'

'Stop living hypothetically! This is it. You're on. The clock is ticking. At least go somewhere. Your adult life has been travel – doing it, then selling it. You have no idea what to do with your life now, so just go on a trip. Anywhere. Go somewhere and see what happens.'

'Can you stop talking?'

'Who knows? I've never tried.'

I watch the flames. Incredibly, Niall remains quiet for an extended period of time. At a certain point he leaves and later he calls out, 'Goodnight.'

'Come here a sec,' I call back.

He returns.

'Do something for me?'

'Sure.'

I watch the glow of a dying fire and can't believe I am about to admit this to him, but I need to go, and I can't trust myself to do so.

'I have an appointment at two o'clock tomorrow with a hypnotherapist.'

I wait for him to laugh.

'I have to go to it, but I'll not want to.'

'Cool, cool,' Niall says. 'Night.'

I have no idea what 'Cool, cool' means and I'm nonplussed by his lack of shock at the seismic admission of weakness that I need therapy. It's as if it's no surprise to him at all.

Chapter 21

I discover what Niall means by 'Cool, cool' the next day when he walks me to my appointment.

'This is fine, Niall,' I say, as we walk along the river. 'I've got it from here.'

'I'll come in with you.'

'Incorrect.'

'Moral support.'

I stop dead. 'Thanks for walking me into town. Now go away. And don't tell anyone about this. Not my daughter, not my ex-wife, not anyone.'

'Can I tell the estate agent?'

'*No!* Christ!'

'He talks to me quite a bit. I like him. And I really hate keeping secrets.'

'When? When do you even see him?'

'At viewings. He does viewings and tries to tiptoe in. See? I can't keep a secret. I've bumped into him showing people in a few times.'

I bow my head and take a deep breath. 'Niall, are you listening?'

'Yup.'

'Don't, please, don't—'

'I can hear a sand martin.' He swivels round and looks at the riverbank.

'Are you listening, Niall?'

'Yuh . . .' he says, studying the water's edge.

'Don't tell my ex-wife's estate agent I'm seeing a hypnotherapist, okay?'

'Sure.' He doesn't move.

'You turn back, I've got this.'

He looks at his watch. 'You asked me to make sure you don't skip this. I'll see you to the door then I'll go.'

He's not going to back down, so I walk on. When we get to the high street, I stop in my tracks. On the opposite side of the street, a building that has been inhabited by a stream of pound shops and pop-ups for the last decade, is being refitted. I recognise the deep-blue and mustard-yellow paintwork on the shopfront and on the large poster pinned to the window announcing, *CAFÉ DES VIEUX AMIS, COMING SOON!*

I watch three men fitting out the restaurant interior, and a man and a woman on the pavement applying shiny gloss paint to the ornate frames of the large shopfront windows. I gaze at the poster, with a picture of the interior of the other Café des Vieux Amis, in Shepperton, the one Claire and I knew well. I feel a little bit sick.

'What is it?' Niall asks.

'Nothing,' I say. But I don't move.

'Really, what's up?' Niall says.

'Nothing,' I mutter. I walk away. Niall follows and sees me to the door, where I turn to face him and look as if I'm really grateful, then say, 'Fuck off.'

He laughs. 'Sure you don't want me to come in with you?'

'You haven't asked me why I'm here.'

'I like to mind my own business.'

'But seriously.'

'I'm not shocked. Let's leave it there.'

I hate that.

'It's a shame you're not a smoker,' he says.

'Why?'

'Two for the price of one,' he says.

'What do you mean?'

'Kill two birds with one stone. Make two friends with one gift. Two needs, one deed.'

'Niall, I understand what two for the price of one means. I just don't get how it applies here.'

'Hypnotists are good at getting you to quit smoking – he'd be able to sort that out too.'

'It's a she, and she's a hypnotherapist not a hypnotist. And, yeah, it's a real shame that I don't have a life-threatening drug habit I need help getting over.'

Niall steps back and clasps his hands together in a *courage-mon-brave* gesture. 'It's like you're changing but you're still totally you,' he says.

'What is that meant to mean?'

'Enjoy therapy,' he says, and laughs as he goes.

I turn and look at the grey door. There are three buzzers and the top one reads, *MARY BLAIR*.

I am still climbing the stairs and breathing in the smell of incense when she calls out, 'You did it! You're here.'

'It's not too late to turn back,' I reply.

But who am I kidding? I want to be here. I love the smell of the place and all this crap about not wanting to share my feelings is exactly that. I'm desperate to share them, I just don't know who with.

The room is nice. It has the feel of a big, converted attic, largely due to it being a big, converted attic. I don't know how to sit on my chair – cross-legged, upright, hands on thighs, hands under thighs, one arm over the back, all casual.

Mary hands me a clipboard.

'The consent form, Peter. I've filled in most of it.'

Mary has filled in my name and address. I add 'Flat 1' to the address, and in a box inviting me to describe my reasons for being here I write, *DIVORCE / WORK / GENERAL.*

'Sometimes,' Mary says, 'people come to a hypnotherapist with a specific concern or problem they want to address. Plenty of times, it's not so clear.'

'I want to feel happy,' I remind her.

'And even being able to say that is a heck of a thing,' Mary says.

I shrug. I'm still trying to work out how to sit and where to look. Still and at Mary is the mature and rational choice but it's not coming easily to me.

'I'm going to describe what this process is, and, importantly, what it isn't. And we'll do some visual hypnotherapy, very gentle, aimed to help you view things differently. But it might be good to have time to talk today, so we can discover what you want.'

'I want Claire back.'

'And what you can actually have.'

'Ah,' I say.

'You don't look comfortable,' she says.

'I'm about to pour my heart out to our old babysitter. I'm *not* comfortable.'

'I mean, that chair isn't your friend.' She leads me to a massive beanbag by the window. 'Use that,' she says. 'I think it's what you need.'

I lower myself onto the Jabba-the-Hutt-like beanbag with all the grace of a camel on a dinghy but none of the discomfort. I slouch, because the beanbag gives you no choice, and feel the sun on my face.

Mary pulls her chair across the room to me. This might be a tactical diversion which she uses, to start someone in an uncomfortable chair and then lead them to the beanbag of comfort, a way of creating an immediate problem which she can solve, of appearing indispensable to my well-being within five minutes of arriving. Clever? Manipulative? Who cares.

Or perhaps I'm over-thinking.

'I'm getting me one of these beanbags,' I say. 'But I'm on the brink of moving Susie's ex-boyfriend out of the flat. I cannot afford to get one of these in until he's gone because if he sees this, he'll never go.'

'Is that a cause of stress for you, Susie's ex?'

I look at Mary. 'Don't say this to anyone, but without him these last few weeks, I think I might have gone insane.'

'Peter . . . what would you like to talk about, to begin with?'

'There is something that's come up, it might be a bit of an anecdote, a distraction, but it feels like something I could tell you.'

'Sounds good,' she says.

She is poised and comfortable in her chair. The clipboard and pen have been put aside, which I like.

'There's a café opening in the high street, called Café des Vieux Amis.'

She nods. She's probably seen it. It might even vie for her attention with the Boatshed.

'The people who run it have another Café des Vieux Amis, in Shepperton – it's been there for years and years. Claire and I liked it.'

I stop, unsure exactly where to start this possibly unhelpful story.

'I'm worried we'll run out of time,' I say. 'For you to do your other stuff.'

'You don't have to worry about time, Peter.'

I do actually. I'm fifty-three and it's running out.

'This thing happened ten years ago, when the children were teenagers. I was trying to make contacts in Cuba to offer dive packages there and Claire told me I should take a week away and go there and do it properly. I had always wanted to dive the Embudo de Coral, the funnel of coral, out there. I booked it. Then, not long before I was going, Claire got asked by work to go on a long-weekend work thing to a Formula 1 testing centre in Germany. I mean, she was a data analyst for an accountancy firm and all of a sudden her job threatened to be seriously more interesting than she imagined.'

'Sounds very cool,' Mary says.

'It was. It is. And I said, obviously, I'd cancel my trip so she could go. Claire didn't want me to, she felt I needed to get back to doing something for myself not related to the children. My parents offered to stay at ours whilst Claire was away in Germany and take care of the kids. You actually babysat Susie on the Saturday evening because my mum and dad were out with friends and Erland was at a mate's.'

'I do remember. I thought you and your wife had a very cool life, which your dad told me all about in proud detail.'

'There you go, didn't know if you'd remember.'

The room falls quiet for a moment and I feel the weight of having to continue. Talking is quite hard work when one is generating the words, not just responding to someone else.

'So . . .' Mary says.

'Claire and I were flying back into Heathrow the same afternoon and we decided to meet at Café des Amis for dinner. I couldn't wait to see her. It was like we'd been away for ages, the way we hugged and kissed and the fact that she screamed with delight when she first saw me after a week apart. Her eyes had that spark in them, when she's full of ideas. I've seen that spark when we've planned holidays, treats for the children, things to do with the house, special occasions for her parents. She snogged me right there in the restaurant. She had two glasses of champagne on the table for us and she said she couldn't wait to tell me about her weekend.'

I try to sit forward on the beanbag, but it's not easy. It's what the thing is designed to prevent you doing.

'Can I ask you a question?' I say.

'Yes,' Mary says.

'What do you think this is going to be about, what I'm telling you?'

She shrugs. 'I'm not sure if that matters. I don't have preconceptions. I listen.'

'Fair enough. I need to sit on that chair, same height as you.'

'Go for it, whatever works.'

But I find I cannot get to my feet from the beanbag. I try twice but get nowhere and, before I can stop myself, I am instinctively rolling sideways off the bag onto my knees and crawling to my feet. I will never be able to reverse or erase this moment. It is what I will remember on my deathbed.

'Actually, I might stand, if you don't mind.'

She doesn't.

'Claire was an accountant. She became a data analyst. Her company were approached by F1 because they were making the link between F1 and data and engineering and stuff I still don't totally understand, applying their ways of developing technology to all sorts of amazing stuff like medical equipment and irrigation. She was put on the team and this thing blew her mind. She talked and talked over dinner about what she'd been shown at this innovation lab, apologised for doing all the talking but I asked her to keep going, said I loved listening to her talk about this.'

'And was that true?'

'Hundred per cent. It was interesting – and seeing her so fired up, I always loved that. She hides it from me these days to be kind, but I love that about her, she's very cool.'

Mary smiles. I fall silent. I gaze at an indistinct spot on the floor behind the legs of Mary's chair.

'What happened in Café des Amis?' she says.

'I can tell you what didn't happen. What didn't happen was me being honest with my wife about my week in Cuba. When I told her the diving had been great, I lied. For the second half of the week, I wasn't in the water, I was in my hotel room.'

I can see Mary's expression change, although she is almost hiding it.

'Before I went to Cuba, I had about two thousand hours of dive experience under my belt. I knew my stuff. Cuba was beautiful but I was lonely the moment I got there. I hated being away from my family. There's not much to do on the Isle of Youth apart from dive or sunbathe. From day one I was thinking about how many nights until I flew home. On the third day we dived the blue cave, where you go vertically down, head first, through a funnel for forty metres and come out in this translucent blue space. In the funnel it's a solid wall of fish that part as you move through them. It's hectic and tight and panicky. I was aware that I was gulping my air. You think it's never going to end then finally it opens out and deposits you in the cave and you are in pure colour, no features, no coral, just blue. No sense of what's up and what's down. And I had this sensation of being incredibly close to Erland and Susie, of them in their mother's womb. I stared at the blue and floated. I felt so connected to them. I just floated and then suddenly it didn't feel nice – I missed them so much that I felt scared. I looked around and I couldn't see my buddy, who I had teamed up with on the boat and didn't know at all. Something felt terrifying. I thought it was the children, then I realised I couldn't breathe. I wasn't getting any air. I looked at my regulator and I was out.'

Mary is leaning forward, her elbows resting on her knees, watching me intently.

'I tried to fill my lungs with the last vestiges of air in the tank and I turned three-sixty, looking into the blue, and I saw the vague shape of my group far away and higher. I started moving towards them. My heart was thumping, it was all I could hear. I fought the urge to move fast because it only slows you down and I had one breath in my lungs and nothing else. I felt that I was getting no closer. I had as much time left to live as I could hold my breath. And I heard Susie crying from somewhere in the water around me. When they were little, Susie and Erland would sometimes wake in the night and cry out for one of us. It didn't happen often but when it did, the sound would break my heart. "Daddy, Daddy." One of us would go in. I loved going in, the way they stopped crying the moment the door opened, their snuffly breath as they settled, the sound of their breathing as they slept and the rise and fall of their body beneath my hand. One night, I couldn't wake myself up properly, but Susie was calling out my name, "Daddy, Daddy . . ." and I was half-asleep still and it turned into a nightmare, in which I had died and Susie didn't understand and at night she lay in bed crying and calling out for her dead dad. That's what I could hear beneath the water. My lungs and my heart wanted to rip open and let the water in and all I could hear was my little child's voice, out there in the blue, sobbing my name. And finally, after what felt like a few minutes but was probably a minute at most, one of them turned. It was the dive master. He was huge, a free-diving champion in Cuba. He came towards me. I signalled that I was out of air . . .'

I find myself doing the signal to Mary, instinctively. It's a slashing motion across the neck.

As he got nearer, I saw the expression in his eyes change through his mask – he could see I was in desperate trouble. Now all I could hear were the sinewy, throttling sounds of my body trying to hold its breath. And suddenly his hand was on my face, pushing his mouthpiece into my mouth, holding the back of my head with his other hand. I drew in the air from his tank. I was calm. Despite this monumental mistake, I was hugely experienced, and I knew now to take in his air slowly. It had to last the both of us, even though he could go without any for extraordinary lengths of time. When our slow, staggered, air-sharing ascent to the surface was finally complete, and I took my mask off and breathed clean air, I was calmer still. I turned to him and said, "Thank you," and he patted my shoulder and helped me onto the boat and said something in Spanish to the crew, then he circled above the rest of the dive group on the surface, watching until they had all returned.'

I go back to my chair. I sit back on it, feeling comfortable now. I look out of the window at the blue sky.

'I lay down on the deck for some time, wrapped in a towel. I was in shock. A fat man in an apron brought me sugary coffee. I moved my head in slow motion and smiled at him. You know what he did?'

Mary shakes her head.

'He leaned over and kissed my forehead. As he stood above me, he smiled and in a husky Spanish accent, he said, "Safe." And when he did that, I knew I had nearly died.'

297

Mary smiles. I smile too, the same deeply content, joyful smile I had on my face back then as I sat up and drank my coffee on that old Cuban boat.

'I looked at the water and I knew that I would never dive again. I said my goodbye to the deep. All I could think of was my children being told I was never coming home, of them growing up without me.'

I stop talking for a moment. I have never told anyone what I have just told Mary. Nobody knows a thing about it.

'Claire said, "I've been talking all evening." She has a sweet tooth, I don't. Her pudding arrived. Her eyes lit up at the sight of it. She dug her spoon in and rested her arm against mine. "Cuba," she said. "Was it amazing?"

'I pressed my arm against hers, rested my head against her head.

'She whispered, "Can't wait to be in bed with you."

'I whispered back, "Can I just say that Cuba is beautiful and leave it at that? I would not be able to do it justice."

'She smiled and kissed me then said, "That's going to be a nice short brochure. Save a fortune on printing. 'Cuba is beautiful, that's all you need to know, book here.'"

'She laughed and ate her pudding and we went home and got on with our lives and occasionally Cuba would come up, and I'd be able to honestly say that Havana is amazing and the diving is stunning but the dive centres need better equipment, because, guess what, yes, I dived badly and got distracted, but when the boat got back to the dive centre it turned out the gauges were faulty and my tank had been half-empty from the start. But it changed me totally. I lost all confidence in myself, I felt useless and old. And I felt my only job in life was to stay alive for my kids. Now I realise that was my main job, but not the only one. Too late.'

I look at her. She looks back at me intently and her eyes might even be close to tears.

'It's never too late,' she says. She sits back, moves her head to loosen her neck. 'Well, actually, that's not true. It is sometimes too late for some people. But not you.'

'After that, on dive trips with work I said I couldn't dive due to an ear infection or an injury. I did that for years. I have felt scared ever since Cuba, and I've never told anyone.'

Mary's tone and her body language change subtly, to something more forensic. 'Describe your marriage in one word,' she says.

'Perfect.'

She nods to herself. We sit in silence. I'm drained and want to go now.

'Until the divorce, obvs,' I say.

She nods again and looks me in the eye. 'Between now and our next appointment I want you to ask yourself why you didn't tell Claire. And I want you to tell me the answer when I see you.'

I didn't know there'd be homework and the request unnerves me. I stand up. I smile at Mary, with an emerging sense that I'm never going to come back here.

'I need some air,' I say.

Pardon the pun.

I go to the door. 'Thank you,' I say, and I leave.

On the pavement, I'm concerned that I have just been very rude. I text Mary:

Sorry, I didn't mean to leave so abruptly. Apologies if I was rude.

That's me to a tee. Do something a tiny bit dramatic because I feel something strongly, then immediately apologise for it and feel like a tool.

Mary replies:

You have nothing to apologise for and you weren't rude. You were brave and strong today and said so much, no wonder you needed to skedaddle.

I may have found the only hypnotherapist in the world who uses the word 'skedaddle'. I can contemplate this and a few other things over a reassuringly expensive coffee in the Boatshed. Claire and I drank Stella in the nineties for the simple reason that we loved their ads on TV. The marketing bods labelled Stella as 'reassuringly expensive', showed us a bucolic old France shot like a movie and bathed in the music from *Jean de Florette*. When I watched *Jean de Florette* and *Manon des Sources* on VHS, I thought the movies had stolen the music from the lager ads. Adverts in the nineties were big events. We would watch them the same way we watched the actual programmes, with anticipation beforehand and opinion after. Claire had young Brad Pitt getting out of jail without his Levi's on and I had Nicole in the Renault Clio. We had Guinness surfers and Caffrey's hip hop.

There are no events in my life any more. The new car registration; I have no idea what we're on now. The start of a football season, because it never ends. I don't queue to see a much-anticipated film at the cinema because I know it'll be in my living room in a matter of weeks. Adverts are total shite. I don't have sex. I don't travel. I am known amongst my mates, family and colleagues as someone whose main passion is scuba diving and, unbeknown to them, I haven't done it for a decade.

Three things occur to me as I enjoy the buzz of this café and of being somewhere other than my flat. The first is just that: that I would like my home more if I wasn't in it all day. The second thing is equally obvious as the first: I want to sleep with someone. I want to have sex with a woman who likes me and is nice and funny and interesting. It's ungentlemanly and boorish to talk about one's love life but it is relevant to mention here that Claire and I slept together a lot. I didn't ever poll my friends and peers but ten, twenty years into our relationship we would still make love two or three times a week. I think that's a very healthy amount. There were times when it was less, but all I'm saying is, to suddenly go more than a year without making love, without being touched or held tight, with no one to whisper goodnight to, it's miserable.

Thirdly, and this is not thought out and I'm not even sure what I think about it myself, but when asking myself what I am hoping to get out of seeing Mary Blair, and what specific thing hypnotherapy could do for me, and given that I disappointingly don't need to give up smoking, I wonder if what I could do, or should do, is ask Mary to help me get back in the water, forty metres under it, to be precise.

I'm going to park that thought there, drink my expensive coffee and send Claire a text I've been meaning to send for a couple of days.

Come and have a drink with me, no weirdness, no big chats, just some entertainment, something I really want you to see. I promise no deep conversation. Px

Predictably, unable to handle the lack of detail, because mystery is not a data analyst's thing, Claire calls.

'I believe you, Pete, when you say there'll be no deep conversation,' she says. 'But I'd love a deep conversation. I'd love a clue how you are and what you're thinking.'

She does this on the rare occasions we talk on the phone, launching in as if we're picking up on a conversation we were having an hour ago. I love that.

301

'Hi,' I say.

'Yes, hi. Sorry.'

'You know Josie at work?' I say.

'Quiet-little-mouse Josie? That Josie?' Claire says.

'Yeah. I mean, I only have a staff of three and you know the other two quite well.'

'What about her?'

'She's doing stand-up. Come and watch her with me.'

'Josie is?' Said as if I must be mistaken.

'Yup.'

'Josie?' Said as if I must be mad.

'Yes.'

'Little quiet Josie?'

'Can we skip through this bit?'

'You got her a job as a comic? How did *you* do that?'

I don't understand what she's talking about. 'I didn't.'

'Oh, just . . . you texted me about finding her a job, so I thought this was—'

'No. She does this on the side, and you never replied.'

'Yeah, I know. Weird, isn't it, that I don't have a list of jobs I can put total strangers into. But I've got to see this. I mean, I can't quite imagine her . . . but, you know, good for her.'

'If you could work on being even more patronising, I'm sure she and all nineteen-year-olds would appreciate it.'

Claire laughs. We have a date.

Chapter 22

I'm at the bar of the Railway Tavern and text Claire to ask her what she wants.

Pint of most expensive lager please x

On arrival, she does that thing again, launches straight in.

'I know you lured me here with the promise we wouldn't talk about anything major, but I'm not going to let you get away with that.'

I smile politely and begin the highly enjoyable game of being tight-lipped to annoy her. We find a table with a decent view of the stage and sit opposite each other. She removes her coat, takes a breath and starts her pint.

'You win,' I say. 'I love you.'

Claire's face drops. I immediately feel guilty. There's a silence between us that is treacle thick. An evening-ruining silence, potentially.

'I really did just want you to see Josie and to hang out with you, but if you're pushing me to say something major, that's it.'

Claire's voice almost fails her. 'Anything but that,' she says.

'Okay, sure . . .' I say, being stupidly buoyant with my voice. 'But that's the most interesting thing about me.'

'It can't be.'

'Not up to you.'

'You've got so much else.'

'Anything else is private.'

'How are we going to be okay if you don't talk to me?'

'Because the private stuff is about life without you, finding a way to live without your counsel. You don't get to rubber-stamp that.'

I really did just want us to watch Josie.

'I don't want to rubber-stamp anything, but we can still share stuff.'

I shake my head dubiously. 'That'd be you winning, getting everything you want.'

The uncomfortable silence returns. A spotlight fires up, aimed at the stage.

'Ready for some comedy?' I say.

Claire shakes her head and drinks.

Josie is first up. There are four comics each doing two five-minute sets. She looks no less terrified than before. I have no idea how many gigs she has done since the one we watched at the Grasshopper. She might not have done any. I might be about to hear the titanium-arsehole routine again.

She goes up on tiptoe to address the mic and adjusts it down as she starts.

'I recently went to the funeral of my friend's grandad. He, you know, died of old age, so not a tragedy. Sad but not tragic. His two carers were there, crying their eyes out, I mean bawling. People there had known this man fifty years and they're keeping it together.'

Suddenly, Josie glares out at us all and her timid voice is overcome with indignation.

'The carers have known him six months and they're purple-faced, sobbing, snotty. Even the wife isn't crying as

304

hard as these two. And the carers, when you think about it . . . THEY'RE THE REASON WE'RE HERE!

'THEY HAD ONE JOB!'

Josie calms and takes a deep breath, as if to contain her anger.

'Carers who out-grieve the family, right up there on the list of things I dislike.'

She paces the stage, pulls a face as if contemplating the list.

'A list which includes but is not limited to . . .

'Toddlers watering plants on the leaves not at the roots.

'People offering to help you find a lost object.'

She looks at us knowingly.

'"Well, where did you last see them?"

'"You must have put it somewhere."'

She rolls her eyes and bites her lip, counts to ten with her fingers, exhales heavily.

'Okayyyy, I'll remember where I put it and then look there. Thanks.'

Josie mimes watching her helpful friend go.

'You annoying cunt.'

Claire laughs into her pint.

'And people who wear running gear to spectate at marathons. They're on my list too.'

I take a drink. Josie swigs from a bottle of water and paces around the stage as a wall-to-wall buzz of anticipation moves through the audience. '*Keep going*,' the room is saying, '*we like this*.'

Josie puts her water down and rests her hand on the mic.

'My four-year-old half-brother . . . look, this is a middle-class pub and I'm not going to try and explain my family to you. We live on an estate so that means we have uncles and aunts younger than us, that's all you need to understand. Archie, who is four, I was looking after him last week and he was being bolshie so me and my boyfriend said, "Look, Arch, we know what you're allowed to eat between meals, and it's not Haribos. We know and we're right so let's just play and have fun and you eat your fruit." So he starts playing again and ten minutes later he just stops and looks at us and says, "Before I was a toddler, I was a baby and before I was a baby I was born and before I was born I was a little old man with a different name so I know more than you."'

Josie looks at us, spooked. The pub smiles back at her.

'Christ! All right, Benjamin Button! I gave him Haribos and backed the fuck away. He's not mine, it's not my job to fix him. My rule with children over the age of two is not to get into long conversations with them, 'cause they just find you out.'

A few minutes later Josie leaves the stage, to applause. Claire raises an eyebrow, impressed. She goes to the bar as the second comic comes on. We watch the other acts. They're all pretty good, although the guy wearing a tutu over a boiler suit never says anything to explain why.

Josie and Grant come across during the break. I am a bit nervous about Grant's reaction to Josie losing her job, so I concentrate on Josie's other career.

'Fantastic!' I say. As before, she is trembling with nerves.

'Thank you,' she says.

I introduce Grant to Claire and I try to say the 'ex-wife' bit so clearly and naturally that it might make Claire feel assured that I am not going to revisit what I said earlier. I want her to feel comfortable, despite having a prick for an ex-husband.

Claire is effusive in her praise of Josie. 'Just brilliant,' she says. 'I can't imagine trying to do that and you are so good. You've got people in the palm of your hand.'

'It doesn't feel like it,' Josie says, smiling and shivering.

We all fall silent for a moment, and I notice that Grant is shifting on the spot a bit and that Josie is looking at him, expectantly.

'Look,' Grant says, the ease and confidence gone, 'I wanted to say . . . and I'm not speaking for Jo-jo here, I wouldn't—'

Josie cuts in, 'When I told Grant about losing my job –'

Claire looks at me, her face a question mark.

'– he said something to me and I said to him, "I wish Mr Smith could hear that because it's true."'

'And she told me to tell you,' Grant says. 'Next time I see you. What I said was, this job has been so brilliant for Josie and you're the perfect boss, trusting her, making sure the other two trained her up. I hope you realise that and don't feel bad.'

It's unfathomable to me how Josie feels so positive about working for me. I'm embarrassed, knowing that I trusted her because the alternative was turning up for work myself. Mrs H and Si trained her up because I wasn't there.

'You're the perfect employee,' I say to Josie.

She wraps her arm around her boyfriend's waist. She is beaming with happiness.

'Then why did you let her go?' Claire says.

'She wasn't funny enough,' I say. Claire and Grant laugh. Making Claire laugh is an event, a wonderful one. Josie pulls a face at me.

'You're allowed to hit him,' Claire says.

We chat a little more and then Josie and Grant leave us.

'Believe it or not,' I say, 'I did not pay those two to say all that so that you'd see me in a good light.'

We take our seats.

'I know you didn't, Pete, because that would involve you having an ego.'

It's a nice thing to say. And true. I have no ego, I'm brilliant that way.

Claire leans forward. 'Peter Smith, I see you in the best possible light. I could not have a higher opinion of you. I often don't think of myself so highly for leaving you and wanting a different life, but it is what I want, and I have to get on with it.'

'You might be helped in that regard if I had a life of my own.'

'I would just feel happier if you did, and happy for you.'

'Because you do love me,' I say, realising it.

'Of course I do!' she says, exasperated.

'So, as you've probably surmised, I'm shutting down the business,' I say.

She looks at me, right at me. The corners of her mouth rise to the faintest of smiles. 'Good,' she says. 'Tell me all about it, now or as and when you're ready.'

My smile thanks her for not pushing me for details she knows I probably don't yet have. 'And don't worry,' I say, 'I'm never going to say what I said to you earlier again and you don't need to worry that I will. I'll be fine. I am fine.'

'Thank you,' she says. 'Even though I will miss you saying it.'

The order is reversed for the second half of the show, so we have to wait fifteen minutes for Josie. At Claire's suggestion, I join her on her side of the table so that I can watch without twisting round. We sit side by side and I think she feels as comfortable as I do. After the second act, she slides her empty glass across to me and whispers, 'Get me another drink, you tight git.'

Where will I find a lover who can drink three pints of lager and look so elegant and cool?

'Still a desperate alcoholic then,' I mutter, as I get to my feet.

The start of a third pint is where I tend to start feeling pissed. Two and a half pints in and I'm anybody's. So I sip slowly, and am still compos mentis when Josie returns.

She begins, 'Can anyone tell me why it is that whenever I'm going for a special evening out and I'm wearing my best stuff, someone who smells of urine carrying an open carton of yoghurt always sits down next to me on the bus?'

People nod knowingly, some laugh. She's got them instantly. Claire sits forward. She is smiling and her lips are parted, in anticipation.

'We say such weird things to each other, don't we?' Josie says, looking down at her feet as if this carefully prepared (in a Moleskine notebook) material is just occurring to her. 'We lie. Let's face it, much of the time we lie. "How's life?" "Good, yeah, good." If we didn't lie, conversations would be different. "How are you?" "Fine. You know, touch of cancer but fine."'

Josie goes quiet, adopts a power stance and holds her hands out in front of her; then parts them and draws an imaginary line with them.

'WE SLEPT TOGETHER,' she says, in a booming voice. 'Those words. We slept together. If what we're saying is really what we mean, would it be soooo bad when a person says to their partner, "We slept together"? "Oh, so you missed the last train and were too pissed and tired to get home or book a room so you stayed at your colleague's and she slept in her bed and you slept on her couch so you slept . . . together. You lay down under the same roof and you slept?"'

Claire's laughing and so is most of the pub, that ground-swell laugh where people watch and smile and their mouths are fixed open and a constant low ticking engine of laughter comes out.

'But we hardly ever mean what we say. "I'm fine." "Busy-busy." "Weighing up my options." "Never better." "Really like your new boyfriend."'

Josie takes the mic off the stand and moves around a bit. She still looks nervous and moves apologetically, in contrast to her confident, sassy verbal style and I wonder if she is doing it deliberately or not.

'"We slept together" means that the last thing you did was go to sleep together. Fucked till dawn. Slipped back to your own flat on the first bus after grinding each other to a smooth finish. At no point when two people sleep together are they asleep, unless you're really unlucky. But if a man actually slept when I was sleeping with him, I'd never offer him the honour of sleeping with me again, the fool.'

A woman whoops and cheers at this.

'My mother,' Josie says. 'Really.' People turn and look at the woman who shouts out, 'Keep going, gorgeous!' Everyone applauds and cheers. Josie talks on through the cheers, not allowing the place to fall silent mid-set.

'It's so British to take the action of having sex and describe it as "sleeping together". No wonder the French and Italians pity us.'

Claire smiles at this and takes a swig of beer. I know her so well. I know just why this humour appeals to her, because it's truthful and clever without being intellectual and it's about sex and it's joyful and it's not mean. It appeals to the side of her that work doesn't get to. It feeds her insistence that people shouldn't think differently just because they age. They should only think differently because their thinking changes. And I realise that we're in this together. She and I are doing this thing together. It's unbelievably painful because, one, it just is and, two, it means we're never going to reunite, but we are being divorced together and it's ours and if we do it well it'll mean that one day we're good friends, who Erland and Susie will like being with.

Claire and I have always been a team on a project: travelling, falling in love, marrying, raising a family. And now we are doing this thing together and tonight I believe that we are going to do it well; kindly and with generosity. This can be a project for the rest of our lives, which we take time to perfect and is no one else's business. This is us being good at being divorced. And a man who didn't want to split up in the first place can still make a decent fist of being divorced with his wife.

It is no different to Claire and me allowing Susie to do things in the safety of our house which we would rather she did not do, and finding she remained close to us because we had. Susie was respectful and so is Claire. She's not going to rub my nose in it when she's having a wonderful time, just like I wouldn't, should I ever do anything interesting again in my life. And the four of us are and will always be the four of us. I don't have to co-parent with any man Claire loves. I'm lucky, I can enjoy my family and my life and I can love being with my ex-wife. It's all there for me, if I want it.

And, being a mature male, I see that if I were to be enjoying myself and getting laid and feeling good about myself, then being civil with Claire's future boyfriend(s) will come easy because I'll be fine with the whole thing as long as I can be seen by everyone to be winning or at least drawing at divorce.

That's what's been missing – any mention of divorce as a competitive sport. I can so nail this shit!

'Such weird things we say,' Josie says. 'I went to a yoga class the other day and the teacher kept telling us what to do next, like the pose or whatever, and she'd say, "If that's available to you . . . " Such a nice phrase. Such a kind way of approaching the mission impossible of yoga. "Now, move straight into standing half-lotus, wrapping your legs behind your back whilst humming Wagner in Latin and shutting your eyes on one leg, if that's available to you today." "Oh! You know what, it was available to me yesterday, I can do that normally but it's not available to me today." "If that's not

311

available to you, go into child's pose. Do the pose of shame, you fucking LOSER!'"

Josie points to the front row of drinkers watching her.

'Men who are really into yoga, always front of the class, baggy tracksuit bottoms, bald, but not just bald, shiny bald, buffed – my friend Lou calls them The Varnish – stay behind after for a chat with the teacher . . . all those guys?

'They're the guys who were TOTALLY SHIT AT REAL SPORT.'

This gets a good laugh.

'They've finally found something. Useless at football? No hand–eye coordination for tennis? A bit scared in general?

'YOGA!

'If you can breathe deeply through your nose and not laugh when someone tells you to send the breath up to your earlobe, you've found your thing. And none of us are ever going to come watch you from the sidelines or play in a team against you on a Sunday morning, so you're safe, you can say you're good at it 'cause nobody will ever find out you can't touch your toes without breaking wind. And you can go off on retreats, weekends in Devon or a fortnight in Sri Lanka, for an immersive experience which you sign up to only really because you're hoping it turns into an orgy. Because being shit at sport, you've not had much sex in your life.'

Josie sees the compere halfway up the stage steps. She puts the mic back on the stand.

'I'm Josie Bird and you've all been lovely, apart from . . .' She squints into the spotlight and points at her mum. '. . . her . . . she's been perfect.'

We all cheer and the cheering turns to applause as Josie leaves the stage.

And then there's a certain deflation in Claire and me. Josie has been a high-calibre distraction that has allowed us to sit

312

together, drink together, laugh and smile. Without her, we might be pushing our luck.

Claire finishes her drink and says, 'It's time to go.'

I have half of mine left. 'I'll stay for a bit, so there's no awkwardness walking you home or to the bus stop.'

She cocks her head and looks to one side and I see the buffering wheel in her eyes as the sarcasm loads. 'Yeah, awkwardness would be out of the question between us, wouldn't it?'

She gives me a big hug and I hug her back. I say to her as she leaves, 'Claire, it's not going to be awkward any more, I promise.' She smiles at me and squeezes her eyes shut for a moment. It's Claire's equivalent of the Paul Hollywood handshake, without the self-satisfied, self-aggrandising, over-paid, over-fed, over-hyped, fake-tan elements.

So, different, really.

I watch her leave the pub. I watch the door close behind her. I gaze a moment at the space she has left and, although my heart breaks again, something is different. After a rocky start, this evening was good. I think I got it right. I think I see that the more of a life I have, the freer she will be and the freer she feels the better we will be together, because I will have contributed to her happiness in that small way. In other words, Niall was right about loving her by letting her go, and, to borrow a phrase I regularly slag off, *there are no words* to describe how fucked off I am to admit he was right.

Claire and I just need to keep understanding each other. That way, we'll be good friends. Good at divorce. Joint best at it.

I stare at the door she has disappeared through for a second more and then I follow after her. I leave my drink on the table and my coat on the back of the chair because what I need to say will only take a minute. Claire has stopped up the street outside the chippy. She puts her hands on her hips, taps her foot and looks the place up and down as she decides whether or not a bag of chips is in order. Claire Smith's love of chips, one of the many things I adored about her. She steps inside.

I join her at the back of the queue. 'Hey.'

'Hey. Hungry?' she asks.

I shake my head. There are five people in front of us. Very soon, there are another two behind us.

'I wanted to tell you something,' I say.

'Shoot.' She digs into her bag and takes a fiver from her wallet.

'When I went to Cuba, all those years ago, something happened . . .'

She raises an eyebrow. 'Oh, yeah?'

She's thinking I'm going to tell her I was unfaithful. Well, of course she is. She's going to be so pleased when she finds out I wasn't, it's going to load even more affection and sympathy onto her reaction to what did happen. I accept that she doesn't want to be married to me, but she'll finally know everything and love me more. Hooray for me, I wasn't unfaithful – what a guy!

She folds her arms and leans back. 'Yes, Peter?'

'I had a diving accident. I nearly died. I haven't dived since.'

Her mouth drops open and makes a faint, breathy sound.

'You haven't dived since . . . ten years ago?'

I nod. Her eyes seem to glaze. She's incredulous. She looks past me, uncertainly. 'Why . . .' She trails off, then returns, speaking distantly. 'Why did you still go away if you weren't diving? Why was I left alone doing the kids and work and . . .'

I wait a moment before replying, in case she hasn't finished. 'I still had to do the trips, set up the business. They were shorter, I didn't need decompression days before flying home.'

'I remember asking you about that. And for ten years you've been thinking what, feeling what?'

'I don't know. I lost my nerve. I didn't want you to feel you were with someone weak.'

She covers her face with her hands. 'Christ . . .' The word squeezes out between her fingers. 'Right . . .' she says, but her voice is vague. She's thinking. Her face darkens. Her expression is a total stranger to me, and I don't like it; it suggests a version of the future in which we don't know each other. I cannot bear that future.

This is already feeling a bit more complicated than I had imagined. I thought I would be being comforted by now, but Claire's body language is not the best and I'm wondering if the queue for fish and chips is the ideal place for this conversation.

She stares blankly at me. 'How nearly did you die?'

'Very.'

Her cheeks flame and her nostrils flare. 'Why didn't you tell me you nearly died halfway through our marriage?'

Everyone in the queue looks at us because, although Claire has said this through gritted teeth, she has said it loudly.

'I didn't know we were halfway.'

She glares at me.

'I didn't, you know, want to . . . worry you.'

She relaxes. Her face opens up and she smiles, and I know I'm in deep shit.

'Oh, thanks,' she says. 'Because I could never handle worry, could I?'

'Can you not talk too loudly?' I say.

'I'm happy for anyone to hear this. I sacrificed my body and set back my career, twice, for us and you witnessed every single moment of worry and fear I went through. But you lied to me for ten years because you felt a bit squeamish about letting on to me that you're not invincible?'

315

'I ran out of air. I was scared. It changed me.'

'So what? You were scared, so what? I was scared for years. Scared having kids would derail my career, scared I'd become irrelevant, brain-dead, boring, fat, ugly, less appealing than whoever the bikini-clad fucking hell you met on all your scuba-diving work trips.'

'Yeah . . .' I mutter.

(I mean, you know, yeah, when she puts it like that.)

'Did you know that on average it takes twelve extra years for a woman to get to where she would have been in her career if she hadn't had kids? That women lose twenty per cent of their pay in the ten years after maternity leave? Now, that's scary.'

'Can we just keep this chatty and nice?'

'I'm a data analyst, Pete, this is chatty. D'you see? I've been scared a few times over the years, and I changed too, and I shared it all with you, 'cause that was the deal. You were there when I was sobbing with fear at going through a second labour. Because when they say you forget the pain of childbirth, it's a lie. How the hell could anyone possibly forget pain like that! You were there when I got undressed at nights after a total of eighteen months breastfeeding and my tits hit the floor. I had no privacy, I just had to hope you'd remain more interested in me than my employers seemed to be after I had the cheek to go on maternity leave. It's scary, when you fall in love, have babies, raise teenagers, it's all scary but we were in it together, sharing, talking, not lying—'

'I've never lied to you.'

'Apart from pretending to be scuba-diving for a decade and not telling me you nearly died. Sorry, but I'm in a nit-picking mood. We always said we shared everything! But something changed, you changed. It made me doubt myself. It made me unsure. Most of the time it was fine but occasionally I'd ask you if you were okay and you'd say, "I'm fine," but gradually, drip, drip, drip, it went away from us. And now, after ten fucking years you tell me there *was* a reason, something *did* happen, it wasn't me being paranoid.'

'Sorry.'

'Oh, that's all right then. Apology accepted, let's move on.'

'It's not too late.'

'It is, actually. And all because you had a bad moment. The first time you had something essential to share with me you hid it and look what it did.'

'I'm really sorry.'

'So am I, but I'm not turning back.'

'I do get that. We're divorced.'

'I'm so angry with you.'

'I get that too. Everyone in here does.'

'Try listening to the man I love ask the midwife, "Is that crowning?" thirty times before labour starts. Like listening to a child say, "Are we nearly there yet?" every two minutes. "Is that crowning? . . . Is that crowning?"'

'You've always said that was cute!'

'Try having your vagina torn open and then as you're being sewn up in front of half a dozen strangers being told this isn't that bad and to be grateful it didn't tear all the way to your arsehole. Try experiencing pain so bad that you are mentally scarred by it for two years right up until the moment you choose to go through the same pain again so that the fruit of the first horrific life-changing pain doesn't have to be an only child, and because the man you love can't get through a single day without mentioning the possibility of having another baby.'

'Which you wanted too.'

'BUT I DIDN'T WANT THE PAIN! . . . or the stony, hostile silence when I told my boss, who was a fucking woman, that I was pregnant again.'

317

Why did I interject then? Why did I speak? This is a listening situation. My perspective is not called for. There's a line of complete strangers here wearing expressions confirming that I should be listening. My ex-wife's tone of voice is another indicator. Shut the fuck up, me, I'm begging you.

'Waves of pain, like when we went to *The Blair Witch Project* and it keeps getting towards dusk and you know dark shit is going to happen when it's night, you know it's coming and you're shitting yourself and terrified even though you keep telling yourself, "I'm in a cinema, this isn't real, Woking Broadway is fifty feet the other side of those walls."

'YOU WHIMPERED WATCHING THAT FILM!

'So don't look like you don't remember. Same way you know night-time is coming in a horror film and bad shit is going to go down, I knew the next wave of pain was coming and how much it was gonna hurt 'cause I had it fifteen minutes ago and it was brutal and worse than anything I had ever imagined. You think you could die of pain and a part of you wants to be shot in the head. And you're not shitting yourself metaphorically, you're actually doing it, in front of people including the man you love who is whispering, "You're beautiful," thus rendering any compliment he has ever paid you and will ever pay you utterly redundant.'

People in the queue are looking less hungry than when they entered. The bloke serving asks Claire if she wants salt and vinegar on her chips.

'Yes, please,' she says calmly. Then turns to me, 'Oh, and don't forget the haemorrhoids.'

'I accept everything you have said,' I say.

'I advise you against a "but" here,' Claire says, taking her chips and stepping aside to let the queue move up. We lean against the wall beneath a muted TV (bloody hell! I think they've muted it to listen to us) and Claire blows on her chips.

318

'But . . .' I say, very politely.

'Motherfucker . . .'

Claire doesn't say this. It comes from a woman in the queue. She looks like a librarian, or a nun wearing civilian clothes, but she's staring at me with pure hate in her eyes. There's an old, very old, woman next to her with a scarf wrapped around her head watching us too. She has the sort of moustache Erland was proud of when he was sixteen and she is so bent double by age, she has to crane her neck upwards to watch us. It looks extraordinarily uncomfortable, but she apparently considers us entertaining enough to be worth the pain.

'But,' I repeat, with gritted teeth, 'all I am trying to mention is that, although very different to childbirth, running out of air deep beneath the ocean with no one in sight and it seeming as if death is certain – is a little bit scary also.'

Resigned, weary, Claire says with a sigh, 'That's why you should have told me.'

'Yes,' the old woman says, 'you should have told her, you cunt.'

There is nowhere for my life to go from here but up. An eighty-year-old, moustached woman living in a permanent downward dog has just called me a c★★t and a line of strangers smelling of batter and vinegar are nodding in agreement. It's time for me to leave and for Woking to become European City of Culture.

I walk out of the shop. Claire follows and we stand outside. She offers me a chip.

'I see what you mean about it not being awkward any more,' she says.

I take one and blow on it.

'But thanks for giving me something to be mad at you about,' she says.

'No probs.'

319

She hands me another chip then turns and walks away. I watch her go.

That went well.

I return to the pub, to my half-drunk pint. Sat alone, I ask myself why I didn't tell her? Is it because beneath the family-centric new man was all the old rubbish about wanting to be a rock for my woman? Did I see myself as the tough, solid, unemotional Marlboro man from the ads of my youth, despite the fact that even if you waxed me, put me in a dress and tattooed my membership number of the Anti-Nicotine Society on my face, I could not be less like the Marlboro man than I already am?

What made me think it would be a good idea to lie to my wife for years? I nearly died. It stopped me doing the thing I loved most outside of marriage and fatherhood. Maybe Claire would have liked to know about that man who saved my life. Claire, Erland and Susie were all I could think of in my last moments, and I didn't tell her any of it. Why? So as not to worry her pretty little head? Obviously not. So as not to seem pathetic? Then maybe we weren't the couple of the century, if I was so scared that a single failure might mean Claire went off me. Why the hell didn't I coil up in a ball and tell her how terrified I was and how much I love her, the same way she did with me from time to time? What is it with men like me who get to go home with the Claires of this world because I am not a dickhead but then, when it really matters, behave like one?

Or perhaps Cuba was an excuse I'd been waiting for, a way out. I once loved to travel and to dive. Airports, aeroplanes, hotel rooms, heat, the ocean, they were my breeze. I loved taking them in my stride, racking up the countries and the miles. And then, suddenly there's another human being in your life and he is tiny and dependent on you being there. Not dependent in the same way he is on his mum, but dependent on me not to create a tragedy of his childhood by dying on him. And now being thirty-eight thousand feet up in the air feels reckless, stupid, unfair on him. So does forty metres beneath the surface. An exotic beach is no more to me than the place my little boy and his mother are not. And maybe if I rush all the meetings and duck out of some of the hospitality, I can fly home a day or two early. Maybe that's my story, that having children changed me beyond recognition, not the diving incident.

And it is possible that for a man like me, who just wants to be a father and finds other things less interesting, the structures and the understanding and support isn't there? That, or I was too dim to find them. This is not a quiz, I'm not tweeting, don't send in your views.

I finish my pint and am deciding against having another when Josie's mum, the now famous Josie's mum, comes over and introduces herself. She is effusive about me.

'My girl thinks you're the bits, Pete. It's been great for her, she really came out of her shell. I'm so grateful to you.'

There's coming out of your shell and there's talking to audiences about arseholes.

'She was a delight to have in the office and I'm sorry it couldn't continue.'

'It might be good for her to move on, and we're just so grateful.'

Josie's mum, which is how she's introduced herself – I still don't know her name – is handsome and relaxed and athletic and sexy. Her voice is hoarse. She grips a vape. Her eyes are furious and kind. She gives me a hug me and I suspect she could crush me. I wouldn't want to piss her off.

'Thanks, Pete,' she says.

She keeps one hand on my arm after she's hugged me and looks for someone in the pub. I'm enthralled by her, flattered, to the extent that I feel a bit weird. And then it strikes me, I want to go to bed with her. Through the all the emotional rust and the cobwebs of desire, I really, really want to fuck her. And I also realise this: that *Cobwebs of Desire* will be the title of my first album, if I ever show an interest in playing music, take up an instrument, have lessons, get good at it and form a band.

A man comes over and says hello and shakes my hand.

'Peter, my husband, David.'

We shake hands and start to chat and of course, but of sodding course, he's a really nice bloke.

Chapter 23

I spend the next day in the shop continuing the clear out. The phone seems to ring a helluva lot more than it ever did. Fortunately, I have one of the machines where you don't hear the message being left. I dip out to the Boatshed on two occasions to get coffee which gradually sorts out the hangover bequeathed to me by the three pints I had with Claire last night and the two I had with Josie's dad.

I FaceTime Susie. Her smiling face appears as she walks along a corridor at work.

'Can you talk?'

'Sure, defo, just stepping out.'

She stops on a stairwell and points the camera out over a panorama of Stockholm. 'Like the view?' she says.

'Great,' I say. 'Looks cold.'

'It's still freezing but so clear and sunny. You at work?'

'Yup,' I say. 'Want to see what I've done with the place?'

I flip the screen and pan it around the empty shop.

'Very minimal,' Susie says.

I put the camera back on me. 'Very closed down,' I say.

'Oh, my God! You look really happy.'

I tell her that it's just what had to be done and I've no plans but it all feels right. We talk about fixing a date for me to visit but we agree we can't yet, whilst Susie's still getting settled into life there. She also tells me that she's doing bar work at the weekends.

'It's so expensive here, Dad, I have to.'

After our call, I worry about her money and I feel a bit paranoid about her not having time for me to visit, but over a few minutes I feel these ideas talk themselves down from the ledge; isn't it great that my daughter has found a second job to make it possible to live in such an expensive place? She's independent and she's sorting it out. It means she's working every day, so there's no time to host her dad and show him around. That's not rejection, it's life. The time will come. I've no idea if I think this or am telling myself to; this trying to be positive is all new to me.

I get home at four and have a long nap and then I take a bath. There is no sign of Niall and I'm missing him by the time he bounds in.

'Yo!' he says, throwing himself onto the sofa and almost, kind of snuggling up next to me. 'Miss me?'

'Nope. There's a host of other chairs in this flat.'

'But this is the nicest. This is our spot.'

I pull a face.

'Given my imminent departure . . .' he says.

I fist-pump.

'Yes, that's always funny when you do that. Given that I'm leaving soon, shall we go out? For a pint? We've never done that.'

I stare at him in stunned silence. It's not something I have ever considered.

'Let's go out, now,' he says.

'I went out last night,' I say.

'Oh, yeah, then it's out of the question.'

I seek clarification of his idea. 'Out?'

'Sure.'

'Out of the flat?'

'Yes, Peter, out of the flat.'

'Out, as in . . .' I gesture with my two hands, leaving the flat and going in opposite directions. 'Or out, as in together?'

'Together, Pete. Shall we go for a pint together, leaving the flat together, going together to the same place and sitting together in it drinking a pint or two in each other's company?'

'Bring my book?'

'No. Not bring book.'

I bow my head in contemplation and sit in silence. I'm not going to tell him this, but he had me at 'Yo'.

We walk to the Pelham and it feels weird to be in public with Niall.

'I'm going to call you Drew,' I announce, as we turn the corner, 'like in *Minions* and short for Drewid. Brilliant.'

He stares at me in disbelief. 'It's only now occurred to you to call someone called Drewid, Drew? *And* you think it's witty? No wonder no one wants to do business with you or live with you.'

'You want to live with me.'

'Yeah, I do, true, but you really do not want to set your bar this low.'

I hold the door open for him, allowing him to enter first and do the honours.

'It's kind of weird being out in public with you when you're the dirty, unpleasant secret in my flat,' I say.

'I get that,' Niall says. 'But try and enjoy it. I'll be gone soon.'

I fist-pump before I can stop myself.

We take our drinks straight away, instinctively, without discussing it, to a sofa so identical to the old sofa in my kitchen that I think a psychologist would have something to

325

say about it. Niall has bought two pints and four chasers, to kick things off. That is not my idea of going for a quiet pint, but, on reflection, I don't think Niall used the word 'quiet'. It's twenty years since I was involved in a round of drinks like this.

'What's the chaser?' I say.

'Jameson.'

By eight-thirty I am pissed, Drew is my best mate and we have a pound on the pool table booking us the next frame. From our all-seeing vantage point on the sofa, as I contemplate a quick power nap before the pool, Niall spots someone. He sits upright and gasps, spilling beer over his lap.

'That's Ros!' He points with his beer arm, spilling more. 'My first girlfriend.'

He goes over. I observe from the sofa. The ex seems thrilled to see him. She screams and they hug and she introduces the guy she's with. Niall and the guy shake hands and then they embrace, compelling me to ask, What's wrong with the traditional thing of going all sullen and pouty and offish when you meet someone who has slept with your girlfriend or wife before you did? It always worked for me.

Instantly, it seems, the three of them are in animated conversation. I watch Niall and I see the charm that he has. It's genuine, not smarmy. He is so open. His face says, *'I'm listening and isn't life awesome!'* It also says, *'I talk bollocks and never stop and have no boundaries,'* but you take the rough with the smooth. I can see what Susie liked. And I wonder if she doesn't miss him, at least a bit.

Niall calls me over. I spread my jacket across the sofa before going in the hope of keeping it and as a way of announcing to the pub that I am old and small-minded.

'Guys,' Niall says exuberantly, pulling me in to their gang, 'this awesome human being is Peter, and he's my ex-girlfriend's dad and he has allowed me to stay with him until I found somewhere. Pete, this is Ros and her husband, Matty.'

I offer my hand to both of them. 'Lovely to meet you,' I say. They shake hands, like it's a cute ancient ritual they're respectful of. I ask them what they 'do' because that's my level of patter. They work for the same company, locally, a crypto start-up. I nod like I know what that means, but my understanding of that is like a two-year-old's; I get the gist and I could possibly point to a drawing of crypto if it were put in front of me amongst some bunnies and cars.

'What you up to, Nially, you old hippy?' Ros asks.

'I run an ethical landscaping business. Basically, I'm a superhero passing as an ordinary, everyday, good-looking guy.'

They laugh. 'How about you, Pete?' Matty asks.

'I'm getting over a painful divorce I didn't want and looking for a job at the age of fifty-three having destroyed the business my parents started. They're dead.'

I smile as the conversation grinds to a halt. I thought that the clean mix of the truth and a confident delivery would be amusing. I was wrong.

'Really got to finesse your pub chit-chat there, Pete,' Niall says.

Naturally, that gets him a laugh. There is no God.

'We're out for the first time in ten months since having our first child,' Ros says.

A bit pissed, Niall and I explode excitedly at this news. All of a sudden, we're a bouncing party of four happy faces and I'm hugging two strangers and congratulating them and, weirdly, feeling desperately emotional about their happiness. Maybe, if I hug them long enough, I can catch it.

'Congratulations, that's wonderful!' I say repeatedly, as if trying to use these words to fill the hole I created by telling

327

them how fucked my life is. Niall's face seems consumed with happiness for his first love.

'A boy, Larry,' Matty says proudly amidst all the yelping.

'Mum is babysitting,' Ros says. 'Staying the night, so we can have a proper evening out for the first time.'

'So weird to be away from Lazza, even if it is only four hundred yards,' Matty says.

'Where do you live then?' Niall asks.

'Don't tell him!' I say. 'He'll move in.'

'True, actually, especially as I still fancy your mum a bit,' Niall says.

Matty pulls a face that suggests either he's not pissed enough to hear that or that he is a bit more proper than Niall.

'My mum's very fanciable,' Ros agrees.

'But, Pete,' Niall says to me, 'I didn't fancy Ros's mum when I was going out with your daughter.'

'What about when you were going out with her daughter?' I ask.

Ros laughs. Matty still looks alarmed that anyone could fancy his mother-in-law.

'Eh?' Niall is confused.

'Listen,' I say to Matty and Ros, 'the last thing you want is your first night out in ages ruined by having to talk to us . . .' (I desperately don't want to lose the sofa.) '. . . but please will you let me buy you a bottle of champagne or whatever you'd like?'

They accept and from the bar, I see Ros, Matty and Niall go to the sofa. They are talking excitedly. Ros and Matty are clearly not with a group of friends. This evening isn't a baby celebration, it's two young blurry-eyed parents who have been told by Granny they need to get out of the house and have a few drinks followed by a good night's sleep. Granny for her part wants nothing more than to be the one who answers the baby's call, feeds him, listens to his crying abate and turn to the hallowed steady breathing of slumber. And Granny wants to see her daughter be a young woman again for a few hours and get dolled up and go to the pub. That's how I see it: two young parents with nice little jobs in whatever crypto is, earning just enough to pay rent on their first flat with, hopefully, a second bedroom for the baby. It all strikes a chord and fills my heart with nostalgic happiness and yearning.

I offend the barman by asking if they do champagne, rather than just ordering some.

'Yes, we "do" champagne.'

He's an arse, so I ask him, 'What sort?'

He glares at me. 'We've a Taittinger Brut Réserve, a Taittinger Nocturne, the Ruinart Brut and a Billecart-Salmon Rosé.'

I blink first, naturally. 'I think —' I scratch my chin — 'the cheapest one, please.'

'Indeed,' he says, and turns away.

I hear my name being called, by Ros, from the sofa. 'Four glasses, Pete, get four.'

She makes room for me by sitting on Matty's lap. I sit down next to him. Niall makes as if to sit on my lap.

'I'll kill you,' I say.

He takes the arm of the sofa instead, but it leaves him looming over me, so I tell him to get a chair.

'Okay, full disclosure, I don't understand what your jobs are,' I say.

'Sure,' Ros says, in a businesslike manner. 'It's a crypto start-up, two years old, sixty-five million turnover. We specialise in blockchain democratisation. I know it sounds boastful but I love my job and Matty never admits how clever he is, so I do it for him!'

'So, you work for the same company . . .'

329

Matty nods and Ros grins from ear to ear.

'. . . but what do you do there?'

'To be honest,' he says sheepishly, 'joint CEOs. We had the idea when we met at university in Colchester. I worked in San Francisco for two years whilst Ros did a postgrad at the LSE and then we set this thing up and it just went bananas.'

He seems embarrassed by his success. He'll be a great dad.

'Good God,' I mutter.

Niall drags a chair over to our sofa and sits. I take a moment to consider how normal these two ridiculously capable, successful young people appear to be. I take another moment to forgive them for earning a fortune already. 'I would ask what blockchain means but I'm a bit tiddly and a bit thick and it just won't stick.'

They laugh. They think I'm joking.

'And I'd rather ask you about little Larry, if I'm honest – that's more my area of expertise and interest.'

'Mine too,' Matty says. 'Well, interest, not expertise.'

'And it isn't little Larry,' Ros says, 'not by a long way. My little bundle of joy, who was the size of a blueberry at six weeks in the womb, was delivered naturally at a whopping twelve pounds.'

'Christ almighty!' Niall shouts, spilling champagne on the beer stain on his jeans.

'I know,' Ros says. She will have had this conversation more than once in the last few months but doesn't seem to mind.

'Mad, isn't it?' Matty says ruefully. He looks haunted by the thought.

'That's insane!' Niall says. 'How are you still in one piece, woman?'

We fall silent, perhaps in contemplation of the image Niall has conjured up. His mouth, having dropped open, has not shut. He stares at the floor and it is possible to see his mind at work; it's drawn on his face, his efforts to come to terms with the size of the thing that his ex-girlfriend pushed out of her body. And then Niall smiles to himself. No, it's worse than that, he laughs to himself, and it makes me nervous but I'm too slow to react, too slow to bring him down, pin him to the floor and wedge my arm in his mouth – all in slow motion, with me shouting, 'NOOOOO!' as I take him out before he can speak.

'I like to think I paved the way for that, you know?'

He winks knowingly at Matty and, to my horror, glances down at his own crotch area. Matty seems suddenly very sober. Tumbleweed blows across the now arid plain where conversation and laughter once lived. I watch Matty and see that not even a sixty-five-million-pound turnover can stop him wondering if Niall did indeed do some way-paving for big Larry's surprisingly smooth entry into the world.

'I think it's our turn, fella,' Niall says, seeing the previous game of pool end. He leaps up, slaps Matty on the arm and heads jauntily to the pool table.

Matty stares at his shoes. When he finally looks up, he has a shell-shocked expression on his face. He goes to the pool table, grabs a cue and plays a mute, aggressive game of pool with Niall that I keep an eye on whilst trying to make conversation with Ros. But both of us have dried up. Matty's mood is dominating, and it is a relief when I see – I'm convinced – Niall ease off and let Matty steal the frame.

'Well played, mate,' Niall says.

'Time to get back,' Matty mutters. He smiles briefly at me and heads for the door. Ros smiles bravely at us both – 'Lovely seeing you –' and hurries after her young husband.

So, this is what it's like to be out in public with Niall. Armageddon.

'Let's go home,' I say.

The fact that Niall is silent as we head back suggests that he – even he – has worked it out. I feel sober of mind, drunk of body. Halfway home, as I identify more and more with poor insecure Matty, I cuff Niall across the head.

'What the hell was that for?' he whines.

I don't answer.

'Actually,' Niall says, 'I know. Shit! It just seemed so funny as I said it.'

He cuffs himself across the head.

'I mean,' he says plaintively, 'it kind of was, wasn't it?'

'Not if you're Matty.'

The next morning, I wake feeling hungover, again. Today's is worse than yesterday's. Soon after I shuffle into the kitchen Niall does so too, damaged to an identical degree.

'I'm really pleased we chose to have a few more shots back home,' I say.

'It was a brilliant idea, I'm proud of it,' Niall says. 'We have no milk.'

'Please let there be milk,' I say.

Niall is kneeling at the open fridge door, staring inside. 'I so desperately needed there to be milk in this fridge so I can make tea but there's no milk. We're without milk and being milk-less was absolutely the last thing I wanted to happen.'

'Shut the fridge door and open it again,' I say.

Niall closes the door, waits a beat and opens it again. He looks inside and slumps. 'Didn't work.'

'I'm going to get milk.'

'Get some bread too,' Niall says.

It's a massive struggle for me to get dressed, wash my face, and brush my teeth.

'And eggs . . .' Niall calls out.

'Okay.'

'And some mushrooms . . . beans, baked beans I mean, not actual beans, not green ones or anything . . . bacon, obviously . . . a cheeky pork sausage would go down a storm. You get it, I'll cook it.'

'You're on.'

Feeling very unsteady, I unlock the front door and shut it quietly behind me. I have a moment of whatever the exterior equivalent of room spin is. Planet spin. Just spin. I have spin.

I stare at the ground to steady myself and when I look up, I see that Matthew is pinning an *Under Offer* sign up on the board.

Nervously, he says to me, 'Your wife has accepted an offer.'

I gaze at the board, wasted and hungover. I shrug and place my hand on his shoulder.

'Good for you, Martin.'

'Matthew.'

Then I throw up. I manage to turn away and not hit Matthew with it, but my head movement produces an unfortunate sprayed-arc-of-sick effect on the footpath.

'Good God!' Matthew says, and looks at me with what seems a hint of respect, even admiration. 'You must really love her.'

Chapter 24

Change is slow, is it not? Ideas come at speed, then I have to wait for everything else about me to catch up.

Recognising that it would be nice to make love with someone does not, in itself, do anything other than prompt me to dust and hoover my bedroom because – well, you just never know.

And waking up at five in the morning with the terrors – that does not suddenly go away. But the stuff knocking against the inside of my head, waking me up so it can scare me and then dissolve, is becoming more specific. I wake this morning with a dread of the shop looking sad and pathetic, a monument to my failure. This feeling has the relative luxury of a definite and simple fix.

I am in by six and continue clearing the place out. Only one swivel chair remains, thanks to Josie's Gumtree sales. That chair is Si's and he has mentioned wanting to keep it. It is knackered and ugly and creaks. It does not surprise me that he likes it.

I call him at eight.

'How is the world of painting and decorating?'

'Don't know yet, I've been on holiday.'

'Where to?'

'Namibia.'

'Really? Bloody hell!'

'Is it a huge shock to you that I like travel, Pete?'

'You got all the gear?'

'Gear and a van.'

I detect some pride in his voice.

'You up for two days' work, starting today? I want the shop looking fresh and to paint over the name outside.'

'Be there in an hour.'

Si's Ford Transit is a little dented here and there, but nothing too serious. It is red, almost totally red and covered in the livery of a company called Filson's Organics, with whom I am not familiar. The slide door, however, is white. Also, a bit scratched but, I'm guessing, in better condition than the Filson's door that has been removed at some point. I don't know the full identity of the organisation that the white door originally belonged to, but I do know that the result of this marriage of two vans is that one side of Si's vehicle now has the word *FISTING* in large letters across it.

He unloads his gear as I admire the chariot.

'"Fisting", Si?' I mention.

Si is matter-of-fact. 'I know, not ideal.'

I follow him inside.

'Still, great van, isn't it?' He is bright and breathless.

'As great as a dented van with the word "Fisting" on it can be,' I say.

'It would be better if the fonts matched.'

'Wouldn't that be so much worse?' I ask, but he's gone, back to his van to unload more stuff. I grab my phone and take a photograph of Si's backside sticking out of the back, bum-crack resplendent, and the logo alongside. I text it to Peggs.

Si paints the shop frontage, including the name sign, in a pleasingly thick dark grey undercoat. I fill the back of my car with boxes and bags and go to the tip, and I buy a tin of dark purple gloss exterior paint from Homebase. Over the course of the day, I watch the family name disappear from the high street, as if averting my parents' gaze from what's happening, the same way a teenager puts a T-shirt over the framed photo of his parents before having a wank. But that only happens in films; in real life, no teenage boy has a photo of his parents in his bedroom. The purple is lovely.

'You heard from Mrs H?' Si asks, during a tea break.

I nod and pull a face.

'Oh, dear,' Si says.

'Got an email from her. It was like getting bollocked by Mrs Thatcher.'

'Ah.'

'I've not replied. I'm not sure how to or even if I want to.'

Inside, I go around the walls of the shop with a scraper, removing Blu Tack. I get rid of every cable and last piece of detritus. Tomorrow, Si will whitewash the walls and I will be able to leave this place as a fresh, bright, open space with potential (for, you know, that massively buoyant high-street shopping culture we currently have).

In the movie version of today, old friends of my parents and loyal customers would stop as they pass by and we'd reminisce. Funny and touching anecdotes about the shop, my parents, me as a child, Susie and Erland on their visits here, would pepper the day. The sequence would end with me standing alone in the shop, a smile to myself at the emotional closure those good people out there have helped me find, and excitement at the new life ahead of me. I'd sling my jacket over my shoulder and stroll off down the middle of the street. I'd be whistling. The day wouldn't end, it would fade to black.

In the real version, I am sitting on a crusty but coveted swivel chair, sipping an extra-hot flat white, watching a middle-aged man's bald spot as he paints the low part of the shopfront, with the word 'Fisting' reflected in the window.

I swivel three-sixty and the headrush produces a brilliant idea, pertaining to my ex-wife. I own this shop. Not the building, but the leasehold on the ground floor. It's not worth a fortune for a number of reasons, including the fact that I – and this will come as no surprise to you – failed to extend the lease. But it is worth something. And as I turn in circles on Si's chair, I decide to sell it, not rent it out, and to give Claire half the money. This is only right because she topped up our joint income when this shop was not producing enough, or, specifically, when the bloke running it wasn't.

When I say 'topped up', I mean she single-handedly supported us.

The brilliance of my thinking is this: one of two excellent scenarios will unfold. Either I offer her half, she accepts and it adds ballast to the possibility that I am an outstanding guy. Or I offer her half, she refuses, is still reminded what a standout human being I am whilst I get all the money. I text her immediately.

Selling the shop. Half for you of course. X

Pure genius.
She texts back straight away:

So hot for you right now. This is so like you, Pete Smith. Generous, proper, good, kind. If I leave work now, are you free in an hour to meet up for a shag as a way of thanking you for being you?

Bugger. Busted.

Very funny.

I thought so.

Quiet day at work then?

No, in the loo catching up on texts. Thanks for the offer, however insincere.

The offer was sincere. Half of it is yours.

No way. You don't owe me anything. X

That's right, you owe me. I gave you the best years of my life.

Those were your best?!

Bugger off.

Okay. But thanks for offering Pete. XX

Heartbreak is so nearly a legitimate medical term. How the hell am I going to love someone as much as I love her?

I walk home and answer the question for myself. I am not going to love anyone else the same way I love Claire. That's not the aim of the game. The aim is to love and to be loved. And not to compare. Thank you all for bearing with me whilst I reached this very basic level of understanding.

I call her, as I walk by the river.

'We weren't perfect, you know,' I say.

'I agree,' she says.

'We weren't a national institution.'

'You're right.'

'You agreeing with me doesn't really allow me to build up to my point.'

'Sorry. Okay, do your point now.'

'Now, or more build-up?'

'I'd go for now.'

'What's the rush? You got data to analyse?'

'Yes. Loads of it. So, do the point.'

'Okay. You can't blame Cuba. I didn't shrivel up after that.'

'No, you didn't, you were brilliant.'

'I loved being a dad and a husband . . .'

'You're a fantastic dad.'

'. . . and we had so much fun way after Cuba. The four of us went to every continent on the planet together.'

'Except for Antarctica.'

'Antarctica doesn't count – no one goes there.'

'I'm going there.'

'When?'

'Next year.'

'Oh, what?! That's ridiculous, that's just taking the piss.'

'You never took me so I'm taking myself.' She laughs.

'It'll be shit,' I say maturely. 'Point I was trying to make is that we rocked. Cuba was not the beginning of the end. You're right I should have shared it but you're way wrong thinking that was what killed us.'

'I don't think that.'

'You wanted something else – that's your right but don't pin it on me failing to share something years ago.'

'I'm not. Not at all. No one thing causes everything else. Cuba isn't why I left you ten years later and me leaving you can't be your reason for never getting back to your feet.

You're becoming pathetic and it's a tragedy because you're wonderful.'

'Fuck you, Claire. How dare you?'

Pathetic is a bit strong, surely? And yet, I needed to hear that, and she is the only person with the guts to say it despite the high probability of being told to fuck off.

'Thank you, though,' I say, beneath my breath.

'Possibly a bit harsh,' she mutters.

'I wish that were true,' I say.

It will do me good not to be crippled by the idea that I've lost something that was perfect and that nothing will ever compare.

'You still there, darling man?' Claire asks.

'Yeah, I am.'

'Pete, you're not pathetic, I didn't mean that. But you are allowed to want some respect, some money, some sex, to be heard, to have a laugh. You're allowed all that, but you have to make it happen. No one else is going to give that to you.'

'Not even in return for money?'

'You haven't got any money.'

We are silent for a while.

'Hey,' I say, 'thanks for refusing half the shop.'

'It's not mine,' she says. 'It's yours. You need to realise that.'

I walk as far as the Boatshed. I look through the window and a bundle of images enter my head: some are of what that building looked like when I was young, others are of me and my adult daughter stepping into it a few weeks ago and being reunited with Mary. I remember Mary as a teenager and try to get my head round what it means that she is now a woman with children and a marriage behind her and the knowledge and training to help me. What it means, of course, is that time passes with alarming speed. And what that means is that the funk I'm in is dangerous. It could eat up the next chunk of my life and spit me out as an old man.

There is no more leave-it-till-later left to me. There can't be. I did glimpse this when I reached fifty, but I ignored it. Fifty is a bit of a game-changer. Or should be. But I didn't make any changes because I was happy and comfortable and lazy and I possess less foresight than anyone I know. Instead of looking at my life three years ago, I celebrated my half-century with a weekend away at the Ram in Sussex with Claire, Erland and Susie. We stayed there two nights and went walking on the South Downs and had a day out in Brighton; it was exactly what I requested. Susie and Erland stayed out in Brighton for one evening and I didn't drink back at the pub so I could pick them up at one in the morning from the club they had found and got drunk in. Driving back to the pub with the two of them asleep in the car, Susie next to me, dribbling, Erland lying across the back seat, I was happier than I could ever begin to describe, and Claire was alone in the four-poster bed she had booked for us. I tiptoed back into bed so as not to wake her, thinking I was being considerate. We had breakfast the next morning by a roaring fire in the pub and Erland told Claire and me what he had told Susie the night before, that he was going to New Zealand to work on a wine estate.

I realise now what I chose to ignore then. There's a time in your life when, if you're a privileged middle-class man like me, educated well at a decent comp, and raised by parents born with little who worked hard to give you more than enough, you feel that you can do anything with your life. At fifty, or, in my case, today, here on the riverbank, you understand that the potential to do anything does not mean you'll do everything. In fact, you'll do just a few things. Hopefully you'll do them well. But if you lose your spark, one day you run out of chances to do anything at all and you become the new version of yourself you're not happy with but presumed was temporary.

Si's van is great to him because he owns it and it's going to move his life forward — today, not tomorrow, not later. This time next year, people will be sitting in the Boatshed paying three quid for a coffee saying, 'You should use Fisting Si — he painted our house and he was good and very reasonable.'

At home, I find Niall asleep on the kitchen sofa, legs slung over one end, his belly exposed, and his left hand in its go-to resting position on his crotch.

I take a shower and hang out in my room for a while. I am restless. In the kitchen, I find that Niall has woken up and evolved to a sitting position, legs stretched out in front of him, arse nearly slipping off the front edge of the sofa, gravity-defying, in fact, and gazing empty-eyed at his phone. I sit down next to him.

'What you doing?' I say.

'Looking at women.'

'What is that?'

'Tinder. Don't pretend you don't know.'

'I'm not pretending, I can honestly say I've never looked at it.'

'But you've never taken it off your phone either.'

'She's too old for you, Niall.'

Niall looks at me, like I'm an idiot. Something I no longer bother objecting to or consider particularly unfair.

'She's for you.'

I give him a hard stare (not as hard as Paddington but fucking hard nevertheless), then peer at the woman on the screen.

'Fran, forty years old,' Niall informs me. 'Lives pretty much on the doorstep, it would seem, estate agent, into Indie music and modern art, proudly working-class roots. Promising-looking cleavage.'

'Don't be disrespectful.'

'Sorry.'

'They are nice, though.'

'Green eyes.'

'Is that her natural hair colour?'

He repeats the idiot look. 'No,' he says, open-mouthed at my ignorance. 'No one is born platinum blond. I give up.' He shakes his head as if washing his hands of me. 'She's nice, I'm going to swipe right for you.' He does so with a flourish. 'You're welcome,' he says.

I freeze. 'Wait a minute. Is that my phone?'

'Course it's your phone. I said it was for you.'

'For Christ's sake!'

My phone pings. 'And she likes you too! That was quick.'

'Give that back.'

Niall holds the phone away from my grabbing hand and leaps to his feet. I go after him, but he runs and bolts himself in the bathroom.

'Out here now, young man!' I call.

'One sec.'

'No. Now!'

'Okay, I'm coming.' He says this with a teenage whine.

'Now, Niall!'

'Coming! Good thing you put a bolt on this door.'

'I'm counting to five.'

'Congratulations.'

'Seriously, Niall. My phone back, please.'

'Just doing a . . . you know.'

'You'd better not be holding my phone.'

343

'I'm not.'

I hear him put the phone down. It falls to the floor.

'Shit!' Niall says. 'Nothing.'

I return to the kitchen and open up the doors, stand on the threshold of the garden and assume the pissed-off and angry stance only to find that I'm not feeling it. He's out of order, but at least I'm not bored. And, anyway, he can swipe right as much as he likes – I'll delete the whole thing when I get my phone back. I hear a flush, the tap and Niall returns without his belief in what he's doing dented by my hostility.

'You have a date at the Pelham with a green-eyed girl in forty-five minutes' time.'

'I presume you are joking because if not you are dead.'

'I'm not. It's time to lock and load. This shit is real.'

'Give me my phone back.'

Niall creeps towards me and hands it over at arm's length.

'So I can bludgeon you to death with it.' I take my phone. The Tinder app makes as much sense to me as the DNA helix. 'How do I cancel?'

'That would be incredibly rude.'

'I think she'll get over missing out on a drink with me.'

'Or it'll be the final blow to her fragile confidence.'

'She doesn't look fragile to me. Now cancel it.'

He dares to join me and takes hold of the phone. We are both looking at Green-Eyed Girl – that's her profile name – and I mistakenly mutter, 'I like the look of her.'

Niall shows me how to send a message. 'Just type there to cancel. You can tell her the truth, blame me, or make up some shit about having just had a call from your aunt locked out of her house or something, but be kind to her.'

'You should have thought of her before this stupid prank.'

'I should but unless you're now writing Billy Bunter books for a living can you not use words like "prank"? I was arsing

344

about, being a twat, but I'm not doing pranks or having jolly japes or being bummed by sixth-formers.'

'She's nice-looking,' I say again.

'Nicer-looking than me. You can choose between looking at her or me for the evening.'

'You've both got good-sized bosoms.'

'She's less hairy than me.'

'She's less of a wanker than you, too.'

'You don't know that. But if you're so sure, go spend an hour or two in the pub with her, instead of here with me.'

'Two hours?' The panic in me rises. 'What do I talk about for two hours?'

'Not your divorce and not your work. Anything else. But not your dead parents. And mostly listen. Listening plus natural pauses and breathing will cover ninety minutes of the two hours.'

I step into the garden to have a word with myself. Do this, Pete. Do this and don't make a big thing of it. Just go for a drink with Green-Eyed Girl and be glad she wants to, however it goes.

From my bedroom, I send her a message, asking if she'd like to meet somewhere else as it's quiz night at the Pelham and it tends to make conversation tricky. There is no quiz night but the thought of Niall popping along for a drink to observe my dating skills makes me shudder.

Fran, my green-eyed Tinder date, suggests a bar on the other side of town called the View and that is where I walk to, without too much faffing about, and without over-thinking it, because to do so would be to back out.

Chapter 25

Setting eyes on my first date since the late Neolithic period (an era I thoroughly enjoyed) reminds me of playing football for my school. Whenever I clapped eyes on the opposition, they always all looked bigger, stronger and more confident. And better at football. And like they wanted to be there. Fran isn't bigger than me, but she appears cool, calm and, frankly, unbothered.

And it might have been that I was looking the same way to her until I stubbed my toe on the anvil holding the inner door open. I see her wince as it happens and, as I approach her at the bar with my eyes welling up with pain, I comfort myself with the fact that she only winced, she didn't roar with laughter.

I offer her my hand. 'That didn't hurt,' I say. 'I'm just feeling very emotional about meeting you.' I am taking short, punchy breaths to deal with the throbbing in my big toe. She takes my hand and holds it softly for a moment before letting go.

'Who the hell puts an anvil in a bar in Woking?' she says.

'Exactly,' I say.

And I know this is going to be fine. I mean, I'll be rubbish at it, of course, but it doesn't matter because however it is, it'll be fine.

'I'm sorry I wasn't here first,' I say.

'You were early, I was earlier, but thank you. They've got blankets and outdoor heaters on the terrace.'

'Sounds good,' I say. 'You get us a table and I'll get us a drink.'

'Can we have one each?'

'Go on then.'

She wants a glass of Picpoul, which I discover is white wine, and I have the same, but only after an internal crisis about whether to get a large measure or a small one. Is large presumptuous? Is small mean? Does large put me in a corner if we don't get along? Does small risk the implication that I think she should drink less, rein it in a bit?

'Do you do a medium?' I ask.

Or does that suggest I am incapable of making a decision, don't know my own mind, am boring, middle-of-the-road? All things she can find out for herself in the next ten minutes, but why make it easier for her?

'No, just large or small.'

'Large then, please.'

'Sure thing,' the barman says. He pours the wine in front of me. He smiles at me and asks, 'You on a blind date?'

He's about Erland's age and has such a nice manner, the same open, kind features my son has, that I don't mind him asking.

'First one in thirty years. Shitting myself.'

'Lovely eyes.'

'Thank you.'

He laughs. He has no idea how much he's just helped me.

Fran has a blanket over her knees and does a very sweet little movement as I approach, hunching her shoulders and clapping her hands together excitedly at the sight of the wine. Her face creases into a gorgeous smile and she makes confident, sweet eye contact as she says, 'Goody! Thank you.'

347

'You're welcome,' I say, taking the seat next to her so we can both look at the view over the Surrey Hills in the spring evening gloom. 'Good idea coming outside,' I say.

'Nice, isn't it?' she says. 'Cheers.'

'Cheers.'

We chink. She does a shiver under her blanket but it's one of feeling cosy, not cold.

We get on well. It's easy to chat with her. Mostly, I listen. Ten minutes in, we are talking about Australia (she was born there and lived there until she was fourteen, and I had my time there working as a diving instructor on the Great Barrier Reef) when she does the conversational equivalent of a handbrake turn.

'It's a country of such contradictions, the quality of life, the amazing way people have out there, but the racist undertow . . . I struggle with the history. But I do think, if I'm going to be honest, that the age thing is going to matter to me. I mean, the age gap, as I sit here now with you, I realise it does matter. I think it's a cultural–historical references thing.'

'Oh,' I say, blindsided by the manoeuvre. I nod sagely as I take this on the chin. I'm twelve years older than Fran. I feel a bit grumpy and a bit unable to hide that fact.

'Don't sulk,' she says, possibly the most annoying thing she could have said.

'Look, for me,' I say, 'it's just about having a drink with someone. I wasn't even thinking about age or anything beyond having a chat so it's less of an issue for me.'

'You weren't interested in sleeping together if we wanted to?'

'On a first date?' My voice squeaks. I could kill it.

'Remind me, 'cause I get the two apps confused, did we meet on Tinder or on English Country Cottages?'

I laugh. And laughing allows me to relax and think, Sod it, who cares? It's good to be out. And then I realise something else too, so I ask her, 'So, are you saying that when you saw my photo and read my profile—'

'Your incredibly short profile with no info on it,' she reminds me.

'You thought you'd possibly want to sleep with me?'

She nods, 'Yeah. Until you started talking.'

I beam.

'You were meant to find that offensive and fight back,' she says.

'Why? All I'm hearing is that even armed with a visual, you might have wanted to sleep with me. That's wonderful. That's all I need right now. Thank you.'

She smiles at me. 'Keep being this weird and I might want to fuck you again.'

'I'm not ready.'

'And I'm not serious.'

We choose to have another drink, and without the potential of getting even a little bit involved with a woman who isn't Claire hanging over me, I enjoy myself.

We part on the far end of the high street. She gives me a peck on the cheek, and I walk home feeling like I've just completed the first module of a Stage 1 course in re-entering society. The quickest way home takes me past the church so I pay a visit to my folks. I remove the flowers I left on their grave a month ago and say hello to them (my parents, not the flowers – not that one is less odd than the other) and tell them my news, specifically that I've closed down their shop.

I am possibly the first man to begin an evening on a Tinder date and end it in a graveyard, and not in a having-sex-with-your-date-on-a-tombstone sort of way.

Niall is still up when I get back.

'How did it go?'

'Brilliantly, she's in my room now getting undressed.'

Niall pulls a yuck face. 'I can't be expected to listen to you having sex, you're over fifty.'

'Which brings us neatly back to the subject of you moving out.'

'Tuesday,' he says.

I detect in his tone that he is serious and find myself strangely dumbstruck.

'Honest. Tuesday.'

I look at him. 'Really?'

He nods. 'I found somewhere nicer. A little bedsit.'

I swallow. I nod, as assuredly as I can. 'Good stuff,' I mutter. 'Good.'

We stand there, in silence. I don't know why I'm speechless. He is looking at me as if waiting for me to do something.

'Shouldn't you get going?' he says.

'Where?'

'Bed? Sex?'

I stare at him, incredulous. 'You actually think that gorgeous-looking woman would want to come home with me and go to bed with me, you deluded hippy?'

'Yes, I do. Why not?'

I sweep my hand in front of me, to produce the evidence. 'You're too nice for this world, Niall.'

'I'm moving out because I can't listen to your self-deprecating garbage any longer.'

'You're moving out because this is my home and I'm in control and I'm kicking you out. Sit down, I want to ask you something.'

'Is it quick or long?' he asks.

'Medium. It's serious.'

'Then hang on a minute.' He leaves the room and reappears moments later holding a very ornate-looking bottle. 'Client

350

gave this to me last week. It's toffee vodka and, apparently, it's incredible. Shall we?'

I nod. 'Why not?'

He pours a shot for each of us and hands one to me.

'Sit,' I say.

He sits on the sofa. I draw a chair up and lean forward to talk to him. We chink glasses.

'Here's to your new home.'

'Thanks. Want to see it?' He reaches for his phone, but I put my hand on his arm to stop him.

'Show me tomorrow,' I say. 'Niall, have you thought any more about an injunction against your stepbrother? Or a warning letter from a lawyer? Deborah will help if you want her to.'

'If you'd got laid tonight would you be asking me?'

'No, I wouldn't care.'

He smiles. He knocks back his shot. 'I mean . . .' He stops to think. Then he smiles at me. 'We've ended up talking about him like he's some scary ogre whereas in fact he's just pathetic. He's a really small-minded man who likes bullying me. There are loads of men like that – usually it's their girlfriends or wives or ex-wives they like to control. But picturing you and Ed's wife in a posh office talking about me, doing all this for me . . . Thank you. That's enough. That's all I needed.'

I smile at him and nod and what I am doing is telling myself to learn a thing or two from this, from Niall, about ignoring stuff, leaving some of it to deal with itself.

'I'm going to kind of dump him. Starve him of oxygen,' Niall says. 'Thanks to you, he's just . . .' He mimes picking a piece of dirt off his clothes and flicking it away.

When I was at sixth-form college, I had a friend called Mel whose parents I adored. Mel and I are still in touch but she and her family live in Northumberland and we never meet up. I thought her parents were fantastic and I wanted to be liked by them so much, even though I had no gap to fill when it came to parental affection. I remember this feeling now, how good Mel's parents made me feel about myself when they talked to me and listened to me.

I move across to the sofa and put my arm around Niall and tell him I'm proud of him and he tries to say the words 'thank you' but chokes.

We sit there for a few moments.

'I didn't think this through,' I say. 'Now I'm just stranded sitting right up against you on the sofa.'

'It is awkward,' he says, his head bowed.

I'm tempted to take the piss out of him and use that as an excuse to get to my feet, but I stop myself. Niall has never in his life had a decent conversation with his father or stepfather. I squeeze the back of his neck.

'If things ever change, or he does something, tell me and I'll defend you.'

He nods, and sniffs. I rub his back and then say goodnight and go to bed.

Next morning, I call Peggs and ask him if he has time for a coffee, because I'm going to have to miss our lads' breakfast next week.

'I'm being cancelled by the least socially active man since J. D. Salinger,' he says.

'Get over it and meet me for coffee so I can see that gorgeous boy.'

'You betcha,' Peggs says. 'Why are you cancelling, out of interest?'

'I've got a school governor training day at the Local Education Authority.'

'Whoo-ooo!'

I absolutely, categorically knew that would be his reaction.

On my way to meet Peggs at the Boatshed, I call Ed to cancel.

'Whoo-ooo!' he says.

We sort of make up, in that Ed mumbles, 'Sorry if I was abrupt and a bit useless,' and I tell him, 'Don't worry about it, you can't help being a prick,' and we move on. But the call still feels like it's caught him at the wrong time, like he's busy and can't talk for long. There's a sense that he finds it all a bit irksome.

I feel differently about him and me. There's something about being on the end of a friend's sharpness, their irritated businesslike approach to things when it is not the appropriate response, that sticks. I love him, but it's different and I cannot afford to ask him again to be something for me he is either incapable of or unwilling to be. I need to be strong and independent and selective about who I lean on. I would rather turn to Mary Blair for fifty pounds an hour than ever feel the way Ed made me feel when I turned to him. And I am aware that I am failing to be the friend he wants and needs me to be at this stage in his life. We're both different now.

I ask him if he's backing Niall, and he says yes and I tell him I'm glad, which I am, and I want to tell him not to mess Niall about in any way, but that would not go down well. Ed doesn't like to be told.

After the call, I sit on a bench by the river and think about Ed. I ask myself, If there's never a good time to talk, are you still good friends?

Ed can't handle difficult stuff. It's been a long-running joke between us who know and love him, his acute fear of death and inability to even talk about the subject. I mean, I'm not looking forward to it, but I can tolerate talk of it and do not shy away from its presence when loved ones die. But Ed can't handle it. If he could have missed his dad's funeral, he would have. Ed doesn't like sticky subjects or doubt, and a friend like me going through a bad patch that threatens to be long-winded and existential, well, he just doesn't 'do' that. And if I complain about that, it is no fairer of me than him complaining that I am going through it. He pulled out of being there for me because he's terrified of ever being remotely like me. I need better than that and I can have it. Niall has been a better friend to me than Ed.

Bloody hell, that's true.

It's great to see Peggs, who still wants to take the piss out of me for cancelling breakfast.

'You are busy! You! Pete is too busy for breakfast, because he's busy!'

Anyone who thinks *The Inbetweeners* is for teenagers doesn't know what being middle-aged is like. Peggs's piss-take is justified. I haven't been busy for years. I let him indulge in this for a couple of minutes before we get down to the serious business of me playing with the baby and him nodding off in his chair.

Later, I write an email to Mary, saying that I would like to book another appointment and I have thought about asking her to help me go back to diving. *If you want to dive again*, she replies, *I think we can get you there.*

She doesn't make big claims about her capabilities; it's all about us working together, and what I can achieve. It might be a load of bollocks, but it's what I want right now.

Chapter 26

At seven the next morning, Erland calls. It's eight in the evening for him. I step into the garden. It's grey and chilly but the fresh air feels good. Niall is on the sofa, working, so I slide the doors shut behind me.

'Lovely to hear your voice to start the day, darling boy.'

'Got to be honest, Dad, I get a bit sick of FaceTime. Sometimes I just want to chat to you, not me and Susie to entertain you like a double act.'

'I know what you mean but I like both. You okay?' I ask.

He sighs, 'Yeah. Actually, I've been offered a promotion here, quite a good one, assistant manager at the estate, and we're all going out later to celebrate and I just kinda stopped in my tracks because if I take it I'm kind of saying this is where I live and am going to live and I love that but I also feel weird about it.'

I feel nauseous but I don't want to say the wrong thing. I play safe, concentrating so hard on not saying, '*Please come back, don't make New Zealand your home,*' that, as a result, I don't really say anything of any use.

'Well done. That's just fantastic.'

'Thanks. Need to think.'

'You'll make the right decision, Erls.'

He goes quiet. So do I, as I fight the selfish demons inside me, the ones fed by how much I miss my boy.

'I heard about the business closing,' he says. 'Are you okay?'

'Yeah, all good.'

'Dad, I wish you'd told me and not Mum. This is a big thing and I didn't want to hear it second-hand.'

'I'll tell you next time, promise.'

'Next time you run a business into the ground?'

'You'll be the first to know.'

We both laugh under our breaths but I feel empty after the call. I remain in the garden, staring into space, taking the idea of being subdued to a whole new level.

I don't tell my son and daughter stuff because my job is to protect them from worry. That's a decision I made when they were children and, who knows, maybe it's time to trust that my adult children want to know the good and the bad, that they have cottoned on to the fact that I am not Yoda, and that life throws some curveballs. Maybe the most boring dad in the world is the one who pretends all is well.

I look inside at the kitchen clock and realise I have been out here for an hour. Niall has gone. I cannot account for the last hour, save for about sixty seconds' worth of introspection. There's sunlight on the garden and a sense that this is slowly bringing it out of hibernation. Spring is taking hold. I should ask Niall to tell me a bit about how to keep this garden looking nice once he's gone. It will be nine o'clock in Cable Bay now and the sun will be setting over Erland's vineyard, or maybe it is dark there already. He will be out celebrating his new job.

I call him back, expecting to get his voicemail and intending to leave a message congratulating him more convincingly and telling him I'm here for him if he wants to talk it through. But he picks up, and all sounds quiet around him.

356

'Hey,' he says.

'Hey. Thought I'd get your voicemail. Aren't you meant to be out?'

'Yeah, but we all worked late this evening. I'm sitting on the veranda with a beer in my hand, looking at the fields, before I head out. So you couldn't have timed it better.'

I launch into what can only be described as full disclosure about the shop, the way the business slid downhill and my inability to see how to change things. This isn't why I rang at all, but maybe this is what he wants to hear.

'The premises are worth a little bit,' I tell him, 'and I got to the point of thinking I have to leap into the unknown. I haven't spoken to you about it because I don't really have a plan and shutting down a family business is a bit embarrassing, and I never want to worry you or Susie – I'm your dad and it's your job to worry me.'

'I don't worry about you,' Erland says.

'Good,' I say. 'Why not? I'm an imbecile.'

He laughs. 'Because you'll sort something out. I'm glad you've shut it down, you hated it. And even though you'll never say it, I also get that you're still reeling from Mum going. Why should that be easy to get over in a hurry?'

I look over my small back garden in Surrey as Erland looks across the wine estate that is his home. He's right about talking like this, with no picture – it's better. We can do silences.

'There's so much I have to say about your job news, Erls. But I'm scared of saying the wrong thing and of being selfish because obviously one of my main thoughts is not wanting you to live on the other side of the world at all, let alone long-term. But that's not fair.'

'I'm not sure I do, Dad, that's why I called for your advice. I think if you're scared to talk to me or Susie, or to Mum for

357

that matter, about what you think, well . . . you seem a bit detached.'

'Which couldn't be further from the truth.'

'I know that, Dad, but I'm the bright one. Remember that Susie and Mum are a bit thick and need stuff explained to them.'

I laugh.

'Mum said to me a few months ago that she sometimes feels hurt how unruffled you are by the divorce, that she has no doubts but feels incredibly sad whereas you seem . . . indifferent.'

'No comment,' I say, 'other than that is the most ridiculous thing I have ever heard. And we've had some interesting chats recently, I think she knows how much I care.'

We fall silent for a bit.

I amend my last comment. 'How much I love her.'

'I know you do,' he says.

'Would this promotion make you better qualified for a job back here one day, do you think?'

'It can't harm, can it? But that's the sort of thing I'd like to be able to sit down and discuss with you.'

'Then we'll do it. Like you say, some calls just you and me, as well as the FaceTimes.'

We share another nice, easy silence. I hear a voice in the background, from a field on the other side of the world, call my son's name. He calls back, 'Be with you in ten minutes.' It makes me proud. I don't know why. No, I do, it's obvious. He's liked. I can be certain of that. He's out there and he's liked and valued. He's my lovely boy.

'You're doing so well, Erland.'

'Thanks, Dad.'

It's my favourite word in the English language. Dad.

'You know . . .' I say to him, calmly, softly. 'What you can't understand is that every time I am with you or speak to you or see your face on this little screen, or think about you, I have you in my arms as a baby, I have the feeling of you as a toddler wrapping your legs around my waist as we walk, the sensation of your weight resting against my shoulder and the fingers of one of your little hands playing with my hair or stroking the back of my neck. And sometimes it is breath-taking and almost makes me buckle because it is such a happy feeling, but a loss too. And parents are battling with that and the joy of watching you go into the world and, all I am saying is, it's . . . it's a lot. And it's a bad parent that weighs their child down, and this isn't anything to do with me and Mum not being together, I felt like this long before all that. It's just about bringing another life into the world and spending a couple of decades desperately hoping it won't ever come to any harm and finding the time you spend with it the best fun of your day, of your life. You shouldn't have to listen to all this, but I love you. I love you and your sister more than it is possible to say and a part of me is absolutely one hundred per cent guilty of wishing you were three again and I could carry you everywhere I go. I've reached a certain age and you are an adult living your own life, but I don't want to play golf or see more of my friends. I want to be your dad.'

There's silence and then I hear my twenty-six-year-old son on Waiheke Island in New Zealand say, 'Then come and see me. Please, Dad. I miss you.'

I can't really remember what we talked about after that. I was already opening my laptop as he told me to give it a think and mentioned some of the things we could do together, that it was early autumn and the perfect time to come, the sooner the better. I don't really know exactly what he said – my head was buzzing and my eyes were scanning the screen impatiently as I started looking at flights. And it felt so obvious and so, so easy.

I spend the rest of the morning feverishly looking up the best deals to Auckland until weighing up between stopovers and best price and best airline and changing my mind a hundred times threatens to sour the whole thing. I hit the wall and turn to an idea I had at the outset but ignored for fear of being turned down by my old contact at BA.

I go and check that Niall is out of the flat, just in case this goes badly, and I call Ben. I probably haven't spoken to him for two years. We've done a lot of business together over the years and he has put me and my family on a couple of BA holidays I never got sent an invoice for, but I fear that things have shifted in terms of the balance of power in our business relationship.

He picks up immediately. 'Didn't I used to know you?' he says.

'I think you did,' I say.

'Peter! Lovely to see your name come up. How are you?'

'I'm great, how are you?'

'All good, my friend, all good. You touching base or can I help you with something?'

'I am ringing to ask for a favour, a deal, but I have to be totally upfront and say that I'm also in the process of closing down the business.'

'Oh, well . . . that's either bad news and I'm sorry, or exciting news and I'm pleased for you.'

'Ben, honestly, it's more exciting than sad. I'm not going to claim it was going brilliantly, but it's very much my decision.'

Please don't ask me what I'm going to do next or what my plans are.

'Fair enough. As long as you are okay. What's the favour?'
Good man.

'I want to go and visit my son in Auckland, very soon, for a few weeks, a month.'

'Excellent,' Ben says. To the same extent that my enthusiasm for the job waned, his grew.

Thirty minutes later, Ben emails me a return ticket to Auckland, for a price that embarrasses me with its generosity, and I receive a text from him telling me that if I turn up in a suit I can expect to be upgraded.

I take a photo of the booking confirmation on my screen and text it to Erland. He sends me applause, about thirty rows of it.

Ten minutes later I get another text from him: *JUMPING AROUND WITH HAPPINESS AT TWO IN THE MORNING. SO EXCITED.* And beneath his words are rows and rows of hearts. I am grinning like a lunatic.

I email Mary Blair and cancel, with the best excuse I've had so far.

Being an international jet-setting man of mystery, I then go for an afternoon nap, for fear the excitement will give me shingles. As usual when I lie on my bed, I think of Claire. Possibly because of the picture of her I have on my bedside table. I text her.

Going to NZ x

I know, Erland called me straight away. He's so excited x

Me too. Going Sunday x

Fantastic. Want to meet for coffee on Saturday morning?

Yes

Want me to check the flat for you whilst you're away? X

That'd be great. Thanks x

Well done Pete Smith xx

I can't sleep. I go to the pub. I take my laptop and sit with a beer and a bowl of chips and research Waiheke Island. I look at the window seat where Claire and I often used to sit and I send her another text.

Look . . . when the day comes that you're seeing someone, I don't want you feeling weird about it with me or not feeling able to tell me xxx

I don't get a reply. And I don't think much about it because I am thinking about the Kauri Grove forest, where Erland and I will walk next week.

Fittingly, I am back home in the smallest room in the house when Claire replies.

Okay, thanks xx

No . . . I explain, with my pants and jeans around my ankles, . . . you are meant to reply by making it clear you haven't yet slept with another man . . .

She texts back:

Oh, right. I see xx

Yet again, I lose at divorce-text. And the pulsing dots that show me Claire is writing more suggest she's about to start a lap of honour. Incoming . . .

I see you with another woman I'll kill you both

What time on Saturday? I ask her.

When's good for you?

Any time after 5 a.m.

Eleven. Can't wait x

Can't wait x

I can't wait. I cannot afford to wait.

I email Ben at BA. I thank him again for the ticket and ask him if he would give Josie half an hour of his time, give her some advice and some contacts. And I know he is going to say yes.

Chapter 27

After my dad died, for a few months I had lucid dreams in which he'd appear in the distance and we'd walk towards each other. Sometimes, we were on the marshes at Snape, in Suffolk, sometimes we were in places we had travelled to as a family, sometimes in a poppy field on Salisbury Plain. And he would be smiling, and my smile was so broad it would hurt my face and joy would surge through my body like a drug, but I would always wake up before we got to each other.

The last time I had this dream, I was clambering across orange rocks in a desert. The air was yellow and stifling. There was no water and no plant-life. Dad appeared. He was wearing an old cardigan and he looked thin and his skin was pale. I clambered down off the rocks and walked towards him on the flat, dusty plain. I wasn't smiling because I was scared that he would feel skeletal if I touched him, or that he would turn to dust. As we got close, he smiled at me. It was his old smile, the one I miss so much. I knew I was asleep, but I felt the tears rising in me and I could hear myself sobbing in my bed. I strode towards him and threw my arms around him, sure that the dream would end but it didn't. And he felt wonderful. Not bony, not weak. I hugged him tight and felt his arms hold me in to his body and we both wept together, and he cuddled me and I nestled my head against him and he was strong and big and fleshy and warm and he smelled good. Then I woke, and I was smiling, and it was the last time I had the dream.

I woke this morning at four o'clock and as my eyes opened, I felt that same smile spread across my face as I realised that in a few days' time I am going to hold my son.

I find myself in the kitchen bathed in sunshine, holding the jar of teabags, with two mugs on the counter. As I leave the tea to brew, I turn on the speaker and pick up my phone and unleash the playlist I have carefully, lovingly and maturely made for this morning. I turn up the volume and track one is the score to me taking Niall a morning cuppa: Bananarama's 'Na Na Hey Hey Kiss Him Goodbye'. I hand him the tea without kissing him and leave his door open so he can listen.

Niall joins me in the kitchen as track two kicks in: 'Go Your Own Way' by Fleetwood Mac. He smiles patronisingly, says, 'Old music,' and takes a look inside the fridge.

'Have a bubble bath or something while I cook breakfast,' he says. 'Get dressed at least.'

As I make my way to the bathroom, Bill Haley and His Comets come on: 'See You Later, Alligator'. Niall turns it up. I dress to '50 Ways to Say Goodbye' by Train and 'Good Riddance' by Green Day, both of which I found when googling *songs about saying goodbye*. New music, by my standards.

I open the doors to the garden and drink the coffee I am going to miss so badly when Niall has gone and my neighbours get treated to Simple Minds' 'Don't You Forget About Me' and Tom Petty's 'Time to Move On' but the best comes when we are at the business end of a huge, superlative fry-up and Gloria Gaynor joins us. Neither of us blinks: Niall immediately reaches for my phone and ups the volume.

'I Will Survive' booms through the flat and out across the garden. I am belting along within seconds and Niall joins in with a mouthful of food. We sing along and bob around in our chairs and suddenly we are both on our feet, Niall still holding his knife and fork, and in perfect time and imperfect tune we bellow out the words as we laugh at each other and dance around the kitchen.

When the song ends, Niall takes his plate and flops onto the kitchen sofa in a deep sweat and uses his hands to feed morsels of bacon and black pudding into his mouth as he regains his breath. It is, quite simply, one of the grossest things I've ever watched. I take a mental photograph and resolve to look at it if I ever find myself missing him.

I look at the sum total of Niall's belongings in my flat: one sports bag and one small cardboard box full of books. He has left them on the hallway floor whilst he goes to his ex-wife's place to collect the rest of his possessions.

His bedroom is empty, the bed stripped and the whole space immaculately tidy. It is, by far, the cleanest room in the flat. His bedding – Susie's, actually – hangs drying on the washing line in the garden.

I walk around the flat and get used to the place without him. I read an email from Mary suggesting that we do FaceTime sessions for the month I am in New Zealand. I am making things in my life start to shift, she says. But she warns that going away does not cure depression overnight. I have admitted I want to be happy. I need to keep working on it for when I return.

I email her back, that I agree. I don't argue with her using the word depression.

When Niall gets back, I tell him I'll come with him, to lend a hand at the other end. It's my first time in his pick-up, which is as neat and clean as his room. If his personal grooming was merely a shadow of his domestic cleaning, he might not be single.

I wind down my window, rest my arm on the door and feel the breeze on my face.

'Thanks for coming,' Niall says. 'There's no way I'd be able to get one box of books, two bags and six black bin liners moved on my own.'

'I can't stay long,' I say. 'I'm holding the mother of all celebration parties later on, best day of my life this. Big, big party.'

'Big enough to contain all your friends, like *all* of them? Let's face it, you're going to crash this evening – it's going to hit you that I've gone and you'll be in pieces.'

We don't talk after that.

Niall's new place is too small to be called a flat, but with a bedroom the size of a double bed separate from the kitchen–living room, is too big to be a bedsit. It's a pad. It's going to be okay, but for now it's empty and a testament to the fact that one can reach the age of thirty-one and not own a single piece of furniture.

'You don't own a bed, then?' I ask, looking around at the bare walls and bare rooms.

'She wouldn't give it back,' Niall says. 'Says she sleeps in it.'

'Not unreasonable.,' I say.

Niall tips one of the bin liners upside down and a large plastic thing falls out, with a pump.

'Ta da!' he says.

I watch as he connects the pump to the plastic and inflates a large surfboard in the little bedroom.

'That is, what?' I say.

'My stand-up paddle board, aka my temporary bed.'

I roll my eyes before I can stop myself. 'Do you own a kettle?' I ask.

'Certainly do. It's in the blue sports bag.'

'I'm going out to get you some tea and milk,' I announce, 'and one of those boxes of Fox's biscuits where you open them and find there are six tiny bite-sized biscuits inside, and that eighty per cent of the packet is packet.'

'Get Hobnobs,' he says, going red in the face as he pumps.

I take a look up and down Niall's street and see a shop canopy at one end. It is a corner shop in the old tradition and has exactly what I need. I get some extra things, to stock his cupboard; cereal, sliced bread, butter and Marmite. When I get back, I see Niall has wedged two cushions against the living-room wall.

He has unpacked. We open the windows, let the air move through the place, and have a cup of tea. It's time for me to leave him. Moving into a new place on your own is always a strange day. Hopefully, he has plans for later.

As he drives me home, he turns to me and breaks the silence.

'I wish you were my godfather.'

'Thanks.'

'I'd love to have a name for you that isn't your own name but is a pet name and kinda shows everyone we have a special bond. Like an uncle or a godfather. But not one of those nicknames for a male relative that kinda implies a little bit paedo.'

'Yeah, let's avoid those.'

'I'm gonna call you . . .'

No words come to him immediately, which is an event in itself.

'I'll call you G'daddy, like P. Diddy. No. I'll call you . . .'

'Call me God.'

'I think not,' he says. 'I'll come up with something.'

We both go silent as he turns into my road. He parks up and turns to me. 'My thank-you present is that I will send someone over once a month to tidy up the garden. It'll probably be me, so I can spy on you and annoy you. Anyway, I like your garden and I want to save it from you, so please accept.'

'I accept. Thanks.'

He holds a set of keys out to me.

'And it is not beyond the bounds of possibility,' he says, 'that I might ever lose my flat keys. Could you look after the spare set for me?'

I take them. We hug and we don't say another thing. I get out and after I have shut the door, I pat it. He drives off, grinning from ear to ear. He waves out of the side window and when I see him look back at me in the wing mirror, I give him the middle finger. He beeps and accelerates away.

And it turns out the movies do get this bit right; I really do stand there for a while and watch the empty road long after he has gone.

My flat is quiet. The sun is off the back of the building and only the side window in Niall's bedroom is bright. It's a beautiful day. The bedding billows on the line. I hang Niall's flat key on the hooks in the kitchen. I fill a glass with water, take a sip and carry it with me into my bedroom, get a blanket from the cupboard and lay it across the unmade bed in Niall's room. I put on some music and spend the next hour or so walking from my room to Niall's, laying out clothing and other stuff for my trip. I get my suitcase out, dust it and unzip it on the floor by the spare bed, so that I know what I am aiming for.

In the late afternoon, I light a fire. I move the standard lamp in the kitchen to the living room so that I will be able to lie on the big sofa in there later and read. I do everything with a quiet calm – you could even call it solemnity – because as of now everything I do matters. There is no more winging it, not facing up to things, no more leaving it to later. I'm on my own now. And I'm excited to be packing a bag again. I'm good at it. I've done a lot of it in the past. It has seemed like the long-distant past for some time, but this evening it all feels like yesterday.

In the kitchen, I put on the TV and decide to catch up on a chunk of TV by watching *Gogglebox*. I microwave a frozen pizza and some frozen potato waffles and I heat a tin of beans in a pan. I've missed proper food.

There's something anthropological about watching other human beings watch horror films. It would be equally telling, for a neuroscientist, to watch me put so many carbs in my body that I nearly lose the will to live, and still debate whether or not to eat the single remaining slice of pepperoni pizza just out of arm's reach.

I imagine what I look like to an observer: in the next-door room, there is a roaring fire, a very comfortable sofa that I can lie on with room to spare, and in a pleasant pool of lamplight lies a book that will nourish my brain and feed my spirit (by Anjali Joseph, if you're interested). But here I lie, slouched diagonally across a sofa too small for me, watching shite and eating junk.

I get up and put my plate on the worktop. I feel full and slothful. I do a couple of stretches and sigh heavily. I look at my trusty old kitchen sofa and feel a stab of affection for it. I go next door and put another log on the fire. I return to the kitchen and take another look at the sofa. I call Fisting Si.

'Are you busy?' I ask.

'The working day is over, so that would mean me having a social life. No, I'm not busy.'

He's like a retired Cabinet minister; as soon as he leaves his post he becomes witty and interesting. I could have spoken to this man for years.

'Quick job, right now, need a man and a van to take a sofa somewhere.'

Niall is out. Either that or his buzzer isn't working. I decide not to call him. I like the idea of leaving a surprise. I get the spare keys out of my jacket pocket and let me and Si into the building. We carry the sofa up two flights of stairs and I feel seven-eighths of a cheap pizza moving its way up through my major arteries in preparation for a Saturday-evening heart attack.

We put the sofa down in Niall's living room in the spot where it looks best. I take a card from my inside pocket and prop it up on the sofa cushion.

It says: *Yours. Peter x*

Then I take a food bag from my pocket and from it the slice of pizza I couldn't eat, and I tuck it down the side of the sofa cushion. Si watches me do this and nods to himself approvingly without seeking any explanation from me, and it is this that leads me to believe we'll become good friends.

Acknowledgements

I am grateful and proud to be represented by Becky Thomas at the Lewinsohn Literary Agency.

I'd like to thank my editor Jon Elek, Annabel Robinson, Rosa Schierenberg, Rachel Hart, Rob Cox and all the team at Welbeck.

For their encouragement and notes at the infancy of this idea, my thanks to Rochelle Stevens and Hugh Dennis.

My thanks also to Saliann St-Clair at the Lewinsohn Literary Agency.

And finally, to those beautiful boys, Otis and Jamie, thank you for making the whole thing so much fun.

About the Author

Joe Portman is a writer and a colossal disappointment to his mother.

He raises kids, takes photos and windsurfs on the south coast.

WELBECK
PUBLISHING GROUP

Love books? Join the club.

Sign up and choose your preferred genres to receive tailored news, deals, extracts, author interviews and more about your next favourite read.

From heart-racing thrillers to award-winning historical fiction, through to must-read music tomes, beautiful picture books and delightful gift ideas, Welbeck is proud to publish titles that suit every taste.

bit.ly/welbeckpublishing